FIVE BY FIVE

TARGET ZONE

3

FIVE BY FIVE
TARGET ZONE
3

REMAINS OF THE DEAD
Michael A. Stackpole

AND NOT TO YIELD
Sarah A. Hoyt

GOLIATH
Doug Dandridge

TEACH YOUR CHILDREN WELL
Eytan Kollin and Dani Kollin

ESCAPE HATCH
Kevin J. Anderson

WordFire Press
Colorado Springs, Colorado

CONTENTS

REMAINS OF THE DEAD   1
Michael A. Stackpole

AND NOT TO YIELD   61
Sarah A. Hoyt

GOLIATH   115
Doug Dandridge

TEACH YOUR CHILDREN WELL   155
Eytan Kollin and Dani Kollin

ESCAPE HATCH   207
Kevin J. Anderson

REMAINS OF THE DEAD
A STAR TIGERS STORY

MICHAEL A. STACKPOLE

I

The tip of Thomas Firefly's tongue poked pink out of the corner of his mouth. He looked up from the sketchbook, squinted at the liftloader Meka, then penciled in more detail on the machine's arm. He used a finger to smear some of the graphite, roughly matching where a leaking hydraulic line had splashed dark fluid. When he looked up again, the Meka had vanished into the freighter's hold.

Alicia plopped herself down on the packing crate beside him. "Not bad."

"Thanks."

"I still don't get the *why*."

He glanced over at her. "I like the feel of the pencil scratching on the paper. It adds tactile to the visual, makes it more real."

"Not that, dummy." She frowned, which somehow still didn't diminish her cuteness. "And don't give me the 'action and adventure' crap. That might work for Captain Hudson."

"It's not because I'm running away from you."

She dug an elbow into his ribs. "Nice try, but not all clips have abandonment issues. The 301st, really?"

Thomas sighed and closed the sketchbook. "First unit, third planet …"

"Which is wrong since scientists have figured out that life actually began on the fourth planet. Mars, right?"

His brown eyes tightened. "And you a navigator."

"Not like the Qian let us any closer than the far edge of the system." She scratched at the back of her head. "You're too smart to be doing something this stupid. You owe them nothing."

"What *them*?" He shook his head. "You're blonde-haired, blue-eyed, just like the folks back on Terra. If they dropped you in Iceland or Scandinavia, no one would look twice."

"Until I opened my mouth."

"Sure, we all have *that* problem, but look around you." In the spaceport's docking area, countless non-humans wandered, chatted and loitered, just as he and Alicia were doing. Thomas studiously avoided thinking of the others as *alien*, both for politeness sake, and on the basis of seniority. Humanity had been in the stars for nanoseconds compared to some of the species lurking around the landing pad.

"I'm looking."

"You and I, even though we come from different Terran stock, are tons closer to each other and Terrans than we are to any of the species here. Just because the Arwarzhy clipped us from our home planet and sold us as pets doesn't mean we're not human."

"But that's not how the Terrans see it, is it?" She raked fingers back through her pixie cut. "They don't want to acknowledge we exist."

"Half the people in my enclave don't want to acknowledge *the Terrans* exist."

"Point."

"Our people are furious that once Terran leaders made contact with the Qian, our brethren didn't demand our immediate return. But, really, they couldn't. It took them fifty years to prepare humanity to realize that there was life outside our solar system, and that we were going to be slowly worked into the Qian Commonwealth. Bringing us back, after generations of us had lived among the stars, would screw that plan up. I also think that lots of Terrans would have thought that we looked down upon them, since our people have been raised with Qian technology for centuries."

Alicia stared at him openly. "You're making my case for me. They've not done anything for us, and now you're going to join a fighter squadron calling itself the Star Tigers? You know what most folks call it."

Thomas sighed. "The Suicide Kitties."

"That's the polite translation." She shook her head. "And they've already lost a pilot, even before their roster is full."

"I heard." Thomas looked down at the black, pebbled cover of his sketch book. "When the Qian cracked down on human trafficking, then took us and sorted us out, and put us in our own little preserves, my forbearers did their best to reconstruct our culture. We'd been clipped from all over the North American continent, but the Qian tossed us all together; so I was raised in mismatched stew of dozens of Native American traditions."

"And according to Terrans, I speak Nor-Dano-Swedish with a Finn's accent." She raised an eyebrow. "And despite that mix, we don't have a word for 'you're not making your case.'"

"Nor one for patience."

"Ouch."

"My case is this: my people have reconstituted a culture out of the half-remembered beliefs of kidnap victims. Most of them were outsiders anyway—the Arwarzhy knew enough to pick off folks who wouldn't be missed or believed—so their grasp of traditions was weak at best. Or extreme. Sum it all up, though, and you get a culture that believes that some Great Spirit lives in the universe and is tightly tied to whatever rock you're standing on."

Alicia glanced at her chronometer.

Thomas chuckled. "So my point arrives. I got my surname, Firefly, when I became a man because I was smart, and I studied things like astronomy and because I wanted to fly. Really it was because I didn't want to be tied to a rock. Some of the Elders understood—that about me, and what the reality of space meant for their beliefs. If I'd not run away to the spaceport and hired onto the first freighter that would have me, those Elders would have driven me there and paid for passage."

"So, among your own people you're an outsider, too?"

"Yeah. But with you and Captain Hudson, other spacers, I found my place."

"And now you're leaving it."

"Because the 301st is something bigger than Terra or the clip colonies." Thomas nodded toward one of the diminutive, large-headed, grey-skinned humanoids sitting across the hangar. "You think that Arwarzshy wouldn't take us away and sell us to a collector if he had the chance?"

"He would." Alicia nodded. "And there are collectors who would pay."

"There are collectors that still have their collections. Likely have all the forms right, too, showing how they are paying humans to be test subjects, or actors in some slowly-unfolding drama. Point being, for a lot of these beings, we're just pets that have slipped the leash."

"And you think getting vaporized in the cockpit of some Shrike fighter is going to convince them otherwise?"

"*Them*, no. Those who turn a blind eye to what they're doing, you bet."

"That's incredibly brave, or incredibly stupid. Maybe both." Alicia checked her chronometer again. "Cap needs us back at top of the hour."

Thomas tucked his pencil into a slot in a leather case, then rolled it up and tied it off. He tucked it and the sketchbook in a satchel and looped it across his body. "Might as well head back now. Traffic is light enough we can get quick exit clearance for the shuttle."

As they started across the spaceport, a couple of the Arwarzhy began to parallel their journey. Thomas would not have given it much thought save for the conversation just ended, and the fact that the Greys had one person on each side and two trailing behind them. *If two more come up in front, we're going to have trouble.*

"Think they're buying or selling?"

Alicia shrugged. "That or spying?"

Thomas considered the third option. Rumors were rife about this species or that straddling the line in the Qian-Zsytzii war. Many individuals played for immediate reward, while governments looked at long-term gains. The Qian Commonwealth was meant to benefit all, but species like the Arwarzhy chafed beneath regulations that stopped profitable things like trafficking in sapient species.

For them to be watching us means they believe that knowledge that I'm joining the Star Tigers is valuable. He didn't think that was very likely. It wasn't much of a secret that the unit had been formed, or that members were being recruited from among clips. *And anyone smart enough to be spying would know that my value would be nothing until* after *I join the unit.*

His dismissal of spying as a motive didn't mean they were in any less danger. "Selling, I would bet."

"I'm not inclined to take chances."

He smiled. Her earlier shrug had dropped one end of a short, dense metal rod into her hand from within her flight jacket's sleeve. Alicia might have grown up in the colonies, but whenever she tangled with Greys, she treated all of them as they were the Arwarzhy who clipped her ancestors.

And given those buggers' longevity, any of them could be.

Four more of the black-eyed humanoids appeared to cut them off. Granted the shiny domed top of their bulbous heads would barely reach Thomas' chin, but the Greys had a wiry tenacity that made them hard to put down. Four to one odds would give the Greys an edge. *And experience will even things out.*

Thomas and Alicia had fought with Greys before, together and separately. What the Greys had a hard time understanding was that in some colonies, martial traditions often centered themselves around preventing more kidnappings. Plenty of disobedient human children shivered to tales of Greys coming to get them and, later on, took deep interest in learning how to kick what passed for Arwarzhy ass.

He tightened his grip on the sketchbook. No species willing to call itself sapient was going to feel threatened by the book, but Thomas understood it for what it really was. In size and weight it compared well with a block of wood. Grey skulls were hard to miss and the book was heavy enough to deliver a nasty blow.

The Greys started to tighten the circle. If any of the other species noticed, they gave almost no sign. Those who did shifted to where they could watch the battle, or huddled together to place bets. Thomas might have thought them callous, but for many years, man-fights were popular amid the sporting classes within the Commonwealth.

Yet before the Greys could close and engage, a piercing scream echoed through the docking bay. No throat could have made that sound—and every spacer knew it well. Somewhere, deep in the bowels of a ship, an engine pod had overspun and was ripping itself apart. Right on cue, as the scream rose up and out of Thomas' hearing, pinging and popping triggered banging and clanging. His head snapped around. Back from over near where he'd seen a Grey lounging beside a ship, a dark curl of black smoke began to rise.

The Arwarzhy saw what he saw, their dark, unblinking eyes growing even larger. The eight of them froze.

Thomas cut to the left, getting out of the line between the Greys and the damaged ship. Alicia followed tight in his wake. He rushed at the lone Grey on that side. The Arwarzhy gave way, darting back toward his ship. His move was enough to convince the others to retreat as well.

Alicia frowned. "I thought we were in trouble."

"Better to be lucky than good."

"And we're both." Her frown melted into a smile. "They don't know how fortunate they are."

"True." He gave her a wink. "So let's get to *Swift* before they make us prove it."

<h2 style="text-align:center">II</h2>

Captain Gregory Allen dropped to one knee on the repair bay deck of the *Unity*. He steadied himself with his left hand. The decking felt like wood, matching the red-cedar appearance. It wasn't wood—not wood grown the conventional way at least—but the Qian had chosen it to make the humans feel more comfortable.

He ducked his head, looking in toward where small, spider-like repair automatons skittered over his *Shrike's* belly. The little silver and black machines seemingly moved at random, their actions dictated by the RA107 repair automaton hunched behind Greg. The RA107 was the size of a small pony, but matched its arachnid charges in design—which is why Greg didn't like it lurking at his back.

The fact that it spoke in a mechanical approximation of human speech did nothing to quell his unease. "Systems repair, 75% complete. Cosmetic repair, 74% complete. Completion estimate at two Terran Standard days."

Greg studied the tiny sparks marking the smaller spiders at work. "Thank you."

"Gratitude is superfluous. We are just an adjunct to the *Unity's* command system."

"Gratitude is just being mannerly." Greg straightened up, running his left hand along the ship's skin. Up there, by the cockpit, his name had been painted in a clean, flowing hand. *Just as my wife had painted it on my first fighter.*

He looked away. His left hand balled into a fist. His right hand, which initially appeared to be as flesh and blood as the left, tightened into a crystalline mace of ice blue. One of the small spiders leaped from the *Shrike* to his sleeve, its forelegs tapping delicately against the prosthesis.

Greg flicked the automaton off with the snap of his wrist. It spun through the air, but landed on four legs. The other four slowed it, then the thing galloped back toward him, but leaped onto the RA107's broad back and remained there.

Greg frowned. "I'm sorry. Is it okay?"

"Performance is undiminished. Your limb is functioning within normal parameters."

"Great. Thanks."

"Gratitude is …"

"Got it." Greg concentrated and forced his Qian hand back into its original configuration.

The RA107 stepped laterally. "Data recovery and replacement to pre-damage state was 100% successful."

Greg nodded. That meant that a picture of Jennifer and their daughter, Bianca, would be available on his fighter's auxiliary monitor. He had no doubt that the Qian could have implanted a lens into his eyes that would allow him to call that picture up any time he wanted. Had they done that to him, he wasn't sure he'd ever look at much else.

"Your ship is coming along, Captain Allen."

Greg forced a smile onto his face, and drew his hands to the small of his back. "It is, Mr. Yamashita. How goes your reporting?"

The young Asian man shrugged. "I file the stories, but I have no idea as to when they make it back to Earth, get run, or have any feedback."

"We *are* at war, Mr. Yamashita. There is bound to be some delay in communication for the purpose of security."

"I know. I'm just not used to it." Jiro shrugged. "Even when I was reporting on mining troubles in the asteroid belt, feedback came fairly quickly. I think my editors just aren't sending any of it along. Instead they send things they want me to question the 301st about."

"Such as?" Greg walked toward the lift. "I could use some coffee. Join me?"

"Sure." The reporter reached the lift control panel first and hit the button. "To answer your other question, they've sent reports about the reaction to Maddie Fields' death. Mixed bag. Most of the United Kingdom is sad because their pilot has died, but they're also proud. Politicians have noted she's keeping with the proud tradition of the RAF and the Battle of Britain. Lots of speculation on who will replace her. Two minorities—pacifists and the Earth-Firsters—are protesting any human death. A couple radical religious sects say they'll protest the funeral."

Greg preceded the reporter into the lift, then sent it down toward the galley. "That sort of thing still garners publicity. I mean, I understand they protested at my wife's …"

"I shouldn't have mentioned it. Forgive me."

"No, it's fine. I trust you didn't do that to get a reaction for a story, right?"

Jiro's eyes widened. "God, no. Look, I know that my presence isn't the most welcome thing here, but …"

Greg rested his real hand on Jiro's shoulder. "It's fine, Mr. Yamashita. I do trust you."

"To a point."

"I *am* my father's son. There's always a point." Greg nodded toward the lift's opening door. "Your job is to report. Mine is to fight. We both know that we're shaping opinion. We also both know that there is a particular opinion which is the narrative Earth's leaders want to be accepted as the truth. I have no problem lying, so you don't have to."

"And that's off the record, right?"

"Take yours black, if I recall correctly?"

"Thanks."

Greg smiled, but refrained from quoting RA107 back at the reporter. Jiro Yamashita had been chosen as the only reporter from Earth to be imbedded with the 301st. What their home world knew of the Star Tigers could go through him—and countless censors between reporter and citizen. While Jiro was looking for stories, he and Greg had reached something of an accommodation, which allowed them to enjoy each other's company.

Greg set the coffee mugs on the table. As with the rest of the *Unity*, the Qian had fitted it out in woods and brass, creating a massive art-deco warship that would have been at home in the works of Victorian novelist George Chetwynd-Griffiths. Actually, it owed more to the Disney version of Captain Nemo's *Nautilus* than anything else, but Greg found that perfect. *A fantasy set for a fantastic adventure.*

Jiro accepted the coffee and wrapped both hands around the barrel. "Ever get the feeling that this is one giant experiment?"

"How so?"

The reporter frowned. "Ever since the 301st got ambushed, I've been asking for updates on who did it, how it happened, and I'm getting nothing. I mean, if it was the Zsytzii who tried to kill the Haxadissi ambassador, why wouldn't the Qian tell us that? They recovered the enemy ship fragments. You can't tell me that they don't know."

"I *can* tell you that." Greg shrugged. "Three scenarios. First, it was the Zeez, but the Qian don't want to panic folks by noting an incursion so deep in Commonwealth space. Second, it wasn't. It was an internal matter based on Haxad or showing a rift within the Commonwealth itself. Either one of those are not going to be good for public consumption. Even if you did learn the truth there, your report would never make it back to Earth with that information in it."

Jiro sipped his coffee, then lowered the mug. "The third scenario?"

"That they don't know who it was, and that has the Qian terrified." Greg exhaled slowly. "Probably the only time my father was candid about a problem in the White House was when he told me about a situation his father faced. It was after the Aeroflot jet went down over Samarkand."

"Turcoman separatists used a captured Chinese SAM to shoot it down. That put your grandfather in the hot seat."

"Blazing. And, yes, rebels was what it turned out to be, but no one knew it in the moment. No one knew it for certain for a week. And all that time there was pressure on my grandfather to act. Folks didn't want to accept that he didn't know the truth because, for their own sense of security, they *needed* him to know. Pressure was on, but he didn't want to act and be wrong simply because it could ignite a war."

"It did."

"But later, and more controlled. It limited the panic, limited the damage. Folks had time to act and react."

Jiro nodded. "Just like the decision to keep the Qian's contact with world leadership quiet for a generation or three."

"Yeah." Greg smiled. "Of course, had things really gone to hell in a hand basket in central Asia, like as not we'd not be here. The Qian never would have brought us into the Commonwealth, even as a Protectorate world."

"And that brings us back to the central question: why did they?"

Greg shook his head. It couldn't have been because they needed troops, or needed *human* troops. They were allowing only a handful of humans to fight; and they could have drawn all the humans they needed from the various clip colonies scattered throughout the Commonwealth. No one on Earth had a good answer for why. Earth-Firsters figured it was a plot. Science Fiction geeks figured it was destiny. Various religious folks figured this was something between damnation or revelation. Most people, as long as they had food, beer, and holovids in abundance, really didn't seem to care.

"I know you're not comfortable with the idea that they have a reason they'll share with us later, Mr. Yamashita. Neither am I. I tend to believe that they'll share it with us once they figure we can handle it."

"I suppose we don't have a choice in the matter." Jiro's eyes narrowed. "So here's another question, a minor one."

"Yes?"

"Why did you even bother with a mug for your coffee?"

Greg glanced down. His right hand had flowed around the mug, absorbing the handle. He tried to open his hand, but he couldn't feel individual fingers. Not at first. He fought panic, then full feeling came back into hand.

Fingers redefined themselves and slowly came away from the mug. Still, his grip had left an impression in the ceramics, as if he'd gripped the mug tightly before it ever got fired. Still, the red, white and blue coloring remained, as did the Star Tiger emblem.

"I don't know what that was." Greg recalled that the RA107 said his prosthesis was working properly. "I guess, subconsciously, I didn't want to spill and my hand ..."

"That makes sense." Jiro stared at the mug again, then sipped more coffee. "Will you report that to Xin when you get checked out for flight duty?"

"Don't have to. I'm sure he knows." Greg waved the artificial hand toward bulkheads. "The *Unity* keeps an eye on things."

"Are you ever worried the ship knows more about you than you do?"

"Back to this being an experiment, are we? Where humans are being tested for unknown and nefarious reasons?"

"You make it sound like I'm an Earth-Firster."

"Not my intent." Greg shook his head. "Ridiculing their ideas just makes it easier for me to dismiss the possibility they might be right."

III

Colonel Nick Clark read the message on the viewscreen built into his desk one more time. "The Haxadissi Ambassador has filed a complaint about our giving orders to her pilot, even though if we hadn't given those orders, she, her staff, and members of her family would have died in that ambush? Not to mention the fact that her pilot followed so slothfully that he almost cost Captain Allen his life. And Command is using this complaint to suspend our operations?"

Vych Thziilon, the squadron's Qian liaison officer spread her open hands. Little lights, like electric freckles, flashed along her cheekbones and forehead beneath lavender skin. Some even shot up into strands woven into her dark hair. "Colonel Clark, reading that message yet another time will not change the meaning of it."

"Rereading certainly isn't injecting any sense in it." Nick sat back, relishing the squeak of a chair that needed just a touch of oil. The Qian never would have allowed that imperfection, save that they'd built his office to very precise instructions. Though the office overlooked the *Unity's* flight deck, the decor had been modeled on that of a rustic lake cabin in Maine. The Qian had recreated it to perfection, right down to that squeak and the faint scent of pine.

He regarded the other female in the room. "Thoughts, Major Taine?"

Damienne Taine, her black hair woven into a thick braid, frowned. "If you expect, Colonel, outrage, I shall disappoint you. I *am* angry that Lt. Fields' death is tarnished by this, but it is not out of character for the Haxadissi, I am given to believe."

Vych nodded in agreement.

"On the other hand, sir, we *are* at half strength. Elizabeth Windsor is on her way to join us. Captain Rustov should be with us soon, too. In two days we should rendezvous with Thomas Firefly and Captain Allen should again be flight ready. Our other three pilots are inbound. Within the month we would be at full strength and able to train as a unit."

"I've done the math, Major. Being under-strength hurt us at Haxad—but being full-up wouldn't have helped much." Nick tapped the viewscreen with a finger. "I should have seen this coming before anything that happened at Haxad. Ambush aside, we were set up. The Haxadissi would have complained about Terrans being their escort no matter what. There's probably some number-superstition or symbolism in all this, too, right? Seven is not good, six is worse, plus Haxad is the system where the first Terran died, right?"

Vych's hands came back in, slipping away into the folds of her robe's overlarge sleeves. "Among the Haxadissi, seven is an auspicious number. Six is the equivalent of your thirteen. That a human died, but no Haxadissi did put them in debt to humanity."

Nick closed his eyes for a moment. "So this is the best possible outcome for *someone*. The Haxadissi are humbled, we're hobbled and the Star Tigers have been exposed as a political toy. Damn. Your Qian politics is a contact sport."

Vych glanced at Major Taine for a heartbeat, then back at Nick. "Colonel, you must understand that politics is not being deployed alone against you. It is being used in your favor. As Major Taine pointed out, you have new personnel coming in. The Haxadissi complaint means you're not being thrown into battle while hobbled."

"I get that. I do." His nostrils flared. "I know we have to refit, but when and where and how we go into action should be a decision made *with* me, not in spite of my wishes."

"I shall make this known to Admiral Ghaetr."

"No."

The Qian's head came up. "No?"

"No, I'll tell him when he gets here."

The lights on Vych's face flashed more quickly. "Am I to convince you that you do not want to take an action, or am I preparing to deal with an action taken?"

Nick met her gaze easily. "You remember all the visits I made when I was appointed to command this unit? I got lots of awards and medals and things for having done nothing. One of them was to get inducted into the *Mnemnar-vyste*."

"No, Colonel Clark, that is not something you want to invoke."

"I do, and I will." He tapped the screen again. "This accusation against my squadron is an affront to my honor. I will challenge the Haxad pilot to a duel. My membership in the *Mnemnar-vyste* makes this possible. Actually, it demands it, doesn't it?"

Vych hung her head. "It does, provided your superior in the society does not dismiss the dishonor."

"I'm guessing Admiral Ghaetr will be happy to get here double-quick to do that." Nick nodded toward Major Taine. "Major, you'll want to prep Lieutenants O'Leary, Sun, and Early in protocols and formations for escorting the Admiral's shuttle here."

"Yes, sir." She drew herself up to attention and snapped a salute.

Nick stood and returned the salute. "Dismissed, Major."

The hatch had barely closed behind her when Vych looked up again. "Nicholas!"

He came out from behind his desk and took her hands in his. "I know what I'm doing."

"You know what you think you are doing."

"I've read the rules."

"In translation, Nicholas." She rubbed a hand along her brow. "The *Mnemnar-vyste* has existed for millennia. It was old before your Neanderthal and Denisovan species ceased to exist independently of your dominant humanoid species. The translation you were given is infantile in simplicity, devoid of nuance. And you have not seen the volumes of commentary and Court of Honor decisions rendered down through the aeons. What you propose to do is not as simple as you imagine."

"And I'm sure the admiral will be happy to explain all that to me."

She looked up at him. "You make an enemy where you need not."

He gave her a wink. "There are only two types of fights worth fighting: those you *can* win, and those you *must* win. The first are optional. The second are vital. He's got to see that we're more than numbers and forms. If I have to be a thorn in his side to make that happen, I will be."

"Yours is a philosophy about fighting with which the admiral will agree—because you cannot win this fight."

Nick laughed. "It's won the second I send a message to the admiral. If he upholds the dishonor, then I am free to fight a duel with the Haxadissi pilot. We know that won't happen."

"Perhaps it will. Perhaps that pilot will kill you."

"I've seen him fly. If he kills me, I'm better off dead." The human took her by the hand to the viewports looking out onto the launch bay. "We know that can't be allowed to happen. Me killing a Haxadissi, and one killing me, are outcomes that create plenty of Chaos. So the admiral has to tell me that it's not a dishonor. He'll dismiss the Haxadissi charge, which frees us to act again."

"But you agreed with Major Taine that waiting is best for the squadron, waiting until you get more pilots."

"It is, but that leaves the choice to act in *my* hands. If I can't establish and maintain control over my people, I lose." Nick ran a hand over his jaw. "My grandfather fought in our First World War.

General Pershing was in charge of the American Expeditionary Force. The French and the British both wanted to control our troops, and use them however they damned well pleased. Pershing knew that if he allowed that, Americans would be wasted. He didn't let it happen and Americans ended up doing what the French and British had failed to do in a very long and bloody war."

She reached a hand up and stroked his cheek. "You cannot imagine that your squadron, no matter how good, can win this war by itself."

"Nope. But I have no trouble imagining some commander somewhere using us to plug a hole so his people can escape." He raised his hand to hold her palm firmly in place. "You know me better than any Qian. You know me better than anyone. Perhaps even better than I know myself. Can you fault my logic?"

"No, but I can fear for your application of it."

"Your admiral is not the first superior officer I've had to deal with."

"As you have said, Nicholas, I know you. I also know much of him. He is not stupid. He knows what you are doing. He will feel he must break you."

Nick nodded. "He'll do his best, but he has a weakness."

Vych's facelights slowed their dancing. "Yes?"

The pilot pointed to the flight deck. "I'm betting he has no more of a clue about why we're here than we do. He feels he has to act, but doesn't want to get things wrong. I'll make life hard for him, then give him an out. Unless he's more dialed in than I can imagine, he'll take it."

"I do not know if he is privy to decisions made at a higher level than his own. Regardless, he will follow his orders to the letter. You best hope that his superiors—those who do know why you are here—provide him leeway."

"If they don't, it tells me even more." He smiled against her hand. "So, will you help me craft a message that will annoy without blatant insults?"

"Yes."

"And help me through nuances?"

She laughed almost humanly—in a manner that she'd never exhibited when they first met. "It will be a ... pleasure is too strong a word."

"An education, maybe."

"Definitely that, Nicholas." Vych nodded solemnly. "Sooner started, sooner sent."

He turned back toward his desk. "Then let the games begin."

IV

Thomas waited for Captain Richard Hudson to slide his seat forward before he slipped into his place at the auxiliary pilot console. Hudson, a rather large man with thinning brown hair and a bit of a belly, dominated the transparent forward cockpit dome. He fastened his restraining straps and laughed aloud. "No finer a day possible than flying."

Alicia entered the crowded cockpit and took up the navigator's station to the captain's left. She sat with her back to Thomas, but they'd set up little mirrors that let them exchange glances. The one they shared now was the one they always shared after Hudson made his declaration. His joy teased big smiles from both of them.

"Mister Firefly, is the shuttle made fast?"

"Aye, sir. In the last pod. We had fourteen greens on the way forward. The visual run had everything looking good."

"As expected. Do you concur, Miss Yorgensdottar?"

"Aye, Captain." Alicia hit a couple of buttons on her console. A schematic of the ship came up on a secondary monitor. It showed the cockpit at the head of a long string of pods. One engine component sat behind the cockpit, and another seven pods back. The pods glowed green and their external hatches burned red. "Everything is in order and I have a course plotted."

"Satisfactory." Hudson looked to the right. "Bring the engines on line, please, Mister Firefly."

"Aye, sir." Thomas's fingers played over his console. Instead of a ship schematic he got a spreadsheet full of numbers. He started the forward engine pod first, then brought the second engine pod along at two percent behind the first. A low thrum worked through the hull. The engines would cycle up and sync at 75% of capacity, which was all they needed to haul this load. "Five minutes to maneuvering, eight to speed."

"Course requires us to come about to 315.3 degrees, up 21.76."

"Noted, Miss Yorgensdottar." Hudson unlocked the helm controls. "Departure Control indicated an Arwarzhy ship had an engine failure down there. You had nothing to do with that, yes?"

"No, sir." Thomas glanced at the mirror. Alicia just shrugged. "We were there, and there might have been trouble, but their engine ripped itself apart, so they all ran off to check it."

"Good."

"Was there a reason you asked?"

"Might could be Departure Control had some questions asked of it about us." Hudson brought his command chair all the way around. "I wasn't worried about you kids. I am just glad I didn't need to come down there and pry you out of some lock-up."

"We're happy you didn't have to do that either, sir." Alicia smiled. "We don't know what they were up to, but it's over now."

"Don't think that, Miss Yorgensdottar. With them, it's never over." He brought his chair around. "Am I good to throttle up, Mister Firefly?"

"Yes, sir."

Hudson reached out with a massive hand. White scars twisted over the knuckles. He eased the throttle forward. The thrum increased, then the starfield beyond the cockpit began to shift.

Thomas's console beeped. One of the cells in the spreadsheet showed red numbers instead of green. "Hang on. The rear engine just had a power drop. Off .21 percent."

He hit a few more keys, bringing up a diagnostic image of the engine pod on his primary monitor. That shifted the spreadsheet to the secondary. "That's weird."

"More informative, Mister Firefly."

"Sir, in the time it took to bring up the engine's diagnostics, the problem corrected itself." Thomas squinted at the screen. "In fact, it seems like the engine is running leaner. It's picked up 2.31 percent efficiency. And ..." More keys clicked beneath his fingers. "... and it's matching the forward pod."

Hudson looked over his shoulder. "They've never paired."

"Yeah, I know."

"Anything anomalous, Miss Yorgensdottar?"

"Green and red right where they are supposed to be."

"Satisfactory. Coming about to 315.3 degrees, up 21.76."

Alicia hit a button on her console. "This is transport *Swift*. Requesting clearance on outbound vector 315.3 by 21.76 up."

"Clearance granted to jump at AU 1.73."

"Copy command. AU 1.73. *Swift* out." Alicia smiled. "We are good to go, sir. Wait, what's this?"

She hit another button on the communications console. "Transport *Swift*."

A melodious voice floated through the speakers. "Permission to come aboard, *Swift*."

"We're underway and outbound. Please identify yourself."

Thomas pulled data from the navigation console. "No ships near us."

"This is *Corzt-tan Kyan*. In your tongue, *Ship of Shadows*. My request is sincere and urgent." The cockpit hatch hissed open. "And perhaps a bit late."

A humanoid figure stood in the hatchway. Tall and slender, with features soft enough to suggest it was female, the creature had blue flesh covered in tiny, scintillating scales. They became red and yellow around the face and on the backs of the hands—each of which had three fingers and a thumb. The red and yellow colors also swirled up the stalks of the two antennae atop her head. The compound eyes were the color of cold water at midnight, but glossy and alive. The creature wore rough-spun clothing, including a collared cloak. It had been thrown back over one shoulder, revealing the hilt of a blade at the creature's waist.

Captain Hudson came around in his chair. Thomas expected him to bellow, pop the release on his restraining harness, and launch himself at the humanoid. His right hand rose toward his breastbone to do just that, then he stopped.

"You're why my engines just got efficient?"

"It was the least I could do after binding my ship to yours."

"You carrying anything that will blow my ship up?"

A webbed crest rose on the creature's head between the antennae, but settled back quickly enough. "I have no intent to cause you or your ship harm. It is that you bring Thomas Firefly to a place I need to reach, and your ship is faster than mine. I will save time and fuel. You will save fuel. It benefits us all."

Hudson looked at Alicia then Thomas. "Eyes on your stations. We're making the jump. Miss Yorgensdottar, count us down to jump."

"Aye, sir."

Hudson pointed to the chamber aft of the cockpit. "Strap in there. We'll be with you once we've made the jump. I don't reckon you're going to tell me much, but I'll have questions a plenty for you to dodge."

O   O   O

Once they made a clean jump into hyperspace, Captain Hudson engaged the autopilot. He spun his chair around and released his restraining straps. "Mr. Firefly, with me. Miss Yorgensdottar, if you don't mind …"

"I have the con, sir."

Thomas brought his seat around. "Sir, why aren't you a lot more agitated about a creature that can park a ship on your ship, defeat your entry systems, modify your engines, and get inside the *Swift?* Do you know her? Is she even a her?"

Hudson tugged at the hem of his jacket. "I don't know her. I've never seen her species before. But your question has the answer in it, doesn't it?"

"I don't know …"

Alicia turned around. "She did all the things you listed. She could have done more. What's the use in getting upset?"

"Good point." Thomas frowned as he freed himself from the restraining straps. "I guess I don't like someone I don't know, knowing about me."

"Son, if that truly concerns you, your life will be long and sad." Hudson patted him on the shoulder. "C'mon."

Thomas followed him into the freighter's small canteen. Their guest had removed her cloak. That revealed a second, shorter dagger bound to the upper portion of her left arm. Thomas checked for any others, but didn't see any. Nor any blasters or odd items that might have been a weapon of some sort.

The creature dropped to a knee and bowed to them. "Your hospitality honors me."

Hudson bowed his head to her. "You're welcome here, of course. Didn't see the second dagger before."

She rose. "That you recognized one was enough."

Thomas looked from Hudson to their guest and back.

The guest noted his apparent confusion. "I am of the Qwelanji peoples. I am known as Vreshvala. Neither of you have encountered my kind before."

Thomas shook his head.

Captain Hudson folded his arms over his chest. "Not the Qwelanji."

"We are much as you humans. Our world was also a protectorate, and many of us were journeyed to far-away by the Arwarzhy." Vreshvala canted her head slightly. "That was long ago. We have since joined the Commonwealth as members."

"So it as you did for the Grey's ship down there, pulled them off my crew?"

"Distracted them, yes." Vreshvala nodded briefly "But you, Captain Hudson, you left unsaid that you have seen the *thenzar-dat* before. You understand the meaning."

Thomas shook his head, suddenly feeling like he was five years old again. "I don't."

"The knives mark her as one of the *Njatta*. They're an organization of all peoples."

Vreshvala's mouth opened in an approximation of a smile. "We have an affinity for machines."

Hudson nodded. "A talent. A genius, I guess. They are to machines and code what Martha Higgs-Hawking was to physics."

"You are being too kind, Captain."

"The other *Njatta* I saw only had one knife. He would have ranked below you, yes?"

"Rank is a concept with much fluidity among us." A clear membrane nictated up over her eyes. "He would have had less experience than I, as perceived by our superiors, in that situation. You aided him, yes?"

"I got out of his way."

"Often all the help one needs. I am sorry to burden you as I have." She turned to face Thomas. "And I apologize for your distress at this conversation. You are anxious about how I know of your destination."

"Pretty much."

"I can only assure you that your enemies do not have it."

Thomas raised an eyebrow. "I have enemies?"

"They are of no consequence."

"That doesn't help."

Captain Hudson gave him a sidelong glance. "You volunteered to join a fighter squadron, and it surprises you that you have enemies?"

"I guess being surprised about that *is* kind of dumb."

"I won't let your commanding officer know." Hudson slapped Thomas on the back. "Vreshvala, all you need from us is a run to the rendezvous with *Unity*?"

"That will be sufficient, yes." She nodded solemnly. "But I shall leave you to your work. You will not even know that I am here."

V

Greg had just come around the tail end of his Shrike when he saw the young man enter the flight deck and stop. The canvas kit-bag slipped from the young man's hand as his eyes widened and mouth opened. He just stared, clearly not seeing much of anything, and Greg actually envied him.

Greg had first seen the flight deck back when the *Unity* was orbiting the Earth. He's stood where the newcomer had, taking in the length of the deck and, at the far end, the opening that revealed the black void of space. For Greg, a portion of the view had been taken up with a crescent moon. Here a gas giant with rings and a couple of moons the size and color of Mars enhanced the view.

That little bit of envy triggered something inside Greg, something that slithered up ugly into his mind. It colored his assessment. The young man had shoulder-length black hair, wide face and dark eyes. He wore a flight suit from the freighter that had jumped into the system. He looked wrong. He had no discipline, no awareness of how silly he appeared, with his mouth open and his eyes unfocused.

He dares presume to be worthy of joining this unit?

Greg shivered. *Where in hell did that come from?* He looked down. His prosthesis had shaped itself into a crude spearpoint—one that looked as if it might have been chipped from stone. *Like something his people might have made long ago.*

Greg shook his head to clear his mind, then forced his hand back into a normal shape. "Can I help you?"

The young man looked at him, blinked a couple of times, then nodded. He took a step forward, then realized he'd dropped his bag. He hesitated.

"Just leave it." Greg advanced, offering his hand. "I'm Greg Allen."

The young man started to take his hand, then stiffened and saluted. "Captain Allen, sir. I'm Thomas Firefly."

Greg returned the salute. "Glad to have you with us. You were with the freighter."

"Yes, sir." Thomas looked back over his shoulder. "I was trying to find my billet. I'm sharing a cabin with Lieutenant O'Leary. I got directions, but some Qian security officers wouldn't let me get there."

"Colonel Clark is meeting with senior staff. Their launch would have been down in the lower docking bay where you came in." Greg jerked a thumb toward the stars and dark. "O'Leary is out on patrol for as long as we have guests."

"Is there a place I should wait?"

"If you give me a minute, we can get coffee in the galley. I was just finishing my inspection of my Shrike."

"Oh, wow." Thomas drifted forward. "The holos don't do them justice. I mean, the brass and wood, I know that's all cosmetic and, at least among my people, this sort of style didn't … wasn't … a *thing*. But boy, those lines, the scalloped edges on wings and tail, it looks like a raptor."

Greg smiled, the last traces of his negative reaction evaporating. "Have you flown one, or only simmed?"

"Only simmed." Thomas' brow furrowed for a moment. "I hadn't put in to join the 301st. I didn't even know about it, not really. I had just completed my testing to upgrade my pilot's license. You know, maybe get a ship of my own. I passed, and then I got an invitation to join the unit."

Interesting. Greg nodded. "You must have tested out incredibly well. You're a Pioneer, right?"

"A clip, yeah. We don't call ourselves Pioneers. Grew up in a colony. You're Terran?"

"An Earther. And I've been told that calling someone a clip is impolite."

Thomas laughed as he ran a hand over the Shrike's tail. "Most of us don't really like Pioneer. Sounds like we wanted to be out here. I mean, I *do*, but my ancestors didn't have much of a choice. Plus, being of Native American stock, the word 'Pioneer' isn't very popular."

"Roger that. Just be aware that Lieutenant Early really doesn't like to be called a 'clip.' She's *Pioneer* all the way, and proud of it."

"Thank you." Thomas sighed. "And so you know, I joined the 301st for the sake of humanity, not wanting to prove myself or anything."

And there you and Lieutenant Early part ways again. "Your knowing that means you're a step ahead of most Terrans. Mind you, we're all proud of where we've come from, but we know the score. Humanity is being judged here."

"So where are you from?"

"North America. The United States. My father is the President."

Thomas' expression slackened. "Is that good?"

"You really don't know?"

"No. I mean, I wish no offense or disrespect, but …"

Greg laughed. "None taken or imagined. Frankly, I'm relieved."

"Because I'm ignorant of Terran politics?"

"Because I'd hoped all of that had been left back in Earth orbit." Greg turned and pointed toward the lift. "Your admission just made me think I might have been right. Let me buy you a cup of coffee."

"Yes, sir, a pleasure sir." Thomas darted back and retrieved his bag. "Just one thing."

"Yes?"

"What's coffee?"

VI

Nick Clark had never warmed to the male of the Qian species. He found them to be arrogant, stubborn, willfully ignorant, intolerant and generally disagreeable. He'd have happily killed one or more because those that didn't make it into the Warrior Caste dominated the bureaucracy. It wasn't enough for them that you dotted Is and crossed Ts—you had to do it in the right font, with the right color, in the right file format and within some archaic calendar timing scheme that had nothing to do with reality.

Most of them are enough of a pain to be fighter jocks.

The only reason he'd not gone on a murder spree was that he dealt mostly with Qian females. They formed the ruling class. Even though the males stood half-again as tall as the females, and massed more than double than they did, the matriarchal nature of their society kept the males in place. Nick gathered that the women controlled all reproduction; so the males toed the line in order that their bloodlines would continue.

Aside from being physically bigger, with a deeper purple hue to their flesh, the other thing that marked males as different—at least among the Warrior Caste—was the lack of cybernetic augmentation. He'd never seen a Qian male as fully integrated as someone like Vych, but the warriors had no lights beneath their flesh. What they did, they did with nerve and sinew alone.

Admiral Rygh Ghaetr dominated Nick's office, as if a demon summoned by some unholy ritual. Seamless flesh gave no clue as to his age, though the hair at his temples had lightened to a midnight blue. His uniform, black, had no decoration save for some red piping around the cuffs, collar and hem. Nick knew the Qian could see in the ultraviolet range, so he suspected rank insignia might be plain to Qian subordinates. The lack of adding anything Nick could see was simply meant to mock him.

Fine.

The Qian shook his head. "I will not be here long enough to enjoy your hospitality. Your petition for a duel is denied."

Nick affected an expression of bewilderment, letting his face slacken and his eyes widen. "Admiral, sir, I am distraught at not being able to pay you proper courtesy and respect as dictated by *Mnemnar-vyste* protocols. I would not have you think me disrespectful."

"Colonel Clark, in a time of war, polite gestures can be a waste of time."

"I understand, sir. I had hoped to thank you for having given us the assignment, which, I am sorry to say, resulted in the accusation by the Haxadissi Ambassador." Nick clasped his hands behind his back. "I hope I did nothing wrong by issuing a challenge. I felt it was necessary, lest the shame of our performance should ascend to you, sir."

The Qian's dark eyes narrowed. "How could you imagine your shame would rise to shroud me?"

"Was I wrong in thinking that our orders passed through your office? Is it another officer I should apologize to?"

"They came through my office."

"Then we have dishonored you." Nick hung his head. *Come on, take the bait.* "I cannot imagine how you can bear that shame."

"Colonel Clark, while your Star Tigers are of paramount importance to your world, what they are able to do is of minor consequence to the war effort. This much is not beyond your grasp." Ghaetr's chin came up. "There is nothing your unit could do that would shame me in the least."

"Then there is nothing, sir, which we could do to increase the esteem in which you are held."

"Quite probably not."

Nick's eyes sharpened. "So that puts you in a very crappy situation, doesn't it, Admiral? But we knew you were there, because you got saddle with us in the first place."

"What is this nonsense?"

Now set the hook. Nick spread his arms wide. "It's pretty plain, Admiral. Your leaders, one and all, want humans as part of your war with the Zeez. Why, I don't know. And your brothers in arms clearly don't want anything to do with us. Even out here, even on *Unity* we hear about how we bounced around and down in tables of organization. We ended up with you because you didn't have enough power to pass us off to anyone else. You would have made us stand down completely and would have forgotten us, save that I dared use my membership in the *Mnemnar-vyste* to force you to act."

"Guard your mouth, Colonel. This is insubordination. I can have you removed."

"No, actually, you can't; and that's your problem. If you can't handle me and my unit, your career is dead. You're not moving anywhere. Your fleet won't be involved in any action that could bring you glory. You will be done."

Ghaetr stabbed a finger at him. "You think you can pressure me into letting you act, no, *dictate* your fate? Do you really know why you fell to me?"

"Enlighten me."

"You fell to me so I could smother you. And so that my sister's son, who is in rank equal to you, and who has his own squadron of fighters, could be moved from my command to that of an ally of mine. My career might be over, but my family's glory will shine through my nephew."

Acid bubbled up from Nick's stomach and burned in his throat. *This isn't quite going the way I wanted it to.*

"Smother you I will, Colonel Clark. I set readiness standards for your unit. You will *never* measure up. You will never be cleared for full action. Your escort job was the highlight of your career. From this point forward, you will be a parade unit only. That *is* understandable to you, yes? Parade, never to see combat, just to pretend that you are warriors.

"You were correct that my leaders want you as part of the fight, but you failed to understand that what they need from you is not *victory*, but a lack of failure. I can guarantee that. Supplies arrive slowly. Maneuvers are rescheduled. Your training, testing, and maintenance cycles will speed up, but the vital demands of the war will slow service."

Nick snorted.

"I believe that denoted amusement among your kind."

"How do you know that, Admiral? Recent study, or did your family *own* some of us?"

That set Ghaetr back for a heartbeat, but no real sign of discomfort flashed over his face. "Your species was always known for being clever and inventive, but to be doomed by impatience and impulsivity. I would tell you that I had thought of giving you a chance, and that the incident at Haxad had forced me to reconsider, but we would both know that to be a falsehood."

"If you smother us, you are making the worst mistake you can imagine."

"My imagination is quite vast, Colonel Clark." The Qian shrugged. "I have made mistakes before, but I have never erred when being cautious. Removing you is just being cautious. Risk you, I risk much. Your victories would be minor, but your losses major."

Nick heard a finality in the admiral's voice which started his stomach collapsing in on itself. *I wanted to be in charge of our fate, now I am. I am not, however, in control of it.*

The door to Nick's office hissed open. A tall, slender humanoid entered. Nick noticed the knives immediately. He'd have gone for the small blaster in his desk drawer, except that the interloper didn't reach for a blade and the Qian security officer outside his door had descended to a knee and had lowered his head reverently.

And Admiral Ghaetr had assumed the same position. "You honor us, *Njatta*."

"The honor is mine, Admiral." The melodious tone of the voice tagged the visitor as female in Nick's mind. "I must ask of you a great service."

Ghaetr looked up, all traces of anger and contempt gone from his face. *Hell, he looks like someone who just got himself a pony for his eighth birthday.*

"If what you wish is in my power to grant, *Njatta*, it is yours."

"Thank you." A webbed crest rose along her skull, and her two antennae quivered. "I have need of this ship, and of the 301st."

Ghaetr blinked, and his lower lip quivered. "But, *Njatta*, this ship, this command, it is beneath your notice. The 301st is understrength and is not prepared for battle. I can recommend for you the *Seyjat-yin*. They are without equal."

"I am well aware of your nephew's unit, Admiral. You honor me with offering them. I am also aware that they are involved in vital operations elsewhere." She turned and smiled at Nick. "But the 301st are known to be as yet unready for operations. Thus their participation would be a complete surprise to adversaries."

"Yes, yes, of course. Of course." Ghaetr lowered his head again. "Whatever you need, *Njatta*, it is yours. Will you wait until they are at strength or …"

"I fear my mission is immediate. We will depart as soon as you have boarded your launch and head back to your flagship."

"I could, *Njatta*, remain to assist."

"I would not keep you from your vital duties, Admiral." She rested a hand on his head. "And I would delay your departure no longer."

"Yes, *Njatta*." Ghaetr rose, shot an unguarded glance at Nick, and wandered from his office.

Nick shifted his gaze to the visitor. "I don't know what you have on him. I'm not even sure I want to know. He may be happy to turn us over to you, but what makes you think I'm going to do the same?"

"You will do it, Colonel Clark, because I know your secret." The visitor nodded. "And it is that knowledge that tells me you are vital to my mission's success."

VII

Nick sat at his desk and stared at a bottle of thirty year old Scotch. He wanted a drink badly, but not because he wanted to release tension or process emotions. If he had taken to drinking to relieve stress, his liver would be the size of Jupiter and he wouldn't have drawn a sober breath in decades.

He wanted it because he understood the flavor, the smoothness of the alcohol. It would be something normal. *The only thing normal in the last two hours.* Despite that desire, he didn't pull a glass out of his desk. He never drank alone. That, too, was normal, and he'd settle for that level of normal at the moment.

Vych entered his office, taking the bottle in with a glance, but without a comment. "Admiral Ghaetr's launch is away."

"What happened here?"

"Your meeting was not monitored, Nicholas."

He leaned back in his chair and stared at a picture on his office wall. It depicted a man in a boat, doing his best to land a big fat trout. "You're smart enough to know that I thought I had Ghaetr hooked, but he really had me."

"I did try to warn you."

"I appreciate that. I'll pay better attention." Nick frowned. "The 301st was done, then that ... person came in. Ghaetr was more in awe of her than a kid visiting Santa. Sorry, that's a ..."

"I comprehend the reference, Nicholas." Vych gave him a gentle smile. "The person is named Vreshvala. She is of the Qwelanji. They are long lived and she is far from her home."

"He called her *Njatta.* His security people let her in here with two knives visible." He shook his head. "You don't have to explain it all, Vych, just enough."

"It is an infinite universe, Nicholas. Incomprehensibly old. Full of chaos and yet, the laws which govern it shape life in common and parallel pathways. There are many species, and yet among them are common beliefs and philosophies. Those beliefs and philosophies— though each species would like to believe they discovered them— form a continuous thread that perhaps even predates the creation of the universe."

The pace of lights playing across her face increased, but swirled through calm whorls and eddies. "The *Njatta* are a people who transcend species. You would call them a sect or cult, perhaps an order or fellowship in the sense of religious or familial organizations. The *Njatta* existed before even the Qian ventured from our first world. Honored are those who are called to join them."

"What do they want?"

She hesitated, and the lights flashed bright before diminishing. "Knowledge, which is a most unsatisfactory answer. My apologies."

"Why did the admiral agree with her request so quickly when she was asking him to let us do *something* and he'd decided we would never do *anything?*"

"Nicholas, you need not be concerned with *Njatta* seeking power."

"In my experience, those who say they aren't seeking power usually are."

The Qian nodded. "And in most cases, your concern would be well placed. But, you see, the *Njatta* have power already. They direct it for the benefit of all."

Nick heard in her voice complete conviction. She believed exactly what she was saying. He knew she understood the wider universe far better than he did. He'd learned to trust her judgment. *I'll trust it now; or* for *now, anyway.*

"She said she had a mission for us. Do you know what it is?"

Vych shook her head. "She is working with our navigators to plot multiple courses in multiple stages. The journey should take between eight days and one of your fortnights."

He chuckled. "You like that word despite it having absolutely no meaning out here."

"The feel of it is very human." She smiled and the lights slowed. "You will have ample time to get Thomas Firefly flight ready."

"I'll want more, but I shall take what I can get." Nick opened his bottom desk drawer and returned the bottle to it. "You will let Vreshvala know that I want to review her plan before we execute it."

"I am certain she comprehends that." The Qian pressed her hands together. "And you must comprehend that if you are successful in this mission, Admiral Ghaetr will never again be an impediment for the 301st."

VIII

Thomas settled into the Shrike's cockpit and exhaled the breath he didn't realize he'd been holding. Though the simulator cockpits had been identical to the one in the fighter, just sitting in the real thing felt different. He knew it to be a matter of perception, but what his brain accepted, his heart ignored.

Because now I can fly.

The pilot's seat had been covered in maroon velvet, and the interior done in woods and brass. The control console itself had a plethora of modern screens, but toggle switches and buttons had an ancient feel. Thomas had never seen their like on the command consoles of any ship he'd flown in but something just felt right about it all. *Even though I have never seen Terra, something that appeals to Terrans also appeals to me.*

Greg Allen, who stood on the stepped platform, leaned on the edge of the cockpit. "Good enough for you?"

"Yes, sir." Thomas laid his left hand on the throttle assembly and grabbed the stick with his right hand. The cold metal spoke to him of power, yet he liked how it warmed to his hand. "Commo, auxiliary monitor, targeting lock, and damage template left; local sensors center; weapons, fuel, and flight control monitors right."

Greg nodded, then pointed at the auxiliary monitor. "You can use that for displaying diagnostic subsystems if needed. I usually have a picture of my wife and daughter there."

Thomas frowned. "I didn't know any of us had left anyone behind."

"They died a couple of years ago." Greg held his right hand up. "In the accident where I lost this. I think a goal of organizing the unit was to have us all unencumbered, but some choices were made politically...."

"I understand, sir. I'll put a picture of my mother there. She died about ten years ago. I've not been back home since." Thomas looked at Greg openly. "I'm sorry if I caused you any pain."

"You couldn't have known." Greg shrugged. "In fact, I'm okay with your not knowing about that or who my family was. It's not that I was running away from things when I chose to come out here. At least, I don't think so. But having everybody see their death as a tragedy means my life gets defined as a tragedy. That would really dishonor my wife and daughter."

"You're very kind, sir." Thomas gave him a solemn nod, then pointed to a slot on the console's right side. "That's the nomad dock?"

"Yeah, the ship's brain. The simulators get data from the central computing resources, but the nomad just boxes it all up. Everything from astronavigation to family photos." Greg smiled. "You've been simming well enough that I'm sure you get one on our next mission."

"You don't know what it is?"

"Nope." Greg glanced toward Colonel Clark's office. "The colonel generally doesn't bother us with details that aren't relevant."

"But he must know."

"Maybe. Then again, the Qian play everything close to the vest." Greg's green eyes narrowed. "You know that expression? From playing cards?"

"It's usually said, 'Qian secrets are never discovered by accident.' Most people say that with some relief in their voices. You sound more suspicious."

"Many of us are."

"Of?"

"Of why they want us helping in their war." Greg nodded at him. "You've been out amid the stars for ten years, did you say? Can you guess why they need us?"

Thomas scratched his head. "Sir, I can't even tell you when the war began. I've been working haulers for, yeah, about ten years. I think I remember a navigator saying he had to plot around some restricted space maybe five years ago. The word 'Zsytzii' wasn't anything I'd heard until three years ago."

"About the time that news went public on Earth about the Commonwealth's existence." Greg ran a hand along his jaw. "We were told it was an invasion."

"Could be." Thomas blushed. "Among the haulers, politics isn't talked much. Space stations and freeports kind of exist in a universe of their own. Sure, a fight somewhere might mean that we get a premium for something we're hauling, or that a cargo is now contraband. Could be the Zeez are invaders, or someone pulling out the Commonwealth, or forces loyal to a military governor who's rebelling. Stories about that sort of thing crop up here and there, but I mostly ignored them. I'm sorry."

"Don't be. I lived in a household that was steeped in politics. You're not missing anything." Greg patted him on the shoulder. "Does make me wonder, though, why you'd volunteer for the 301st."

"Will you accept 'action and adventure' as an answer?"

"If you can get Mr. Yamashita to buy it, sure."

"I've been pretty much avoiding him, sir."

"Evasive maneuvers when dealing with journalists are definitely a survival skill. And it doesn't really matter why you're here, Mr. Firefly. You're a good pilot and clearly an asset to the squadron. That's more than good enough for me."

IX

Greg slipped the translucent block that was his nomad into the rack beside the briefing room's door and took a seat at Colonel Clark's left hand. He sat across from Major Taine. The rest of the squadron sat around the lozenge-shaped briefing table. Vych Thziilon and another non-human stood opposite Colonel Clark.

Greg rested a hand on the table. It looked to be made of walnut, with wood-grain easily visible; and certainly felt like wood. Greg smiled involuntarily because it reminded him of the bedroom set Jennifer had bought to furnish their first home. And when Bianca came along, he'd vowed to learn enough woodworking to make her a matching set.

But I never had the time.

Colonel Clark nodded. Lights flashed over the Qian liaison's face and the hologram of green-blue world blossomed to hover of the table. "This is Thjenza 471.03. The name has no meaning, it's just a catalog reference. There's nothing terribly remarkable about the world except that the CO_2 content makes it warm and we'll be wearing scrubber masks so we can breathe. Earth gravity normal, a variety of wildlife and plants, but no native sapient species. It's off the beaten path.

"From what I've just said you'll have figured out that we're going down there. Atmosphere is a little thick, but that shouldn't be a problem for any of you. Perhaps, *Njatta* Vreshvala, you would care to expand on what we will be doing once we are down there."

"Thank you, Colonel." A webbed crest rose on the non-human's skull. "On the world we will conduct a survey."

Lieutenant Conn O'Leary, raised a finger. "Are you sure it's us you'll be wanting to do that? Wouldn't there be some robots or graduate students who'd have a better grasp on what they were seeing?"

The colonel shook his head. "Within the last century there was a fairly extensive survey of the flora and fauna. Your nomads are pulling down those reports right now."

A wave of impatience flared Greg's nostrils. "What is the threat assessment? If there isn't a threat, you wouldn't want fighters."

Vreshvala turned her face toward him, and he caught himself reflected in the compound eyes. "To my knowledge, there is no threat."

"Then why ...?"

She continued. "It is my feeling that you will be needed."

"Feeling?" Something in her voice drained away Greg's irritation. "So we're coming along against the possibility of trouble?"

"That's roughly it." Colonel Clark's eyes hardened. "Your nomads will have our training schedule. We have two days until we reach the system. You'll each be drawing a rifle, pistol, and mobile sensor array for your nomad. I want you checked out on the firearms. I want you to have eight hours simming in that atmosphere. I want you to study the previous surveys—do that by wings. One of you gets flora, the other fauna. Captain Allen, I want you familiar with the geography. You'll also liaise with *Njatta* Vreshvala as needed."

"Sir, yes, sir."

"One thing for all of you: this may seem like a nothing mission, but it's only a nothing mission if you treat it like one. I don't care if there is no threat down there, I want you acting as if that's just a hive loaded with Zeez. You're going to be sharp and prudent and get back here in one piece. We didn't do badly last time out, but we're doing better this time out. And better the next time. Look around this room. If you half-ass this stuff, one or more of us isn't going to make it back. I know you don't want that to be you; and you sure as hell don't want it to be *them*. Understood?"

"Yes, sir."

"Good. Dismissed."

Greg rose from his seat with the others, then looked at his two superior officers. "Is there anything else you need from me?"

Colonel Clark shook his head. "Not at the moment, Captain. Do your job and we're fine."

"Yes, sir."

He slid his chair back into place, and retrieved his nomad. He grabbed it with his left hand, not wanting to tempt his artificial hand with it. Instead he let the fingers of his right hand drag along the table, relishing the sense of wood that they so faithfully reported to him.

"Captain Allen. May I impose on your time?"

"Yes, *Njatta*, is it? Is that a rank or your name?"

"It is an honorific. Please to be calling me Vreshvala."

"Well, Vreshvala, I am your liaison officer, so I will help as I can." He slid his nomad into a pocket, then waved her toward the door. "What is it I can do for you?"

They moved into the passageway outside the briefing room. "If I might, I would very much like to examine your hand."

Greg hesitated for a heartbeat. Every since the Qian had helped pry him from the wreckage of two aircars and put him back together, people had been curious about the prosthetic he'd been given. The shapeshifting capabilities alone so far outstripped anything humanity had developed that his hand was practically a circus attraction. He firmly felt that people should mind their own business, and usually glowered when someone made that request.

But she's not human. Orientation for all of the 301st's pilots had included briefing about non-human cultures and their particular brands of etiquette. He couldn't remember ever seeing or hearing about whatever Vreshvala was; but a number of species showed how much they valued someone by asking questions which, on Earth, would be considered rudely invasive.

He assumed it was something like that, so he peeled back his grey flightsuit's sleeve and willed the arm to shift from pink to a light blue to mark where it joined his body.

She looked up. "Remarkable control, but that was not necessary. I can see in what you term 'ultraviolet.'" She reached out with both hands and drew them from seam down toward wrist on both sides.

The pilot didn't pull away, though he wanted to. He wanted to because her touch *tickled*, and that was a sensation he'd not felt ... *since Jennifer died.* Then his arm numbed, but didn't feel heavy. Instead, just the opposite. Had it not been attached to his arm, he was certain it would have floated to the passageway's upper reaches.

Vreshvala canted her head to the side. "You have achieved excellent integration. It is beyond what diagnostics would have predicted possible."

"Thank you, I guess." Greg rolled his sleeve back down and fastened the cuff tight. "I don't know that I've done anything special."

"There are those who would disagree, Captain Allen." Vreshvala opened her mouth slightly, simulating a smile. "I would ask you a question."

"Yes?"

"Who are you?"

Greg closed his eyes for a moment. He'd heard that question asked in a hundred different ways. Most often it was a casual request for information. Occasionally journalists would ask it in hopes some penetrating insight or gaff would be the result. He remembered his wife asking it in a multitude of ways, from gentle to angry.

Vreshvala's intonation imparted a dozen different possible meanings for the question. Greg supposed that in her culture, such a question was meant to elicit a family history, so as to fix him in his own social context. But he also heard the request for serious thought. She wanted insight, not a gaff.

"I'm human, from Earth—Terra, if you wish. I am a pilot. I am a widower who has also lost his only child." His eyes opened. *Is this how I truly see myself? As human first, then my job? Is the only family I will mention the family that died?*

Vreshvala laid a hand on his prosthesis. "You are not responsible for the deaths of Jennifer and Bianca Allen."

He started. "I know that. It was an accident. A drunk in an aircar hit us. I'm lucky to be alive."

"You are saying you *know* it, Captain Allen. Do you *feel* it as well?"

"I don't know that there is a difference."

She canted her head. "There is. To *know* is to accept another's report of truth. To *feel* is to establish your own truth as reality."

"I'm not certain I follow."

Vreshvala clasped her hands together at her belt. "Peoples who are being able to see on a sub-atomic level, to be watching quarks combine, elements to combine, they *know* what they have seen. For you, for me, we must accept that what they report is true, but we cannot *know* it is true. Moreover, phenomena in the universe are not all composed of quarks and bonds. For example, did you *know* your daughter loved you, or did you *feel* it?"

"I, ah …" He thought hard. *Can a person ever truly* know *what goes on in the mind of another? And are* feelings *not facts, too? Feelings clearly were facts, to deny that was to deny any validity for emotions. Do I concentrate on* knowing *because I don't want to examine feelings?*

"I feel that she loved me. I believe I *know* it, too."

"Then you are not being unwise." Vreshvala nodded quickly. "The reason I am asking this, am asking you to think on this, is that we are to liaise. This universe, you know of the existence of dark matter."

Greg nodded. "And dark energy. Our senses and instruments can't detect it, but mathematics and physics predicts it must be there."

"That explanation will be sufficient." She held her mouth open in imitation of a smile. "As I said in the briefing, I *feel* there is a threat.

I do not know it. I wish you to understand that if I would tell you of a feeling, you would comprehend a greater validity to it."

The pilot rubbed a hand over the back of his neck. "I'm getting the impression—okay, *feeling*—that in your language, there is a native term for what you are talking about and that we don't have it." *Just as our ancestors who lived before the invention of the telescope never had the word* asteroid. *For those people asteroids never existed, so a word wasn't invented for them.*

"I are correct."

"I'll suggest then a word: gut-feeling." Greg smiled and patted his stomach. "Humans tend to act a lot in concord with gut-feelings."

Vreshvala glanced at his stomach. Some emotion or other played across her features, but Greg had no way of working it out. "Gut-feeling. I was unaware humans had sensory organs located deep within their body cavity."

"Outside my area of expertise."

"Except as being human."

"True." Greg nodded. "Is there anything else I can do for you at the moment?"

"No, Captain, you have been very helpful." She rested a hand on his prosthetic. "If you find any way in which I can be of service to you, please do not hesitate to come to me."

Greg watched her turn away, her dull robes obscuring all but the back of her head and the twin antennae. He wasn't certain what that had all been about, other than maybe establishing rapport. *I don't* know *and am not sure what I* feel.

He ran things back in his mind, and found himself lingering on memories of his wife. Her touch. The sound of her voice. His artificial hand, which had never touched her, warmed as if it safely tucked around her belly in bed. He could feel Bianca kicking in her tummy. He stared at his hand because that simply wasn't possible, and yet he felt it.

He also heard her ask that question, "Who are you?" in a variety of ways. Innocently, when they first met, because she didn't know. And again, at various points. Inquisitively. In mock surprise as he acted out of character. *And angrily.*

He couldn't remember the circumstances surrounding her anger. He just heard it. She asked in a tone that made the question really into "Who do you think you are?" *Why? What had I done? What did I fail to do?*

He focused and tried to remember. He got nothing. No impressions, no flashes of vision. Nothing but a sinking, sick feeling in the pit of his stomach.

Greg leaned back against the passageway bulkhead. "Jennifer, I'm sorry. I never wanted to make you angry."

Her warmth still lingered on his arm. He took that as a sign that her anger hadn't lasted, and hadn't been invoked that often. That made him feel better.

He even dared hope he had been forgiven.

X

Nick Clark couldn't tell if the expression on Vreshvala's face was one of consternation or bemusement—and he wasn't certain he liked either. "I really don't think I can break it down any more simply, *Njatta.* During our discussion about the mission prior to the briefing, you made no mention of a threat. I don't like the idea that you would hold that back from me, then spring it on my people."

"Colonel, when you and I spoke previously, I did not feel there was a threat."

"And that further concerns me: I'd like to see the evidence which underscores this feeling of a threat. I need things to reassess our plans."

The visitor nodded once. "I assure you, Colonel, that your preparations are sufficient."

"And you know this how?"

"If they were not, I should feel a greater threat."

Nick covered his face with his hands. *You cannot blow up at her.* He really still didn't know what she was, but he recalled how Admiral Ghaetr reacted to her and knew that to go off on her would not work. It wouldn't change her mind, and it would kill him in the eyes of Qian leadership.

"*Njatta,* I am certain you meant that as a vote of confidence in my people. I will take it like that. I would hope that you also understand that because the Star Tigers are my responsibility, *I* need to feel comfortable with what we're being asked to do. We're less than a day out from Thjenza 471.03. If we have to change things, I need to know now."

Vreshvala raised both hands. "I understand, Colonel, what you are asking. I would be reassuring you. I fear that I have exacerbated the situation because I told you that I know your secret. Allow me to explain, to give you context."

Nick was pretty certain he wanted to be sitting down for this, but forced himself to move away from his desk and toward the viewports overlooking the flight deck. *Context is what they always provide when they're not going to give you the answer you want.* "I'm listening."

"In the history of the universe, Colonel, civilizations define themselves by their relationship with machines. They are consumed by them, transformed by them, or transcend them. Transformation can be a step on the road to consumption or transcendence."

"I can see that."

"Civilizations also accept or reject machinery, whether a mechanical age, an age of information, or an age where machinery and information are integrated. You would call that artificial intelligence. And there have been civilizations which have created technology which has consumed them."

Nick chuckled. "Holovision has often been decried as such a technology on Earth."

"So it is vilified by every civilization. It provides a false sense of omniscience. It provides much knowledge, but no wisdom; but people believe themselves wiser because they believe themselves better informed. They forget that they do not see everything, just those things others wish them to see."

"And I wish to see more than you've showed me so far."

Vreshvala nodded as she came to his side. "I know, Colonel. What you must understand is that the *Njatta* have an affinity or talent for machinery and information. Our capacity for understanding and seeing and analyzing data is quite vast. Civilizations which have come and gone may not be producing data now, but the simple reality of their having produced it in the past leaves shadows. The situation where someone tells you something and you say, 'I didn't know that,' does not mean that fact did not exist, or that it is true, it simply means that you had a deficit in that area of knowledge."

"I don't want deficits in areas of knowledge as concerns this mission."

"I am understanding that, Colonel. I also understand that any deficit in knowledge will not affect this mission." She held a hand up. "Permit me an example. I said I know your secret. I do not need to know the particulars of your secret, just that you have one. It is a secret you have hidden from your people, yet it is a secret you remind yourself of because it is necessary for you to remain true to who you are. That person is the person who was chosen for this mission; and is the person who will keep your people alive. Their lack of knowledge will no more doom them than it will save them. It is immaterial to their success."

This can't be making sense … and yet … Nick's eyes tightened. "What you are telling me is that we already have all the information we need to succeed in this mission?"

"Yes. Your people have the data and training which would enable them to defeat a Zsytzii force were one to be encountered."

"A force of a certain size. What if they come with twice as many, or four times as many?"

"They do not have those resources, Colonel."

Nick turned to face her. "If you can say that, it means you have solid intel on their military including deployment and orders. That's enough to win the war."

"The *Njatta* do not take sides in this conflict. We have been and will always be devoted to aiding civilizations in reaching their destiny. Victory of the Qian over the Zsytzii or the opposite would work against that."

"You're telling me that despite having the power to end a war and save lives, you'll allow people to continue dying because you believe each race has a pre-determined fate in store for it? And you're asking me to trust the lives of my people on your feeling about what will happen?" Nick shook his head. "There's so much wrong with that I don't know where to begin."

Vreshvala brought her hands together against her stomach. "Do you recall, Colonel, when you watched your children play a game? Perhaps your chess. Or watched them put together a puzzle? You could see how things would turn out, but they could not. You could predict things with certainty which they never could have seen. You might even have warned them and they might have denied it. And yet you would be correct because of experience and superior reasoning and even a mind which was better developed to deal with puzzles and strategies."

Nick saw where she was going and was of a mind to protest, but he wasn't going to fall into her trap. Not only had she been right about watching children, but he'd seen the same when fighting against other nation's pilots. Their methods, their doctrines, their weapons had all defined them; and his greater understanding of all those things had made him a superior fighter. Moreover, in the time he'd spent in the Qian Commonwealth, he'd run into non-humans that made him feel like a child.

"You're telling me that I have to trust your superior judgment?"

"As a soldier, this is not a foreign concept to you."

"'Ours is not to reason why....' No. I guess it isn't." He exhaled slowly. "And yet, with all you know, you can't tell me for certain that none of my people will die."

"I cannot tell you that *I* will not die, Colonel. Yet I shall be there with your people and feel we will be safe."

"I guess I've gone into battle with worse intel." Nick refused to let his hands curl into fists. "I just better not come out with my people being worse for the wear."

XI

If grinning like a fool had been made a capital crime, Thomas Firefly would have continued smiling all the way to the gallows. His Shrike shot from *Unity's* launch bay, inverted and swooped down into an orbit between the ship and the blue-green planet below. He tightened his turn and leveled out on O'Leary's wing just as if they'd been flying together for years.

Simming has nothing on reality. Thomas had piloted freighters and loved flying the shuttle. He'd even spent time in some high performance air-cars, but they were all like walking compared to the Shrike. It responded to the slightest pressure on the controls and almost felt alive.

And I feel more alive flying it.

They settled in, waiting for the rest of the squadron to launch. The planet's rings cut a delightful crescent through the void, shining brightly. Some of the asteroids and stones glinted brightly as they rolled through their orbit. Part of him wanted to head off to fly through the middle of them, but he knew that the visible rocks were the least of the dangers lurking there. For every stone he could see, there were thousands of micro-meteorites that would grind his Shrike to nothing.

He rubbed a hand along the wooden console. *Not going to let that happen to you.*

Clear of *Unity*, he hit switches to bring his weapons online. The nose-mounted Meson Cannon went green first, then all four of the wing-mounted lasers. The Baryon rocket launchers both lit green, and the magazine showed eight missiles fully functional. His shields reported back operational.

Colonel Clark's voice came over the radio speakers in his helmet. "Five and Six, you'll lead us in."

O'Leary replied for the two of them. "Roger, Lead. Five, you're on me."

Thomas nodded, then keyed his radio. "Roger, Six."

Thomas' sensor panel showed seven shrikes and the small launch *Vreshvala* flew. To his mind it wasn't a very remarkable ship. It looked like a cylinder that had been split top from bottom. It had a rounded taper at each end, with three engine pods grafted to the aft section. If it had any weapons, he couldn't see them and his sensors didn't report them.

Thomas and Lieutenant O'Leary led the way down. Lieutenants Early and Sun ran cover above while the colonel and Major Taine each took a flank. Captain Allen brought up the rear, and the *Njatta* ship ran in the middle of the formation.

Once they'd arrived in the system, *Unity's* crew began downloading data from the handful of satellites the Qian survey team had left behind a century ago. The Qian pulled lots of meteorological data, but Colonel Clark had them concentrate on any ship data. Analysis had shown a few ships bouncing through the system, but none of them getting close to the third planet. Most never got closer than the gas giant orbiting ten times as far as the third planet because coming in closer created all sorts of gravitational problems for a smooth and swift jump back out into hyperspace.

Thomas kept his hand steady on the stick as his Shrike entered the atmosphere. The fighter bucked a bit, but settled down as he eased the throttle back. Lights flashed in his nomad as the ship reshaped the shields to help with aerodynamics. Soon the ship cruised through the atmosphere as easily as its namesake might ride an updraft.

He adjusted his inertial compensator to account for the world's gravity, then followed O'Leary down through a layer of clouds. A kilometer and a half down they punched into clear air and came out bearing directly on a mountain.

"Five has visual on Olympus. It's closer than expected."

"No, it's not, Five." Captain Allen's voice carried a note of amusement. "It's just bigger than anything you've seen before."

Thomas checked his sensor ranges. *Damn. It is huge.*

Snow capped the mountain and drew white veins down to where rainforest began to take over. Visible rock appeared grey, but had a soft glow to it—looking more like polished granite than any natural stone had a right to. The trees, Thomas came to realize, had been what fooled him because they grew on a massive scale. They could have hangared all the Shrikes in a hollow at the base of one of the trees. *One of those hollows could house the town where I grew up.* Snow disguised the depth of the mountain valleys and what appeared to be a stream curving around the mountain's base had to be a truly grand river.

As they came within range, a red shape painted itself on Thomas's head's-up display. It corresponded to a plateau they'd located in the survey data. Vreshvala had chosen it as the place she wanted to set down.

"Five, take us into the landing zone."

"Roger, Lead."

The easiest way to guide the others down would be to blast a path through the undergrowth. With a flick of a thumb switch, Thomas could quad up his lasers and start landscaping. The trees might be tall enough to rival buildings which could house thousands, but the lasers would raze them in no time.

In his flight element, he'd gotten to study the flora on the planet. While the canopy appeared, from above, to be thick and impenetrable, the century-old survey indicated it was anything but. He shifted power to his belly shields, then chopped back his throttle and kicked the grav-lift generators in.

Dialing back the lifts, his ship descended slowly. The first carpet of leaves parted easily, letting him into a world of shades of green and blue. Tree boles grew more thick as he descended. Every hundred meters or so he passed through another foliage layer.

Finally, on the ground, he discovered a vast hollow beneath the roots of the tree he'd come down through. A quick scan indicated it was empty. He keyed his radio."

"Conn, anything about fauna big enough to excavate a den in the roots of one of these trees."

"Not that I saw, but such beasties might have been hibernating when the survey was done."

Thomas flicked on his landing lights and added enough thrust to move into the organic hangar. He did a full circle and didn't see anything out of the ordinary. Deploying his landing gear, he touched down and the soft earth gave about a half meter before stabilizing.

O'Leary brought his Shrike down and parked it near the entrance. The other Shrikes swooped down and in. Thomas smiled. It seemed appropriate to have Shrikes nesting in a tree. *Well, close, anyway.*

As the other ships landed, Thomas pulled on his breathing gear, slipped his nomad from the ship into a portable sensor package, and popped the canopy. He climbed out onto his wing, grabbed his laser rifle, and leaped to the nest floor. He sank into the soft loam to his ankles.

He joined Conn near the opening, crouching across from him, laser rifle at the ready. The undergrowth formed a solid green wall. He couldn't see anything but rainforest, even though they'd landed on a plateau halfway up the mountain and no more than five hundred meters from an escarpment.

Unbidden, the lessons his Elders had taught about how life existed on a spiritual level came back to him. They'd pointed it out on an arid world where plants and animals clung to life and protected themselves with venom and thorns. That made it easy for him to discount what they were saying. *But here?* Here the abundance of life made their case wordlessly.

This place strengthens their case more than they could imagine. He smiled. *I wish I had my sketchbook so I could show them.*

O'Leary's voice crackled inside his helmet. "Look alive, Firefly. The colonel catches you acting like a tourist, that's what you'll be once we're back on *Unity* again."

"Roger that, Six." Thomas gave his wingman a thumb's-up as Vreshvala's launch squeezed through the opening. "Our tourist is here. I hope she finds what she's looking for."

XII

Greg Allen did his best not to gawk at the trees soaring overhead. It had to be his imagination, but it seemed that the hole in the canopy had closed just a little in the short time it took for the squadron to land. He told himself it was just branches settling down and out, but he didn't wholly believe it.

He couldn't help but smile beneath his breathing mask. The rainforest and the size of the trees reminded him of a story he used to read to his daughter, about a girl who had become tiny and her adventures in the woods behind her house. He felt that small—and had no desire to meet hedge-hogs in waistcoats or gallant mice with swords and a sense of chivalry. Still the size of the trees humbled him.

Colonel Clark keyed his radio. "Major Taine, you'll remain here with O'Leary and Firefly. Lieutenant O'Leary, deploy your external antenna array. Monitor comms. Let *Unity* know we're down. Also pull data from the satellites and see if you can find out if we're detectable down here."

"Yes, sir."

The colonel pointed toward the tunnel with his laser rifle. "Captain Allen, take point. You two will have our backs. Ready, *Njatta*?"

"Yes, Colonel."

Greg checked his rifle, then headed across the landing zone and out into the rainforest. Traversing fallen foliage and other debris reminded Greg of walking on a trampoline. Things skittered and slithered beneath the leaves, the smallest of which was the size of a snowshoe. He didn't see any signs that they'd been gnawed on much by animals. Mold and fungus seemed to be enjoying the feast however, with red and white spotted mushrooms rising waist high, with the diameter of a decent umbrella.

Maybe I am in that story.

He led them north-northeast and after a short walk they stopped at a rock face at the base of the escarpment. Tree roots hung down from above, or from smaller plants which had grown in niches here and that, but the roots had no purchase on the stone. Moreover, a rectangular space roughly four meters wide and twice that tall remained unobscured.

Greg studied it for a moment, then scanned it with his sensor-pak. "I can't detect any sign of weathering. The survey team didn't take readings on this rock, but stones had weathered normally otherwise."

Vreshvala reached out with a hand and brushed her fingertips over the smooth surface. "It is stone except in the most important way."

Greg frowned. "That being?"

"That it is not stone." Vreshvala nodded toward him. "Touch it, Captain. With your hand that is a hand except in the most important way."

"Sir?"

Colonel Clark nodded. "Unless you have a compelling reason why you shouldn't...."

"No, sir." Greg clipped the sensor-pak back onto his belt, then stripped off his right glove. His hand maintained all appearances of flesh and blood until it got to within a centimeter of the surface. His fingertips began to take on the glowing grey sheen. He wasn't certain if that was better or worse than it jumping immediately to the jagged crystal form. It didn't feel different—*It doesn't feel* anything.

Then his hand met the wall.

He tried to classify what he felt. None of the normal tactile descriptors worked. It wasn't pressure or heat or cold. It didn't feel soft or hard. No pain. *Just a buzzing or tingle, but not a vibration. Nothing is moving, at least not on a macro-level.*

The *Njatta* canted her head. "That sensation, the nearest word in your tongue is *cascade*."

"Yeah, cascade, that works." He glanced at his commanding officer. "It feels the way water burbling up from a spring looks. Not a geyser, just a continuous rolling, swirling."

"Thank you, Captain." Clark looked at Vreshvala. "What does it mean?"

"It means we are safe to enter."

The stone split down the middle and parted, not with jagged edges, cracking and rumbling, but with the soft silence of velvet curtains parting. Ambient light poured in, but the passageway's ceiling remained shrouded in shadow. Even when Colonel Clark turned on the flashlight attachment for his sensor-pak, the light couldn't reach the roof.

Greg followed Vreshvala into the passageway. It grew to accommodate them, giving Greg the sense that they had been swallowed by a snake and were being sped into its gullet. Yet even as that idea came to him, he felt no threat. The *cascade* continued and reassured him that they weren't trapped.

Lieutenants Early and Sun remained at the doorway as the others explored. The passageway walls had a translucency which seemed to allow for the play of shadows within them. It reminded Greg of looking into a muddy lake and being able to see for the meter or two that sunlight penetrated, then all grew dark. The fleet shadows defied description, and Greg purposely didn't try to ferret out meaning.

Colonel Clark slung his laser rifle over his back. "We're inside a machine."

Vreshvala turned, her mouth open, but not in a smile. "Very good, Colonel."

"Obvious. You have an affinity for machines." He glanced at the data screen on the sensor-pak. "Did you know this was here?"

Greg looked at her. "Did you *feel* it was here?"

"This system, this place, felt as other places have."

"What *is* this?" Colonel Clark rubbed a hand over the back of his neck. "It seems like the heart of a glacier, but it's not cold."

"Colonel, you recall my saying that some species *transcend*. By this I mean that they move beyond necessities and limitations of physical forms—at least as we understand them. The people who created this place are such a species."

As she spoke a tall, slender, ghostlike creature floated up through the stone in the glare of the colonel's flashlight. It stopped as if trapped beneath a translucent layer of ice. Though twice as tall as Vreshvala, and a luminescent white, the creature closely resembled the *Njatta* in form. It had two antennae and the sail on its head stood a bit taller. It had the same three fingers and thumb on each hand, and compound eyes which featured four extra domes.

Vreshvala pressed her hands together. "That, I believe, is being a representation of the creatures which created this place."

"Looks a lot like you. Is that why we're here?"

"No, Colonel." She bowed her head. "You have seen, in your travels, enough non-human life forms to recognize the functionality of what you are calling the humanoid shape. Some people believe that life was seeded throughout the universe, thus to be accounting for the commonality. Others believe that physical laws of the universe dictate practical pathways for evolution, and this determines the shapes we inhabit.

"There is no connection of which I am aware between this species and my own. These people have been ascendant for millions of years. My people, like yours, have been present on our world for far less time."

Greg had drifted closer to the creature. "Why did they build this place?"

"I believe it would be, in your idiom, because they were hedging their bets. While a species may approach transcendence As a unit, some individuals will travel more swiftly toward that goal than others. This would be a place where they were storing their memory, their essence, against failure."

Greg spun, his eyes narrowing. "You're saying this is a seed bank. If they wanted to repopulate their world, they could do it from here."

Vreshvala nodded. "That would be the purpose. The motive remains infinite. This could have been a museum. It could have been a project conducted by rebellious forces who stored an army here. This mountain could contain an army and all that is necessary to make that army function.

Greg shivered. "The lack of weathering is because this machine preserves itself. That cascade is this machine renewing itself."

Colonel Clark frowned. "That would take incredible power."

"It would, sir. I'm willing to bet that is what the forest is. It functions as a monster photovoltaic array. The roots run deep, and run into this mountain. All the plants could be connected, so everything feeds into here. As long as the sun shines, this place will preserve itself."

The colonel nodded. "Until it gets a signal to decant or rebuild whatever it has stored here. Or, if it detects a loss of power, it probably is programmed start sending spores out, or to create and outfit survey teams to find other worlds."

Greg turned to Vreshvala. "That's what you came to look at. If these people, people who had enough mastery over their circumstances to harness the power of the solar system, were to burst out, it would be like a pocket of disease bursting into a population with no chance of opposing it."

"I am not disputing your assessment, Captain. Likewise, recovery of this society's military assets would be problematic."

Colonel Clark scratched at the crescent scar on his chin. "Though I doubt we could do it, destroying this place and the weapons is unacceptable since it would be genocide."

"We could not, Colonel." Vreshvala stroked the passageway's smooth surface. "Opening this site would be possible, but with the potentially horrible results we have been discussing."

Lieutenant Sun Lan joined them. "Colonel, Major Taine tried to reach you. She is in communication with *Unity*. There is something you will want to see."

Clark nodded. "I'll leave it to you to learn what you can. I don't mind admitting, I'm not seeing a simple solution to this problem. Hell, I'm not even sure if I can define the problem."

"Your wisdom is a credit to you, Colonel."

Greg let his artificial fingers brush the wall as the colonel departed. The cascade still thrummed through it, and another current ran beneath. For a moment he thought it was his heartbeat somehow reflected, but it wasn't in sync with the throbbing in his neck. *Not my heartbeat, but their heartbeats.*

He shivered. After the accident he'd been in a coma for the better part of a year and a half. The Qian had rebuilt him. He couldn't really remember anything from that time. He just had a sense of floating in a void, waiting for something. *Is that what they feel?*

"*Njatta*, do you know anything of these people?"

"Nothing."

"Have you found other, similar, repositories? Could you tell me if you had?"

"No, and yes." Her shoulders rose and fell. "Whether or not I would be telling you is another matter. The *Njatta* know of many traces of lost civilizations. The universe, to be using a word of yours, is *littered* with them. Some ruins even indicate that those species had known of even older species, and so on. And we have found repositories, usually connected with colonies or lost world-ships; but I am unaware of evidence that another species hedged its bets this way."

"There's another question here, isn't there?" Greg's green eyes narrowed. "Colonel Clark said it would be genocide to destroy this place. Does that suggest that we have a moral responsibility to revive these people? Back on Earth, the debate has long raged over bringing back extinct species of animals. While the technology exists to do so, people have pointed out that whatever socialization these creatures knew would be denied them. While a beast might be a mastodon in form and genetics, it wouldn't learn what it is to be a mastodon. The environment would be different, and there would be nothing there to teach it."

"You would be correct, Captain, at least partly so." She opened her arms. "This world is probably nothing like the one on which they evolved. There might not even be original genetic material here, but programs and machines that would rebuild them on a molecular level. Would they be the people they were? Did the best of them leave only their evil behind, or vice versa? I do not know if we have an obligation to resurrect them because that may run counter to whatever intentions they had in placing them here."

Greg's guts twisted. "What if this was meant to be a prison, to forever hold those who had committed horrific crimes? What if they were placed here and forgotten when the rest of them transcended?"

"Your suggestion is most intriguing and not a small bit terrifying."

"I'm just thinking that what might appear to be the right thing could easily be a very bad thing."

She tilted her head to the side. "What do you *feel*, Captain?"

Greg hesitated, then touched the wall again. "I *feel* they want to be alive again. And I feel that is a decision that I cannot make."

"Our feelings coincide."

Sun Lan came running back down the passageway. "The colonel, he wishes you to come. The Zsytzii have arrived. They've launched a survey ship, and they've got fighters covering it. Many fighters."

XIII

"If *this* was the threat you were feeling, *Njatta*, you underestimate the Zeez or overestimate our skills." Nick touched the screen on his sensor-pak and projected a larger image against a pale green leaf. "The Zeez entered the system with an *Amcharac* class battlecruiser. It masses three times what *Unity* does. It's launched a survey ship and a squadron of fighters to cover it."

As he spoke, the images changed from the long, rectangular starship to a representation of a standard Zsytzii "fighter." Each one of their aerospace combat units consisted of an cruciform command ship—codenamed Crux—and five smaller ships which weren't much more than a cockpit with a laser cannon on one end and an engine on the other. A Zsytzii squadron consisted of a half-dozen of the command ships, which meant the 301st were outnumbered five to one.

And that's if they don't launch more *fighters.*

The Zsytzii reproduced in litters of six males or up to three females. The females remained equal, but within a male litter, one child was the superior, and the five functioned as juniors. The juniors would never mature, physically or mentally, and had formed a very useful labor pool in Zsytzii history. Qian sources believed the superiors and his juniors had a basic psychic link but cybernetics had been used to upgrade the link and give the superior direct control over his brothers.

Nick looked at Greg. "Here's the bad news. *Unity* is pulling this data through the survey satellites. The world is masking her presence, but the Zsytzii capital ship is parked on the route out of the system. We are outgunned and outmanned, even if five out of six of those 'men' are feral first graders. Would I be correct in assuming, *Njatta*, that letting the Zeez in here is unacceptable?"

"This was not the threat I felt, Colonel. And you are correct."

Greg Allen held up a hand. "*Unity* can't run out of the system sub-hype and find another jump solution?"

Nick shook his head. "Not without us, I have been told, and I'm taking that to mean we're not leaving *Njatta* Vreshvala here. Immaterial, really, since running would concede the world to the enemy."

O'Leary folded his arms. "Looks as if any donnybrook ends up with them taking it anyway."

"They do have one weakness."

Greg Allen looked at the projection again. "Sorry sir, I'm not seeing it."

Nick brought the survey ship up. "You're on a mission during a war. You're here to find something. You can imagine there's some urgency. You're sending in a survey team that's valuable enough that you screen them with fighters. Strikes me that the survey crew is your best and brightest, so they get things right on the first pass."

Greg nodded. "All their eggs in one basket."

"Exactly." Nick killed the projection. "Two and a half hours until they hit atmosphere. That's when we hit them."

O O O

Nick glanced at his Shrike's auxiliary monitor. It displayed telemetry coming in from the Qian survey satellites, via the external antennae array. It showed the Zsytzii ships coming in fast and still on their original approach vector. Their heading would take them to the plateau he and his squadron had just quitted.

Had that been his flight incoming, he'd have knocked the satellites down. The only reason they might not have was that a previous scouting trip had pulled telemetry from them, and the Zeez were still using them as a source of intel on the planet. To protect themselves, the Star Tigers had activated protocols which erased any sign of their presence.

Nick had dispersed his forces carefully. *Njatta* Vreshvala had followed his recommendation that she should take her ship, work her way around to the opposite side of the planet, and get out to report her findings to the rest of the *Njatta*.

He'd tried to get *Unity* to head out the same way, but Vych had refused that order. Though her refusal probably doomed *Unity*, she explained simply that to run and abandon the humans would undermine the Star Tigers' legacy. While they both knew that no official record of this mission would ever exist, within the Qian hierarchy they would know the truth, and that counted for a great deal in the grander scheme of things.

Nick shook his head. He hated the very idea of "the grander scheme of things," because most folks put the emphasis on *grander* when the important bit was *scheme*. He'd known from the start—*all* the Star Tigers had known from the start—that they were pawns in some great game. *But even pawns can become Knights if they survive long enough*. To enable them to survive had been his goal.

They'd settled on a basic plan. The Star Tigers would hit the incoming Zeez hard, then burn for *Unity*. Once all the fighters had been recovered, the crew would make a micro-hop to what appeared to be a gravitationally stable spot in the system. From there they would make a run at getting all the way out.

But if that spot doesn't exist.... Fact was, the presence of rings around the planet played hob with gravitational solutions. Collisions between rocks could shift profiles and invalidate a solution in the blink of an eye. He shook his head. *First problems first.*

To wait for the Zeez, Nick had sunk six of the Shrikes in the large lake on the approach to the plateau. They'd inserted below the algae layer, sinking to a depth of ten meters. There the sunlight just made the water above glow with a milky jade light. It undulated a bit, almost like an aurora.

He looked for fish, but didn't see any. Still, he smiled. "If we get out of here, I'm coming back and hooking something."

The layer of water above would have made any sensor signals unreliable—at least from fighters at that range. Nick hit a switch, severing the cable to the external antennae array. The floatation collar on the device popped, and the antenna slowly sank into the darkness below his ship.

As the Zeez began to enter the atmosphere, Nick increased power to the grav-lift arrays. His Shrike slowly rose from the depths. Algae and water sheeted off as he broke the surface. Port and starboard, fore and aft, the other five pilots came up.

Greg Allen and O'Leary were ahead and to the left, Major Taine was off Nick's right wing, and Sun and Early were back right. As per their plan, the Shrikes kept low to the water, skimming the surface, picking up speed. Then, three seconds from what had been the far shore, the fighters went vertical, aiming toward a shower of bright lights burning into the atmosphere above.

Nick brought his shields up to full and pumped all the energy into the front hemisphere. With the flick of a thumb he paired his Baryon Missiles and began to pick targets. Major Taine would be focused on the Superior in the last flight element, while he'd pick up the juniors. Likewise the other two flight elements would target the hindmost Zeez flight elements.

The second and most dangerous mistake the Zeez had made concerned their entry. Their shields allowed them to enter the atmosphere, but the friction between shield and atmosphere generated a lot of heat and a fair amount of plasma. That tended to interfere with sensor arrays. Either they'd been very careless, or were relying on the survey satellite data to show them what was going on down below. Regardless, they were coming in hot into an area that was about to get much hotter.

Nick flipped his radio over to Tac-three. "Mr. Firefly, you are clear to move."

"Roger, Lead."

The colonel shifted back to Tac-one. "Engage on my mark. Mark."

O   O   O

Thomas nudged power to his grav-lift arrays. His Shrike began to rise. Using pedals and stick he navigated by pointing the ship's nose up, then threading his way through branches and leaves. He could have blasted straight up through—his shields would have more than sufficed for preventing any damage—but he couldn't bring himself to do that. Even if Greg Allen was right and the trees were just a mass of solar cells, something about the forest itself demanded respect.

Thomas smiled. He'd seen a lot to marvel at in his travels, so the wonders of nature weren't foreign to him. But this was nature on an industrial scale, which was ancient, and it sent chills down his spine.

He popped up through the foliage and immediately locked onto the survey vessel. It glowed very brightly. About twice the length and four times the girth of Vreshvala's launch, it was pushing a lot of super-heated air in front of its forward shields. The targeting computer immediately identified it, displaying a boxy ship with two engines at the back, four grav-lift generators on the bottom and ...

What the...?

Launch-warning klaxons blared as the survey ship launched two Baryon rockets. Thomas yanked his stick to port, kicking the Shrike into a barrel-roll, then ruddered around back onto his attack vector. The klaxons still sounded, but his console reported no missile lock.

What are they shooting at?

The missile streaked past him, then vanished into the forest. An eyeblink later light flashed. Fire ripped a rectangular scar in the world's green flesh. Flames rose and curled into black smoke above the Zeez charred landing zone.

No, no, how could they....?

Thomas punched his throttle all the way forward and brought his Baryon rockets online. Pulling back on the stick he flew up above the survey ship's glide path, letting the hot gasses in front of it shield him. He inverted, then tugged back more and dove straight at the coffin-shaped ship's aft. At point blank range, his middle finger tightened on the firing button.

The Baryon rockets streaked in at the Zeez ship. The first slammed into a shield, but the explosion shredded it. As nearly as Thomas could figure, at the last minute the pilot had shifted energy to his aft shields, but they'd not reached anywhere near full capacity when his first missile hammered it.

Though blunted, that first detonation evaporated the ship's thin armor and thinner hull. That breach, in the engine compartment, would have been more than enough to suck out crew members and any loose equipment. It wasn't enough to destroy the ship, but it would have crippled it.

The second missile shot through the hole in the hull and exploded within the engine room. The blast melted the engines and destroyed the magnetic containment vessels which managed the fusion reaction. The super-heated plasma, freed of all restraint, expanded much as had the fireball in the forest below.

The ship's internal bulkheads and hatches had been engineered to withstand the vacuum of space, not to contain the heart of a miniature sun. The heat vaporized them in an instant, and quickly thereafter gnawed through the hull's support structures. Auxiliary engines and battery packs—which were all that powered life support and shields—vanished next.

The world's atmosphere had its revenge. The survey ship broke apart roughly five kilometers above the surface. The pieces and parts sailed along on momentum alone, crashing into the fiery hole in the forest.

Thomas keyed the radio. "Lead, the lab is down. Repeat, the lab is down." A light lit on his console, and a new warning klaxon began to blare. "And it looks like I could use some help."

O   O   O

Greg replied to Thomas's message. "Lead, Nine has him. Six, on me."

"Roger, Nine, on you."

Greg kicked his Shrike up and over, then dove. He shunted power to his aft shields just in case any of the juniors decided to follow him. He loaded two Baryon rockets, then picked out a senior and shot O'Leary the targeting info. "Take him with two."

Greg shifted aim for the senior diving his flight on Thomas. "Nomad, prox-blast, four meters from target." Once he got a confirmation light on the weapons' display, he hit the trigger button with his middle finger.

The twin missiles lanced forward on bright flame, curving up from Greg's line of flight as they tracked their target. The senior juked at the last second, rolling left. The first missile went past and exploded harmlessly. The second lit off closer, pinging shrapnel off the senior's shield. A couple fragments made it deep enough to scratch paint off the ball cockpit.

While Greg could have hoped he'd take out the senior, he got the effect he wanted. The juniors, following in a tight pattern, followed their senior tightly as if they were fish in a school. The second missile exploded in the middle of their formation. Two of the smaller darts snapped in half. A third rolled away lazily, the pilot dead. The last two scattered and Greg flew through the heart of the explosion, rolling to drop onto the senior's aft.

Below him Thomas' Shrike danced through the air like a kite in a gale. The senior hung with him. Laser bolts sizzled past, but never so much as brushed one of Thomas' shields. The Zsytzii senior aped Thomas' movements, which had Greg doing all he could to stay on the Zeez's tail.

"Five, break right to 45.1 on my mark." Greg hit rudder pedal. "Mark."

Thomas rolled and dove right. The senior inverted to follow. The second he started to dive, Greg hit the Meson Cannon's trigger. The golden beam scintillated off the Crux's shield, then punched through. The beam sliced one weapon pod off close to the fuselage, then cored through the armor over one of the engines.

A secondary explosion started thick, dark smoke trailing from the Crux. The Zsytzii ship began a long spiral down toward the surface. The ship straightened out and headed toward the black gash in the forest.

Red laser bolts crackled against Greg's aft shields. He stood the Shrike up on its port wing, then completed the roll and swooped down toward the starboard. The two juniors in his wake had broken to port, not anticipating his full roll. If he pulled back on the stick, he could come back up hit them from below.

Before he did that, he took a quick glance at his threat monitor. They'd launched against thirty-six Zsytzii ships. Two seniors survived. Fifteen of the juniors were still in the fight. All of the Star Tigers remained operational, though sensors reported that Early's Shrike had lost aft shields and one engine.

Which means the chances of her making it to Unity *for evac are tiny if she has to fight her way clear.*

He keyed his radio. "How are we playing this, Lead? It's a target rich environment."

"Problem is, Nine," frustration ran through the colonel's voice, "It just got a lot richer."

o o o

Nick's auxiliary monitor still pulled telemetry from the satellites. The Zsytzii's *Amchara* battlecruiser had been lurking two and a half hours away—at least as measured by the possible arrival of fighters to reinforce the original squadron. That margin had been the only thing which gave the Star Tigers a *chance* of getting to *Unity* and making the micro-jump to safety.

The Zsytzii captain made a decision. Exploiting the same anomaly which *Unity* would have used to jump *out*, he jumped *in*, tucking his ship inside the planet's rings. While that opened the way for *Unity* to make a run for safety, it also allowed the Zeez to dump two more fighter squadrons into the theatre. To make things even more exciting, the cruiser cut loose with several heavy Meson Cannon batteries, stabbing gold energy columns into the atmosphere.

If we had ground troops, they'd be mighty uncomfortable now.

Nick opened his radio to all tactical frequencies. "Tigers, break off, head down. Lose yourselves. *Unity,* evacuate. We'll wait for you to come back for us."

"Negative, Tiger Lead. That will compromise this world. We cannot let that happen."

"No stopping it."

Vych's voice betrayed no emotion. "There is. We're working out the solution now. We will destroy the cruiser."

"It has bigger guns and range on you. You won't get that close."

"We will if we jump into it. There is a narrow gravitational window."

Nick rolled his fighter, chopped back the throttle, waited for the junior on his tail to flash past, then burned him with a quad laser burst. *"Unity* you can't do that."

"Those the protocols, Lead. We will send for help for you." Vych's voice faltered. "Remember us well."

O   O   O

At the colonel's command, Thomas had rolled his Shrike and dove for the surface. Two juniors followed him. He pushed power to his aft shields and raced into the smoldering hole the Zeez had carved into the forest. He chopped the throttle back, then banked to starboard and plunged into the living forest.

In getting to his position to attack the survey ship, Thomas had noticed that the foliage had distinct tiers and tunnels. Gaps opened between the upper level, middle and then forest floor. Given that the uppermost leaves were a dark green, and the middle tier had more of a blue tint, he wondered if the seasons caused some leaves to fall and others to grow, continuing the energy harvesting.

Maybe I'll escape to the southern hemisphere and see if it is different down there.

Laser bolts streaked past, lighting guttering flames in branches and boles. Thomas banked starboard, reversed his throttle, and dropped his Shrike a hundred meters. He made a flat turn to port and throttled up. He watched the junior ships adjust to follow and he smiled. *I can lead you on this merry chase all day.*

Apparently that conclusion occurred to one of the juniors. While they might mentally have been no more intelligent than a human in kindergarten, they clearly had that much cunning. While one pursued him, the other ship rose above the canopy and just started shooting.

Angry red darts laced the forest with fire. Thomas broke to port. Fire from behind spattered against his shields. The ship above him, apparently hovering and spinning, angled more fire from above. He rolled to starboard and dropped. *That'll work until I'm on the forest floor, then it's just a matter of time.*

He shifted power to his top and aft shields to buy himself some more time, then a brilliant white light flashed above him. The hovering Zeez junior vanished from his sensor screen. A heartbeat later the light representing the second one likewise died, but without any explosion.

Thomas hit his radio. "Thanks, Nine, for getting them."

"Love to take credit, Five, but we're still busy up here." Greg's voice tightened. "But if you're free...."

O O O

Nick rolled and broke for the atmosphere. "*Unity*, do not make that tactical jump."

"We will evac non-essential personnel, Lead. They're now yours."

"Vych!"

"Ships away." The Qian's voice softened. "Save them and yourselves."

Ahead, coming up over the curve of the planet's disc, *Unity* appeared. Dozens of evacuation pods burned away hard. They headed straight toward the planet, and two Zsytzii fighter squadrons broke off to pursue them.

Nick keyed his radio. "Evac pods incoming. Protect them at all costs."

He glanced at his threat display. *More of them than there are of me. Time to bag my limit.*

Hauling back on the stick, he came in at a shallow angle at the atmosphere. He punched power to his belly shields and skipped off the planet's gaseous shell, then boosted power forward. A junior that had been on his tail exploded behind him when its angle of attack drove it too steeply into the atmosphere.

He flicked his lasers over to pairs, rolled to port, then punched his throttle full forward. He shifted power to his forward shields, then tightened up on his trigger.

The lasers pulsed red fire into an oncoming cluster. The juniors jinked, which saved their lives and spoiled their aim. The senior at their heart cycled his lasers, then hit rudder to pull his fighter out of Nick's line of fire.

Nick reversed his throttle, then brought his ship's nose up and hit rudder. As the Zeez laser fire burned through where he should have been, he triggered his Meson Cannon. The gold beam linked the two ships. Much of the energy skipped away from the angled shields, then they collapsed. The beam scorched a black scar on the Crux's nose.

Not enough.

Then the Crux exploded.

Nick glanced at his threat monitor. None of the other Tigers were even close. Moreover, *Unity* still appeared on his scope.

Worse yet, the stars are moving.

The radio crackled. "Lead, *Unity* cannot jump. The window has closed. We have failed."

Nick's heart leaped despite the resignation in Vych's voice. He didn't reply, however, because nothing he was seeing made any sense.

The stars, or what appeared to be stars, were indeed moving. A portion of Thjenza 471.03's inner ring had detached itself. Thousands, perhaps tens of thousands of rocks, varying from things the size of a grain of sand to one captured asteroid larger than Nick's Shrike, tumbled through space. They glittered and flashed in sunlight, deadly diamonds accelerating down into the planet's gravity well.

That's why your window closed, Unity.

The stone shower swept through space. Traveling at incredible speeds, each grain slammed into shields and ships with a force that collapsed energy fields and pounded straight through armor and hull.

Cockpit canopies shattered. Engines exploded. Magazine detonations ripped fighters apart from the inside.

The asteroid broke against the battlecruiser's shields, but battered them harshly. Shield projectors exploded. Nick's monitors showed the battlecruisers shields to be so weak that his Meson Cannon could have cored its way into the hull. *That wouldn't be enough to kill it, but it* would *leave a mark.*

Fist-sized stones fell in the asteroid's wake, doing quickly what Nick's energy beam would have labored to accomplish. Armor plates shattered. Rocky debris punched through the hull, leaving holes with glowing red edges. Smaller stones, and a few bigger, pummeled the Zsytzii ship, abrading all the armor, then grinding through whatever remained. In the blink of an eye the relentless assault cut away enough that Nick got to study the battlecruisers structure. The ship rolled, engine pods tumbling toward the planet, with equipment and crew members spinning into space.

In under a minute the battlecruiser went from a formidable engine of war to a cloud of debris indistinguishable from the storm of stones which had destroyed it. And it, with the remains of the fighters and the ring fragments themselves, made for a beautiful spray of shooting stars as they burned into the world's atmosphere.

O O O

Greg Allen looked down into the steaming depths of the coffee Jiro Yamashita had brought him. The journalist sat opposite him at a round table in the galley, with Thomas Firefly taking up a third seat, hunched over sketching. "I appreciate what you're telling me you saw from the evac pod, Mr. Yamashita, but I really cannot comment. You already know this mission is completely embargoed, and any attempt you make to relate what you saw will be suppressed."

"I'm a journalist. I have to try."

"I know. Fact is, I *don't* really know what happened down there."

Jiro looked at Thomas. "And you, Mr. Firefly?"

Thomas looked up from his sketchbook. "Captain Allen has it right. I can't explain any of that. Not scientifically, anyway."

Jiro leaned in, and Greg's stomach tightened. *Where are you going with this, Thomas?*

"Tell me, please, Mr. Firefly."

Thomas shrugged. "Traditions I was raised in stressed that everything has a spiritual life, and we're just part of it. Look, you were down there for a bit, before your pod got recovered. Couldn't you feel something *more* in the forest?"

"It's not about me. You spent more time down there, saw things I didn't."

"Okay. My sense is that the planet's spirit didn't like it being attacked. What you saw, I guess, was the planet's immune response."

"Immune response." Jiro frowned. "How exactly would that work?"

Thomas shook his head. "If I knew that, I'd be more than a fighter jock." He looked stricken for a moment and faced Greg. "I can say that, right?"

"Call yourself a fighter jock." Greg nodded. "Yeah, you earned that. Of course, your *only* kill was kind of hard to miss...."

Jiro sat back, folded his arms over his chest. "What happened down there is only part of the story. I got evacced with all non-essential personnel. That means *Unity* was going to do something that would doom it as far as the Qian were concerned. Only reason they'd do that would be to protect something huge."

"You don't think a planet that's alive would be huge?"

"Oh, I do, Captain Allen. I do. But ..." Jiro arched an eyebrow. "It does make me wonder what other secrets the Qian have, and to what extreme lengths they'll go to keep them hidden from the rest of us."

O O O

Nick suppressed the urge to shake his head. "I think my people understand the need to keep knowledge of what we saw to ourselves. I do wonder one thing, though."

Vych and Vreshvala both nodded toward him.

"How soon does a Qian ship arrive to do some damage and teach that world that we can't be trusted, either?"

The *Njatta* raised a hand to shoulder height. "There is no need. There is no trace of this planet's existence in any accessible database. It's all been done away with. Instead, on navigational charts, Thjenza 471 is shown to be a collapsed star. It is a navigational hazard. No one will ever visit. No one will ever know."

He laughed. "Our navigators know. My pilots know."

"None of them could plot a course back to that world. No nomads or navigational computers will be able to successfully manage that task."

"Someone could see it with a telescope."

Vych shook her head. "Nicholas, you must fully appreciate what *Njatta* Vreshvala has told you. There is no location where an optical telescope could be placed which would detect that system. More sophisticated telescopes could collect data *indicating* it is there, but the *Njatta* have made it such that any analysis of that data would simply erase evidence of the system's existence."

"And you're sure there's no chance it will be discovered?" Nick read shock in the asymmetrical play of lights over Vych's face. "Not to question your honor, *Njatta*, but it's my experience that secrets don't like to stay secret. And, frankly, given that the *Njatta* have their own agenda in the world, I *know* you have the information stored away somewhere in case it becomes vital later."

Vreshvala nodded. "I did say 'accessible.' You are wise to question, but you should not worry."

Vych smiled. "The *Njatta* are never wrong in matters such as this."

"I've never had good experience with claims of infallibility." Nick gave Vreshvala a hard stare. "Remember when you talked about my secret, my children?"

"Yes."

"I don't have any children."

"Indeed, Colonel Clark." The *Njatta* cocked her head to the left. "My mistake. You *do* have children, and grandchildren; you just have not yet had the pleasure of meeting them."

AND NOT TO YIELD

SARAH A. HOYT

The trial starts with a sad-eyed major sitting behind a desk. My desk. My office has been commandeered for my own martial court. We're almost alone. The new laws require trial by jury—trial by twelve as the people call it—but that rule is for civil trials, not for military trials, where autocratic rule prevails. It's not as bad as it was under the regime we overthrew, the regime of the Good Men, mind. You won't get condemned and killed because one man, the sole, undisputed hereditary ruler of the Seacity, is having a bad day. No. Though there are two privates by the door, both fully armed, ready to shoot me down if I should make a run for it, I'm not treated like a criminal.

Instead, I'm presumed innocent until proven guilty, and I stand in my full uniform, with the colonel insignia at shoulder and sleeve, above the patch showing the legendary mountain from which my land gets its name. And I have a defense council, a judge advocate. He's not a lawyer but an old friend, Royce Allard, looking hot under the collar and a little afraid.

He should be afraid. The procedures might be impromptu, the courtroom an office, but the results of this trial are full and binding and final. I stand accused of going AWOL in time of war, of disobeying the direct orders of my superiors, of unlawful kidnapping and assault, and of "conduct unbecoming," which covered everything else of note. I guess military lingo didn't have a term for going crazy and hurting important people. Then comes the bagful of minor sins, including theft, kidnapping, breaking and entering into a secure facility, menacing, risking important information falling into the hands of the enemy and risking being taken hostage, and a few other things, possibly including, but not limited to, using bad language and being seen in a ragged uniform. All together those are worth little. A few days in jail, a reduction in pay.

It doesn't matter, because the major charges, if proven, will see me hanged by the neck till dead.

And they will be proven, because, you see, I am guilty.

○　○　○

War for me began ten years after revolution had freed Olympus Seacity; five years after I'd been made a colonel and head of our propaganda machine.

It is not war to pilot a desk. It's not war to think up clever holocasts and sneaky methods to subvert the enemy's carefully planted idea that their regime has given the Earth three hundred years of "peace and security." It is not war to wait, to hope, to search the casualty lists every night, to pray to a God I wasn't sure of believing in that *his* name wouldn't be among the dead and missing.

Though we were both technically believers in the long forbidden Usaian religion, he was the believer, and I believed in him. And though both of us had been instrumental in the revolution that set the Seacity on the path to restoring the ancient principles of *life, liberty, and the pursuit of happiness,* the truth was that Nat—Nathaniel Green Remy—fought. I stayed home and planned and waited.

Home had been reduced to a small part of what had been my ancestral palace.

My name is Lucius Dante Maximillian Keeva. I was born to one of the fifty men who between them ruled all the Earth—the Good Men, as they were called—and raised as heir to Olympus Seacity and its subject territories. Or not quite. It turned out the intolerable rule of the man whom I have to call Father had other dimensions, other implications. Some of which led me to solitary confinement for fifteen years and to the raw edge of what I must, for lack of a better word, call sanity.

Nat—and his family—had hauled me back to life and humanity, and if what it cost me was surrendering power and position I never wanted and helping them install their government based on the principles of the long vanished United States of America, I could do that.

Two rooms in the house and the use of an office were all that would have been truly mine, anyway, had I ascended to rule as the Good Man of Olympus. The absolute ruler of that kind of vast empire is no more free than a slave. Oh, his particular whims and his odder tastes might be catered to, but like a slave he is the prisoner of his role, occupied with it from morning to night, his every minute poured into that role.

So, I wasn't any the worse off for my change in roles, from would-be heir to the territory to officer in the revolutionary army of Olympus Seacity, which, with its allied territories and seacities comprised what we called The Freedom Army. And other people were happier. Probably. Almost certainly.

Only the Good Men had not let things go lightly. Authority and power are not surrendered willingly, unless it is meaningless and the rule of the Good Men was very meaningful indeed.

For ten years we'd been involved in a war; we'd lost countless people. Young people had been killed in the army, and people of all ages had been killed as the Good Men resorted to terror tactics on the territories; released bio-engineered viruses; destroyed crops and generally made the life of the citizens of Olympus and our allies hell. Against this Nat fought. Against this I composed a war of words, a concatenation of holograms to make it clear to the people under Good Men Rule that we were the better choice; that they should rebel and come to our side.

It worked. Sometimes. Entire cities and seacities had come to our side. But not enough to end the war.

Which meant Nat continued fighting, and I continued to check the casualty and missing list, every night, after a full day of work, and just before turning in.

This brings me to that August night. It was hot, and I was asleep, uncovered, in my too-large bed. My room was at the top of what used to be the palace, and the door opened to a terrace which in turn looked down all the way to the sea. That door was open, to a smell of salt air, and at first I thought what I heard was the cry of seagulls.

o o o

"How do you plead?" the sad eyed major asks, after the litany of charges against me is read. "On the charges leveled against you?"

"Guil—" I start. And my judge advocate is there. Royce's hand clasps around my upper arm so hard that he will leave bruises. Which takes effort, since I'm six seven and built like the proverbial brick shithouse, and though Royce is not a small man, his hand doesn't even fully go around my arm.

"Sir," he says, and I am not sure if it's to me or the major. "Sir," he says, and this time he looks fully at the major. "Sir, Colonel Keeva pleads not guilty due to extenuating circumstances."

The Major opens his mouth. For a moment I think he's going to say I'd pleaded guilty, but of course he doesn't. Instead, he closes his mouth and looks at me, eyebrows raised. Royce's hand is like an iron band around my forearm. "Yes," I stammer. "Not guilty due to extenuating circumstances."

The Major nods. "Very well," he says. "Do you swear to tell the truth, the whole truth, and nothing but the truth?"

"Yes."

The judge gestures, and one of the privates by the door, a young man who looks too young to grow a beard and too innocent to be in any military, comes forward with a small, dark box, which he opens. Inside the box is my piece of flag. Not the flag of Olympus, which is a blue flag with the representation of the mythical mountain, but THE flag, the one sacred to every Usaian. At some time in the twenty first century, after the fall of the United States of America, and after the founding of the religion based on the founding documents of that lost country, someone had put all the flags they could find that had once flown over American territory before the fall into a climate-controlled room. Since then every member of the religion got a little piece of the flag. Some were inherited within families. Mine had three stars, and a blood stain. The stain had been acquired when a past owner had been martyred to the faith. Another past owner, martyred to the faith, was my only friend growing up, and Nat's uncle, Benjamin Franklin Remy. Ben has been dead for twenty five years. Which is good because he might very well think I'd disgraced him and our shared scrap of flag.

The young man hands me the flag. I know what to do. Usaians have sealed all their oaths with a kiss on their piece of the flag, that visible symbol of their allegiance, for centuries.

I press my lips against the flag, and then it is set on the desk in front of me. I look at it and mentally I ask Ben's forgiveness. "I never meant to sully the flag or the Usaians by association," I tell him. "But you see, I had to save Nat."

o   o   o

The crying of a seagull resolved itself to the scream of a woman, and before I was fully awake, I thought I'd fallen asleep naked with the covers thrown away from me and some cleaning woman must have come in. I reached for the covers, pulled them over me, but the woman was yelling "Luce," and shaking me.

I opened my eyes. The woman was Martha Remy. She's a Lieutenant in the propaganda department, and my subordinate. But she's also somewhere between my best friend and my sister. She is Nat's twin, though she looks nothing like him. While Nat is tall and lanky and one of those rare brown-eyed pale blonds, Martha is short, softly rounded despite continuous exercise, and has mouse-colored hair. Only her eyes are the same as Nat's, dark brown and deeply set, giving the impression of unexplored depths and something like an abiding and unshakeable sadness. They were filled with alarm now.

"Luce," she said. "Did he contact you? Was there a change in plans?"

"Who?" I asked, sleep stupid, my voice slow, my tongue stumbling. And then, as my wits caught up with my wakening, "Nat?"

She nodded. "He's five hours late," she said. "I thought he'd come in. I thought he'd be—Did he tell you about changing plans?"

"I didn't even know he was coming home," I told her, and noted her surprise. It was hard to explain to her that our relationship didn't work like that. He did what he had to do, and I was glad to see him when I saw him.

"He was," she said at last. "He was flying back with … with something. Some mission. I'm not sure what it was, but he was bringing something from Field Marshall Herrera, I think to General Cranston, but he never arrived. They called me to see if I heard from him and I hadn't, but I thought you might have."

By then I was fully awake. I said, "If something happened to him, then his chip would have reported his status to headquarters, and he'd be on the casualty list. He wasn't. I checked before going to bed. Unless his chip was deactivated because he was on some sort of secret run?"

"Not that I know," she said. "But it wouldn't show on the casualty list, anyway, not by last night, because I talked to him at twenty three hundred, and he hadn't left yet."

"Oh," I said. "Have you checked now?"

She shook her head. "And it's weird," she said, babbling. "Why is Field Marshall Herrerra using Nat as an errand boy to someone of a lower rank, too? It makes no sense at all."

I rose from the bed, taking care to drag the sheet with me, though as I said, Martha was like a sister to me, and she'd probably not have batted an eye if I'd got out of bed in my birthday suit. But I'd spent fifteen years in a cell, under constant observation by cameras. Had to have been, because all the times I'd tried to commit suicide they'd come and *rescued* me before I died. Now I relished my modesty, such as it was. I pulled the sheet around my waist, and dragged it behind me, as I got to my desk, and pushed the accustomed buttons to bring up the hologram of the latest casualty list. Early on, these had been compiled by the week, but now every one of our fighting men and women had a chip implanted in their body which transmitted on an encrypted frequency. If the transmission were interrupted, we knew what had happened. Or at least we could presume it, even if we'd been wrong a few times.

Knowing at all times that your relative or loved one wasn't on that list and therefore must be presumed to be well made the war bearable.

As the hologram of names solidified in the air, in front of me, I closed my eyes and did what passed for prayer for me, "If he's not on the list, if he's well—" I didn't finish the promise because it wasn't needed. If there was a God he knew what I was willing to do for such a boon. Anything. Anything at all.

I opened my eyes. I paged down through the As and on through the Ps and Qs. To the Rs.

I blinked. There, midair, was the line I'd dreaded seeing for ten years. Gen. Nathaniel Green Remy, Missing, presumed dead.

From behind me Martha made that sound like a seagull again, and her hand rested on my shoulder. Warm and far too moist. "No," she said. "No."

"No," I said, more firmly. "No. Look, he's not dead. And the chip is not sending the distress signal indicating he's wounded. He's just missing. That means the chip malfunctioned."

"Or he was captured and someone is blocking transmission. Someone is holding him hostage."

"Let's not scare ourselves with worst case scenarios," I said. "Do you know where he was coming from? What transport he was using? It's likely just a deviation in course taking him through an area where transmission is blocked. He'll probably get back into range soon enough." I didn't believe a word I was saying, and there was a reason I didn't believe it. If Nat had said he'd be here, he would have been here. No two ways about it. So something had happened to Nat. But what? And where was he? And was he alive or dead?

I'd been hot when I went to bed, and objectively I knew the room was still hot. It was August, after all, even if dawn wasn't even a rosy glimmer on the horizon. But I felt very cold. Cold and clammy, like someone suffering from a fever. At the same time I was eerily calm.

For years I'd feared to find Nat on the casualty lists. Now I had, and I felt nothing.

"Even if he's alive and missing, unless he makes his way back, he'll die," she said. "Because we don't have anyone available for rescue, not now. And they wouldn't allow anyone to risk themselves, not as things stand."

My mind captured that "as things stand" and held it. I knew next to nothing of how things stood and wondered if she did. My rank was superior to hers, and both of us worked in a department which wasn't briefed with the latest news of the battle front, but there were two sets of imponderables.

The first was that Nat and Martha seemed to tell each other everything. Understandable, perhaps, for twins, even if it would give General Command kitten fits over the official secrets thus leaked. The other was that the religious structure of the Usaian sect bled through and through the official army of Olympus. The Usaians had started the revolution and held it to their—our—belief structure and then, technically, they had melted into the background and become officers or civilians serving the war machine.

Theories are very good, but theory and practice rarely meet when it comes to that sort of thing. I was an adult convert to the Usaian religion, but all the Remys had been raised in the faith, and the faith was a militant one. Part of waiting and believing that a revival of the old United States of America was prophesized and inevitable, was the practice for the revolution to come. Generations of my co-religionaires had grown up training for stealth warfare and sabotage and other military action. Their structure permeated the army too, and everyone knew that members of the same Usaian group talked to each other and leaked information. It was accepted as an endemic problem by our command, which took the downside of a pre-trained force with its upside, which was their efficiency and knowledge.

So Martha probably knew better than I how things stood. And probably things stood very badly indeed if someone of Nat's rank wouldn't be worth looking for when missing. I reviewed in my mind the news of the war I'd seen in the last few days, and there was nothing special. Which meant nothing, and was why I rarely troubled with news reports. Because they wouldn't say anything worth knowing, after passing through several levels of censorship and spin, some of it put on by my own people.

But even so I was aware I hadn't heard one thing: there had been no reports of victories, however small, of any outpost captured, however remote. Since it was the job of my department to make sure those were all over the news when they happened, and given that my subordinates were quite capable of doing their duty without my direct supervision and hand-holding, if no reports of victories had been in the news, that meant no victories had happened for a few weeks. Which meant that things were very bleak.

Of course, to an extent, they'd started out bleak. We were outnumbered ten to one, at the very beginning. But we were well trained and enthusiastic, and it wasn't normal for us to have weeks with no victories.

"Where was he flying from?" I asked.

She hesitated only one second. In the infrequent letters I got from Nat, who was the world's worst letter writer, the place he was writing from had been covered in a censorship band. And in his com-calls, always aware we were listened to, the place where he was and any details of it were omitted. It was only when we met in person that he would tell me where he'd been. Sometimes. Sometimes he just shuddered or let it accidentally escape he'd been at the scene of a massacre, a massive defeat, an atrocity. He didn't talk much about that. Sometimes I thought those things he'd seen, that he didn't wish to talk about were the reason that he talked very little about anything else. As though the wall of silence he'd built up must suffice for everything he might say.

"Condor," Martha said. And then "It wasn't a secret."

Condor was a base South in the North American continent. Most of the continents had been rendered uninhabitable by clean-up bacteria released before the Turmoils back in the twenty second century. Most of the population had died, save those in coastal areas and those who'd taken to the seacities. But three hundred years later, the bacteria had worn themselves out, and trees grew there now, making it a virgin land, just getting resettled.

A lot of our people lived there, both those under the jurisdiction of Olympus Seacity and those who belonged to the Usaian religion, and whom we treated as our dependents, and our responsibility. We had bases out there, to protect out people, and other, secret bases where our military personnel planned and did whatever the hell it was they did. I rubbed the bridge of my nose. Condor was a known base—known by code name, but not by coordinates. I had an idea where it was, but only because of something Nat had let slip when off his guard. Something about taking time off to go visit a sacred site, nearby, and about a city.

"Go," I told Martha. "I'll figure it out."

She looked more worried. "You'll figure what out?" she asked, her voice outright alarmed.

"Where Nat is. How to rescue him."

Her eyes were wide, "Luce, he might be dead."

I lowered my head, once, not quite an acquiescence. "He might," I said. "But I don't think so."

"You don't think so?"

I couldn't tell her that I'd seen Ben's ghost for years after his death, and that I was morally certain if Nat were dead, I'd now be seeing his. You can't be a rational human being and proclaim a belief in ghosts. You can't even be me and proclaim a belief in ghosts. And if I flapped my lips about anything like that, Martha would have me in a psych ward so fast my head would spin. And I couldn't be in a psyche ward right now. I had work to do. For the first time in ten years, I felt I had work no one else could do. I had to rescue Nat. If there wasn't anyone else free to do it, I could do it. I was expendable.

Oh, sure, because I was a Good Man who had switched sides, I was prominent and a bit of a propaganda coup for our side. But that's all I was. They could probably use a hologram of me for years, before anyone noticed.

"Call it a hunch," I said. "Go. I'll figure it out."

"I don't want you to do anything," she said. "I only came to you because I thought you might know where he was expected to be, and if—Luce." She grabbed my wrist, hard. She looked up, managing to look very stern and forbidding for someone who barely reached up to my shoulder. "Listen, Luce, you're not going to do anything stupid, are you?"

"No," I said.

I won't say that what I planned to do was very smart, but I sure as hell hoped it wasn't stupid.

She was barely out the door and I was on the com to my superior. Another Colonel, but ranks were all strange and wobbly in our organization right now. I was a Colonel in charge of propaganda, and my immediate superior a Colonel in charge of psychological warfare. His jurisdiction went just a little further than mine.

The com rang ten times before being answered, abruptly. I had the feeling that someone on the other side had punched the receiving button without getting up, a feeling supported by the fact that I was staring in almost complete darkness at what appeared to be a bit of wall. Then the lights came on, and Colonel Hanson was staring at me. He was a small man, with dark hair and the expression of an harassed accountant. Now he looked even more harassed and squinted at the holo of me. At first I thought he was having trouble focusing, and then I realized he probably wasn't used to being addressed by one of his underlings wearing a blanket sloppily wrapped around himself. It was all made worse as I saluted automatically and the blanket fell. I bent to retrieve it.

"Colonel Keeva?" he said, as if he'd conjured up the words from some deep well of memory. Truth be told, though he also lived on Olympus Seacity, I didn't think we'd seen each other more than twice. Most of our communication was indirect, through our underlings.

"Sir," I said. And then in a rush, because I'd never fully managed military speak, "Sir, I need permission to—I need to go on leave." I'd averted the sentence before I told him exactly what I meant to do, because I had an instinctive feeling he'd disapprove.

"Leave?" He pronounced this as though it were alien. "When?"

"Starting now, sir," I said. "For a couple of days."

He frowned. He looked aside and seemed to consult something. "For what reason? What do you wish to do in that time? You do know we normally have a two week filing requirement for any sort of leave short of family emergency."

"It is a family emergency," I said. "General Nathaniel Remy is missing."

His eyes widened a little. I could see he meant to say something or ask something, but he closed his mouth without speaking. He seemed to be struggling for words, and failing to find them. At last he said, "General Remy is missing ..." he repeated. And did something with his fingers then turned to look to his right side. I knew what he was doing. Reading some hologram. Maybe the list I'd given him, maybe some dispatch. I saw him in profile as his mouth tightened and the muscles on his face clenched, and then he said, "Shit." He said it under his breath and in a whisper, so I likely wasn't meant to hear it. But I did.

When he turned his face back to me, it was impassive. Impassive in a manner of speaking, at least. I could still see the tautness of his facial muscles, but it was clear he was trying to look impartial and official, as though nothing existed but a robot who fulfilled a military role. Yeah, right.

But the truth is that the masked feelings served him. I had no idea what he was thinking or feeling as he said, "Colonel Keeva, from … information I possess, since he's missing it is highly likely that General Remy is dead. There is nothing you can do. You couldn't trace him or even find his body." He hesitated a moment. "I'm sorry." Another small hesitation. "You'd be better served, and Olympus would be better served as well, by your staying at your post. We do have counselors if you—"

I'd already turned the com off, which I was fairly sure was against thirteen regulations and five procedures. But I really didn't care about that, or Colonel Hanson's bright idea that Nat was likely dead. Nat couldn't be dead. I couldn't allow it. And I didn't much care what anyone thought.

My fingers were already halfway through the dial sequence to the supreme military officer on the island, General Cranston, head of home defense and nominally my boss's boss since in the inscrutable spiderwebbing of the ever mutating revolutionary army, my department fell under defense.

This time I remembered to hold my sheet as I saluted, but the resulting stare was no less shocked. And the answer to my stammered request was "Stay on your post." This time I could tell what the man was thinking. At least if a mingling of pity and alarm counted as thoughts.

I thanked him meekly and this time waited till the man I'd called turned off the com, before turning it off myself.

Which is not to say he'd convinced me. Or rather, he'd convinced me of one thing: in a minute or less there were going to be psych officers crawling all over my bedroom. And then they were going to tranq me, soothe me and medicate me till a year passed and Nat was dead for sure and there was nothing I could do.

And that was not going to happen.

O O O

"… And on said date, you willfully ignored the orders of your superiors, and left your post against orders."

I set my jaw. I try to think of the proper lingo to explain that I'd had to, but all I can say is, "You see, I knew they were wrong."

○ ○ ○

Okay, so I didn't know that General Cranston had called the psych techs. I didn't know that the sun would come up tomorrow, either, but there was every reason to suspect so.

Before I had fully thought this, I'd crossed the room, thrown open my closet and pulled out my uniform. In retrospect this was a bad idea, as the brass hats tend to get all bent out of shape when you tear or stain the uniform. It probably wouldn't have been half as bad if I'd worn civilian clothes while doing things they disapproved of.

The problem is I didn't really have many civilian clothes after ten years.

Once upon a time, long ago, when I was someone quite different, before arrest and time in prison, before I'd been forced to kill my only friend, to end his suffering after extensive torture, I'd been a bit of a peacock and worn whatever was in fashion. But then I'd also been seventeen and skinny. The time in between had changed me and put flesh and muscle on my bones. And after I'd gotten out of jail, I'd gotten a new set of clothes, but that too had been in another life, when I'd been the ruler over the city of Olympus and its associated territories.

Then had come my time in the army of Olympus. And it had left me with nothing but uniforms. The few civilian suits had been shoved to the back of the closet and they didn't come to my questing hand. So I donned the sky-blue tunic and pants, with the Olympus patch on the chest, and the colonel insignia on the sleeves.

Then I'd gone through the sequence—open faucets in the fresher, push a panel on the wall, turn the lights on in a certain sequence—needed to open the secret compartment on my ceiling where I kept the black, padded suit designed to wear while riding a broom. The antigrav wands weren't supposed to be used for anything but bailing out of flyers. They were illegal for riding around, because they couldn't be traced. Which was fine and dandy because while I suspected that they could, given some thought, figure out where I was headed, they wouldn't be able to trace me that fast. And it would take General Cranston a while to make it through the bureaucracy enough to even decide to intercept me.

I hoped.

And as I hoped, I'd put the padded suit on, and grabbed my broom, packed next to it. Next, I grabbed my burner from beneath my pillow, checked it for full charge, slipped it into the suit's pocket, then got its twin from the bedside table to join it. Last of all, I got the one from my dresser and slipped it beneath the suit, into the holster built into my uniform pants. I'd been caught unarmed once. It was never going to happen again.

When I leapt from the balcony outside my room, someone was knocking politely on the door to my room. Thank heavens Olympus Seacity and certainly its military forces were largely Usaians. They could never convince themselves of the rightness of a no-knock raid.

O O O

Does theft, too, fit under conduct unbecoming? Or did they never figure that one out? I'd reimbursed the owner, but I had first stolen her flyer.

O O O

Flying through the warm night air, above the crashing waves, I realized that while I knew that Nat had been at Condor, and had presumably been headed here, I had no idea what pattern he might have flown. And I certainly didn't know where he'd been intercepted.

I also realized that taking a broom all the way to the North American continent was delusional. Oh, you could fly that sort of distance. When I'd escaped prison, I'd had nothing but stolen brooms on me, and had used them to fly that sort of distance. Twice.

But I was not thirty six anymore. In reality I felt more than ten years older. Not saying I'd felt young and spry when leaving prison, but I'd been numbed to reality and to the world and the whole thing had seemed like a fantastic dream.

Now my body would make me pay for that kind of unprotected, protracted ride, but more importantly, I didn't have that kind of time. Brooms, even when flown high enough you had to use a mask and goggles and an oxygen tank, were not as fast as flyers.

I needed a flyer.

Some thought took me away from the areas around what had been my palace, all of it military installations and official buildings, and to the area under the Seacity where working people clustered.

I touched ground underneath a bridge, happy to be wearing a dark flight suit.

When I was young, not out of real need or real viciousness, but out of a sense of freedom and escaping the stifling confines of my public life as the heir to the Seacity, I'd been an illegal broomer. Ben Remy and I had been part of a broomer gang. While our gang was mostly composed of the children of rulers and their immediate aids and servants, and while none of us were particularly inclined to crime, we'd done our share of hijacking the occasional transport and stealing the occasional transport.

The body remembered almost better than the mind did.

I knit myself with the bridge, and walked down the road, keeping close to first the bridge pillars, and then to the wall that supported the level above. The Seacity was built like a wedding cake, in layers, each layer supporting the one above. And while the uppermost layer, where I lived, was almost permanently in the sun and the fresh air, the area here, at the bottom, was almost completely subterranean. Between the pillars and walls that supported the next level, and the buildings that lined the roads, there was very little space for the piped-in sunshine to find its place here.

But of course it wasn't dark, not even at this time of night. Though the area was mostly home to servants and manual laborers, it also housed the places where the upper classes came to play: bars, seedy restaurants, and less savory establishments lined the roads, and were lit, night and day, by brilliant signs and advertising holograms. Even in these days of war and austerity, the place was boisterous and loud. Music assailed my ears, and some of the signs promised delights I wasn't sure I even understood, much less having ever considered sampling.

Which is why I had landed near one of the external supporting walls. Those walls were supposed to be kept unimpeded by permanent construction. Once upon a time, there had been tents lining the walls, but that was before the war and more careful policing of these levels, because it was an obvious way to invade the seacity. Thinking of this, as I walked along, closely knit with the dark wall, reminded me that I had to watch for patrols.

I thought it just in time, and knit with the wall, as the rhythmic sounds of army boots approached and walked past.

They were two young privates, much like the ones who normally guarded the door to my office or the door to my lodgings. Too young, too clean, much too innocent to be involved in war, and yet probably to be dead before too long.

These two were talking, as they walked, and looking towards the lighted shops and laughing at a bright hologram that promised

"Boys, boys, boys" and "Girls, girls, girls," in shimmering blue, intercut with images of the aforementioned boys and girls—fortunately in this case definitely men and women—in state of undress.

There was no reason the two should remind me of Ben and I, twenty five years ago, but they did. It was something to the easy comradery and the laughing at silly things. It felt very lonely all the way out here, in the dark, with no friend. At least for my years in prison I'd had the company of Ben's ghost, even if I sometimes suspected he'd been an illusion of my unraveling in mind. He might have been, but still I hadn't been alone.

The young men passed out of my range of hearing and I moved again, sliding next to the wall and a way down the road. I was looking for specific things, before I could acquire a flyer. First, it must be a common enough model and color that it would attract no one's attention. Second, it must be at least twenty years old, so I understood its schematics and knew how to disable the tracking devices and could be sure to get all of them. And third, I might find it in a place where it would be easy for me to make it to a point of take off unnoticed.

I didn't find anything fitting my criteria for a good long while. I walked the entire length of that street, then turned to the right at semi-random. Semi-random, because I knew it would take me nearer the sea on that side. Going towards the inner part of the island would make it harder to escape.

Walking out of the bar and entertainment area, I found myself in an industrial area. Once upon a time this zone had been occupied by places manufacturing illegal substances or alternately by places manufacturing cheap articles. Both had functioned mostly by day. The increased patrolling had turned the shops to legal industry—burners, burner chargers, the various detection and navigation gadgets used by our people—but had also turned them into twenty four hour establishments.

Down this second road, I'd come across a factory from which emanated the sound of heavy industrial equipment and of conversation and laughter. Mostly female laughter, because most of our factory workers were female, just like most of our soldiers were male. There was nothing against a woman serving, certainly not in units that employed little or no physical force. We had excellent female pilots, outstanding female snipers, and a lot of our electronic intelligence units were women. Most of these women, too, were of long-standing Usaian families, and as devoted to the cause as any man. But in the end, by law of averages, outside the religious conviction and the people who could use a talent or another in their service, working class men enlisted, and working class women manned factories.

I stopped outside this factory because there was a row of flyers parked in front of it, and pretty much all of them would serve my needs. I picked a battered white one and approached, in the shadows. I was about to shoot the membrane of the genlock through with my burner, when I heard muffled sounds and realized there was someone inside it.

Damn, I thought dropping to the ground, because it would have been all too easy to see me through the windows of the vehicle.

On the ground, I'd lain very still, almost not daring to breathe, while the voices continued inside it. When it started a gentle, rhythmic rocking, I figured that the people inside had better things to worry about than looking out the windows. But I didn't stand. Instead I crawled, very fast, on hands and knees, three flyers down the line, to another white, non-descript flyer.

This time, as I rose, just a little, I put my ear to the shiny white carapace and listened. There was no sound from inside the flyer. Of course, with my luck, someone was probably asleep inside. I bumped it slightly. It was a flimsy vehicle and my bump made it rock gently and would almost for sure have disturbed someone inside enough to make them move around at least a bit. But my ear, flattened to the shell, revealed no sound of movement.

I let out breath I hadn't been aware of holding, grabbed my burner, and burned out the membrane that would normally read the proprietor's genetics before unlocking.

If you're ever in a position where you have to steal a flyer, supposing you can find one of that vintage—the new ones are more sophisticated—it's important to remember that genlock are alarm-wired. That is, you can easily cut through a genlock, but if you do the flyer is going to start screaming for help, not just audibly but in every com of the local police force. Which is why it's important to use a burner. But there is an art to that, too. You have to set the burner on burn, you have to set the heat depth to no more than two inches, or you'll set the flyer on fire, as I'd done with the first one I tried to jack, way back in my callow youth, and you have to tilt it slightly to the left as it starts to burn, or it will not disable the chip, and the alarm will still go out.

It had taken me about five tries to learn, and even after that there had been some false starts, but of course, back then, back when I was still in my father's favor and the acknowledged heir, the worst that such failures caused me was a scolding in my father's office.

Now—Now it would be quite different and a far more dangerous game, which is why it was a good thing that the body remembered and executed the maneuver perfectly.

Getting my fingers in through the narrow canal thus opened to flick the open button from the inside was something else again. My fingers were no longer the slim instruments they'd once been. Not that I'd grown fat, but my fingers had finished growing, proportionally to my body. I finally found the catch instinctively, and released it, causing the door to pop open.

I got in very fast and closed the door, so that from outside and without coming up close to look at the door, everything would look normal.

The inside of the flyer was standard with two seats facing each other and the column with the navigator for programming course and route to the left, easily accessible to the two people sitting nearest it.

I could find the cylinder that beamed back coordinates and identification to the control towers by hand and I did, removing it from the panel with a twist and beating its brains out with the butt of my burner before opening the door enough to toss it out on the pavement. You see, if you didn't beat its brains out, it would be broadcasting from the location where you dropped it, and that would let the authorities know the flyer to which it belonged had been stolen, and to send out alerts for apprehension.

I couldn't take off straight up, not from here, but I backed up slowly, then moved, at a measured pace down the street, trying to think and act like a citizen going about his own lawful business.

By the time I took off with no one sounding the alarm, I let go breath, explosively, aware for the first time that I had been holding it.

o   o   o

"But why Lieutenant Madeiras?" the Major asks. "He couldn't have known anything."

o   o   o

I was in the air and flying away from Olympus, at a level just slightly too low to be picked up by the automatic sweeps which would find it odd I wasn't identifying on all frequencies, when I realized that I was not an invading force.

I don't know how else to explain it, but when you're six seven and built like the proverbial brick shithouse, you're not used to thinking of yourself as someone who can be subtle or careful in his approach. No, you learn pretty much at the age you stop growing up that the way to achieve something is to go charging up to the next—inevitably smaller—person and demand it.

This wasn't going to work that way. Look, yeah, I was in the military, I worked in a command center. I worked in a command center for propaganda, and we would sharpen our words and hone our sentences really hard.

None of which could face up to what they did down at Condor, which was mostly planning, yeah, but took place among front-line commanders. People with lots of experience killing other people. Mind you, the most I'd gotten of that from Nat was when he would shake and say a couple of cryptic phrases. But I'd gathered from other people who'd been at battles where he'd been in command that he was quite capable of killing. And of risking death.

I was handy with a burner and all, but it takes a different kind of courage to go up to an enclave of armed, trained killers and say, "Hi, I'm here to demand some answers."

Sure, of course, military aren't just trained killers. They're disciplined trained killers, and most of them do it for a reason, and risk death in the process. But they're still trained to kill rather than surrender.

And Condor was, at the moment, our forward base of operations, as such, though of course, since we could deploy troops from anywhere at a moment's notice such terms meant somewhat less than they had in the twenty first century.

It was a place filled with highly efficient fighters.

So, I needed to be sneaky. The problem was that I had zero understanding of how to do this.

As I flew blindly in the general direction of Condor, it occurred to me it shouldn't be that hard. After all most of my job in the army of Olympus could be described as being sneaky with words. And then I thought, *Lieutenant Madeiras.*

The reason I thought that, of course, was that the young man had been transferred into my department from Condor, at Nat's recommendation, due to Madeiras being able to take words and make them spin and then sit up. And I guarantee any young Lieutenant who'd resided in a base or compound will find three sneaky ways out of it and ten ways in that his superiors know nothing about. This is a necessity if one is to hit the watering spots and more than watering spots nearby without getting written up for one of the milder forms of conduct unbecoming. Besides, I had heard the young man talk about a girl he had down there, and it sounded to me like they met a lot more than the every six months or so that such people got leave.

I chewed the corner of my lip, thinking that making my way to the lodging of Lieutenant Madeiras would have been easier before I stole the flyer. I knew exactly where the young man lodged, because he had been very happy to be able to rent a single room, off military housing, when it turned out his placement in Olympus was at least for a year.

But then I realized that taking Lieutenant Madeiras with me while stealing a flyer would have proven complicated. I didn't know how he'd react to being kidnapped, but doubtlessly I'd need to keep a burner on him—a difficult thing to do while burning out a genlock.

So … mentally I plotted my course back to Olympus, and the particular approach to take so that no one would think it was me—not that they would think that while I was driving the stolen flyer, not unless someone had given alarm. Even then they wouldn't think of my returning to the Seacity, which of course made it the most cunning thing I could do.

Almost proud of myself, I entered the Seacity not far from where I'd left, and took the spiral path of city traffic to the top of the city, using all the designated ramps flying about two feet off the road surface as the authorities preferred flyers do in populated areas, unless on a long-route flight.

I couldn't congratulate myself on where Lieutenant Madeiras lived, but I was glad it was private housing. A rooming house, five stories high and a block wide, renting one room-one bath accommodations to all the young men who'd volunteered to serve but were sick and tired of communal lodging.

Which meant, in my broomer suit, taking care to keep my face in shadow, I could make it unnoticed to his northwest corner room. I took the gravity well up, and headed for the room door, glad that he'd told me exactly where the room was, because he'd told me he could see my terrace from his room.

It wasn't until I was knocking on the ceramite door that it occurred to me he might not be home. It was, after all four in the morning. Or he might be home but accompanied.

It proved too late to turn back, as rustlings and shufflings echoed through the door and then, "Yes," in Lieutenant Madeira's voice, in an hesitant tone.

I wondered if I should identify myself. If he weren't alone, that would mean I'd need to take his girlfriend with me, just in case she overheard me.

But if I didn't tell him my name, would he open the door? At least he sounded sleepy which meant he was unlikely to have heard any request for my capture. "Colonel Keeva," I said. "There's an emergency."

The bolt slipped on the other side of the door, and the door opened first a sliver, then his eyes widened, probably at the fact that I was wearing full broomer's leathers, which made my already towering height more so. Then he threw the door fully open, and I pulled my burner and pointed it at his belly, at the same time I put my foot in the door to keep it open.

"Colo—Colonel Keeva!" he said, shock and dismay neatly blended in his voice.

He was not a short man, but he was shorter than I. Almost everyone is. Slimmer and less bulky too, and only came up to about my shoulder. My hand looked disproportionately large, as I grabbed his shoulder, pushed him in his lodging, while keeping the burner on him, then shut the door behind me with my foot.

The room was typical young bachelor lodging, and remarkably neat, from the single bed, that looked like he'd just got out of it, but like it had been made with perfect corners before, to the cooking area with every surface clean and shining. I looked towards the door, presumably to the fresher. "Do you have anyone with you?"

His eyes were very wide, and fixated on my face, as though he were trying to figure out exactly how insane I was. He started to open his mouth, then shook his head.

"Sure?" I asked.

He nodded, then took in a deep, sucking breath. "What's wrong? What have I done?"

"Nothing," I said. "I need your help."

He looked at the burner, then back at my face. "My ... help?"

"I need your help finding a way into Condor."

"Into ... Condor?" the last was said in a tone of disbelief. And then, proving he wasn't just an echo machine, "For heaven's sakes, why?"

"General Remy left there to fly here and went missing," I said. "I need to get in there and crack their computers. I presume his flight path was secret, but once I get there I can crack the computers. But I have to get in there. And to the computers."

"To the computers!" he said. His voice was faint, as though he were ill. "How—" He looked up at my face again. "General Remy is missing? Or dead?"

"Would I be in such a hurry to rescue him if he were dead?" I asked.

He shook his head. "But how do you know—"

How did I know? Well, I wouldn't be going through all this trouble to rescue a dead man, so Nat must be alive.

Some part of me knew this was specious reasoning. But it also knew that I could not survive losing Nat. I'd lost Ben and spent fifteen years in solitary confinement, barely at the edge of reason. I couldn't do it again. And in my mind losing Nat and solitary confinement were inexorably linked. Which was likely, considering what I'd been doing in the last hour. Though the way the army dealt with such things, death was, thank heavens, more likely.

"I just do."

He bit his lips together. "And you ... what do you want me to do? Tell you how to get in?"

"No, I want you to show me. Chances are I wouldn't know how to do it without seeing it. And besides ..." And besides, unless I took him along he might give me away.

He seemed to understand my unspoken demur. "And you intend to hold me at burner point, all the way there?"

I looked at him. He looked back at me. For a moment neither of us spoke.

Then he reached over, grabbed the muzzle of my burner and turned it aside. He looked back up at my face, "Colonel Keeva, you wouldn't shoot me."

"I would if you stand in my way and cause Nat to die."

He blinked. He took in a deep breath. "You say General Remy was flying here—alone?—and is missing?"

I nodded.

"He shouldn't have gone over any disputed areas," he said, in the tone of a man thinking to himself. "If he had some sort of problem he would communicate with someone, certainly. Did you know what he was coming here to do?"

"He was bringing some sort of information," I said. "To General Cranston."

He nodded. "Since he didn't go over disputed territory, the most likely way he disappeared is sabotage, then. It would have to be sabotage, or he would have communicated. If he didn't, something was done to his communication equipment. By someone who didn't want the information to reach us? An enemy agent? Or of course fire from a troop of enemy agents forewarned where and when to expect him to fly over."

"Yes," I said, my mouth dry. I hadn't put it in so many words, but of course that had been in my mind all along. "That's why I think we should figure out his exact flight plan."

"We," Lieutenant Madeiras said. He looked at my burner. "Right. Colonel Keeva, holster that thing and give me five minutes to dress. I won't leave your sight. And I won't try to do anything funny. If the situation is as you say I would never forgive myself if I let General Remy die."

As he was finishing fastening his uniform, similar to mine but with a different insignia, he said, "What made you think you needed to hold a burner to me?"

"I … I want to kidnap you," I said. "I figure my conduct this night is going to get me in serious trouble. No reason to drag you into the same sort of trouble with me."

Royce's voice, loud and formal, says the words I talked him into saying, despite his protests. "The Colonel wishes to stress that he kidnapped the lieutenant and forced him to help in the plan against the lieutenant's will. Lieutenant Madeiras is to be held harmless."

The look on the Major's face is almost amused. "That is not the lieutenant's story."

"Call me George," the young man said, after I took off from the seacity again. "This is not exactly an official situation. What coordinates did you program in, Colonel?"

I told him, and added, "Might as well call me Lucius. Colonel is a mouthful."

He looked over my shoulder and shook his head. "Those coordinates aren't even right."

"Well, Nat never gave me coordinates. I deduced them from other stuff he said."

"Right," he said. He didn't exactly push me aside, but displaced me. His fingers flew on the keyboard. I looked at the coordinates he programmed and said, "Well, it could be that." What I'd deduced from proximity to certain cities and availability of certain fruits in the surroundings would fit there, too. The new coordinates were about three hours flight from the ones I'd guessed, and I suspected I could have found Condor anyway, but it would have taken me days flying criss-cross above jungle and farmland. And hell, I didn't have days. Sooner or later someone would figure out what happened and send people after me. I had absolutely no doubt that the same bureaucracy which found it hard to spare a man or two to look for Nat could and would spend a group to look for me. To be fair, they thought Nat was dead. They probably thought I was crazy and dangerous. And I wasn't at all sure they weren't right. Not that I cared, if I found Nat, and if I could save him.

"If." He stepped back from the programming and looked up at me.

"You could be leading me into a trap," I said, matter-of-fact.

He gave me a long, wary look then snorted. "Not likely. I'm not that tired of living or that brave." An hesitation. "Besides, something about this whole situation smells to high heaven. I liked General Remy. He was the one who said that I should be transferred to your department. He said I had talent that way. And he was right. Even if it took me away from Sherry."

"Sherry?" I raised an eyebrow.

The young man's olive completion flushed the color of a dark sunset and he looked absurdly young. "We're going to get married when the war is over," he said. "And get a farm in the new territories, and raise kids and sheep."

This was so much like my plans—and Nat's—when the war was over, that it made my heart clench. Who knew if both or either of us would be alive when the war was over. Or if the war would ever be over, for that matter. For us or for Lieutenant Madeiras and his Sherry.

He stepped away from the programming and flopped, lengthwise, onto one of the benches supposed to accommodate three people. "That," he said, as he buckled a belt around his middle, "solves one of our problems. We need someone on the inside if we're not to blunder about and raise all kinds of alarms. And anyway, from what I understand you want General Remy's routing, and that means you'll need to get not just into the computer, but into the classified parts of the computer. Sherry can do that. I've set us to land a bit off the base, and I'll have her meet us."

I blinked at him. "If this comes through," I said. "And worse if it doesn't, it could get you both court-martialed. I'll tell people I kidnapped you and forced you, at burner-point."

He frowned at me. "We'll just keep Sherry out of it," he said. "And now if you excuse me, I need to sleep. I won't be any use if I don't."

He fell asleep. I verified the coordinates and frowned at the sleeping Madeiras. I hadn't meant to involve anyone else in this folly, and hated the idea of being vulnerable to betrayal. And why would this kid be helping me?

Except that he seemed to have some personal loyalty to Nat. That was a thing Nat did. His first handpicked fighting force, recruited when we'd been hiding out in the territories, the summer before the war broke fully, had been so loyal to him that the problem was not motivating them. The problem was convincing them not to walk through hell for him.

I chewed on the corner of my lip. And yet, our side was willing to let Nat disappear, unmourned, one more "missing and presumed dead" of this war. *Stinks to high heavens,* Madeiras had said. And he was right. All of it, starting with Nat acting as an errand boy for someone who was at best an equal or, given the high power the aides of the Field Marshall had, a superior.

If someone had plotted this, I wondered why. Was it because of what he'd been carrying? Would people in positions of power be much more grateful if he did disappear forever? Possible.

More possible, though, perhaps, that they knew the stuff he was carrying was so dangerous that they knew or thought they knew that if he didn't arrive then he must have been put down, dead.

Which made a certain sense, because Nat was possibly the most stubborn person alive, and the only way to permanently stop him would be to remove his head and bury it at the headlands and basin of a river.

So why was I still sure he was alive?

○ ○ ○

"So how could you be sure he was alive?" the Major asks.

"Because he had to be," I say. "Because if he wasn't alive, then neither was I. Because that's—That's how it had to be."

The Major exchanges a look with Royce. I can't quite read it.

"Did anyone else help you acquire secret information?"

I shake my head. My mouth is too dry to talk.

○ ○ ○

I didn't think I could sleep, but I did. At some point I must have laid down in the open seat and fallen asleep. The course that Madeiras had plotted took us over dense forest. I woke as we started descending, with an exclamation on my lips and my burner out.

George Madeiras was standing, doing something with a ring. Focusing my eyes I thought it was one of those cheap communicator rings, with a link buried in them. My mouth went dry.

He looked up, past the burner, at my face, and said, "I'm calling Sherry. We use these cheap disposable coms, because they never monitor for them. They're like children toys, you know?"

I lowered the burner. Did I know it was true? No. But I was going to have to trust someone if I was going to get Nat's itinerary and the details of whatever it had recorded of his expedition. Oh, I could handle at least most encrypted systems. I dealt with a number of them and could extrapolate others. But I could not on my own penetrate a military base and get to the computer that had the data. That would take being able to fight off several men trained to fight. No. I was not that delusional.

Frankly, even with Madeiras, a mere Lieutenant, on my side, I was banking on the observed sneakiness of all young people, and their ability to get in and out of anywhere they worked or lodged, unobserved. But if this was a mistake on my part, then my entire quixotic attempt to rescue Nat was doomed from the beginning.

The flyer had landed, and the place we had landed gave me hope. Madeiras had to have used this place before, and it had to be carefully studied to get in under the systems of Condor. It also had to be familiar enough that he knew the coordinates by heart. They had to be precise coordinates as, in the middle of a verdant and tightly-packed jungle, we'd landed precisely in the center of a clearing that would barely take a slightly larger flyer.

I opened the door and went out, still clutching my burner.

After the murder of a mutual friend, Ben Remy and I had been blamed for it, and had been sent to prison. After Ben was killed—technically by me, though that was a very elaborate setup—I'd been sent to solitary confinement for fifteen years, until I was freed in a freak prison break.

I wasn't comfortable, still, in large crowds, but I was still less comfortable in a small, enclosed space with someone I didn't know very well.

I was fine in my office, and in my routine, but pulled out of my routine, tortured by thoughts of what might be happening to Nat, what might already have happened to Nat, I was likely to do something I and everyone would regret, without thinking, and just because I was under such great tension that any additional or sudden stress was going to make me react in a very bad way.

I paced the space outside, in front of the flyer.

Madeiras came out, slowly. He was looking at me, and I wasn't sure exactly what he was thinking; and whether he thought I was nuts and would do better with medtechs pumping tranquilizers into me. Frankly, I wasn't sure I wouldn't do better with medtechs pumping tranquilizers into me, only I was sure if I let them take me, then Nat was as good as dead. And that I couldn't allow.

And why couldn't anyone be spared to look for him? What did they know that no one was telling me?

"She'll be here any minute," Madeiras said.

I said "uh?" just as a young female in Olympus uniform came into the clearing, squealed and threw herself in Madeiras' arms. It was probably the least military greeting I'd ever seen but it reassured me. Young people separated by disparate postings, would have found a way to meet, so there was a good chance Madeiras knew what he was doing and was on the level. Why he and his girlfriend should help me instead of denouncing me and getting me under restraint was something else again.

I would have to trust the foolishness of young people, I guessed. Maybe they really liked Nat a lot; maybe they wanted to help rescue him. I'd have to hope that. It was that or go down fighting as the medtechs subdued me.

I'd turned instinctively away from what seemed like a private moment between the two, and now I became aware they were having some sort of low-voice argument. They were being good and I couldn't hear most of it, but sometimes a higher word or other reached me.

"Kidnapped?" from her.

A low chuckle from him and "out of his mind," in the middle of an unintelligible sentence. Then, "Disappeared."

"General Remy?"

More low-voiced murmurs, and then, in a startled exclamation "Secret!"

"Medtechs"

"No rescue?"

More excited argument and "Impossible."

I remained with my back turned by an effort of will. I'm not a good actor. I'm not even good at interacting with most people. I have an eerie ability to predict how information and propaganda will affect crowds, but I'm not so good with individuals. I'm fairly sure that both of them knew my back was too taut, my shoulders too straight, and that both of them knew I was listening to their conversation with intent anxiety. But I would not turn and let them see how hard I was grasping the butt of the burner. I was keeping my hand off the trigger. It was best not to give temptation even the smallest opportunity.

Though if Nat were dead, or if they tranquilized me and I only became myself a month from now, when Nat would surely be dead, I could always put a burner beam through my head. But I was afraid I wouldn't. Because suicide is like that. You can attempt it while you're hot and fired up with despair, but the moment you're not, the moment it calms a little, you can't. Self-murder requires the same passion as all other murder. I knew. I'd tried it twice—no, three times—during my fifteen year solitary confinement. Every time, immediately after, I'd be incapable of any action until despair built up again. I rubbed the scar across my face, from when I'd pulled my bunk down on my head.

"Sir," from behind me, and a throat clearing. "Colonel Keeva?"

It was her voice. I turned. She was petite, dark haired, and was looking up at me with an almost pleading look. "Sir, you have to be wrong. They wouldn't leave General Remy on the missing list without verifying that he was beyond help."

"If they've verified," I said, my voice little more than a low growl, mostly because I lacked the calm to make it louder or clearer. "They have failed to tell me. They told me they couldn't verify, Miss—"

"Lieutenant Jones," she said. "Sherry Jones. Look, I don't mean to be disrespectful, but maybe they didn't tell you the truth?"

"Maybe they didn't," I said, although it seemed to me that that would be possibly the most stupid thing they could do. Had they told me that all efforts were being made to recover Nat—

No. I'd still have demanded to be along on the party to rescue him. I'd have demanded it because I couldn't possibly sit at home and wait one more day. Not with Nat on that cursed list. So, had they lied to me to prevent having me along on a mission that was very far from my specialty? Possible, but somehow I doubted it.

"I, too," I said, "have trouble believing that Field Marshall Herrera would not try to recover Nat, considering that Nat— General Remy, and General Aguillard, and General Nocito were his protégées from the first, and that at least initially they were referred to as his children or his family."

When the war started, Herrera, a convert to the Usaian religion who'd been the military commander of Mazatlan Seacity, had been the only military leader with experience in war. True, the war he'd served in had been a small one, what passed for a trade war between groups of allied seacities. But he'd had some experience with both air and sea combat, and almost none with land combat, but a passing acquaintance with guerilla warfare and urban terror.

He'd also proven to be a genius of strategy and the art of war, which was good, because when we'd found ourselves at war with the Good Men, our troops and equipment one tenth of theirs, it had taken genius to even keep us fighting and prevent our being completely crushed.

Back then, ten years ago, he'd picked the most promising of the raw recruits under his command, Nat being one of them and Aguillard, Nocito, Schwarz, Konstantinov the others. Schwarz and Konstantinov had died, but the remaining three had rapidly been promoted to generals.

Herrera, commanding all the forces of the Freedom Army, had taken the title of Field Marshall. Though it was said he consulted with the other three, the people generally referred to as his "family" or his "children," he made the ultimate decisions. And I had trouble believing that he had no personal investment in a young man he'd taught and trained for ten years and in whom he'd reposed a vast amount of confidence.

No. I'd been mistaken. Or my superiors had lied to me. Field Marshall Herrera would not let Nat die alone in the middle of nowhere.

Lieutenant Jones shook her head, "Uh, sir, Field Marshall Herrera is not in command right now. Hasn't been for a month. He was severely wounded, and we didn't think he'd survive. He's been undergoing treatment, as it happens in Olympus Seacity. He's just been taken from the regen tank, and they think he'll live and return to action, but it will be at least another month."

"Then who's in charge now?" I asked, shocked that I hadn't known any of this. It explained at least part of our string of losses, or at least our lack of victories. But why had none of it been known, even inside the armed forces. Did they trust their propaganda department so little they were afraid we'd let everything leak the moment we knew it? And why had Martha thought that Nat was taking a message *from* Herrera, if Herrera was in Olympus?

"Generals Remy, Aguillard and Nocito have been in charge. That's why I thought—That's why I say—" She seemed momentarily confused, then she wailed. "It can't be true. We haven't heard that General Remy is missing."

"He was on the casualty list," I said.

She squinted at me, as though trying to decide if I were completely insane, then she shook her head. "But then …"

There was a long silence. Then she said. "It's almost impossible to get you into the base unnoticed."

"I know," I said. But in my mind I had registered that "almost." Almost impossible meant it wasn't in fact impossible. Which meant that there was hope.

She sighed, and rubbed at her forehead, a gesture that endeared her to me because Nat was in the habit of doing that too, when he felt like he had a headache coming on. In the next moment she said, "I work for General Remy most of the time. I should be able to get you to his office. If we're very lucky."

I realized she'd probably caught the gesture from Nat which meant she had to be his confidential secretary, and spend an awful lot of time with him.

"Mind you," she said. "We'll probably get caught."

O O O

"If you tell us how you got into Condor, it will be taken in account in your sentencing," the Major says, in a hopeful tone.

"I can't tell you," I say.

"Can't or won't?"

"I don't remember a thing."

The Major sighs.

O O O

We followed a multitude of tunnels, starting with one that I was almost absolutely sure was mostly used to move waste onto large incinerators. And apparently by Lieutenants coming out to meet their boyfriends in jungle clearings.

Even if I had any room to judge, I wasn't in the mood to dwell on the peccadilloes of others just now.

We'd proceeded from that entrance through a maze of tunnels. Twice, we'd ducked into a fresher, or a closet, as a group of people went by. I thought the only reason we didn't have to do this more often was that it was very early in the morning and people would be at breakfast.

Also, possibly because Lieutenant Jones was taking us through the most convoluted, back way she could muster.

We ended up climbing stairs—not anti-grav wells, which certainly everyone else must use here—at a fast clip, three flights, and she used her thumb on a genlock, and a door sprang open.

The plaque on the door read N. G. Remy, Gen.

Inside was a relatively cluttered office with a large desk, a vast armchair, a smaller desk and an upright chair. Both desks were covered in paper. The walls were covered in pigeon holes full of more paper. I fixated on a corner of the room, where an easel stood and the box of pastels Nat carried about with him. The paper on the easel showed a sketch of a flyer. A deep green flyer, taking off.

It was an example of the distortion that war brought to the lives of people caught in it that Nat, a lawyer by training, an artist by inclination, found himself being a general.

Jones closed the door, carefully, then flicked something. "Now we have privacy. I'm sorry I brought you such a convoluted way, Colonel, but I couldn't really hide you on the way here. If we could pretend that you were just another service man—but with your size."

I shrugged and nodded to indicate I understood. I did understand. I was descended—in a manner of speaking—from men who had been created in vats to be sort of super-bureaucrats, government servants par excellence. To that end they'd been made larger, stronger, faster, smarter than any normal human. The only wonder was that those who created them had thought they'd stay servants forever. The resulting regime, by people who'd been taught they weren't quite part of the human race, had been horrible enough to lead to the Turmoils that supposedly had scoured our race from the face of the Earth. Of course it hadn't. Lots of people had died, but not the most egregiously bioengineered. Those had gone underground and become, in due time, the Good Men who, having learned the wrong lesson, were now just oppressive enough to have remained in power for three hundred years, and just smart enough to sell their regime as peace and stability.

Jones didn't need to know all this. Enough of it had leaked out over the years, particularly over the horrible revolution in Liberté seacity, and its aftermath, that she should know exactly what and who I was and why I neither could hide amid normal people, nor was unused to sticking out.

She hesitated a moment, then she said, "The General normally uses this machine," she touched a small link, almost buried in papers on his desk. "We can try to get something from it."

She tried some passwords, and then I pushed her aside, and I tried. Finally in despair I'd tried Goldilocks, the name of our late, much lamented dog, as key to the encryption, and everything had come spilling out. I'd almost cried, then. That Nat, who was so fond of preaching on security and the importance of safe encryption, had used the name of his pet to lock his files was a failing that was so human, so stupid, as to make me fear for his life even more.

Everything was there. Oh, maybe not everything.

From the files locked under encryption in Nat's computer, I deduced that he'd suspected there was a mole at Condor, that this mole was passing details of our operation back to the enemy, that General Herrerra had been not so much wounded as assassinated. Or at least he'd been wounded in an assassination attempt during a larger operation. For the attempt to take place someone needed to have an exact knowledge of what Herrera intended to do. That indicated a leak in the high command, either among the council of generals or their confidential assistants. More data spilled forth. Nat had tried to find the culprit, and was almost absolutely sure he knew who it was, but he wasn't a hundred percent sure, which was why he'd made it a point of going to Olympus to discuss it with the commander there, who was at his level, but not in this tight cell around Herrera.

Um.

He had some notes on when he was leaving and when he intended to get to Olympus, but that was it.

"So," I said. "There was a leak, and he was either shot down or otherwise brought down before he reached Olympus. But there's no indication of the route he'd have taken."

"I can't tell you that," Jones said. "Or not exactly. But I can tell you what areas he'd have avoided and which he'd have tried not to fly over, because I gave him the list of danger spots yesterday afternoon. I can figure the most likely route from his times, too." And then with a frown, "But it makes no sense, you know? Even if he were shot down, unless he was totally obliterated, his chip would radio back his location. We do try to recover the bodies of the fallen, you know? And then there was his flyer. There is tracking on those too. It's encrypted and transmits to us only, but it would transmit."

I frowned at her, "His private flyer? Or a military one?" I looked involuntarily towards the easel where the drawing of the green flyer taking off seemed to be imbued with life.

She shook her head, but said, "His private one."

I bit my lip. "Do you have the encrypted signal for that chip? Or can you find it?"

She hesitated. Madeiras said, "Sherry," and I wasn't sure if he meant it as entreaty or admonishment.

The air smelled musty and disused, with just a faint trace of the cigarettes that Nat smoked almost continuously. I guessed they didn't let him smoke in here, or he didn't do it out of respect for his subordinates, but enough of his cigarette smell clung to him that it had transferred here. It was like a hint of Nat's presence and for a moment I imagined he was here, somehow, waiting for me to figure it out. Then I hoped he wasn't, because if Nat were a ghost it would mean he was dead.

Jones took a deep breath, "I can try," she said. "But not here. You'll have to wait. I'll go down the hall."

She went and was gone an unreasonable amount of time. Or so it seemed to me. There was no clock or watch on sight, and I hadn't brought my private com with me which I normally used to look up time, but which, also, had a chip that allowed tracking me. If I'd brought it, I'd have medtechs all around right now, I'd guess.

She came back at long last, and handed me a small, round data gem. Many of these looked like the children's marbles of years past, having distinctive designs. This one didn't. It was just a perfectly clear crystalline sphere. She hesitated a moment before she handed it to me, as though she weren't sure she was doing the right thing. Then she said "You know, I'm only helping because something about this whole setup stinks."

"Yes," I said, meekly. And then, "Thank you."

She went out the office, surveyed the return route. We first followed, then went ahead of her down the corridor, surveying in front as she surveyed behind.

We'd turned the corner, when I heard a man's voice call behind us, "Lieutenant Jones?"

As she headed back, Madeiras got hold of my arm, and pulled. He whispered, almost soundlessly, "I know the way."

I did too. An excellent memory was part of the skills that had been engineered into my long-distant ancestor who'd become the first Good Man of Olympus Seacity. And like Madeiras I felt we should hurry. Perhaps it was something in the tone of voice that called Sherry back.

We hurried the way we'd come and got aloft with no problems. I realized after we were in the air that I didn't have a locator-chip reader on this fly. At least I presumed I didn't, since it was civilian issue and had only the standard equipment. But my broom had one. It had been, at least once, a top of the line outlaw broom, and we'd used it to fly as a group. We often had to know the location of all the other chips for our band, at least when we were doing something sneaky involving a fight with another broomer lair, or some drug heist. So I could punch the number of that chip, and the broom would locate it. And finding the number was easy, as there was a link on board, of course, nothing fancy.

I realized as I was turning it on, making sure I didn't turn on anything that would transmit outside the flyer, and reading the number, then memorizing it for punching into my broom's search features, that Madeiras had gone very quiet behind me.

I looked over my shoulder. The young man was pale as milk, and turning off a com ring, into which he'd been talking.

"Anything wrong?" I asked.

"Sherry," he said.

"Yes?" I said, afraid something had happened to the young woman.

"She said that the people who called her were military police. They say General Remy had been selling information to the enemy, and that his trip out was a means of committing suicide or trying to escape. They came to seal his office and his computer."

I looked at Madeiras and said, "I see. And are you going to believe that of Nat? Are you going to believe Nathaniel Green Remy is a traitor?"

His eyes flickered to the ring, then to me. He swallowed audibly. But when he spoke his voice was loud and clear, "No, Sir," he said. "Not General Remy. It's impossible."

There was no doubt at all that he meant what he said. I nodded. "Good then. Can you program a course close to what he followed? We'll see if we can find him."

While he did that, I activated my broom's link, without turning on the anti-grav field.

Brooms came in many sizes and shapes, from simple little wands, three feet long, that could be ridden from a crashing flyer to the ground without much trouble, and likely keep the person alive, unless they'd been going really fast or were really scared of heights.

Then there was an intermediate size, also about three feet long, but about as thick around as my thigh, which could be ridden more comfortable, and which usually had a mask and an oxygen concentrator.

At the other end of the scale was my broom, a real outlaw broomer's broom, with a saddle and a for-real oxygen concentrator, with a mask. It also had a pretty good built in link. It was just small enough for me to clip to my belt, but I was an outsized man. I think normal men would have had to carry it.

I entered the number on the chip into the link and set the link on scan.

But we flew the course he'd followed, and looked beneath the whole time, and there was no sign at all of wreckage or of Nat.

I'd calculated that Nat must have disappeared near Olympus because after all Martha had expected him and he'd not yet gone missing officially when she'd started to worry. Which meant not only would he have smashed near Olympus—when his chip stopped answering—but he must have gone off course somewhat, or he would have disappeared before he was expected.

My eyes crossed slightly as I tried to figure it out. We'd fly criss-cross patterns around the expected route until I saw wreckage or caught a hint of something.

Just as I was thinking that, the link on my broom beeped, and pointed south-south west.

Madeiras looked at me, "But there is nothing there," he said. "Just empty ocean."

"I don't think the chip in the flyer would give a signal if it were under water," I said. "Not too far under water."

But I looked at the map that came up on the screen, as Madeiras set course towards the signal. There was no sign of land anywhere. Maybe the flyer was bobbing on the waves and Nat was unconscious inside it.

Right. It was now at least eight hours since he'd gone missing. He couldn't be unconscious for eight hours, unless he'd had a stroke or something, and even then he'd be more likely to be dead.

And why would he head out south-south west? Where could he have been going?

O O O

"Did you not consider that General Remy might have been in the midst of committing treason, making rendezvous with enemy agents at an assigned location?"

"No."

"Why not, if all the evidence indicated it?"

"Because I know Nat."

O O O

We'd turned on the bottom cameras on the flyer and were looking underneath us and slightly ahead as we flew, for wreckage or other signs that Nat might have made a forced landing.

I spotted the flyer first, and blinked at it, seeing the vehicle, the same as in Nat's drawing, sticking out of the water at a crazy angle.

It wasn't bobbing on the water, though. It was just immobile on the surface of the sea, as if the sea were made of glass and the flyer had got embedded in it before it solidified.

The door to the flyer was open, and someone was halfway out of it—a figure, a silhouette, impossible to tell who it was—as though the driver had crawled half out and were lying there, on top of something, I couldn't tell what. Something dark.

I was squinting at the screen and wishing my over-forty-year-old eyes could see better, when Madeiras said, "Sir!" and pointed at the screen.

There was a man on broom, flying towards the flyer. Rescue? An enemy agent? There was no way to tell. In fact, he was still distant enough, and approaching from the west, that only because I'd run with illegal broomers could I tell what he was on was a broom. I knew from the way that dot moved on the screen. Not a flyer, but a man on a broom.

Right. I'd get there first, if it broke me. "I'm going to jump out of the flyer," I told Madeiras.

"In movement?" he asked.

"Do you want to stop on the water? It might be amphibious, but I wouldn't care to test it like this," I said. "You know the brooms were designed to get out of flyers while they're flying."

"I could throttle back a little?"

"Don't you dare. I must get there first."

I closed my leathers, which I'd opened at the chest because they'd gotten too hot. "I'll trust you to open the emergency chute and close it before it takes you down."

He nodded. He was very pale again. The emergency chute was on the floor, a barely visible darker rectangle on the cheap carpet. Probably older carpet that hadn't got replaced in a remodel, because carpeting the chute and having it remain functional was a job for experts more expensive than the owner of this flyer was likely to be able to pay for.

I poised myself at the edge, broom solidly between my legs. The saddle, even on a broom of this type, is not exactly something you sit on, but something you clench. In this case, it just gave me a more solid hold, so I could fight on air if needed.

I was glad of the hold as Madeiras opened the chute and howling wind came in.

I jumped, against the wind, fast, because he had to close the thing fast or compromise his flyer.

The problem with jumping from a flyer in flight is that you need to turn the broom on after you're falling. Brooms are antigrav wands and if you turn them on in or in the close proximity of the flyer, the anti-grav fields will interfere with each other.

I closed my eyes, feeling the air rush around me, and knowing I was rushing towards the sea, counted to ten, then stabbed at the anti-grav button.

Nothing. A moment of panic, because I hadn't used the broom in more than a year and what if—

I stabbed again. The broom caught so suddenly that it felt like I'd just been kicked in a rather sensitive place. I held on for dear life and took a deep breath, reminding myself that after all, sometimes when you're falling fast the broom does take a moment to catch.

In control now, I stabilized the path to fly in a gentle slope towards the downed flyer, instead of falling like a stone out of the sky.

I'd forgotten to bring goggles, and had to squint against the wind, but even so I could see, through tearing eyes, that the other broomer was now about as close to the downed flyer as I was.

O   O   O

"What was your first indication you were dealing with an hostile, Colonel Keeva?"

"When the bastard shot at me, Major."

O   O   O

Fortunately I could reach my burner and I did, and fired back, quickly. Both of us missed, myself probably because of missing the stupid goggles and also because the other thing I'd managed to forget were gloves, and my hands were numb with cold.

And then I was glad that I had this broom, and could fight on broom back. Hadn't done it in years, but it's like anything that gets beneath the level of rationality to the instinctive. It came back.

Good thing it did, because my attacker had friends. I had a moment of hesitation, not being sure on which side the three broomers who joined in were, but then I realized they were pointing burners at me, or taking them out with obvious intent to.

One of the things bioengineered into my ancestors along with high intelligence—not that I've ever seen much evidence of this in myself—and strength and the type of health that allows you to live a long, long time, was super-speed. I wasn't alone in this gift, though.

Supposedly most of the bio-improved people had died in the riots of the end of the twenty third century, the ones that had overthrown the bio-Lords. But that was a very large supposition. Nat himself was descended from extremely bio-improved ancestors who had survived the turmoils. There were others like him.

So I never take things for granted. But as it was I shot two of the clowns down before they could hit me, and then I forgot they existed, because there was a flyer landing, near Nat, so near they might as well have been on top of him.

I sped forward, glad my broom was really expensive. I think I was shot then, at least once. It didn't matter. It didn't kill me. In the state of excitement I was in, it didn't even hurt me and I couldn't tell you where it hit if I tried to.

I reached Nat's flyer first. I could now see that it was Nat spilling out of the flyer, as though he'd tried to crawl out and passed out. There was blood on his pale blond hair, and blood on one shoulder, and on his uniform. There was also blood all down one leg of his pale blue uniform stuff.

Men were coming out of the flyer that had landed ten feet away, spilling out, and they weren't wearing the uniforms of Olympus, nor of any members of the coalition of Freedom.

They also weren't wearing the uniforms of the enemy. I'd seen those in various videos and knew others because I knew the house colors of most Good Men. But that wasn't needed to tell me their intentions. You don't come to rescue a very wounded man wearing combat armor in made of dimatough scales, shiny and black. And you don't carry the most powerful burners with you, either.

I landed between them and Nat. I positioned myself so I served as a shield, on my knees, covering the half of his body that was out of the flyer. I made use of the superspeed to take out two of the bastards with precision shots to the neck. The other remaining dimatough armored guard shot at me, but missed, because he was jostled out by two more of his friends coming from inside the flier. None of them spoke.

I shot the one who'd shot me. The bastards on broom landed. They took the weapons of the fallen.

Shit.

I was somewhere else, as though this were happening to someone else, far away. I had only one thought. I must save Nat.

"He's a traitor, you know," one of the men who'd landed on broom said. I couldn't see his face. He had goggles and a hood, but his lips opened in a savage smile. "He's been selling secrets to the enemy. You'd do better to let him die."

"Nat," I said. I couldn't say anything else. From behind me came a sound like a groan, and I knew it was him, and it was the first indication I had that he was alive. And it was enough.

The burner flared, once, twice, three times. I missed the first, which was the guy that had spoken. I blame my frozen fingers, my stinging eyes, or perhaps just the shock at having confirmation Nat was alive. The first man in dimatough fired on me.

I smelled burning leather. I knew I'd been hit, but it didn't matter.

I raised my burner and was rewarded with the hissing sound that meant the burner had gone empty.

A quick patdown of my pockets revealed this was my last burner. I didn't remember using the charges on the others. But then years of training in aerial combat as a broomer had taught me to discharge and discard, because the burners we used back then were cheap and disposable. Under stress, I'd probably just reverted to pattern.

Two of the men in dimatough uniform aimed at me, but the one in broomer leathers who'd shot at me before, said, "No, let me."

He was smiling.

And then from behind me a beam came, cutting through the air, hitting him in the shoulder. He screamed, and two more deadly shots rang out, hitting the other two men between shoulder and neck, the only way to kill someone in dimatough armor. They fell.

I smelled blood and wasn't sure if it was mine or theirs. I wasn't sure who'd shot from behind me, either. The man who'd been about to shoot me had fallen but wasn't dead. He was scrambling around, trying to get hold of one of the fallen burners, while one of his arms hung limp at his side. And the other one, the still standing broomer aimed at Nat and I did the only thing one can do with an empty burner and threw it at his head.

He screamed and fell on his ass, confused, not dead, and the first one in broomer leathers was grabbing a burner. I jumped forward, kicked the burner out of his hand, and turned to take out his buddy with a kick, but there was someone else there, slugging him.

So I turned my attention to the first one. We were all slipping on salt, and falling. This little islet, whatever it was, must be under water at times, and the salt was thick, a slick coating on its surface. My opponent had got hold of a burner, and was stepping back to aim. Not at me, at Nat. I leapt.

One leap, with strength I didn't have, pushing myself with all my will. Men of my build aren't designed for the long distance jump. We just aren't. But I forced myself, and I realized I'd made it when I felt my opponent's body beneath me, as I landed.

I knocked the breath out of him, as well as out of myself, but then he was squirming madly, and I felt him lift his burner towards my temple, trying to shoot me.

I twisted his arm, wrenching his wrist. I heard bone break. He screamed.

And then I was pulling his goggles off and his hood down.

It was Nocito. I had a moment of surprise, but only a moment, and then I was punching him, "Why, you sack of shit, why?"

It felt good to punch him, and there was blood on my hands, and blood on his mouth, and I heard bone break again. "Say it," I said. I had a vague idea my helper, who had attacked the other broomer, was Madeiras, and I had a sense that I wanted him to know, I wanted someone to know so that if I died Nat would not be saddled with a crime he hadn't committed.

"Tell me why you did it," I said. I dragged him up, with an arm around his chest, immobilizing him. I groped downwards, and got hold of his gloved hands, and twisted a finger back till it cracked. Then another. He screamed. There was blood on his gloves, now. "Tell me. I can do this all day."

My eyes were blurry, but I could see that it was indeed Madeiras, that he had punched the other guy to the ground, and shot him. He turned to look at me, horror and disbelief in his eyes.

I remembered Nat talking about the time he'd tortured someone to death. *It's not remorse,* he'd said. *The bastard deserved it. But it did something to me. It was I who broke.*

But I had to do this, because Nocito had to speak.

Crack went a third finger, and a fourth.

I gripped his thumb and he screamed, "He was going to be promoted over me. He always was promoted over me. And he didn't deserve it. I started making sure his operations didn't do well. I got Herrera in trouble. Remy, too. He should have been dead. He should have been dead. Why did you have to interfere?"

My hands were around his neck, and then someone slapped me. It was the slap equivalent of a fly landing on you, but it was a slap, across the side of my face.

I let go of Nocito and turned—

"Sir." Madeiras was standing by me, his legs wide apart as though he were bracing on a choppy sea, which he sure as hell wasn't because whatever this platform was stood as firm as any seacity. There was blood all down the front of his uniform, and I didn't know whose it was. There was blood dripping down his arm, and from the hand that held a burner. Pointed at me.

"Colonel Keeva, sir. Don't kill the bastard. We need him for questioning." I don't know what he thought he was going to do with that burner. He didn't either, I bet, because as he stood there, his eyes rolled up in his head and he passed out, falling face first towards me.

Nocito had dropped to his knees, but was trying to find his burner with the hand that still worked. I punched him, hard, hoping it wouldn't kill him. Then I tied him with his goggle strap and his own belt. And I kicked him in the balls, which served no purpose but made me feel much, much better. Even if I already had strong suspicions that it was conduct definitely unbecoming.

And then I realized I was on whatever this was, with a bunch of corpses and three grown men, none of whom was going to be walking to the flyer on their own.

I tried my com link, with Martha's code, but could raise no one. Either she was at work and had turned her link off—and I didn't want to call the official office one—or she wasn't taking calls from me, and at this point I didn't even care which.

I looked around. I had two flyers to pick from, but one of them was an enemy flyer. I suspected, from the paint job, that it was from Asgard Seacity. But wherever it was from, it would set off alarms in Olympus seacity. Serious alarms that would probably get us shot down.

However, Madeiras had landed here. I turned, and the battered white flyer was there, landed half in and half out of whatever this odd platform was, supported at a tilting angle.

I looked at the three men, fallen in various positions. Kneeling by Nat, I felt for his neck pulse, and his eyes fluttered semi-open, a slit that showed a dark pupil between his ridiculously abundant pale eyelashes. His lips were parted, which made sense, because I didn't see how he could breathe through his nose, which was filled with dried blood. His lips were cracked and bleeding and almost colorless, but he made a visible effort to open his eyes, and he rasped at the back of his throat, "Luce!"

"Shhh," I said. "We'll get you care."

I carried him in first and set him lengthwise on one of the long seats, and strapped him down in the middle with a safety belt. I opened his uniform to figure out what to do about the bleeding on his hip area, and stared dumbly at a mess of ripped apart skin with white flecks of bone glimmering in it. The chip had probably been crushed and that was why it had stopped transmitting. I had to get Nat to a hospital. Fast.

Then I got Madeiras himself, and tourniqueted his arm to make sure he wouldn't bleed out while I was flying back to Olympus. Last I got Nocito, trussed up and trying to wiggle free. I gagged him with his hood and resisted the temptation to punch him yet again, because there's unbecoming and there's stupid. When your fists are as big as mine, you could eventually get unlucky and kill the son of a bitch.

O   O   O

"At that point, why didn't you call General Cranston?"

"Because I still hadn't talked to Nat and wasn't sure he was clean and besides—"

"Besides?"

"I was almost sure he wouldn't believe anything I said."

"But the chain of command—"

I tell him what I think of the chain of command.

O   O   O

In the flyer, I set course for Olympus, not near my lodgings but near the center. With two injured men aboard, I was going to land as close to the hospital as possible.

I found the emergency medical kit aboard but they had no painkillers or blood-clotters. I'd managed to control the bleeding on Madeiras. Nat was still bleeding freely, even after I clumsily put a large pad of cloth—my shirt—on his hip and applied pressure.

It made him scream, and there was blood on his lips too, and I wondered if he'd bitten his lips, or if he was bleeding internally.

But I did find the water bottles in the compartment beneath the navigator. I was afraid he couldn't drink, but he gulped down the water, greedily, and then opened his dark eyes, and stared at me. "Luce," he said.

"Yes!"

"I didn't do it."

"I know that, you fool."

"Bomb. There was a bomb, and when I removed it … it messed steering. I crashed. I could only just get to the abandoned algae farm."

"Good. Glad you did. Now shut up, we'll be home soon."

Only a flyer with no responder coming in hot, screaming towards the seacity, while we were at war, and more or less continuously under attack, couldn't go unremarked. It didn't.

There were people screaming at me through the com, a babble of voices, demanding I identify myself. Through the noise of the voices and a curious hum in my ears, there was the sound of other flyers, flying way too close to me.

Fighter flyers, from the sound of the engines. Of course, they were trying to force me down, and would shoot me if they didn't manage it this way.

I slammed my voice into the com's speaker button, and screamed, "Colonel Keeva, seeking to land near the hospital with two wounded men and a prisoner of war."

There was a long silence, and then someone came on giving me coordinates in an excessively calm and polite voice.

I punched them into the navigator with unsteady fingers and eyes that felt blurry, hoping against hope that I could land this thing without killing either Nat or Madeiras.

It occurred to me as I settled down, none too gently in front of the hospital, that it was entirely possible the two witnesses to my behavior and Nocito's attempt were already dead. In which case, Nocito would probably manage to blame it all on Nat, and I was going to military prison for a long, long time.

Perhaps I could ask for the death sentence instead.

O O O

"You prefer the death sentence to incarceration?" the Major asks.
"At this point? I don't really mind either. I did what I had to do."

○ ○ ○

We were met by military police, in a circle around the flyer. Beyond the circle I could just glimpse passersby and the good people of Olympus going about their lawful occasions. Save for the usual idiots who'd come close to gawk, of course.

But none came too close, because the men in uniforms and armor were pointing their burners at our flyer like they expected it to suddenly explode or something.

I came out with my hands up. I don't remember what I said. Something about wounded, I know. A break opened in the circle, and through it, men in the yellow medic uniforms came running, with two antigrav platforms. It seemed like only seconds before they ran again, past me, four of them pushing the platform with Madeiras on it, with an IV going into his body, and the other four pushing Nat on a platform. There was considerably more than an IV attached to Nat and the medics looked grim.

Then the MP's closed in. But there were medics behind them, and they were trying to get to me too, only the MP's were in the way. One of the medics shoved the MP's aside, and I thought there would be a slugging match, but the MP's parted, and the medics came through.

"Sir," one of them said.

"What?" I asked. I was bare-chested, and my pants were shredded, but I didn't see where this was a matter for the medics, particularly medics with a platform between them.

But the guy touched me on the shoulder, and showed me a bulbous injector in pale blue, so probably a pain killer, and said, "Sir, we have to get you stabilized and into regen."

"Regen?" I said. Which was the first time in the whole mad rush that I looked down at myself.

I knew the burner had hit me. Twice at least. But I'd be damned if I knew where the puncture through my shoulder, the one through my arm and the two in my stomach had come from. I looked down at the blood soaking my lower half.

Which is when I passed out and everything went dark.

○ ○ ○

"And assault on a superior officer."
"But he was a traitor."
"Had you any way to be sure of that?"

o   o   o

I woke up. I woke up lying in bed, my nose full of the smell of antiseptic. My uniform was over the back of a chair. No, not my uniform, or at least not the uniform I'd been wearing before, but a crisp, clean, near-shining uniform.

Other than that, there was no other furniture in the room, though there were rows upon rows of machines, most of which had at least one sensor attached to me.

On the other side of the bed, looking scared and extremely pale, stood my old friend Royce Allard.

When I'd first started working for the Usaians, before we were formally part of the army of Olympus, Royce had been my nemesis. Well, perhaps not that. But he was in charge of the department of cosmetics and appearance. Useful if you are a spy, and I suppose useful if you are trying to create propaganda too. But I thought his suggestions too mannered, too … not what I was. And he was in a fair way to driving me insane.

But over time we'd learned to work together. Allard was a bachelor in his middle years. The person for whom he'd converted to the Usaian religion and joined our cause had died in our first genuine loss of this war, the Broken River Massacre. Allard had never settled again.

We had lunch together sometimes, and sometimes Nat and I had dinner at his lodgings when Nat was in town.

Other than that we were the sort of friends who didn't have much in common, but who respected each other. And somehow when there was a disaster, Royce was always there, trying to help. He was one of those people.

Now he was looking more dead than alive, which surprised me, and I almost asked him if he'd been in the fighting, but that was impossible. Instead, I blinked at him and said, "Royce? They said something about putting me in Regen?"

He made a noise between a snort, a laugh, and a sigh. "Two months and a half ago, yes. You don't take regen well, do you?"

"No," I said. "Last time I needed it took six months of regen and almost another six to recover. Why?"

He shrugged. "Because they've been holding up your court martial till you were awake and well. And they want to question you and talk to you, because now that you're awake they want it next week. It's unfinished business, and they need to give your department permanently to someone else."

I felt my throat go dry. "Court martial," I rasped. "But … why?"

The snort, laugh, sigh again. "Lucius, you went crazy. You went AWOL, you kidnapped someone, you broke into a military installation, you assaulted a superior officer, you tortured someone, you—"

"Saved Nat."

His face went a weird shade of green and I said, "Nat. Is Nat all right? Is he awake? Good Lord, they didn't court martial him too, did they?"

He shook his head. His lips worked. "Nathaniel was too long without rescue. He … The regen isn't working. His family has given permission to turn off the regen and let him die. They were … they wouldn't let the order take place until you woke, because they said that you—"

"Nat what? They gave order to what?" At which point I realized my hand was tearing away sensors. Alarms sounded.

"What are you doing?" Allard asked.

"Getting up off this bed," I said. There might have been a few swear words there in the middle. "Nat is not dying. Not after everything I did to save him, he's not."

"There were extensive internal injuries. And he had been too long without regen, and was too far gone. They've tried for two months, every technique they know, and there's just no response, no—"

"I don't give a good goddamn what there isn't," I said. I was out of the bed, putting my uniform on. Fastening the tunic, unable to find shoes, I headed for the door, plowed right through three medtechs trying to stop me, turned around and asked Allard, "Where is he?" But I didn't wait for his answer, because outside the room there was an arrow and a hologram directing me to the regen ward, and I loped there, at full tilt. For part of the way at least—might have been all the way, I wasn't paying attention—I was trailing two of the medtechs hanging on my arms like ineffectual ballast. Royce Allard, who knew me better, was running alongside me, saying things like, "You shouldn't even be up." And, "The medtechs agree there's nothing they can do for him."

I ignored him, because Nat was my business, and if the medtechs thought they were done trying to save him, they would just have to think again.

Down a flight of antiseptic corridors, their gleaming ceramite floors slippery under my bare feet, around a corner very fast, and up a gravwell to the next floor, I charged. I continued at a trot down the shut doors of regen rooms, scanning the names on the door, until I came to one marked NG Remy, and then I turned the handle and charged into the room.

Understand, a regen room is spare and relatively small.

The regen apparatus itself is a grey dimatough thing, roughly the size of a coffin, with readouts and buttons at the bottom, and a mess of tubes on the sides. And there is a chair, in case one of your relatives wishes to sit there and look at the regen coffin while you're completely dead to the world inside it.

Inside the regen enclosure, you float in something akin to the fluid that submerged you in the womb, only this one is antiseptic and usually full of nanites that are supposed to fix whatever is wrong with you. More nanites and medicines and who knows what else are pumped into you both via your breathing tube, via your feeding tube, and via intravenous ports.

This room was full. There was Martha, and there were Nat's parents, and there were two medtechs, and they all looked like they were at a funeral.

My heart about stopped.

Martha turned around and said, "Luce. So good you could come, because—"

I pushed past her, past her parents, past the medtechs. I pushed right next to the regen coffin. A glance at the display at the end that read out vital signs informed me that Nat was still alive.

Blood was pumping past my ears so hard that it sounded like I had the sea in each of them. Through the roar I heard Royce say, "I told him, and he wouldn't understand. He—"

I grabbed the chair by the back. I brandished it like a weapon. They all stepped back. "No one," I said, my voice sounding like a roar. "Is going to turn off this regen machine until Nat is well and doesn't need it anymore."

Everyone started talking at the same time, all of them, and then Sam, Nat's father, made a gesture. The others shut up. "Son," he said, softly. "You know this is nonsense. The medtechs say nothing can be done. Keeping him alive will only ensure suffering, and he can't survive outside the regen, and what good would that do?"

Sam had a right to call me son. In the fifteen years I'd been kept in solitary confinement, it had been his sending me, clandestinely, works of literature and music, that had kept me even semi-sane.

He was speaking reasonably, and I knew he loved me, and he loved Nat. He had the grey look I'd only seen once before, when he'd lost his younger son.

But I didn't care. He didn't understand. Nat couldn't die, because if he died, nothing mattered. You can love someone like a father, but you wouldn't let him kill you just for that, and letting him kill Nat felt like dying. "No," I said. "No. I don't accept you've done everything you could. I want to speak to the medtech who looked after me."

"What?" Sam said. But Martha was elbowing him and saying something. I couldn't hear it, because my blood was still thundering in my ears. She left running, and came back minutes later with a tall, spare man about Sam's age.

He walked right up front, looked at the chair and didn't come into injector range, but said, "Yes? Sir?"

"You worked on me," I said. "I know you had problems because some of the proteins are different, because of the extent of my bioengineering. You know both of Nat's parents are bioengineered." And as Sam and Betsy opened their mouths to speak. "I mean, they're descended from bio-engineered people. Have you looked at every protein?"

"We treated General Remy for extensive injuries before? Ten years ago we—"

"Blunt force injuries?" I said. "With extreme internal damage?"

He made a face that meant "Well not precisely that" without his saying it.

"Have you sequenced all his proteins? And remember they change radically if you are designed to heal well and aren't treated immediately."

He made a face. "We can certainly do it, but I doubt that it will show us anything we don't know."

"Then do it. Now. And never mind me. I'm going to be right here, making sure nothing gets turned off." I plopped the chair down, sat, and waited.

It took them a while, before they came back, and it took both Sam and Betsy talking to me to convince me that no they weren't going to turn the machine off and that, yes, they would give the new program parameters a chance to work, before I let the medtech put the new program into the machine.

And then I stepped away, and felt suddenly woozy. I probably hadn't been meant to be up and about yet. As I stepped away from the bed, MPs came into the room.

Before I could even move, I was handcuffed and escorted out between men who were almost as tall and burly as I was.

This was not going to end well, but I didn't care as long as Nat survived. Nat could clear himself. What happened to me was immaterial.

I was escorted briskly across the street and up a flight of stairs, then was held by three men, as we took the anti-grav well to the third floor, and then I was put in a small cell.

Many years ago, when I was arrested for a crime I didn't commit, I'd been confined in a similar cell, where over weeks I'd been tortured in ways I'd never even dreamed of. It turned out they were trying to get me to confess knowledge I wasn't aware of having.

This time, despite my clenched teeth, my fear, the cold sting of despair in my stomach, I was treated politely, courteously.

They made me repeat my version of events many times—first to the MP interrogators, then to some major I didn't know, then to Colonel Hanson, then to General Cranston, then to Field Marshall Herrera, pale and looking like he'd been very, very ill, then to the MP interrogators again, then to what I suspected were medtechs. Then they recorded and transcribed my story, from the moment I'd heard Nat was missing till I landed in front of the hospital. I tried to keep Sherry out of it, and was almost sure I'd managed it, though by then my head was swimming. I did insist that everything Madeiras had done, save for the last shot that he'd arguably fired in self-defense, or at least to save my life while I was helpless, had been done under duress, because I had kidnapped him.

At some point I realized that Royce was in the room, had been in the room through all this, listening to me.

"What are you doing here?" I asked.

"I'm your judge-advocate," he said. "For the court martial."

O O O

I stand there mutely. I've told them everything I could tell them. Now all that remains is the judgment. And I can't imagine how military justice can overlook what I'd done, from ignoring military code, to trying to choke a superior. Conduct very unbecoming indeed.

I know what waits me is dishonor, removal of insignia, expunging of honors and hanging. Flogging before hanging optional. But I don't care.

There's some conversation between the Major and Royce, who has approached the bench, or in this case my repurposed desk.

I hear the words, "Not guilty by reason of insanity."

The Major demurs. "Theft. Kidnapping. Assault." He looks at me. I wonder if I can knock down one of the privates and run out.

"Sir, permission to speak frankly," Royce says.

The Major must have given it, because Royce says, "Sir, the Colonel is batshit nuts, sir."

The Major smiles.

O O O

I walked back through corridors, still in my uniform, absently acknowledging the salutes of my subordinates. A couple of them smiled wildly at me. Someone clapped me on the back. I thought it was Royce. I hoped it was Royce.

There was a buzzing in my ears, and I wanted to cry and the only thing I wanted to know was if Nat would survive. He'd been in the tank over a week, with the new program.

I was to be retired for medical reasons. I presumed for *batshit nuts* reasons.

A young man saluted me, and I realized it was Madeiras. I stopped, "Madeiras. I hope I didn't get you in trouble? Or not too bad trouble?"

He shook his head, looking bewildered, "Oh, no, Colonel Keeva. They ..." He hesitated and frowned slightly. "They gave me a citation for valor, and I'll probably get a medal, but they also sealed the records. I tried to tell them I'd gone with you willingly, that I wanted to save General Remy, but they tell me I was under the influence of pain killers then, and didn't know what I was saying. There was a fight for that abandoned plant, you know," he said. "When our guys arrived there to investigate, it was crawling with enemy. But enough evidence remained to validate our story and show we'd had a hell of a fight against a superior force. So I guess we impressed them. It's all very strange, sir."

I asked the question burning in my mind,

"Do you know how the enemy found Nat? Has Nocito talked? Do you know if they followed us there?"

"No, Colonel, they didn't. They just thought of his flyer chip probably sometime after we did. But they had a better detector for greater distance and found him quicker. Their goal was to dispose of him and his flyer, so people would think he'd run away. General Nocito had already insinuated such things to other people, you know?"

I figured. I'd also figured that Cranston had believed the rumors, which was why he would do nothing to recover Nat. They thought he was a traitor and had escaped. I didn't tell Madeiras that, nor how happy I was that I'd not led the enemy to Nat. I'd been having nightmares about that.

Instead, I just smiled and wished him the best, and continued, down the hall, and across the street, and down another street to the hospital.

I went, by accustomed habit to the regen room Nat occupied. I'd been going there every day before the court martial. Just to look at the grey coffin, and at the readouts saying Nat was still alive.

I hadn't been there for the three days of the trial, and I needed to go in, and look at the dials and make sure everything was okay.

I knew everything was not okay before I entered the room, because the door was ajar and there was no name on the door.

Opening it with a jerk, I found three people inside the room, cleaning the regen tank. They looked up at me.

"General Remy? What? You didn't? They didn't?" There was a stricture at my throat. I was going to be ill. I was trying not to yell at these people, who after all had done nothing to deserve it, but I had to do something and Nat—

"General Remy has been moved to room 204," one of the orderlies said. "In the recovery wing."

I leaned against the door, my legs weak, as I gulped in air like a starving man gulps food. "I … Oh."

I made my way to room 204 on shaking legs.

Nat was sitting up, when I came to his room. He looked small and thin, in a narrow bed. The hospital is strapped for space, dealing with war wounded, but at least he had a private room.

There was a large man with graying hair sitting on a chair by the bed, leaning over, talking to Nat.

I recognized the massive form of Field Marshall Herrera, who stood as I approached and shook my hand and thanked me for saving "Young Nat."

Difficulties with protocol were forgiven to a Field Marshall who could bring in victories on one tenth the personnel and equipment of the enemy.

He left almost immediately and I took his place by the bed, on the chair.

"He's very shaken, you know?" Nat asked. "Nocito's treason was worse for him than the physical injury he sustained."

"Why did Nocito betray him?" I didn't really want to know, but I was happy to be there, happy to hear Nat speak, clearly in command of his faculties. "Betray our side, I should say."

Nat shrugged. "Nocito was convinced he was inferior to me, though only to me, and if I were out of the way, and Herrera disposed of, he'd become the Field Marshall. He thought he deserved to become the Field Marshall and the fact he hadn't risen that far yet must be part of a plot. So he set things up to look like I was giving information to the enemy. In reality, of course, he was doing it, and he cost us many a fine serviceman, damn him."

"So he wasn't paid any great fortune, or something?"

"Nah. It was all spite and malice. There might have been a nominal payment, but it wasn't the reason."

"And now?" I asked. "They're retiring you?"

"Oh, yeah. Aguillard will have to do as Himself's right hand, until more can be trained, and well … I'll be available for consultation, of course, but I'm afraid days of fighting and the ability to run or walk for any appreciable time, or even fly a flyer for very long, are past."

"Ah," I said. "I didn't mean that, though. I presume the war will continue, and I know other men must take up what you can no longer carry. I meant you." I cleared my throat. "Us. What are we going to do now?"

He looked at me, frowning. "Well, you have your work, right, and propaganda to create."

I shook my head. "Invalided. Health. Mental."

He smiled a little, but there was an understanding expression in his eyes. "The forces are becoming more formal," he said. "It's nothing personal. You know your quirks. They wouldn't accept you nowadays."

"I know," I said. "So they're retiring me."

"Luce," he said, and reached for my hand and squeezed it hard. "I want to apologize. Martha says I should have told you. What was happening. Because she says you should have known. She was shocked you didn't. But you know why I didn't tell you, don't you?"

"Didn't trust me?" I asked. "Because I'm batshit nuts?"

He looked appalled. "Oh, hell, no. Not that." His hand squeezed mine. Fresh out of regen, he was about as strong as a kitten, but he was trying to give my hand a reassuring squeeze. "No, I just thought you'd worry. I didn't want you to worry."

"I checked the casualty lists every night," I said. "I thought I would die if I found your name. I did, a little, when I found it. I had to do something or I would. Die, I mean. For good."

He looked at my face, attentive, questioning. "Martha told me."

There was a long silence, then he said, "Ten years ago, you said you wanted to go and get a farm out in the territories when you retired, and raise kids and puppies. Do you still want to?"

I blinked at him. I shrugged. "I guess. There's nothing for me to do here." Ten years ago he'd said he'd go with me, but that was before the court martial and the full revelation of my insanity.

"You said," he said, cautiously, "You would be all right if I came along?"

"All right?" I said. "Nat. Will you really come along?"

"Do you want me to?"

"Of course."

"Well, then I will."

"They'll want me available to consult," I said.

"Yeah," Nat said, "Me too. But I figure we can give them our opinions while we're sowing fields and milking cows and raising puppies."

I nodded. Yeah. The war could go on without us from now on.

GOLIATH

DOUG DANDRIDGE

Two thousand years in the past, humankind began to reach for the stars, using interstellar travel through the dimension of subspace to plant colonies on nearby worlds. Then came the Ca'cadasans Empire, an interstellar force that had existed for thousands of years, conquering all that was in their path. The humans were to be the next conquest, conquered and brought into the Empire as had so many before them. Until they had committed an unforgivable sin, the killing of the heir to the Emperor by a rogue human when he landed with the ground force to accept the surrender of a colony. The human species were declared anathema, to be wiped out, their genetic heritage destroyed to the last microbe. The humans lost every battle, the Ca'cadasans possessing not just the larger navy, but tech more advanced by thousands of years. The humans sent out a number of refugee ships, the Exodus class, to save humankind by re-establishing them at other locations through the Galaxy. Only one ship was known to escape, using the more primitive technology of subspace, which the Ca'cadasans had abandoned millennia before in favor of the faster dimensions of hyperspace.

Moving from the Orion sub-arm to the Perseus, on a trip of a thousand years and ten thousand light years, the lone surviving Exodus vessel, crewed by the great grandchildren of the original crew, finally reached what seemed like the perfect place to settle. Unfortunately, it is also the home region to a number of species who were bootstrapped into space by an extinct race known as the Ancients. The human race soon found itself fighting a series of wars. To lose one would mean the enslavement of the species, so they could not afford to lose. After a thousand years the New Terran Empire has grown to become the dominant species in the region. They have strong enemies and stronger friends surrounding them, and the future looks bright for the human race.

Only then the Ca'cadasans, still expanding, found the hated humans. But these humans are only twenty years behind in technology, and actually their superior in some. The humans have been the victors of countless wars, while the conquerors have rolled over one less advanced civilization after another. The war of extermination is on, the larger Empire against that of the smaller, consummate warriors. And the battle rages across hundreds of light years and a thousand systems, while billions go into the long night.

O   O   O

The twenty-five-million-ton behemoth sent a surge of gravitons ahead and opened a hole into the lower dimension of hyper VI. The battleship *Imadaras* slipped through the opening into a dimension that was no less deadly to its existence than the one it was leaving. Antimatter reactors powered down as it entered the new space, no longer needing the energy to switch dimensions, or the shielding needed to exist in hyper VII.

"We will arrive at the final hyper barrier in two hours," said the Astrogator, four hands on his board, looking back at the big Ca'cadasan male who occupied the commander's seat. All of the crew of the ship were males, no space wasted for the non-sentient females of the species. The bridge was large enough to give each of the large, territorial aliens his own space. The officer's reddish eyes squinted in the harsh blue light of the bridge, a remnant of the home environment that most of the males had never lived in.

The Captain grunted and looked at the tactical holo that showed him nothing. Just the star and his ship. He would know nothing else about the system until he entered normal space at the edge of the hyper barrier. *It's supposed to be a relatively weak system*, thought the Captain, thinking back to his brief. There were not many humans, and not much in the way of defense. The reason the Great Admiral had made the decision to send one ship, even if it was one of the Ca'cadasan's largest capital vessels. The planet wasn't important in and of itself, but it was the home of humans, and so it needed to be visited, and those humans eliminated.

"I want all weapons powered up and all tubes loaded," said the Captain, looking at his Weapons' Officer. "And keep a close watch behind. Remember, they like to hang out at the barrier and catch ships coming in."

"They can't have more than one of their cruisers there," said the Weapons' Officer with a sneer.

"And a cruiser can still put a particle beam and some lasers into our stern," said the Captain, pointing the index finger of his lower right hand at the other officer. "And one of their missiles can do serious harm to us. So keep a close watch. Anything out of the ordinary, any blip on the sensors, and you are to fire."

The admonished male gave a head shake of acknowledgement, scratching a horn with nervous energy, then looked back at his board, anything to remove the gaze of his captain.

"Everybody, stay alert," ordered the Captain. "And we'll accomplish the mission, and get back to the fleet." He left the last part unsaid. They would have rewards, both from the tasty meat of the humans, and honors from command.

o o o

"We have a translation, from the hyper VII dimension down to VI," called out the Sensory Officer, Ensign Emile Schmidt, in his soft New Berliner accent.

"Ours, or theirs?" asked Lt. Commander Cinda Klerk, watching the tactical holo and dreading the answer. She was not a large woman, in fact, the captain's chair still felt too big when she sat in it. And she had the kind of face that attracted men, which she saw as a detriment to her career, not letting her fit the image of the warrior woman.

"Theirs," answered Schmidt, a look of anxiety, no, fear showing on his face. "And it's a big one. Twenty million tons or more."

It would be, thought Cinda, the captain of the HIMS *Joel Schumacher*, one of the only two hyper capable warships in the system. She was the largest ship assigned to the Compton system. There were two more ships, both non-hyper vessels of similar class. *Schumacher* was the most massive of the three ships due to her carrying the extra mass of a hyperdrive. At a hundred thousand tons she was not the smallest hyper capable vessel in the Imperial Fleet. The couriers and fast attack ships were much smaller, as were attack fighters, though only the fast messengers were capable of reaching hyperspace on their own. Still, they were facing the prospect of a visit by a twenty-five-million ton battleship, over two hundred and fifty times her own mass.

And we're more suited to going head to head with pirates, thought the Cinda. That was exactly what her ship had been envisioned to take on, either hunting them, or protecting merchant traffic. It was ludicrous at best to station her in a system as a defense against an opponent whose smallest warship was in the six hundred thousand ton range. Especially with the special orders that came down from the Emperor himself.

Cinda pulled up a side holo and stared at the comp representtation of the enemy that was en route. An image originally taken thousands of years before. *They haven't changed*, she thought, looking at the figure of a tall, furred biped, standing on two strong legs, double shoulders extending from the torso supporting four arms. The head was the horror, a medium muzzled, red eyed carnivore with sharp teeth showing in a grin, two large horns growing from the top of the skull. The creature stood three meters tall sans the horns, and looked very much like the demons of some human religions.

"We're receiving a gravity pulse from *New Kiev*," said the Com Officer, a young man who looked like he had just walked out of the doors of the academy. "Her captain is ordering us to support them in an action against that warship."

Of course he is, thought the Commander, staring at the tactical plot that showed the disposition of all vessels within the system from the graviton emissions of their drives. *New Kiev* was a newcomer, a hyper VI battlecruiser that happened to be visiting the system on her recon patrol. But her commander was a full captain, making him the ranking officer in the system. And a complete idiot, as far as she was concerned. Only a moron would face a ship he knew he couldn't beat, or even inflict enough damage on to warrant an engagement. Especially with orders coming down from an authority higher than Fleet.

Cinda fingered one of the small scars on the back on her left hand. She had been a mass of scars after the first, and only, battle she had been through. As Tactical Officer of the destroyer Kelvin Bunker, she had watched as every other member of the bridge crew had died. Her armor had been penetrated along all of her limbs. Fortunately, the suit had sealed all of the penetrations, and she had lived. Still, the memory of that smashed bridge was the first thing she saw when she closed her eyes. The broken bodies floating in the zero gee of a ship that no longer functioned. Blood globules floating in the air, then dissolving away as the atmosphere dissipated. Only the intervention of another human naval force had caused the enemy to break off the action, and allowed some of the crew to survive, including the once enthusiastic Tactical Officer.

We couldn't beat an equal tonnage of enemy warships, Cinda thought. *Four destroyers against one of their scout ships. We never beat them with equal tonnage. We rarely even beat them when we have the numerical odds in our favor, and only when we set them up. And how in the hell can we expect to beat them when out-massed three to one?*

He doesn't stand a chance either, she thought, staring at the icon of the battlecruiser that was about twenty-five light minutes out from Compton IV, the one inhabited planet in the system. The planet was two hundred million kilometers out from the F2 primary, and the battlecruiser was almost three light hours from the hyper barrier in her current position. There was a small liner and a freighter sharing the orbitals, both doomed. One of the frigates was within several light minutes from the battlecruiser, and starting to boost toward a matching velocity, positioning herself to support the capital ship.

She found the last of the interplanetary frigates on the plot, about two light hours out on the opposite side of the primary. She might escape notice for a while, but there was no place for her to go. *And what should I be doing?* she thought, zooming in the plot and looking at her own surroundings. She was well on the inner side of the asteroid belt, five light minutes from the planet, cruising at point zero one light speed, slow enough for her to get rid of that velocity before the enemy ship entered the system. The inhabited planet was the closest object in her path, and her current heading would take her there. She had enough time to change her heading. But where to go?

"Do you want to send back a response, ma'am?" asked the Com Officer, Ensign Horace Mbonga, giving her an expectant look.

New Kiev's captain is the ranking officer in the system, dammit, thought Cinda. And as such, he is the commander of all the forces in the system. But hell, the Emperor Sean himself ordered for all units to avoid combat, unless we can inflict equal or greater harm to the enemy. There was a good reason for that order. Human units had regularly gotten themselves annihilated in combat involving seemingly equal forces. Too many such exchanges, and the Fleet would cease to be as an effective fighting force. And then the enemy would roll over the Empire.

"Acknowledge by gravity wave only," she replied after a moment's thought. Gravitons traveled in all dimensions of hyper as well as normal space, making them detectable at faster than light speeds. Since gravitons traveled in all the dimensions of hyper, they could travel at equivalent speeds of thousands of times the speed of light, and be detected by ships equipped with systems designed for that purpose. The main deficiency with using them for communication was the limited amount of information that could be sent. Essentially, it was a digital code system. And it was a broadcast system, detectable by everything within the system.

"No vid?"

"No," said Cinda, shaking her head and glaring at the young man to cover her own discomfort at trying to avoid an order, even though she knew it was the wrong one. She ran a hand through her short brown hair as several of the bridge crew turned to look at her. Her hand mopped the sweat that was flowing down her freckled face, and she knew, despite her attempt at control, that her green eyes were wide with fear. *What the hell am I supposed to feel? That's death coming our way, and no damned battlecruiser is going to be able to stop them, much less a frigate. That man is an idiot, and obeying him would be a criminal act.* She looked again at the plot, zooming out and looking at the icon of the enemy ship blinking its way toward the system. *It'll be twenty minutes before they could expect a vid from us. Maybe I can figure something out in that time. Something that will allow us to survive, or at least to die accomplishing more than adding extra atoms to interplanetary space.*

The plot was showing the eight million ton battlecruiser moving out from the inner system, tracked by its grabbers' graviton emissions. The frigate *Monte Barker* was beside her, a dog and its flea moving out to do battle with a tiger.

"Those poor people," said Lieutenant JG Natalia Romanov, the Navigation Officer, staring at the main viewer.

"That's what they pay us for," said the Helmsman, Ensign Garibaldi.

"Not us," replied Romanov, nodding at the screen. "Those civilians, on that planet. The Cacas are going to kill every one of them, you know."

Cinda zoomed in on the planet on one of her side screen holos. It was a beautiful world, with maybe a little more arid area than most. Still attractive enough to entice settlers. Only fifty thousand so far, but fifty thousand dreams that were about to end. And according to the Emperor's orders, we are supposed to abandon them as well, so we won't waste our combat power, small as it is, for no reason. She studied the viewer, her mind trying to grasp any possible action that would actually mean something.

"What's that?" she asked, pointing to the tactical plot. As soon as her finger aligned with the dot it started blinking, so her crew would know where she was pointing.

"Comet C509," replied Schmidt, looking at his board and using the unimaginative system of naming minor objects in minor systems.

"Can we get there before the Cacas translate to normal space?"

"I think so," said Romanov, looking confused. "But, aren't we going to support the *New Kiev?*"

"I asked you a question, Miss Romanov," said Cinda, maintaining eye contact with the young woman despite the urge to look away. Or at least trying to. Shame was warring with fear and anger within her, despite knowing that she was taking the correct action, and she dropped her gaze to the floor. "Can we make it there?"

"I think so," said the Navigator.

"Then I want us behind that thing as fast as you can get us there, Mr. Garibaldi."

"But, our orders," stammered Garibaldi.

"You have your orders, from me," said Cinda in a cold tone, standing up and walking over to the helm station. "Now follow them, or I will relieve you of duty."

Cinda forced herself to walk calmly back to her chair and laid back into its embrace. She forced herself to look straight ahead at the viewer, avoiding the eyes of the bridge crew, yet still feeling their eyes on her. *They think I'm a coward*, she cried within her own mind. *And they're right, to their manner of thinking, the young firebrands. I don't want to die. Not for no reason. Can't they understand that our going out with that battlecruiser will make sure that they don't make it home and see their loved ones. And for no payoff, except* making *the enemy waste some missiles.* She slammed her hand into the chair arm and glared at the plot. *If we're going to die, we're going to accomplish something other than stopping a missile or two. Damn if we aren't.*

"Are you sure you want to do this, Captain?" asked her Exec, Lieutenant SG Marcus Frobisher, talking over the private link from his station in the combat information center, the CIC, which also served as one of the auxiliary control stations on the vessel.

"Those are my orders, Exec," she replied in a cold voice. "And I expect no questioning."

"Just doing my job, ma'am," said the second in command. "That idiot is the ranking officer in the system, after all."

"And our orders from Fleet are to avoid action if we can't accomplish anything," said Cinda. "The most I can see us accomplishing here is to hide and gather data, and bring it back to the Fleet."

"Sounds good, ma'am," said Frobisher in a cautionary tone. "In theory. But the officer you report to after this may not take that view."

"I'll have to take that risk, Exec."

"What do you want us to do when we reach the comet?" asked Garibaldi.

"How big is it?" she asked, wondering if her crazy notion would work.

"It's a big one," answered the Sensory Officer, Ensign Schmidt, looking at a holographic representation on his board. "Over forty kilometers in diameter."

"Get us directly on the side away from the Cacas," she said after a moment's thought. "Match velocities, and then get some drones into the dust tail so we can see what's going on."

"And then?" asked Lt. SG Jakardo, the Tactical Officer, giving her a look of disgust.

And you would just love to go slug it out with something that could swat you out of space in a moment, thought Cinda, looking at the young firebrand. "And then we sit and wait." *And maybe they'll just pass us by, do their business, and leave. Then we can report back to base, and I can go through my court martial for cowardice and disobedience in the face of the enemy, while my crew is safe. And then we'll see if it's more important to obey a fleet directive, or some higher ranking fool on the spot. Or maybe we can actually accomplish what command would want us to do, and actually cause a little bit of harm to this enemy.*

O   O   O

One second space was empty. The next, twenty-five million tons of warship exited at point three light from a hole in space, an almost perfect circle showing the red background of hyper I. The ship was a cylinder three kilometers in length, her grabber units, the space drive of the ship, arranged in a skirt around her length. Forty domes were arrayed on the hull, her light amp weapons, while ports and hatches concealed missile tubes and particle beam projectors. The rest of the available skin, like that of most modern vessels, functioned as a sensor array. It drank in every photon that impacted on it, and gave the vessel a view of the space it had entered.

"There is nothing out here," said the Ca'cadasan Weapons' Officer with a sigh of relief, his eyes locked on the holos hovering above his board.

"Stay alert," warned the Captain, his lower hands gripping his chair arms, while his upper limbs were crossed over his chest. "They have ships that can fade to almost undetectability." Somehow they solved the heat radiation problem with those small stealth ships, he thought, recalling the latest brief on the humans. But not their normal ships. A stealth ship couldn't handle his vessel in a heads up fight, but it could get in a crippling blow from cover, if he didn't know it was there.

"We have a fix on some of their ships insystem," said the Sensory Officer, the lowest ranking male on the bridge. "Or at least where they were three hours ago."

The tactical plot came alive, showing two vessels in orbit around the planet, gleaned from visual sensors. A couple of moments later the plot updated from graviton emission readings, showing two ships coming out toward them about twenty light minutes from the planet, while the two vessels they had initially plotted remained in orbit. And finally, they plotted a fifth ship in the far reaches of the system, on the other side of the star.

"Preliminary identifications," called out the Sensory Officer, looking over at the Weapons' Officer. "The ships coming to meet us appear to be a scout capital and a very small escort. The two ships in orbit are commercial vessels of some type."

"What about that other ship?" asked the Captain, leaning forward in his chair, lower arms still gripping the chair rest, upper arms both pointing at the tactical plot.

"It appears to be another very small escort," said the Sensory Officer. "Nothing to worry about." The officer looked back at the Captain. "Do you want me to do a complete visual sweep of the system?"

The Captain thought about that for a moment. A complete visual scan would entail checking out every object in the system. Every planet, moon, asteroid and comet, including those in the Kuiper belt.

Billions of objects, and still no guarantee they would see anything trying to hide. A waste of computer power.

"No need," said the Captain, giving a head motion of negation. "This is a minor system. What we see is what we get." The Captain pointed his upper right index finger at the plot while his left upper hand scratched at one of his horns. "Put us on a least-time profile to orbit. We'll take those two ships out on the way in, then orbit the planet and kill the humans there."

There were feral grins and looks of triumph across the bridge as the Pilot put them on the ordered course.

"We have missile tracks," yelled out the Sensory Officer. "Ten missiles. No, twenty."

"Give them a couple of spreads, Weapons," ordered the Captain, leaning forward in his seat to watch the red arrows blossoming on the plot. Another ten arrows appeared, and the Captain guessed that the enemy ships were flushing all of their missiles. Missiles were most effective at long range, where they could build to relativistic velocities, making them both harder to hit, and packing a devastating kinetic punch when they hit.

Another moment passed, and numbers appeared under the vector arrows, indicating an acceleration of five thousand gravities, about what he expected.

"Match them missile for missile," ordered the Captain, sure he was carrying many more than the enemy scout capital ship was. According to his intelligence, they carried at most a hundred weapons, maybe half again as many, while his magazines held over nine hundred of the long range weapons, all much larger and much more capable than those their foe possessed. His missile defenses were also an order of magnitude more effective.

His own missiles appeared on the plot, twenty at a time, vector arrows showing an acceleration of eight thousand gravities. They would reach the enemy force well before the human missiles got to his. *They will die a long time before they know the result of their attack.* That thought was satisfying to the Captain in a manner he couldn't explain. Except that maybe it was fitting to let them keep the hope that they might blow him out of space, just before they died.

O   O   O

The bulk of the comet was comforting, in a way. There was no way an enemy was going to see them through forty kilometers of ice and rock, unless they got a look around it with a drone. The drones that *Joel Schumacher* had sent into the tail were getting a delayed visual of the actions the ship couldn't see. The bridge crew sat in silence as they watched the tactical plot that was tracking everything by graviton emissions through hyper VIII, giving them an almost instantaneous look at what was happening. It took the enemy missiles almost ten hours to engage the two human ships. Ten hours in which the crew of the frigate vicariously sweated out the tension that had to prevail aboard those two ships that were targets.

The battlecruiser, of course, kept calling for them on the com, demanding to know where they were, and why they weren't there to die with the other two ships. Cinda ordered no response, expecting any minute for someone on her crew to mutiny. Fortunately, that didn't happen. There was nothing she could do to prevent it. And then some fool would move them out of cover to engage the enemy, and they would be destroyed at a distance.

The crew all watched in horrified fascination as the missiles approached on the plot. They had both ships on visual, but they were now a light hour away, and they were seeing what had happened over an hour ago. They also had the enemy missiles on visual, or as good a visual as they could get on objects streaking in at point nine light, maneuvering furiously to avoid counter fire.

Cinda sweated along with everyone else, with the exception that she also had to endure the stares of her crew, or the furtive glances that displayed the same emotion. There were looks of shame, switching to anger, then relief, and back to shame. The looks of people who thought they should be doing something, but happy that they were not going to die with those they should be dying with.

Some icons dropped off the plot, missiles hit, their destroyed drives no longer producing gravitons. But not enough. A hundred missiles were coming in at the two human warships, and they had only picked off a dozen at long range.

"They're gone," said the Ensign Schmidt with a cracking voice as the icons representing the human vessels dropped off the plot, along with most of the enemy missiles. About thirty of them continued on, without targets. They would continue on through the system, without the energy to decelerate, to become wanderers in interstellar space for the next twenty thousand years, after which time they would leave the galaxy.

Almost four thousand men and women had died in those few instants. People out here serving the empire to the best of their ability, many with families back in the safety of the Core worlds. Some with families out here on the frontier. Never to return to any of them.

Forty minutes later they caught the first visuals of the missile attack. There were some bright flares of light here and there in space, missiles being hit with light amp weapons or counter-missiles, or those same defensive weapons going off on close misses. Cinda sat with clenched fists, hoping that the holo would show enough missiles being blown apart for the human ships to survive, and knowing that it was pure fantasy, since the ships were already gone.

Cinda didn't want to watch the visual of the end fifteen minutes later, but she couldn't force her eyes away. She watched as the missiles came in, a dozen taken out by close in counter missiles, some more blotted from existence by lasers and autocannon. The first strikes were not direct hits. Missiles that missed went for proximity kills, detonating gigaton range antimatter warheads that sent waves of heat and radiation into the hulls of the two ships. The eight million ton battlecruiser weathered that storm. The eighty-five thousand ton frigate spouted gas from multiple hull ruptures before her own reactors went critical, and she flared into a miniature sun for several seconds before the plasma spread into space and the ship was gone.

Moments later two missiles hit the battlecruiser, their kinetic energy making the antimatter warheads redundant as they shattered the capital ship. Its own stores of antimatter breached containment and propelled the plasma into a swiftly spreading cloud.

The bridge crew stared in disbelief. Someone cried. No one knew who. They were too busy staring at the holo. Cinda stood up from her seat and forced herself to walk with steady steps toward the hatch, while her mind tried to force her to stagger in shock.

"I'll be in my cabin," she told the crew after turning to them for a moment. The hatch closed behind her, and she felt the first tear bead in her eye. They were freely flowing by the time she reached her quarters and threw herself onto her bed.

There was nothing we could have done, she thought, laying back and staring at the ceiling. We would have just died with them, and the enemy would still be on their way to kill the people on that planet. Fifty thousand more deaths, and I still can't do anything about it. She had thought about trying to lay missiles in the path of the enemy ship, like mines. But they would most likely be detected before they could do any harm. There was nothing her small ship had that could make a difference. No matter what they tried.

Cinda wanted to save those people. They were civilians, innocents, just regular people out here on the frontier, trying to make a better life. Away from the protection of the Core and developing worlds, with their orbital forts and system fleets.

But I've only got one frigate, with twenty destroyer class missiles. Even if I fired my whole spread at them, they would blast them out of space without even trying. She kept playing the problem over and over again in her mind. Any missiles she sent at them would be detected well before they got to target. And a ship that was designed to handle spreads from other capital ships, hundreds of weapons at a time, would have no problem taking out her paltry twenty weapons. Even at long range and maximum velocity, just like they had taken out all the weapons from the battlecruiser and frigate. There was just no way to do it. Unless. The thought seemed to come out of nowhere, a gestalt.

Cinda was out of her bed and into the seat of her desk in a second. She linked in with the system and the comp holo sprung to life over her desk. She stared at the holo for a moment, then ordered the system to show her the track of the comet, and the incoming course of the Ca'cadasan battleship.

Cinda had been raised Reformed Catholic, the many parables of the Bible were still in her memory, the stories used to teach children about the glories of God. Later scientific education dulled the belief, but the lessons were still there. Goliath was the most fearsome opponent the Hebrews had to face in the Holy Land. A giant, much as the aliens they were now fighting, with heavy armor and deadly weapons, including a spear no other could throw. And David, a shepherd, had killed him with a weapon used to drive off wolves. And we *could be David, and slay Goliath.*

It could work, she thought, getting up from her desk. It seems like a crazy, wishful thinking, plan, but maybe all we have. "All senior bridge officers and division chiefs are to report to the briefing room, immediately," she said into the com link, heading for her quarter's hatch.

O O O

The twenty-five million ton ship shuddered slightly as it released a half dozen missiles through its accelerator tubes. It would take about fourteen hours to close, but the remaining small escort ship was doomed.

"Time till orbital insertion, twenty-eight hours, twelve minutes," said the Pilot, his lower hands playing over his board.

"Weapons'," said the Captain, sitting on his raised chair, looking over the crew who sat at lower stations. "Are there any orbital defenses in place above that planet?"

"None that we can detect, my Lord," said the Weapons' Officer. "There might be some shore batteries on the ground, but this is not a heavily populated planet."

"Not from our sensor readings, my Lord," chimed in the Sensory Officer. "Preliminary scans indicate little industrial activity, probably a very low population planet, with a newly planted colony."

"We could just hit them with some missiles," said the Weapons' Officer quietly, looking back at his captain.

"No," growled the senior officer. "We are not here to kill the ecosystems of planets. Only the humans that infest them. We will go into orbit and blast their settlements out of existence with kinetics, then send down ground troops to root out whoever is left." He looked pointedly at the Weapons' Officer. "And I can assume they don't have much of a ground force presence either."

"Probably a few hundred of their militia," said the Weapons' Officer, giving a head shake of negation.

"Then we will proceed according to doctrine," said the Captain, looking at the planet in the holo. "Then two days back out and into hyper."

O O O

"I don't see how this can work," said Lt. SG Jakardo, the Tactical Officer. "We're depending too much on luck."

"I really don't think we have anything else to depend on," said Cinda, looking from face to disbelieving face. "Look. I refused to sacrifice all of you in what I saw as a forlorn hope. This may be just as forlorn, but I think we might just be able to pull this off." *And it certainly fits the letter of the Emperor's order.*

"They're still a battleship, ma'am," said Lieutenant Romanov, the Navigation Officer. "They outmass us by a factor of over two hundred and fifty."

"Maybe if we just use the missiles," said the Ensign Mbonga. "That would still give us a chance of getting away."

"We need to do everything we can to make sure we get a hit," said Cinda, shaking her head. "If we only depend on the missiles, we are depending on robots to do the job. And I doubt we could get away anyway, if they still have any tracking or weapons ability." She looked at the officers, most of whom were shaking their heads. "Look. This isn't up for discussion. I wanted your input on the plan, but the decision is mine. Now, I'm depending on you to make it work."

The looks coming her way were still full of doubt, and she didn't blame them. She worried for a moment that they might refuse, that she would have that mutiny she had feared on her hands. *Not that I didn't give them a great example to follow with my refusal to obey orders, even if I was in the right.* "Look. If we don't do something, all of those people on that planet are going to die. That's a fact. I won't slight the bravery of the captain of the *New Kiev*, or his people. But basically, the man was an idiot. He wasted his command for no purpose. There might not have been a plan that would have worked, but running a battlecruiser into the teeth of that Ca'cadasan monster was definitely not it. Now it's up to us to save that planet, and I intend to do so. Anyone who doesn't want to participate can get in a shuttle and sit this one out. Not that I think you'll survive us by much."

The crew members looked at each other, some nodding, others shaking their heads, then nodding. "I think we're with you, Captain," said Frobisher, the senior officer of the group. "I really don't see this plan doing much more than getting us killed. But I for one am not willing to let fifty thousand people die without a prayer. That isn't what I swore my oaths for. So let's get the bastards."

o o o

"I'm picking up activity in the asteroid belt," called out the Weapons' Officer from his station, looking back over at the main holo.

"What is it?" demanded the Captain, standing from his chair and stalking toward the central holo tank, upper arms crossed over his chest. He leaned against the rail with his lower hands and stared at the representation of the system.

"It appears to be a small ship leaving the proximity of one of the rocks, a fair sized metallic specimen," said the Sensory Officer, zooming in on a close up of the vessel on the forward holo. The ship looked like a stout shuttle, the kind used in mining operations.

"Is it any danger to us?"

"I wouldn't think so, my Lord," answered Weapons'. "It might carry some mining lasers, but nothing that we need concern ourselves with."

"Launch a quartet of armed shuttles," ordered the Captain after a moment's thought. "I want that craft destroyed, and whatever station they came from, if there is one, also taken out."

"Four shuttles, my Lord?" asked the Weapons' Officer, a questioning expression on his snout.

"Two are to go to that location and take care of the observed problem. The other two can do a close in sweep of that belt, look for other possible hideaways, and rendezvous with us before we leave the system."

The Weapons' Officer gave a head shake of acceptance, then turned to his board to transmit the orders to the shuttle crews.

"And I want the rest of the shuttles and our fighters prepped for action. There's no telling what else we might discover that we need to destroy." *Better to be thorough, even if it takes another half a day. It will be much more terrifying to the humans to come into a system devoid of life, giving them little to hope for when we come and visit their other systems.*

o　o　o

"They're launching shuttles, ma'am," called out Jakardo. "Two, no, four of them."

"Heading?" Cinda stared at the plot that showed the icons of the enemy small craft. They were on an initial heading that could take them close to the comet. *Please don't be heading this way*, she prayed, clenching her hands.

"It looks like they're starting to turn their vector," said Schmidt, the Sensory Officer. "Heading appears to be out toward the belt."

"Why would they be heading there?" asked Garibaldi, looking over at Romanov.

"Most likely they spotted some of the miners," said Jakardo, scowling. "A shuttle, or possibly an energy spike from one of the stations. They're going to investigate."

"There are several hundred people out there," said Romanov, looking back at the Captain with a pleading expression. "We can't let the damned bastards kill them."

"And there's fifty thousand people ahead of that big bastard," said Jakardo, giving Romanov an "I can't believe you" stare.

"There's nothing we can do for those people in the belt," said Cinda, feeling sick to her stomach for what she was about to order. "If we attack them, we tip our hand to that monster. And then we die for nothing. And the people on the planet die soon after."

She sat there looking at the plot, shaking her head, wishing she could change reality, and knowing that she couldn't. "No. We stay put, and make our play for the only target that might make a difference."

The rest of the bridge crew sat there, none of them looking happy, but all nodding their heads in acknowledgement. *They realize there is no other choice,* she thought, feeling the same shame she knew they felt. *Still doesn't make it any easier to make it.*

Here we go, thought Cinda, watching the enemy ship approach on the tactical plot, while a side screen showed an almost real time view of the massive vessel. She shifted a bit in her seat. She had never really liked the battle armor that naval personnel wore into combat. But if the compartment was evacuated and became vacuum, they would allow the crew to still function. And if battle damage had to be cleared, the powered armor suits gave them the strength to do so. It was the smart decision, and the one dictated by regulations, so she put up with the discomfort. *And it saved my life once before.*

The tactical plot showed the twenty missiles sitting in the tail of the comet, moving forward at the same velocity as the body whose ejecta was shielding them. The track of the battleship was closing on the plot, and the enemy ship was starting to enter the engagement envelope.

"Helm," she ordered after trying to swallow with a dry throat. "Take us into position." She looked over at Jakardo. "It's in your hands now, Tac."

Jakardo nodded and turned back to his board. Except for Garibaldi, the young Lieutenant was the only one with anything to do at this time. Everyone else was now just a spectator, sitting there in their own fear generated sweat. And then the frigate poked her side over the top of the comet, David going into battle with Goliath.

O O O

"Is that comet any risk to us?" asked the Captain, leaning forward in his chair and studying the ice ball on the holo. It had a larger than usual tail, which gave it an almost menacing look. *It has been thousands of years since we looked at the Galaxy with primitive superstition*, thought the large carnivore with a snort through his snout. *I do not fear you, ice ball.*

"No, my Lord," said the Weapons' Officer, pulling up a view of the comet on his own screen. "It's larger than the norm for an insystem visitor, and this is an energetic star, so the tail is especially long and thick."

"What will be our closest approach to it?"

"Closest approach will be one thousand two hundred kilometers," said the Pilot. "No danger." The officer looked back at the captain. "Do you want us to change our vector?"

"No," replied the Captain. "What's our current velocity?"

"Three thousand KPS," answered the Helm Officer. "Grabbers are functioning normally, and we are a little over an hour from orbital insertion."

"And the planet? Any changes?"

"The two ships are still in orbit," said the Weapons' Officer. "I'm surprised they haven't tried to get away."

"No," said the Captain, thinking about the small scout ship they had destroyed earlier at long range. "They had nowhere to run. I think the crews have evacuated to the planet. Not that such a course will help them, in the long run."

The Captain looked back at the holo of the comet. The tactical plot hanging in the air next to his chair showed the track of his ship and that of the small system body. The lines would come closest within the next half minute, then separate. Untidy to leave possible planet killers in orbit, he thought, realizing from the track that the planet was in no danger, from this pass at least.

Another thought struck him, and he looked back over at the Tactical Officer. "What is the status of our shields?"

"One quarter strength," said the Weapons' Officer. "Do you want me to … My Lord, we're taking light amp fire."

"From where?"

"There," yelled the officer as a view of a small escort ship came up over the top of the comet. "It's firing both laser rings at us, and we're receiving some particle beam fire. Nothing too severe. Shields are handling it."

"Lock all weapons on that ship and blow her out of space," yelled the Captain, pointing his right index fingers at the holo.

O O O

As soon as she had weapons lock the frigate opened fire with everything she had. Her two laser rings both put out their most powerful bursts, a hundred megawatts of power each in single beams. Her lone particle beam accelerator was putting out a couple of kilograms a second through one of the projectors that branched off of it, concentrating that fire. The ship she was facing had twenty laser domes that could currently take her under fire, out of the forty she possessed, each producing a beam in the gigawatt range, while her multiple particle beam weapons could put out hundreds of kilograms of protons a second.

Some modifications had been made to *Joel Schumacher* while she waited for the enemy ship to arrive. The crew, with the assistance of ship's robots, had moved electromag projectors from one side of the ship to the other. Those augmented fields were raised, a thirty meter wide layer of cold plasma riding in that sheet of negative magnetism. Holes were opened in the field to allow weapons fire to go through, while the computers prepared to close them if necessary to reduce incoming beams.

The behemoth they were fighting had massive electromag shields, even at one quarter strength, though they hadn't had the time to inject cold plasma into the defensive screen. They were still strong enough to attenuate the beams of the frigate, bending them, spreading them, turning them from ravening points of energy to spotlights that did little more than pump heat into the hull. The particle beams, originally made of accelerated protons, were stripped of their charges at the ejector port of the weapon, turning them into neutrons which went through the electromag screens as if they weren't there. Unfortunately, they didn't do much to the ten meters of alloy and carbon fiber composite armor they struck, doing little more than scarring damage.

The battleship returned fire. The one thing that saved the frigate was the understandable reaction of the enemy's crew, only firing what they thought would be enough weaponry to destroy the tiny ship.

Before the beams struck the frigate she sent the signal to the missiles she had deployed in the tail, along with the other platforms stationed there. Twenty missiles, eight sensor probes, and ten repair robots turned on their grabber units and jumped out of the tail, darting for the enemy ship. Each of the missiles was capable of accelerating at five thousand gravities for twelve hours. Instead, they had been jury rigged to pull ten thousand gravities for ten seconds, as long as their internal systems could stand the load of inertia, and more than they needed. The probes could only pull a couple of thousand gravities, and had been set to become jamming and spoofing platforms. The robots could pull even fewer gees, and were there mainly to just add more clutter, and hopefully spoil a killing shot.

It took five seconds for the missiles to close the one thousand two hundred kilometers to the relatively slow moving target, traveling in a mass of dodging targets, using every penetration aid known to the Fleet. They weathered the ill prepared defensive fire, most of them, and struck.

O O O

Lt. Commander Cinda Klerk stared in wide eyed panic at the Goliath they were battling. Everything her ship was putting out was striking the monster, and she saw that it was having absolutely no effect. The *Joel Schumacher* shuddered as lasers struck her hull, tearing through the cold plasma field with some spread. Gigawatt lasers could still do a lot of damage hitting as expanded spotlights, and damage klaxons sounded through the ship.

"We're venting atmosphere," yelled the Chief Petty Officer in charge of damage control over the com link. "Multiple locations."

The ship bucked again, hull breaches turning into atmosphere jets. Casualty figures started coming through the link, and Cinda winced as she looked at the names of people scrolling down the list. A side holo showed a representation of the ship, blinking red showing the damage. The stern laser ring was off line, as was one of the bow grabbers.

The ship shuddered in a different manner as she was struck by particle beams, protons ripping deep into her hull through the weak electromag field. "Get us out of here," yelled Cinda to Garibaldi. "Behind the comet."

The man acknowledged and sent the command, and the frigate started to drop back behind the ice ball. His finger pushing the panel was the last action in this life.

The three meter wide particle beam ripped through the ship, past eighty centimeters of armor and hull, into the ship's machinery, penetrating the thick skin of the central capsule and through the bulkhead of the bridge. The angry red beam appeared in an instant, linking the opposite sides of the bulkheads through the navigation and helm stations. One moment Lt. Romanov and Ensign Garibaldi were at their boards, sitting in their armor in the most protected part of the ship. The next they were gone, converted to vapor where they sat, while the beam continued through the opposite bulkhead.

Cinda stared in horror as two officers she worked with on a daily basis were converted to superheated steam and ash. The remains and the molten metal were immediately pulled from the chamber as all of the atmosphere evacuated. The Captain saw the rest of the crew staring through their suit armor faceplates at the place where their crewmates had sat, and she thought they would all be dead without the armor they wore.

"Auxiliary control," she shouted into the link. "Get us behind the comet, and keep it between us and the enemy." She received the acknowledgement from the petty officers at that station and turned her own attention back to the tactical plot, just before all bridge systems winked out.

"Everyone to CIC," she shouted to the rest of the surviving bridge crew over the link. Without power the bridge hatch refused to open. Then Ensign Mbonga pulled open the emergency crank, pushed an extension of his gloved hand into the opening, and engaged the mechanism. The door slid open, though a little slower than it would have with its own motors, revealing a corridor that had been splattered with pieces of melted bulkhead.

"Where's the nearest working lift?" she called out to damage control over the link.

"There are none, ma'am," replied the Chief, his voice tense with tension. "The corridor you are in is blocked about fifty meters around the next curve."

"Grab the damage control equipment in that locker," said Cinda to Jakardo, motioning toward the small marked door on the side of the corridor.

Jakardo nodded and ran to the locker, pulling it open and removing the pack.

"We're going to try to make it to the CIC," she told the rest of her people. I've got to get to a place where I can do something to affect this fight. She was linked into the Combat Information Center, which was now functioning as an auxiliary bridge, and could see everything they saw through the link into the occipital cortex of her brain. But it wasn't the same as being there.

A moment later they were at the blockage, and Cinda wondered if she had made another mistake by not trying to go around. A thick structural beam was protruding from the bulkhead and forming an obstacle they couldn't get through. Jakardo didn't hesitate. He opened the pack and pulled out the nozzle of the emergency laser that was attached to a power unit in the case. He flipped it to cutting and engaged the beam, sending sparks flying as he started to slice through the tough alloy.

Cinda, linked into Damage Control, saw that many other such small battles were going on all over her ship. People trapped, or trying to rescue crewmates, or get systems online that had been smashed in the couple of seconds she had engaged the enemy battleship.

She glanced at the take from the tactical, at the strike at the battleship, and almost cheered in triumph. David's sling had struck, with results beyond her dreams.

"We have another problem, ma'am," came the voice of Frobisher over the link, and that feeling of triumph was gone.

O O O

The Captain cursed as the tiny enemy ship disappeared behind the great ice ball to his front. A score of lasers and a dozen particle beams struck the comet, burning through the halo and into the ice and rock that were now in the way of the enemy ship. There was no way they were going to burn through that much material in time to engage that ship. Cowards, he thought, dismissing the bravery it had taken for a ship that size to engage his battleship in close combat, when it would have been better served to stay in hiding.

"We have missile tracks," yelled out the Weapons' Officer, his four hands working furiously, hitting the panels on his board.

"Where?" asked the Captain, his horned head turning toward that officer.

O O O

Frigates carried destroyer class missiles, fifty tons of grabber units and crystal matrix batteries, with two hundred megaton warheads. But where a destroyer would carry about sixty of the missiles, most frigates only had magazine space for twenty. It was still enough firepower to devastate a continent, enough to take out a frigate class pirate, but not enough to overwhelm the defenses of a capital ship.

The missiles had a flight time of five seconds from standing start to impact, a distance of one thousand, two hundred kilometers. At ten thousand gravities they built up to a velocity of four hundred and ninety kilometers a second, an insufficient speed to accomplish much in the way of penetration against the ten meter thick armored hull of the Goliath.

The ship's defenses were not ready for the attack from the stern side. Still, in the couple of seconds they had to engage, they took out nine of the missiles. They also targeted and destroyed all of the slower probes and repairbots that had been sent their way. Something that accomplished nothing but the wasting of their firepower on things that couldn't hurt them, just as the human captain had planned.

Seven missiles hit the stern side of the ship. Again, their velocity was negligible, not enough to penetrate the armor of the vessel. The two hundred meg warheads were something else entirely. Each blasted into the hull, their antimatter warheads acting like shape charges, blowing holes tens of meters wide and injecting superheated plasma into the interior of the ship. Hundreds of Ca'cadasan crew died in an instant. Internal machinery was vaporized, and corridors filled with that hellish vapor, making it a living hell for a couple of nanoseconds. Given time, the blasts would have dissipated within the massive structure of the vessel. There was no time.

Hangars, landing spaces for shuttles, fighters and even small hyper capable vessels, had been left open to space, only their cold plasma fields separating them from vacuum. When readied for battle the hangars would have been protected by eight meter thick doors, which had been left open so that the shuttles and fighters could be quickly launched. The brains of four of the missiles located the opening, something they had been programmed to seek and hit. Two missiles hit the hull of the ship along with the other seven of their brethren that had struck the stern, just missing the opening. The other two streaked through the opening, into the hangar, and detonated with four hundred megatons of fury.

Even that would not have killed the massive ship. Two courier vessels in the hangar, twenty thousand ton hyperdrive messengers, added their antimatter stores to the blast, which vaporized several holes through the armored deck and into the missile magazine below. Scores of warheads went off, their antimatter breaching containment and setting off still more missiles.

That was more than even the massive ship could handle, and microseconds after the human missiles detonated the vessel was expanding plasma and particles, a miniature sun that only died when its constituent matter had spread far enough to cool. The thinning blast wave hit the comet, pushing it away while hundreds of thousands of tons of ice flared into vapor.

Just before the ship exploded a quartet of Ca'cadasan missiles sped from their launch tubes, the last strike of the ship, initiated by the alert Weapons' Officer as his last act.

Those missiles, two hundred ton capital ship killers all, left the forward tubes, through one thousand meters of magnetic accelerator at thirty thousand gravities. They also carried the momentum of the ship, point zero one light. The missiles didn't accelerate from this point, they decelerated, trying to kill that momentum so they could head back and look for the target they had been programmed to seek, an enemy ship in hiding near the comet. Their computer brains sent them into a series of changing vector corrections, curving them through space, taking off some velocity here, adding more there, until they were shooting around the comet and scanning for the target. That target was not hard to locate, radiating the heat of a small star against the background of the cold body of the comet. The missiles made the final vector correction and pushed all of their acceleration into a straight line, heading for the damaged frigate.

o   o   o

Cinda blanched as she looked at the profiles of the incoming missiles. Time till impact, forty-five seconds, said the ship's computer in her mind. Cinda looked at the schematic of the ship and her heart sank further. One laser ring out, half the counter-missile tubes on the least damaged side of the ship gone. Hangar deck wrecked, and over half of the life pods destroyed or out of action.

"All crew who can make it off, abandon ship," she called out over the com. "The rest of you, man your stations and fight the ship."

She wondered how many would just run for it, no matter her orders. She was gratified to see the acknowledgements coming back that let her know most of the crew were staying at their stations. She wasn't sure it would make any difference, but there was always the chance.

"We're through," yelled Jakardo over the com.

Cinda turned to see the beam now lying on the floor of the corridor, a couple of bridge crew making their way over. Cinda pushed ahead and jumped over the obstacle next, then ran down the corridor. The artificial gravity was fluctuating, her steps throwing her into the ceiling at times, pushing her hard into the floor at others.

The bulkhead door leading out of the central capsule was closed, and Cinda cursed as she thought how she was going to get that door, as thick as the armor of the capsule, open. In frustration she hit the control opening button, and almost laughed as the door slid open. The CIC was in the rear central capsule, as protected there as the bridge was in the forward one. She jetted through the fifty meters separating the capsules on her suit grabbers. The tube was also evacuated of air, and at first the door would not open, indicating that there was still pressure on the other side. She pushed her code in over the link, overriding the lockout. The door slid open and a blast of air came with it, trying to push her away. Her suit fought the outflow and got her into the capsule, and she boosted away, depending on the crew behind her to close off the door. *If anyone isn't in combat armor they're idiots*, she thought, not really worried about evacuating the corridor atmosphere.

Cinda ran into the CIC, a room slightly larger than the bridge, with twelve seconds on the clock. The central holo showed the same view her link was feeding into her occipital lobe. For some reason it looked more real to see the physical holo, and in that moment she almost wished she was not looking at it.

"All weapons are firing at the missiles," said Frobisher, starting to get up from his chair and sinking back down as Cinda waved him back.

Cinda could see that on her link. The forward laser ring was firing a full powered beam a second, the two remaining counter-missile tubes were cycling weapons as fast as possible, even the close in projectile weapons were blasting on full auto, all trying to stop the missiles that meant to kill the frigate.

"Integrated fire control is down," said Frobisher as the tracks drew closer.

Which means we're really screwed, thought Cinda, staring at the holo, the ticker in her mind counting down to three seconds. Everything was firing on local control, with no integration to take advantage of overlapping fields of fire.

A laser hit one of the missiles, detonating it seven hundred kilometers from target. A gigaton blast spread out from the missile as the antimatter warhead breached contain. There was negligible blast effect, but the hull of *Joel Schumacher* took a wave of heat and radiation that rocked the ship as armor boiled away and atmosphere vented.

The other missiles attempted to change their vectors away from the blast that was frying their own systems. One didn't make it out of the blast before its comp systems fried from radiation overload, and it continued on at an angle that would target nothing. Another ran into a stream of pellets from an auto-cannon, losing two forward grabbers and also drifting off target. A moment later a counter-missile struck the stern of that missile and destroyed the rear section.

The fourth missile made it away from the blast with minimal damage, then tried to reacquire the target. It missed the frigate by a dozen kilometers and slammed into the ice ball. The gigaton blast shattered the comet, sending millions of pieces of ice in all directions. *Schumacher* was hit by hundreds of thousands of chunks of rock and ice, from several kilograms to one twenty thousand ton monster.

Cinda fell to the floor despite her combat armor as the comet exploded. The frigate was only five kilometers from the surface of the ice ball. The blast effect banged on the hull of the ship, obliterating surface installations like grabber fins, electromag field projectors and auto cannon emplacements. The nanoweave outer skin, the sensory organ of the ship, was eroded away. Any escape pods that had survived the fight with the superbattleship were totally destroyed.

Joel Schumacher tumbled away from the explosion, power systems fluctuating, gravity going in and out. Inertial compensators blinked off in some portions of the ship, and some crew were flung into the walls at scores of gravities. Their combat armor survived, becoming the coffins for the smashed remains of the spacers who had sheltered in them.

"Damage report," yelled Cinda into the com as her link to the ship's computer systems went down.

"Damage control is out," yelled Frobisher, his wide eyes looking out at her through his faceplate. He pointed at one of the techs sitting in the room, designating that woman as damage control chief. Which was well and good, except the limited com systems made that an almost impossible job. At this point damage control was more of a local function, crew seeing something that needed to be done and doing it.

Main power came back on, and with it a working schematic of the ship. Cinda studied that schematic on the holo screen, not sure if her ship was going to survive or not. Then her attention was all taken by the blinking red that covered part of the antimatter reactor section of engineering.

"Engineer," she called over the com. "What's your status?"

"The Engineer is dead, ma'am," came back a voice from engineering. "This is Petty Officer First Faraday," continued the young woman. "I've taken over."

"What's your status?" repeated Cinda, looking at that blinking red overlay of the reactor and unable to pull up any other information.

"We're having some problems with the reactor, though I think we can get it under control," said the rating. "But we've got a bigger problem. One of the antimatter storage containers was hit when we were slugging it out with the Cacas. I don't know why it didn't blow then, but I don't think it'll be long."

"Can you jettison the container?" asked the Captain, looking at the schematic and seeing the answer to that question herself. *Christ, but we're screwed again.*

"Maybe. Probably not. I'm not sure, ma'am, but if I had to stake my life on it, I'd say no. There's a lot of damage back here."

"Do what you can to stabilize it, then get out of there," said Cinda, making her mind up in an instant. She looked over at Frobisher. "Order abandon ship. I don't think we're going to save her, and I won't lose any more people in a lost cause."

"Yes, ma'am," agreed the Exec. The call went over the com as soon as his agreement left his mouth, and acknowledgements came back almost instantly.

Strobes flashed across the vessel, and klaxons sounded in every compartment that still had atmosphere. A countdown timer appeared on every implant, though the time was just an estimate. The fact was, the ship was living on borrowed time, and the antimatter could breach at any moment.

"Let's get out of here," she ordered the people in the crowded CIC. "You lead them out, Exec."

"What about you, ma'am?" asked Frobisher, turning his helmeted head her way.

"Captain's prerogative," she said with a smile, wishing she could lead the way off the ship. "First one on, last one off."

Frobisher nodded and moved quickly to the hatch, the relocated bridge crew close on his heels while the CIC people abandoned their stations. Cinda tried to link into the ship's systems and hit a blank wall. There's nothing I can do here, she thought, realizing that the system had gone down completely. As soon as the last crewman left the chamber she followed.

It was eighty straight meters from the CIC to the outer skin of the vessel, about one hundred and ten by the shortest route. That route no longer existed. The corridor toward the stern was a wreck, bulkheads crushed inward to close much of it off. The corridor forward was still useable, by one person at a time. Frobisher led the crew that way, squeezing his armored suit through a space not much bigger than it was. The lights were flickering, even the emergency systems too badly damaged to function without failure.

There was still atmosphere in the corridor, and when they reached a crossway that headed out the sounds of people banging on a door came to their suit pickups. Armored fists beating against an armored hatch that was sealed shut. The suits gave them many times the strength of a normal human, but it was not enough. Metal glowed at the edge of the door, the sign of suit lasers being employed to cut through the hatch. It would also not be enough, not in time. Voices called over the local com circuit, suit to suit, begging for aid.

Cinda recognized the door as leading into the stern area infirmary. There were undoubtedly medical personal behind that door, and maybe some injured. She activated her own suit laser and started to work on the edge of the door. The laser was made to cut through hull metal, but it was asking a lot to cut through this much alloy.

"We're coming for you," she shouted over the local suit to suit com. "Keep working your end."

Frobisher and Jakardo were suddenly there with her. Frobisher activated his suit laser, while the Tactical Officer pulled the damage control cutter he had carried all the way from the corridor outside the bridge. His unit cut through the alloy at six times the rate of the suit lasers, and sparks flew into the air as he moved the beam from the left top side of the door down.

"Let me have that," she told Jakardo. "I'll take it from here while you two get off the ship."

"No, ma'am," replied Jakardo, continuing to work the laser, while Frobisher kept going at the top of the door.

"That's a direct order, Mr. Jakardo," growled Cinda, continuing to cut with her suit unit.

"And you're not the only one who can ignore those kind of orders, ma'am," said Frobisher.

Cinda smiled, and glanced back in relief to see that the rest of the crew had left them, heading out of the ship. They worked in silence, concentrating on making the cuts in the most efficient manner possible, until they had circled the door, all the while wondering how much time they had.

"Shove," yelled Cinda, pushing with her suit arms against the door.

The three of them pushed it into the room, to fall with a hard clang to the floor. There were a pair of sick bay orderlies and one injured crewman, all in battle armor, the two hale crewman helping the hurt one.

"Let's get the hell out of here," yelled Cinda into the com, herding the three they had rescued to follow behind her Exec and Tactical Officer. Shit, she thought, looking at the timer on her implant. Over six minutes had passed since they had left the CIC, well past the estimated lifetime of the antimatter container.

Cinda felt relieved when the airlock hatch of the outer hull came into view. The door to the airlock was still intact, though without power. She wondered why the crewmen who had gone ahead of them had closed it, then realized that it was set to always have one hatch shut to the outside, unless it had been overridden. She tried to signal the override, with no success. Frobisher reached the emergency manual override first, pulling open the panel and pushing the rotating tool on his left gauntlet into the interior and mating it with the ratchet. The door started to slide open immediately, air rushing through the widening gap.

"Lock your boots," yelled Jakardo to the others as the pull increased. It was obvious why when the rest of the airlock was revealed, or the space where one would have been if something hadn't have scooped it off the side of the ship.

"Is anyone still aboard?" yelled Cinda over the local com. She was greeted with static. "Maybe I should do another check of the ship," she said over the com to the people with her.

"Not on your life, ma'am," said Jakardo, grabbing a hand hold on the chest of her suit, boosting his armor, and pulling her out of the ship. "The old girl is going to blow any second now. Everyone's out who's going to get out."

Cinda nodded, knowing the man was right, but still wishing she could go back in. *If the damned ship blew up around me, at least I wouldn't have to worry about the future.*

Everyone now boosted on their suit grabbers, trying to put as much distance between themselves and the gigaton class bomb the ship was about to become. The suits could pull twenty gees with their inertial compensators, twenty-five max, putting the extra gravities directly onto the passenger. All were trained spacers, with the improved systems of all modern humans. They could handle ten gravities for several minutes, while their undergarments compressed and forced blood back to the brains. Still, in space it seemed like they were standing still with only the stars in the background.

Cinda turned her suit around as she boosted, until her ship was again in her view as she backed away. Now she had a frame of reference, the small form of the ship getting smaller by the moment. She zoomed in on the ship, gasping at the revealed damage to its surface. *And this is the side that was facing away from the enemy ship and the comet.* Though it had faced the incoming missiles, which had done significant damage, even detonating hundreds of kilometers away.

There was a small flash about a hundred meters to the stern of the midsection, engineering. The small flash erupted into a large one, and the ship was gone in an instant in a burst of eye hurting plasma. Her faceplate darkened immediately.

"Shit," yelled one of the crewmen close by, and Cinda lightened her visor, then cursed herself as she saw the small dark blotches against the growing, fading plasma field. Those were solid objects propelled outward, pieces of the ship, and where she could see the larger ones there had to be thousands of smaller that she couldn't.

Cinda cringed. Her HUD showed the mass of objects, and there was really nothing she could do about them, other than move her suit out of the way of the larger ones. They passed by without a sound, except for a couple of screams over the com that stopped with chilling suddenness.

"Well, we survived," said Frobisher over the com, relief and fatigue combined in his voice.

"Yeah," said Cinda, checking the emergency beacons of the other crew and determining that over half her crew made it off, one hundred and twenty-one souls. Which meant that over a hundred had already died.

One of the beacons went offline, and Cinda rotated her suit to look in that direction, wondering what new calamity had come upon them. She turned just in time to see something flare in space, her HUD telling her it was about seven hundred kilometers away. The sinking feeling in her stomach told her what it was, even before calls of panic came over the com net.

"It's the damn Caca shuttles," yelled someone, her HUD identifying it as one of the missile crew.

"Try to hit them," yelled the voice of the Sergeant in charge of the small Marine contingent. They were armed with rifles, just as the rest of the crew had particle beam pistols holstered on their suits. And they would be firing at a heavily armored shuttle whose fire control systems could track and kill them with ease.

Another beacon went off her track, then another, and she screamed out in anger as she watched the shuttle, a vessel her frigate could have destroyed with ease, killing the men and women she had ordered to what she had thought was safety. The beacons started to move, the crew going into the drill that had been hammered into them for such unlikely situations, making them harder to hit. Still, not hard enough, as more beacons dropped off.

"Hang on," said another voice over the com, one that Cinda did not recognize. "We're on the way."

The shuttle flared with light, taken under fire by something unseen that had entered the battle. It flared again, then exploded outward, destroyed.

"Who are you?" asked Cinda over the com, still having a hard time believing that there was anything in the system that could have challenged the shuttle. There were only the two commercial ships, she thought, looking back at the bright dot of the planet. And their transfer shuttles.

"This is Attack Fighter *New Kiev* Four," came the voice over the com.

"I thought you had been destroyed with the battlecruiser," she said, trying to spot the six hundred ton fighter against the star field. The battlecruiser would have carried eight of the small vessels, used for scouting and missile attacks.

"We were left behind," said the woman on the other side of the com. "As a last resort defense of the planet. Not that it would have done much good. I have three flight mates with me, while the other flight goes after the remaining shuttles."

"Can you pick us up?" asked Cinda. The fighters carried a crew of five each, and could probably carry fifteen of her crew each in a tight fit.

"We'll get as many as we can, ma'am," replied the pilot. "But we have shuttles from those merchies behind us. Give us a little bit of time and we'll get all of your people out of space."

True to their word, everyone was picked up within a couple of hours. Cinda boosted toward one of the shuttles on her grabbers, insisting that everyone else be picked up first. As she boarded the shuttle she felt total relief for the first time in days. She didn't know her fate, but her crew was safe. And for the moment that was all that mattered.

O   O   O

Four days later there was another visit to the system. There was a moment of panic on the planet as the ships were picked up moving through hyper VI, then people calmed down as the ships were identified as Imperial vessels. A little over an hour later three battleships and a pair of destroyers entered the system and boosted for the planet.

Cinda worried the entire time the ships were on the way. She had been declared a hero on the planet, the savior of them all. But the fact remained that she had disobeyed the orders of a superior officer and had refused combat. It didn't matter that it was a stupid order that would have caused the destruction of her ship, and would not have benefited anyone. It might not matter that the superior's order went against the directive of the Commander and Chief of the Empire. She had committed an offense that could lead to her execution if she was found guilty by a military tribunal. The rest of the crew had already distanced themselves from her, as if she had a terminal disease that they were likely to catch.

Halfway to the planet the Commodore commanding the task force ordered the civilian population to prepare for evacuation. Most of the civilians were relieved. Some were distraught. And there was a vocal few that were angry that the Empire wouldn't devote the resources to defend their frontier planet from the alien menace. Some of those would be talked into leaving anyway. Some few hundred would stay, and the Marines would make sure they had the weapons to hurt the Ca'cadasan ground forces if the aliens came back. They wouldn't survive, but if they killed some Cacas, the Empire would be happy with the return on their investment.

It took sixteen days, galactic standard time, to make it back to a secure base. Due to relativity the time passed much faster aboard the *Duke Georgi Newberry,* the flagship of the battleship squadron. Six days ship time, as the vessel built up to point nine c in hyper VI. The ship was crowded with fifteen thousand extra pairs of lungs, its share of the refugees. Even the large vessel seemed crowded with so many more people on board. Cinda could still get away from some of that crowding at mealtime, when she could eat in officers' country. She had to share a compartment with all the rest of her officers, most of whom seemed to spend the majority of their time out of the former petty officers' quarters, or had locked themselves in their sound proofed sleeping compartments where they could deal with their fears in private. The Lt. Commander felt like she was a leper, and all of her people were afraid that they might contract her disease. They were polite when they had to interact with her, and distant at all times.

Klerk went through many hours of questioning on the trip, with the Commodore, the Flag Captain, the Intelligence Officer, she was surprised they didn't make her talk with the chief cook. Her officers talked with the same people, and she was sure they were making a case against her for disobeying orders. She would not know how good or bad it was until they made it back to a headquarters. She thought it might be good enough to hang her.

Cinda was on an observation deck when the *Newberry* translated into normal space outside the hyper barrier, looking at the system holo as the image of the local space around a developing world came to life.

The Amazon system was the home of over two hundred and twenty million sentient beings, mostly humans, over two hundred million on the inhabitable planet. The orbit of the world was filled with stations, forts, factories, even shipyards. Now that it was the new sector headquarters it was a system that the Empire was not willing to lose without a fight, as shown by the more than three hundred warships around the star. Along with those vessels were hundreds of freighters and liners, as well as quite a few antimatter tankers. What she couldn't see, but was still aware of, were the hundreds of thousands of troops that held the surface of the planet. Men and women manning surface batteries. Ready to fight off enemy ships, or standing by to battle invading troops.

Two hours later Cinda was on a fast shuttle heading insystem. The battleships were needed out here, where they could prepare for their next mission close to the hyper barrier. Cinda linked into the shuttle sensors and saw a trio of liners heading out from the planet to take the civilian refugees off. She wished she could have waited for those liners as well, but someone wanted to take care of her, and quickly.

The shuttle had been configured with actual VIP quarters. What that meant on such a small craft was that Klerk had a tiny soundproofed cabin with barely enough room for a bed, and the space to stand up beside it. At least it allowed her some privacy. Her officers and a few of her crew were also along for the ride, although the enlisted personnel had to use the normal passenger seats that equipped the main cabin of the shuttle.

After a two day trip they arrived at the orbital fort that was the sector headquarters. Over a hundred million tons of station, thought by some to be a waste of resources that could have been put into building hulls. They couldn't move at more than one gee of acceleration, enough to allow them to change orbits, and possibly dodge incoming beam weapons at a distance, though they hadn't a chance against swarms of missiles.

"Lt. Commander Klerk," said a full Commander at the head of the armed Marine detail that met her as she walked out of the shuttle. "You will come with me. The rest of you," said the man, pointing at a party of six naval officers, "will go with these people. They will see to your needs, and will talk with you."

Interrogate is more like it, thought Cinda, falling in behind the Commander while the Marines, wearing dress reds and equipped with side arms, fell in around her. They walked several hundred meters of corridor, crowded with people in uniform who moved out of their way as soon as they saw the Marines, until they came to a lift station in which a ready conveyance was waiting.

"Who am I going to see?" she asked the Commander, who gave her a harsh look and said nothing.

After a couple of minutes on the lift, which went up, then horizontally, they stopped at another station, and the Commander motioned her to follow him. They arrived at a door that opened at their approach. Cinda looked at the nameplate over the door and wondered just what they had in store for her.

"The Admiral will see her immediately," said a Petty Officer who was the flag officer's secretary.

"We'll wait outside," said the Commander, motioning for the Marines to follow him out.

Lt. Commander Cinda Klerk would rather have faced another Goliath, one of the Ca'cadasan superbattleships, than the man she was to face at this moment. But such a ship was not before her, and this door was. She walked toward it on stiff legs, hoping that something might be wrong with the mechanism. The door instead slid smoothly open, revealing the luxuriously appointed office beyond. Cinda stepped through that door, walked the ten paces to the desk, and snapped to attention, rendering a proper hand salute.

"Lt. Commander Cinda Klerk, reporting as ordered, sir," she blurted, her eyes locked to the front.

"Following orders now, are we, Commander?" said the stout man behind the desk.

Cinda's eyes drifted down to see a dark skinned man sitting behind the desk, the six stars of a Grand Fleet Admiral on the shoulder boards of his dress blues. Duke Taelis Mgonda was the commander of Sector IV, the hot district in this war, as well as the flag officer in charge of the sector battle fleet. She had wondered when she saw the name on the door what the man was doing here. Sure, the system was the replacement headquarters for the Conundrum system, which had been lost earlier in the war. He was said to spend most of his time on his flagship, deployed with the fleet. But, of course, the station had a wormhole gate, as did, of course, the Duke's flagship, so he could be here for a short time, then step across the light years to his own vessel.

"Cacas got your tongue, Commander?" asked the Duke in his gruff voice. "I asked you a question."

"I did not think the orders of the captain of the *New Kiev* made any sense, sir," she said, locking her eyes again on the wall behind the man. A wall that contained awards, diplomas, even pictures of the man with the late Emperor, Augustine the First, and his wife, Anastasia. "Besides," she said, taking her cue from the picture of the father of the current Emperor, Sean I, "he was in violation of the orders of the Emperor."

"So you decided to disobey the orders of the lawful superior on the spot?"

"His orders made no sense, your Grace," answered Cinda, knowing that this was her only real defense. "We were not in a position to cause equal or greater damage to the enemy, based on his combat dispositions."

"The Captain of the *New Kiev* was an idiot," said the Duke, nodding his head. "The smart play would have been to have gotten out of the system as soon as possible. The Cacas only had the one ship, and they wouldn't have been able to catch his ship and yours, and attack the planet at the same time."

"They could have still blown us all out of space with missiles."

"And that they might have, young lady. They might also have missed. But he surely doomed his command by boosting into the teeth of that enemy ship."

The Admiral picked up a glass and took a drink. Cinda was wondering if she would be offered a seat, or something to drink. But why waste courtesy on someone who has a date with a court martial, and then an executioner.

"That does not alter the fact that you disobeyed a direct order from a superior officer, young lady," said the Duke, placing his glass meticulously on the coaster on the top of his desk.

"Sir, said Cinda, standing her ground, knowing she was right, "I destroyed that bastard and saved the planet."

"And you hid from the Ca'cadasan because you knew you could do that?"

"No, sir," said Cinda after a moment's hesitation. She looked up at the ceiling for a moment, then back down into the dark brown eyes of the man. "What do you want me to tell you, your Grace? That I was afraid? That I didn't want to die, and to take all of my crew with me? That I used my knowledge of the Emperor's orders as a way to wiggle out of sure death. Well, I was afraid. I was scared shitless."

"So why didn't you continue to hide?" asked the Admiral. "You were in a perfect position to escape notice. The enemy would have continued on to the planet, killed the civilians, and left. And you could have left the system after they had gone."

"I couldn't just let them kill those people," growled Cinda, fighting back the tears that began to well in her eyes. "I just couldn't. What would you have done, your Grace?"

"So you saved fifty thousand people? Good job, Commander. Only we have lost over twenty five billion, that's billion, so far. And I have been ordered by my sovereign Lord to abandon systems with hundreds of millions of civilians in them, so that I could keep my fleet in being, and not waste it in a battle that would give the enemy this sector. So what would I have done?"

Cinda looked into the man's face, seeing the pain and anger, his nostrils flaring as the veins stood out on his neck. How can he live with himself? she thought. But of course the answer to that was duty. He had a duty to the Emperor, and his own feelings had to be subsumed to undertake the necessary actions to make a strategy work against an enemy that so far had all the advantages.

"It was wonderful that you could save those fifty thousand," said the Admiral, looking down at his desk and clenching his fists. He looked back up at her with red rimmed eyes. "Just remember. That is a drop in the bucket as far as this war has gone. We will lose another twenty-five billion in the next year. Maybe more. And if we don't win this thing, we will lose all of us."

Cinda stood silent for a moment, letting that sink in. The Fleet had never lost a war, not in nine hundred years of existence. Now they faced total defeat if they couldn't out think this enemy. Which I did, she thought.

"What's going to happen to me?" she asked the Duke, wanting to get her own fate out of the way.

"Normally, you would go before a board of inquiry," said the Duke, pointing a finger at her chest. "They would probably find enough evidence to recommend a court martial. And then you would most probably be convicted of disobedience in the face of the enemy. Most likely you would be kicked out of the Fleet, though imprisonment would also be a strong possibility. Execution a lesser one. And if the captain of *New Kiev* had survived, he would be facing the same, for disobedience to his Monarch."

The Duke looked down at his desktop for a moment, then back up into her eyes, and there was no trace of anything but determination living there now. "Let me ask you one question, Klerk. What did you learn from your battle with the Cacas? What did you come away with that changed you? And is that change beneficial to the Fleet? Or will you walk into your next command decision with even more timidity?"

That was one question? thought Cinda, while she struggled for an answer. "I'm not afraid," she finally said, looking the Admiral straight in the eyes. "I'm not afraid of the big bastards, not anymore. Oh, I still have a healthy respect for them. But I know they can be beaten. And I know I can beat them."

"The Emperor has a theory that they aren't as intelligent as we are," said the Duke. "Not on an average bell curve distribution at least. I've looked over your data, and the Caca commander came in as arrogant as you please." He pointed a finger at Cinda. "You out-thought that enemy, Captain. And saved fifty thousand people in the bargain."

"I thought fifty thousand didn't matter, your Grace?"

"Oh, it matters," said the Duke. "Fifty thousand here, fifty thousand there. You know, the Empire was founded by fifty thousand refugees." The Duke smiled slightly, and looked up again at the junior officer. "So what should we do with you?"

"You said that normally I would face court martial, your Grace?"

"These are unusual times, young lady," said the Duke, reaching into his desk and withdrawing a small box. "The Empire is in need of heroes. We have had enough goats to last a lifetime." The Duke opened the box and withdrew a small medal attached to a ribbon. The medal was a sun symbol, and Cinda felt the breath leave her as she recognized it.

"A Golden Sun," she blurted, the thing she least expected to see during a meeting like this. It was the second highest decoration that a service member could receive. Only the Imperial Medal of Heroism was considered a higher award, for both military and civilians, and only authorized by a seated Emperor.

"We will have the formal presentation later," said the Admiral, reaching back into his desk and withdrawing another box, which he opened and placed on the desk, revealing the silver oak leaves of a full commander. "These you can put on now, then we will have the presentation of the medal at a news conference."

"A news conference," she said, feeling her legs go weak.

"As I said, we need heroes. So you have to face the music. And for portraying such courage in front of the press, you will receive another reward. One I think you will really like." He graced her with a predatory smile.

"Another reward," said Cinda in shock. She had expected to be punished when she entered this office. Instead, she was getting a promotion, and an award. She couldn't think of anything else she could want, except. Her eyes widened at the thought.

"As you said," said the Admiral, getting up from his desk with the oak leaves in hand. "You destroyed a Caca supebattleship with a pipsqueak frigate. That's a talent we're not willing to waste."

O O O

Commander Cinda Klerk sat in the command chair of her new ship, hands rubbing the armrests, still not sure if she could believe that it was hers. *The Carl Nasher* was a brand new hyper VII destroyer, capable of four times the pseudo-speed through hyperspace as her last command. The vessel was eight hundred and twenty meters in length by two hundred and twenty wide, massing over two hundred and forty thousand tons. Her missile magazines held fifty destroyer class weapons, two and a half times what her old frigate had carried. It was still much less than a hyper VI destroyer carried, but something had to be left out to carry the mass of the more capable hyperdrive projectors. And it's all mine, she thought, looking at the viewer as the planet Amazon fell away.

"She is a beautiful ship," said Lt. Commander Renato Jakardo over the private circuit. The exec was ensconced in the CIC, what would be his normal combat duty station, getting used to the layout and the people he would be serving with, as well as his new position.

"She sure is," replied Cinda, looking over her new bridge crew. Jakardo was the only one they had let her keep, the rest being given promotions and new assignments. She had wanted to keep her exec, Lieutenant SG Marcus Frobisher. That request had been denied. Frobisher had been bumped up two ranks and given a destroyer of his own, an older hyper VI ship. And I bet he is just as thrilled to have her for his first command as I am to have this ship, she thought. To a naval officer, any command was a dream come true.

And they turned me loose for this one, she thought, reviewing her orders in her mind. She would be operating alone, on the fringes of the human controlled areas, at times forging on into enemy territory, the eyes of the fleet. Most times there would be no superiors to bow down to, and she would live or die on her wits, and the capabilities of her crew. She couldn't think of a better way to fight a war.

TEACH YOUR CHILDREN WELL
AN UNINCORPORATED WAR STORY

EYTAN KOLLIN AND DANI KOLLIN

Year 4 of 7 of the Unincorporated War

Fourth Battle of Anderson's Farm

The assault transport was flying through a debris field of similar ships from three battles past—unfortunate victims of a questionable tactics, shoddy armor and a determined enemy. If the heavily armed occupants of the current transport had any reservations about returning to the floating war memorial, they gave no indication. And if any glimmer of hope existed at all it would be that if the third time hadn't been the charm (which clearly it hadn't) then perhaps this, the fourth battle of Anderson's farm would do the trick. The only other advantages they could be said to have was that they were soldiers, very well trained and motivated by an almost unparalleled hatred of the enemy as opposed to a once inestimable fear.

Inside, most of the UHF assault marines were quietly checking their gear and more than one was sound asleep despite attempts by the Alliance missiles, lasers, mines and directed rocks to jolt them awake one last time before tossing them into space. It was the advantage of a veteran crew. The only marine up and moving was the sergeant. Her ancestry was mostly Southeast Asian, which was not a branch of the human race known for its giants. It was however known for its share of implacable warriors and the good sergeant, tiny though she may have been, had no intention of letting her ancestors down. She was absurdly young for the rank but had earned it by dint of not dying in the two years she'd served the UHF. The sergeant was now walking up and down the length of the transport, stopping by every trooper, checking to see if they were ready, looking into their eyes for the emptiness that told her they would kill without mercy. She hadn't bothered performing the ritual with "Daddy" or "Baby Girl," the team's two latest additions. They were only with her unit temporarily and she already knew there was nothing she could teach them.

o o o

"Hey, Cookie," Daddy said to Baby Girl. "Don't forget, we may come in upside down. Do you remember how to detach and flip?"

"Yes, Dad," groaned Baby Girl. "You only made me practice it a dozen times ... yesterday."

"That's 'Corporal Dad' to you, Private Daughter and considering what happened at the last rock we took you have no right to complain."

"So unfair," she muttered.

"How so?"

"I saved your life, that's how so!"

Daddy shook his head, mouth formed into a knowing grin. "Only after I did a *proper* flip from the harness in order to save yours."

"Not going to let me forget that, are you?"

Daddy pointed to the extra stripe on his armor. "Corporal."

"Fine, *Corporal* Daddy. I know how to flip from the harness. I've practiced it so much I could do a double flip in armor and fire from a prone position. Hell, at this point I could probably do it in my sleep. I am so good at the flippin' flip!"

Daddy smiled, content. "That's all I wanted to know."

The transport shook violently.

The soldiers all glanced at their HODs—not ordinance, debris. A second later, the debris was confirmed as pieces of a sister ship; meaning none of its supremely trained marines would ever get a chance to fight for the UHF.

Baby Girl went silent. On a look from Daddy she gave him the reason. "This is where Emily died."

"I know, Cookie," he answered, "but it won't happen to us."

"How can you be so sure?"

Daddy put his hand over Baby Girl's and gave it a squeeze. "Because we're so much better trained than the marines were at the first battle. Because we have actual experience and none of those poor bastards thrown in back then did. And most importantly of all …" he paused until she looked up with a flash of annoyance.

"Most importantly of all what, Dad?"

"I'm your father and I have not given you permission to die. You may think you're an adult and all grown up, but I'll find a way to ground you if you make me."

"Okay," she said, "and thank you, dad."

"You're welcome, Cookie."

o o o

No comments had been directed to the father and daughter while they were having their heart to heart. In fact, with the exception of the sergeant, no one knew Daddy or Baby Girl very well. But they knew what they were seeing was rare—especially in the heat of battle. However the father and daughter had managed their improbable relationship, no marine would dare interfere with it.

"Forty five seconds to landing!" barked the COM.

"Alright you lugs!" shouted the sergeant. "The navy's been kind enough to open the door, but we're damn well going to have to let ourselves in. Helmets sealed and safeties off!"

The transport was soon filled with the familiar hiss of faceplates sliding down and the thrum of weapons powering up. A few seconds later the marines' faces lit up as the beautiful sound was heard of a harpoon being fired from the hull.

"Dad?"

"Yes, Cookie?"

"I don't want Holly or Lee to join the military."

"Don't worry, Cookie. Your mom and I may have had our differences, but I know this—she will not allow anything to happen to your sister and brother. Now look sharp, private."

His daughter's eyes went dark. "Yes, Corporal!" And then her faceplate sealed shut.

The second the marines' HOD's showed the harpoon as "Locked" into the asteroid, they released their harnesses as one, dropped to the floor then flipped upside down to end up crouching the right way up … on the ceiling. The door burst open and the nearest marines fired their personal harpoons into the asteroid, which began pulling them even closer to the surface. As soon as they got their footing, they covered the next group out. Everyone did their job and watched out for each other, but none so much as the father for his daughter and vice versa. Not that it helped.

Year 2 of 7 of the Unincorporated War

With over a million residents, the Highland Living Complex was in effect a city unto itself, even if only as one small part of all the other living complexes that made up the almost 70 million residents of New York City. As Sally Meadows looked around the Highland Auditorium she was amazed at just how many of the thousands present she knew—if not by name than at least by sight. These were not only her friends and classmates, they were her neighbors and the older and younger siblings of her older and younger siblings—faces she'd seen her entire life. The complex and its nosey and boisterous neighbors and the ever-present security that made misbehaving an endeavor that took real planning, intelligence and skill. Yet even with all the comfort and familiarity of home, Sally couldn't wait to get to get away from it all.

At key moments in her life Sally Meadows would look up from washing her face in the sink, see herself in the mirror and realize that she'd changed. It had happened a few days ago, which was why she found herself walking through the vast lobby to get to a seat. The person she'd seen when she'd looked up was not really any different than the one she'd been seeing for the past few months. Her hair was as she'd kept it since before she could remember—long and straight. It was light brown but could alternate to a slightly darker shade depending on room lighting or mood. Her eyes were an admixture of pale green and auburn. Though she could have afforded to have some minor cosmetic changes done, she could not afford to pay for anything really drastic like a sex change or bodywork. Her school had for years played soccer against an upper crust complex and she'd been amazed how many players, at least if their jersey numbers were any indication, would come out onto the field wholly changed from what they'd been the year before. This year's starter was a young Asian male but last year that same person had been a lithe African female. Sally had been tempted to do something similarly radical and could have sold some of her personal stock to pay for it. Few would have faulted her as she was slight and had to work hard to get just the right amount of muscle to stay on her frame to make it athletic. But at 17 her torso grew into her legs and suddenly the gangly girl became a graceful swan so the need became far less pressing. Plus she'd seen some of her friends sell up to 5% of their personal stock only to find that after a couple of months they grew bored with their new bodies and waxed nostalgic about their "old" ones.

Sally's father, Thomas Meadows, had abandoned the family when she was just four. She sometimes envied her two younger siblings. They didn't remember their dad at all accept for the occasional holo-vid call or letter—mostly around their birthdays. But Sally could still remember what it was like having him around all the time. He'd been perfectly wonderful. Her recollections, she knew, were not to be trusted; perfectly wonderful fathers do not run off and abandon their children for other women. It was true that he'd contact Sally more than the others in the family, but that only meant he connected with her two or three times a year instead of once. She didn't know why she'd merited the special attention nor was she pleased at the resentment it caused amongst her siblings. But her father would, on occasion, actually have advice worth listening to. He'd argued strongly that she and her siblings keep as much of their personal stock as possible and had even given them credits to that end. As a result, at a time when most of her friends were in the 30th and some even in the 20th percentile, Sally Meadows owned 43% of herself. But she still couldn't forgive the man for trying to replace his paternal responsibilities with monthly payments and the occasional piece of good advice.

Her older sister Emily had been one of the first to volunteer for the war and had been one of the first to die. Sally had sworn to Emily that she wouldn't follow her into the Navy. It had been a promise both her Mom and Dad had extracted from her as well; one of the few times the two had agreed on anything since the breakup. But Sally's need to avenge an older sister who would never live to get a majority of her own shares, marry and have children was greater than the oath she'd once made. Someone in the Outer Alliance would be made to feel the loss of a sibling and understand what it was like to have a loved one's future snuffed out.

O   O   O

"Hey, Sal."
Sally looked to her right.

"Hey, Gemmy," she answered, remembering the young woman's nickname from their sexuality program.

"It's just 'Gem' now."

"Decided to be more grown up, then?"

Gem paused for a moment. A small smile appeared at the corners of her lips. "Something like that. My uncle was the first one to call me that name, and now that he's gone …" she let the sentence hang. Sally could easily guess at the rest of story. Sadly, one oft repeated in the cursed war.

They'd become good friends during the two-month Intercourse program—mandated by law, at the onset of puberty—but had drifted soon after it had finished. At the time it was all very exciting stuff. In retrospect, though, it had been a bit of a snoozer. They'd all had extensive testing then had all been summarily informed what sexual orientation the tests had revealed. They were then introduced to others of the same orientation and the facts of life where explained in a matter that precluded any need for awkward guessing or confusion.

"Here with anyone?" asked Gem.

Sally shook her head.

Gem's tepid smile suddenly brightened. "Well," she said, taking Sally's arm in hers, "you are now!"

Together they made their way to a pair of open seats the middle of the huge auditorium that was quickly filling to capacity. The din of thousands of conversations carried to every corner. Sally decided to splurge and ordered some soda and popcorn cubes from the seat's concession stand (though she often wondered why it was called that since it didn't concede anything unless you paid it first). A bottle blank was summarily produced from the seat back.

"Mr. Pibb, cold level seven, carbonation nine," she said, pulling the bottle from the tray. It began to transform and assume the coloration and wording of the respective brand.

"That's right," Gem said, wrinkling her nose. "You always used to amp your carb." Sally ignored the slight. Gem then picked up her blank. "Coca-Cola, cold six, carb six."

With the bottle tops now melted over into smooth rims, the effervescent notes of the brands filled the air, competing with all those around them. The girls bit into their popcorn cubes. But Sally stopped after a few bites.

"Why do you eat it like that?" she asked.

"Like what?"

"Everyone I know starts with a corner. Then usually bites off the other three. You started in the center."

"Oh, that," answered Gem. "It's the way my uncle ate it."

"Guess you guys were pretty tight."

"Yeah. Especially since my dad was hardly ever around."

That caught Sally's full attention. She tilted her head slightly, eyes probing.

Gem nodded and continued. "He was always taking any contract that came his way—especially in the outer orbits. The credits were good and he never skimped on sending most of it home."

Sally nodded. "But he was never around to help you spend it."

"Not 'never,' just hardly ever. Thankfully his big brother was."

"What'd your uncle do?"

"Teacher. 5th grade. In our building, actually. L 27. Ever have him?"

"Don't thinks so. Unless your uncle is Ms. Tellesburg. She wasn't so great."

"That's too bad. He was an amazing teacher." Gem paused wistfully. "When the war broke out, my dad decided to stay in the outer orbits. Last I heard he'd joined the OA's Navy.

"Wait," said Sally. "Your dad's fighting for the Outer Alliance?"

Gem nodded, lips pinned together. "Uncle Mel decided what Dad did was wrong so he joined our navy to even things out … they never did get along that great," she added with a half smile. "They made him an officer in marines."

"Guess he was good at leading people," added Sally, desperately trying to find something positive to say.

"He was," conceded Gem, "but never wanted to be. Uncle Mel was happiest teaching kids. I still can't believe he's gone."

Sally's expression suddenly changed from one of sympathy to that of concern.

"What?" asked Gem.

"Nothing."

"C'mon, I remember that look. It's not a nothing look."

Sally smiled awkwardly. "If you join the navy you risk fighting you dad."

Gem stopped nibbling on her popcorn cube and sighed. "Yes. The thought had crossed my mind. But he made his choice and now I'm making mine. What about yours?"

"I'm sure that wherever dear old dad is, it will be as far from any battle as he can manage. He was never exactly good at commitment and volunteering for war is about as big a commitment as you can make."

Gem reached over and squeezed her hand. "I'm glad."

At that moment the lights dimmed and the President of the UHF, Hektor Sambianco suddenly appeared.

Though it was only a holo-display, the crowd was riveted. The President was as compelling in virtual reality as he was in real life.

"We were told," he began, "that this war was going to be quick and easy. Well, I'm here to tell you that's a lie. As you're undoubtedly aware, we're in the second year of a conflict that, according to the experts,"—he said the last word with such contempt that Sally felt a surge of hatred for all experts everywhere—"should have lasted three months at most. Well *I* won't lie to you," he said before he began to lie, "This war will take many years and cost countless lives. And yes, I'm talking *permanent* deaths. Many of you are here because you've already lost loved ones. They can never be replaced. And even though I'm only a minority shareholder of my own stock I am the majority shareholder of the trust and future of every human being in this room, this city, this planet, this solar system." He paused as a wave of applause rippled through the room.

"Under new leadership we've revamped the war effort. No longer will we underestimate the guile and cunning of our enemy. We know the depths they're willing to sink to in order to destroy our beloved incorporated system." He waited for the booing and catcalls to die down. "A system that has brought undreamed of levels of prosperity and happiness to untold billions is now under attack by an evil from the past. An evil that calls itself … Justin Cord."

The enmity towards the father of the Unincorporated revolt was visceral, immediate and bellicose.

"This monster," continued Hektor, "claims to bring the 'gift' of freedom with him from his dark, and until recently, dead past. But what he really brings is discontent, anarchy and war!"

The crowd rose to its feet, screaming its hatred at the interloper from three centuries past. Sally was surprised to find herself shouting with the rest. She wasn't usually so free with her emotions.

"But incorporation is not so easily defeated," continued Hektor. "As long as young men and women are willing to fight for the greatest system of justice and prosperity the human race has ever known, we … will … not … fail!"

The President smiled, encouraged by the cheers and support.

"As you know, we're a market system that rewards what's most valuable, and you," he said, pointing his finger in a cadence that led many to assume the President was talking directly at them, "are now more valuable than ever. The UHF will not skimp on rewarding you for what you're worth." At the smattering of applause, his eyes looked downward and his mouth quivered slightly. "But before I list how we'll reward our heroes, I want to share something." He made a great show of inhaling and exhaling deeply. "I've lost friends to this war; men and women so precious to me as to be more important than family. They gave their lives and because of that, I'll continue to risk mine. So let me say 'thank you.' Maybe your families won't understand."

Sally nodded.

"Maybe some of your friends will ridicule you. Maybe the planets at large will not pay attention to what you're doing. But I will." Hektor pointed his thumb inward. "I know how extraordinary you are. I know the losses you've born and the risks you're about to take, and for that,"—he now bowed his head in humble submission—"I thank you." The President basked in the adulation as the hall echoed in deafening applause. He gave one final wave and then faded from view. Moments later, Hektor's visage was replaced by that of a hardened marine in military dress and sporting a panoply of medals that glittered like stars on a moonless night.

The virtual marine went on to list the benefits of signing up for the war against the Outer Alliance: they'd all get two-tiered salaries. The larger one would be paid directly to them regardless of how much stock they owned. This was a more recent addition as it was found that soldiers could get easily disheartened if every two weeks 75% of their earnings went to stockholders safely on planet while the soldiers risked life and limb out in the depths of space. Now, only the smaller salary was subject to normal stock payments. Further, everyone sitting in that auditorium would get the right to sign up and go through basic training with anyone they wished. This meant that apartments, schools or companies could and would have hundreds of friends, co-workers and families join, train and be assigned to units together. It improved morale enormously. Sally felt Gem squeeze her hand and looked over and saw the questioning look in her eyes. Sally gave a brief nod and was rewarded with smile of such warmth and beauty it took her by surprise.

"I was going to ask you anyways," admitted Sally as they both giggled at the prospect of their new adventure together.

But what Sally was truly interested in was the stock buy-back plan. From how she understood it, if she completed her tour of duty with an honorable discharge, the government of the UHF would match her credit for credit the amount she'd put into a special stock buyback program up to 5% of her salary. And she knew she was going to put in the maximum percentage. With any luck Sally Meadows could finish out war with a majority interest in herself.

O   O   O

It was on the second day of her three-day leave that Sally received a message from the UHF High Command. Her orders had been changed. Instead of training in Camp Pendleton, California she'd been reassigned to Camp Adam Smith in Russia. Sally looked it up. CAS was less than a month old. She wasn't too upset. It was the government after all. A certain level of ineptitude was to be expected. If only the war could've been contracted out to a private bidder. But making war was apparently a sovereign power that even the incorporated system still respected.

Unlike the rest of her family, Sally didn't really have many close friends. She was much more of a loner. Sure, she had plenty of acquaintances but Gem was turning out to be different. In the past few days Sally had found it easier to talk to Gem than to anyone else. Sally knew the world had shifted in strange and terrible ways when her mom was actually eager her to talk to, "that man, your father," which was the phrase Augustine Meadows always seemed to use when talking about her ex to her children.

Sally placed a call to Gem. The line connected but all Sally could see was her friend looking frazzled and all she could hear was the sound of a woman yelling in background.

"And how," the woman said, "can you expect to fight the rebels if you can't even clean your own room!"

Gem rolled her eyes. "Mom," she screamed, looking over her shoulder "I'm on the holo!"

"It's called a phone," said her mom.

"Maybe in the 'old country' but not here."

"Don't you speak to your mother like that!" another woman's voice commanded.

"She's not listening to a word I say," said the first woman.

"Hey," Sally began.

"Sorry," said Gem. "Parents."

Sally laughed. "At least you have both." Gem nodded sympathetically. "Say, would you like to come with me to …"

"Yes," interrupted Gem. "In fact let's go *now*."

O   O   O

They met 15 minutes later and Sally explained her dilemma. It did not improve Gem's already surly mood.

"But they promised we could train together!"

"I know," agreed Sally, surprised at her friend's vehemence.

Gem marched to the street with Sally following close behind. They then hailed an automated taxi. "Let's go!"

O   O   O

The large man behind the desk actually seemed taller sitting down than the diminutive Gem did standing up. Even so he shrank ever so slightly from the righteous anger blazing in his direction. More annoying to Sally was the fact that she couldn't even blame him for the mess. The government had contracted out the training of all recruits to Mudder Inc., a newly merged company of the three former competitors who'd decided the only way to meet the new work orders was to make a larger firm. Gem was not arguing with a hapless government flunky but rather a hapless corporate one.

"It was," Sally pointed out, "a factor in our joining and could be considered a breach of contract which could give us legal grounds to get our enlistments canceled." The combination of Gem's tirade and Sally's calm, legalistic tone, eventually struck a nerve. The man behind the desk blinked.

"Let me see if I can figure out what's going on."

He quickly called up three different holographic interfaces and began a mad scramble to track down the relevant information.

"Ah," he said, finally deigning to smile. "I see what happened. Because Camp Adam Smith just opened, they needed additional recruits to round out the next training cycle. Since you didn't put any specific preferences you were transferred automatically." He smiled as if that explained everything, which it did, and thought he'd actually solved the problem, which he hadn't.

"Well," answered Sally with cool resolve, "you can just transfer me back."

"Um," answered the man, looking unhappily at his holo display, "I'm afraid that's not possible. Pendleton is full up for this and the next two cycles."

"Fine. Then delay our enlistment for two additional cycles."

The man blanched.

"Uh … delay?"

The last thing either Gem or Sally wanted was to spend four more months at their respective homes but the recruiter didn't need to know that.

"Of course," answered Sally. "It's the only fair way to honor the part of the contract that states I can train with family or friends. Clearly, I cannot. Certainly not in this situation. I'm sure your superiors will understand you had no choice but accede to my very reasonable request." Sally knew that the exact opposite was true. That once the wheels had been set in motion it was almost impossible to grind them to a halt much less get them to reverse. But she also knew the last thing this guy wanted was to let her and Gem continue to complain up the chain of command with his name dragged through each layer of it as the guy who should've prevented the headache from starting in the first place.

He looked over to Gem. "Would Ms. Suttikul be willing to accommodate a small change?"

"How small?" Gem asked suspiciously.

"Well, Camp Adam Smith is not yet full. If you were to request a transfer, I could have it authorized before you left the office. Then the two of you could train together."

Sally saw that Gem was about to say "yes" and broke in.

"That is unacceptable. Your solution is that she, like me, will have to give up going to war with her friends and family to support her."

"But … but you're her friend," the man stammered.

"Are you implying she only has one?" Sally asked, indignant.

"I never said …"

"So she should do this transfer to correct an error *your* corporation made just to make *your* problem go away. There's nothing in this for her, is there?"

"Well, I …" He consulted his holo-display. "Perhaps some form of compensation?"

"What kind of compensation?" asked Gem.

"Um …" he said scanning the holo displays for any way out, "I believe I can authorize a payment to the two of you for … let's see here … 500 credits? For the inconvenience, of course."

"A thousand," Sally said flatly. Then added, "each" for good measure.

"Each!" repeated Gem.

"And not any of your brand new corporate script either," added Sally. "GCI credits, thank you very much."

"I'm not authorized to …"

"Then get me someone who is," Gem said, leaning over the big man's tiny desk.

Within two hours, Gem's transfer to Camp Adam Smith and Mudder Inc.'s transfer of 1,000 credits to each of them was complete. All they needed to figure out how was how to spend it all in the 24 hours they had left before being carted off to war.

o o o

"Off the transport, maggots!"

The drill instructor's order seemed a perfect fit to the dark and miserable day that greeted them at Camp Adam Smith. When the thirty recruits had finally gotten off the hover transport and were standing in what was close to two lines, the head instructor took her baton from a subordinate and walked up and down the line shaking her head in disgust.

"It depresses me to think that these plains were once occupied by the fiercest warriors in the history of all the human race. On this very ground rode the Mongols led by the greatest general of all time, Subodai. He defeated the Russians, the Ukrainians, the Poles, the Hungarians and others too numerous to mention. To think that you're what I have to work with, that a race that could produce the Mongol horse archers is reduced to,"—she looked at the group and shook her head—"this. To realize that the UHF must defeat the treason and rebellion of the Outer Alliance with," she paused to spit on the ground in front of the recruits, "you."

She then marched over to a recruit and looked him over as he if were going to be her next meal.

"Well, what have we here?"

The recruit remained stone-faced.

"Ladies and gentlemen, may I present"—she looked at the insignia on the recruit's shoulder patch and shook her head—"Recruit Cody Foster. Looks like all hope ain't lost. This here's a genuine hero from Mars."

The drill sergeant was now toe to toe with Private Foster who stood almost a full head taller than her. She pushed her baton up under his nose.

"Maybe that should be your call sign."

"Uh, I-I-I'm n-n-not a hero."

She pushed the baton up a little higher.

"Not a hero, what?" The sergeant's tone was dangerously gentle.

"Uh, not a hero, sir?"

The baton dropped swiftly from under Foster's nose to the side of his body where it found its mark across the bare knuckles of his outstretched hand. He yelped.

"Not a hero, ma'am?" he whimpered.

She raised the baton to strike his face.

"Not a hero, sergeant!"

The sergeant rewarded him with an icy glare. Another recruit down the line made the mistake grunting a laugh.

The sergeant was in the other recruit's face like white on rice.

"Something funny, recruit?"

"No, sergeant!"

"But you laughed."

"Yes, sergeant!"

"So either you're a liar, or a fool. Which is it, Private"—she read the patch on his uniform—"Jensen?"

"Neither, sergeant."

In the absence of an answer, he stumbled through an explanation.

"He doesn't seem like a hero. He … he … seems like a goofball."

The sergeant nodded appreciatively, then stopped.

"I don't think so." She then turned to the rest of the recruits and began walking up and down the line. "Over the next two months I will have the impossible task of training you from worthless civvies to something that may fool the enemy into thinking you're actual soldiers. I will probably fail. But I'll also get the joy of giving you the appropriate call-sign, which will be your name in the navy of the

UHF for the *rest of your career.* For many of you it will be the last name you'll ever have."

She then returned the full force of her personality back to Jensen. "You …"

"Sergeant!"

"… are hereby known as Recruit Goofball." She did not take her eyes off him. "What do you say, Recruit Goofball?"

Jensen stood there in confusion until Gem whispered at his side, "Say 'Thank you,' Goofball."

This brought a smattering of laughter from the other recruits, though Foster and Sally's faces remained placid.

"Thank you, Sergeant!" shouted Jensen.

But the sergeant was no longer paying attention to Goofball. She was now focused on Gem. "Well what do we have here? Mama's little helper?" And so it went.

O O O

It took two days and ten insulting names being given out until the recruits finally learned the name of their sergeant. She had a first name but only two of them ever learned it. What all of them soon realized was that they weren't going to get cool-sounding call signs, like T-Bone or Razor or Demon Dick. They would only get a call sign after they'd messed up and it would be an embarrassing one. Besides Goofball and Mother's Little Helper, the group had gotten to know Farty, Suck up, Chuckles, Twinkle Toes, Fish Breath, Taco Tony, Dumbass and Cutie Pie. They were eventually issued uniforms and gear and soon thereafter, began to form some group cohesion. Since most had come from the same corporation, the team gelled more quickly. Sally, Gem and Foster were the only ones who didn't know anyone and so, ended up spending most of their downtime together. Sally and Gem discovered that they liked hanging out with the old man, which it was clear by his mannerisms, he was. How old was anyone's best guess thanks to 23rd century medicine and nanotech. Interestingly enough, there were those who pretended to be older than they were in order to appear more sophisticated. If Sally had a credit for every thirty-year-old who tried to pass him or herself off as a seventy-year-old she would've had majority years ago. But Cody was different. When asked his age he'd invariably say he was in his thirties and he said it in such a way as to make it seem he was much closer to 31 than 39. But both Sally Gem suspected he was older, much older. It was the way he moved and what he said—which wasn't much. Most boys in their thirties couldn't wait to tell the universe and every creature in it that they'd figured out everything. Cody mainly listened. That was a trait of the old more than the young. On top of that was the strange fact that he hadn't made a pass at Sally. At first she thought he might have been gay, but after a couple of days it became clear that he noticed women in ways that he didn't notice men. But Sally was pretty sure Cody was more attracted to their drill sergeant and then in a flash she knew why. Older women tended to be attracted to older men. Especially older, confident men and Cody Foster was stacking up to be a lot more confident and brazen then his surface stammering would suggest. For instance, the base's entertainment complex showed patriotic vids. They were expertly conceived, shot and edited. They were able to sway with the precision that centuries of increasingly skillful marketing had begat. Every once in a while, though, Cody would add a word or a phrase to the propaganda and it would suddenly become very obvious that what the recruits were experiencing was nothing more than agitprop. Cody was never loud or overt about it, but the effect was just the same. At the thrice-weekly holo-vid events, Cody, Sally and Gem were the only ones who were not truly hooting and calling for the destruction of the 'vile' and 'heartless' enemy—though most looking on would be none the wiser.

In those initial few weeks Sally began to wonder if Cody wasn't perhaps some type of secret anti-war protester. But she quickly ruled that out—anti-war protesters didn't usually sign up for the wars they protested. So then why the targeted sedition? Sally got the feeling that the only reason she and Gem heard his clever rebuttals was because they were always sitting next to him. Though apparently Sally learned later, not quite as together as Gem would've preferred. Gem and Cody had fooled around once but Cody hadn't allowed the one-night stand to become anything more.

Their training went about as well as could be expected. But it seemed to Sally as if it was a very hurried affair. They'd start each day being woken up from their bio-electric induced sleep. The UHF military loved what the troops called the "must-sleep beds." With a must-sleep, each recruit got the optimal amount of REM state to maximize their training. The technology also ensured that the recruits didn't wander off in the middle of the night and get into mischief (effectively putting to a halt thousands of years of proud tradition). Once a marine was in bed and hooked up, they'd be down for the exact amount of time the base commander wanted. They also had the advantage of stage one electro-muscle sleep generation. Or as the grunts liked to call it, "Night Gym."

But night gym was not all it was cracked up to be. The bed could build muscle while you slept and you slept great. But Sally still found, along with everyone else, that she'd wake up very sore, achy and grumpy—REM sleep be damned. Of course they still had to do a full range of awake calisthenics and general exercise to condition their new bodies. Some of the larger, heavily muscled recruits complained that the new regimen replaced their bigger physiques with those more akin to a swimmer. But in space combat, speed and stamina were far more important than brute strength and Cody gave such convincing and apparently real life examples that even those who'd grumbled the most came to accept that it was all for the best.

It was clear to everyone that Cody wasn't really suffering as much as the rest. If he wasn't in perfect fighting shape on day one, he was certainly close enough. He handled the 'must sleep' beds and the 'night gym' in stride but he was an absolute klutz at anything having to do with actual military training. It didn't matter if that training involved the proper use of an airlock or the operation of marine battle armor. Cody never, ever got it right on the first try. And he asked more clarifying questions than the rest of the training squad combined.

The sergeant would get so annoyed at him that Cody was often ordered to stay after and help with the cleanup and storage of whatever it was they were learning to use that day. He never once complained. Sally found herself sticking around to help because she was genuinely interested in the workings of an airlock control or cleaning and putting away thirty guns or running maintenance checks on the ten suits of training assault armor they had. Plus, Cody always offered to buy the rounds when the task was complete and he never skimped. He must have spent a fortune, because he always seemed to be served the best beer, hardest-to-come-by appetizers and finest cigars. It didn't take long to get Gem involved in the work and post revelry. Though the rest of the team thought they were nuts for taking on additional work, Sally and Gem recognized it for what it was—an incalculable experience. Stripping 30 Assault Rail Guns, otherwise know as ARGs made you better able to work them. The same rule applied to airlock controls, assault armor and yes, even peeling potatoes.

O O O

The sergeant was holding an ARG firmly in her hands.

"This is capable of propelling matter at dizzying speeds. It's why many of the battles out in the great beyond take place with lots of rock to hide behind. If the ships just went up and tried to slug it out, battles would be short and almost 100% deadly. But those railguns are on huge ships with huge launchers and nearly unlimited power. Ours work on the same principal but with much smaller energy outputs."

A hand shot up.

"What is it, Chuckles? And it better not be stupid or you'll be doing laps around the reactors."

"Sergeant, why doesn't some egghead make an ARG that can shoot like a fleet railgun? I think it would be pretty bonus to go into battle with that."

"Five laps … with a shock drone."

Chuckles swallowed hard and took off at a dead run, followed by a floating drone that shocked him if he slowed his pace.

"Now," continued the sergeant, "does anyone care to guess why that was such a stupid question?" But she had no takers. By this point in their training most of the recruits had learned to shut up.

"Fine, I'll tell you. Even if you could warp the laws of physics to create a truly hand held gun that could project matter that quickly no corporation or government on either side of this war would be stupid enough to make it. Your own troops could do more damage to your side with one accidental on planet discharge than a barrage of meteors. It would be so destructive as to be useless on any ship or asteroid in the solar system. But don't you worry you little heads. What you have in your hands is plenty destructive enough." And it was. Their gun could shoot a pellet the size of a grain of rice at nearly 100,000 kilometers an hour. Even more impressive was that it could shoot almost anything that could fit in the magazine. Sally was surprised that none of the drill instructors had taught what she thought would be a vital fact to soldiers in combat. The only reason she knew about it was because Cody had casually mentioned it. And once again, the pattern.

Sally tried to ask Cody about it, but all he said was he didn't want the sergeant to give him some stupid nickname, so he decided it was best to shut up and volunteer. The excuse seemed thin, but she had to admit that after seven weeks she and Cody were the only ones who hadn't been given some stupid nickname because of some boneheaded mistake they'd made. With only one week left to go in their training Sally was beginning to think that maybe they'd actually get out of basic training stupid name free.

o   o   o

Though they'd moaned and bitched for close to eight weeks of training, most of the recruits were smart enough to realize that it hadn't been nearly enough. And that their next phase of training was to be in actual battles made them even more jittery. Sally and Gem took solace from the fact that they'd gained at least a few months more experience by din of their volunteer efforts—still not nearly half as much as Cody's. Which is why the accident was so surprising.

They'd all been training in full marine assault armor—practically a spacecraft in its own right. It was fully contained and could even maintain human life in the vacuum of space. It was magnetized for deck adhesion and was capable of short distance flight in space, but not in gravity. Sally could jump pretty far in it, but was disappointed she couldn't leap fifty feet in the air or across broad boulevards in a single bound. But she was carrying enough firepower to level a small structure.

According to the objective, the target was holding fifty Alliance miners. Sally first had to incapacitate the enemy and then destroy the building. She'd made quick work of the first part with five simulated grenades pumped out of her suit's spring-loaded launcher. She was then given the order to advance and place the charge. She had a disc in her hand that Cody had handed to her only moments before. As her arm swung in a wide, graceful arc her fingers released the disc along its trajectory. Much to Sally's surprise, the now fully armed disc did not budge. It had annealed itself to her gauntlet instead. Sally was still too confused to be scared. Her heart skipped as the countdown timer hit ten and kept on going. Before she could react, Cody burst from the group of trainees and began running towards her.

"Hang on, Cookie, I'm coming!"

That can't be right, she thought. Then Cody was at her side and with a speed that only came from experience, activated the emergency release bolt for her right gauntlet, detached it and flung it into the building. With the 1.4 seconds he had left, Cody threw himself over Sally. The explosion came just as they both hit the ground. Moments later they were buried in the rubble.

All Sally could think about as the world went dark was that Cody Foster had called her a name that only one person in life had ever called her before.

Cody used his suit's power to extricate Sally and himself from the debris. His visor swung open. "Are you alright?" he asked repeatedly.

Sally finally opened her visor. That look he was giving her. Completely wrong face, but that look. To the center of her being she absolutely knew.

"Daddy?" she said, eyes narrowing in disbelief.

"Hey, Baby Girl," he said using another of his childhood nicknames for her.

The moment was interrupted by the sound of nearby laughter. Sally and Cody looked down to see their sergeant standing at the bottom of the pile of twisted metal and stone. Her arms were folded and she was sporting a very self-satisfied grin.

"It took longer than I would've thought and I was even tempted to make something up just to get it done with. But I figured if I just held out long enough you two would do something that would make it easy."

The sergeant waited for the rest of the unit to surround them before completing her thought. "I'd like to introduce you all to our last two call signs, 'Daddy' and 'Baby Girl.'"

And that's when Sally Meadows slammed her ungauntletted fist into her father's unprotected face. At other times and places the man had been called Thomas Meadows. It wasn't his real name in that it wasn't the one he'd been born with. But it was what his four children knew him by. And because of that it was the one name and face that he actually maintained links to. They were tenuous threads at best with lots of precautions to make sure they couldn't' be used to track him. Not that Thomas had ever done anything that could be considered in the slightest way illegal. He made sure to pay all his tickets and fines even when he knew he could've easily won in court. Thomas Meadows did not argue or complain or do anything to get noticed. It was the one identity he maintained that was completely clean.

The irony was that he'd planned on maintaining it for no more than a few weeks. It was the simplest of scams. Steal a valuable piece of property from person or persons who would never report the item missing because they never had the right to possess it in the first place. In this case, it was an actual original of the American Declaration of Independence residing in an apartment in New York City. Not the signed one—that had been vaporized in the destruction of Washington. Thomas was after the one from the same printing press. How the indolent, lazy, bastard he'd stolen it from had come across it, Thomas would never know nor care. He did however know that as harmless, old innocent civilian Thomas Meadows, he could turn it in to the police, wait about a year, then come back to claim the reward with nary a fuss. It was true the reward would only be 1/10th of its actual value, but it was 1/10th he could keep and the system would let him have.

And Thomas Meadows had a great deal of respect for the system. In the 22nd century crime was not altogether impossible, but it was very risky. If you were caught at criminal behavior once too often you'd find yourself getting a psyche audit from the state, free of charge. Though it was a painless procedure, the very thought of it scared Thomas to death—because anything that could so fundamentally change his nature might as well kill him.

It was a good plan and but for the brief dalliance with a woman named Augustine Cooper, Thomas Meadows would have disappeared, never to be heard from again. Augustine was not a particularly attractive or even intriguing woman. In fact it was her overwhelming averageness that made her so appealing. While Thomas was with her, he became as completely average as she was. Their hookup, he'd reasoned, was completely fortuitous as it played in perfectly with his cover. And so, to the allotted two weeks planning the theft, Augustine became an inadvertent bonus. The breakup was easy. He "accepted" a job that conveniently took him to the outer planets. What he did in fact do was drop his name and spend the following year running basic tourist cons in the tropical islands of the Pacific. Nothing major, nothing to get him noticed. Just people on vacation who find that their accounts have been dipped into, but never by any amounts large enough to trigger a major investigation. When that well dried up, he took a ship to Mars to run the same scam at the Thousand Canals resort. The once and future Thomas Meadows did have one rule he always adhered to:

never, ever run a scam or even a fishing expedition while on a ship. It could be a ferry to an island off the coast of Thailand or a starship heading on a three-month voyage to the outer orbits. His logic was sound; it would be foolish to commit a crime where you had no chance of escape. However, in all his expert planning he'd missed the one thing there was no escaping from—fatherhood.

When Thomas Meadows reappeared in New York City to claim his reward, he discovered in the year he'd been gone, Augustine Cooper had given birth to a baby girl and had named her Emily. It was the first careless act Thomas could ever remember making in his adult life. But it didn't matter. The first time he held his baby girl in his hands he knew that something had changed. In one instant he went from being a man pretending to being an average guy to actually becoming one. Of course it took an incredible amount of skill, money and luck to buy a back-story deep enough to survive the scrutiny that inevitably came from domesticity. The biggest problem with being a rube was that you were trapped. Trapped by a job, by family and in the case of the suddenly real Thomas Meadows, by the baby staring longingly into his eyes.

Although the man history would come to know as 'Daddy' ultimately failed as a family man it was not through want of trying. He lasted six years in the role and had a total of four children with the fascinatingly plain Augustine. They were: Emily, Sally, Ashley and then his son, Lee (Thomas could not get Augustine to relent on "ly" sounding names). He loved all his children and became the best father he could. He had an average job but used his reward money to buy his family a nice condo in the Highland Towers Living Complex in New York City. It was a three hundred-story skypiercer that was typical of the breed. Homes and schools and the businesses that catered to them were all maintained in the massive structure. And because the Meadows' owned instead of rented they had a unit on the 237th floor with an acceptable view of New Jersey. Thomas could have finagled a Manhattan view, but he decided that would be just a bit too ostentatious. The meme against New Jersey had survived the collapse of one civilization and the rise of another. No matter how spectacular the view from the home he provided his family, few would envy him—it was perfect.

And his life stayed perfect until a knock on the door reacquainted him with some old cohorts. They had gifts and an easy-to-follow backstory they fed to him so he could maintain the illusion for his wife and children. But the threat was as real and palpable as if they'd burst into his home and put neurilizers to everyone's head.

Later when he and his "friends" went out for drinks, the gloves came off. Either he helped with one last gig or his family would suffer. He asked for promises that this was going to be the last time and because he really had no choice, accepted their assurances that it would be. He of course knew their agreement was worth what it cost them to make it.

The last week he spent with his family was the most difficult of his life. He wanted more than anything to stay with his children. He even loved his aggressively plain wife. But the die had been cast.

So at the end of that week his wife found out that the "friends" who showed up were actually his spouses; that his marriage to her was a fraud. Augustine demanded he leave at once.

As for his comrades, the first chance he could get he turned them into GCI corporate security by hacking into and leaving a warning on the database of Kirk Olmstead, head of GCI special operations. They were arrested and psyche audited in far less time than the law should have allowed for. As for Thomas Meadows, he was wanted for questioning, but not charged with any specific crime. Kirk was willing to let one bird fly for the ones he had in hand.

But now Thomas Meadows had to disappear again. He may have been able to patch things up with his wife and kids but it would've been under the scrutiny of GCI, not to mention being even more visible to any of his other past "associates." So Thomas Meadows went from being the greatest father in the world to being a dad who sent holo displays every once in a while and credit transfers for child support. He could have sent enough to give all four of his children top-level educations and comfortable majorities of their stock. But that would have brought far more scrutiny than was safe. Better for them to think of him as the failed father who sent just enough and occasionally a little more. The one thing he did though was make sure to send each child a personal message on their life day—a celebration of the moment they were was conceived and put into the gestation tank. And that seemed to be that—until the war came.

The man who would become Thomas Meadows again was not even on Earth when the war broke out. He was on Mars and found, much to his surprise, that he'd become involved in the anti-corporate revolt that had swept the planet. It had been folly to stand up to the system, costing him a year of his life as he was forced to go underground in an effort to escape the inevitable witch-hunt for Alliance sympathizers. To add insult to injury, when The Unincorporated Man, Justin Cord himself took over the planet with an Outer Alliance fleet, Thomas almost got himself killed because his cover as a patriotic Core Worlds supporter was just a bit too good. Easily disarming two heavily armed Alliance Assault Miners in front of a crowd of gawkers didn't help either. However with his rehabilitated status, he was once again able to return to Earth as Cody Foster.

It was around that time he found out that his eldest, Emily planned on enlisting as an assault marine in the UHF fleet. She had this fantasy that she'd join, single handedly defeat the Outer Alliance and end up with enough credits to earn a majority of herself, plus, she'd explained to him in their brief, terse conversation, that all her friends were doing it too. Thomas had even revealed his monetary hand by offering to pay for her majority himself, but she'd just scoffed—either out of disbelief or obstinacy. Absentee fathers do not get a say in their children's lives, especially after fifteen years of holo-vid in parenting. He did manage to exact a promise from her that she wouldn't encourage her siblings to sign up. It was an easy one to make. Lee and Sally were young and the war would have to go on for years before they could ever think of volunteering.

After that, Thomas Meadows made sure to keep in regular contact with his family, hoping that more time invested would translate into more influence, or at least more than he'd had with Emily. Though he'd never be stupid enough to reveal his original Outer Alliance sympathies, he did keep his fingers on the pulse of UHF politics—especially anything having to do with the military. Unfortunately, the more he learned the more disturbed he became. It seemed to him that if there was an idiotic corporate executive who had *not* been given the rank of admiral or colonel and allowed to kill untold numbers of hapless underlings, it hadn't been for lack of trying. And then one of those idiotic executives had gotten Emily killed. Even worse, it had been a permanent death. There would be no reanimation because there was nothing left to reanimate. She'd died at the first battle of Anderson's Farm in the Asteroid Belt's infamous 180. The number had been designated because the location was exactly opposite Ceres, the unofficial capital of Outer Alliance. The battle was the first thrust of the UHF's attempt to limit the enemy's economic viability. By cutting off the Belt at the 180, the Alliance would lose half its population and 2/3's of its industry.

Which was why the Alliance was defending it with everything they had. It had turned into a meat-grinder and Thomas's daughter had been ground to bits.

When his second eldest, Sally, came of age the war was still on. Much like her older sister, the fire raged in Sally's belly but with the added impetus of revenge. Thomas tried to convince her not to enlist and failed just as he had with Emily, and mainly for the same reasons. So this time Thomas would be more proactive. He found out what training camp Sally was being assigned to and using some of his ill-gotten if hard earned credits managed to have his daughter transferred to a brand new camp that was filled with lots of brand new people in brand new jobs who had no idea what they were doing. Then as "Cody Foster," the man who disabled two Alliance assault miners on Mars, volunteered in such a time and place as to get sent to the same camps as his daughter. After that it was child's play to get assigned to the same unit.

o o o

The problem with the stockade was not that it was uncomfortable. Any other age would have called it luxurious beyond compare. The bed was body temp adjustable, the bathroom and shower facilities were pampering to a degree that any Roman emperor worth his toga would have sacrificed fifty thousand slaves to possess. It had excellent exercise facilities and was supremely comfortable by the standards of any age and quite nice by the standards of Sally Meadow's. The problem was boredom. Prisoners were not allowed any entertainment options. The only stations Sally could watch or listen to played agitprop programming and the only thing she could access in the library were regulation, maintenance and tech manuals. On the first day, she was actually quite happy diving into it all, starting with the inner workings of a demolition charge with an auto-annealing strip. She soon came to realize just how lucky she'd been. Once the charge had been set and the strip activated, it was impossible to break the bond. If Cody—Sally still couldn't think of him as "Dad"—hadn't known the unlock code for the gauntlet on her battle armor she'd be dead.

But she'd be damned if she was going to owe that man a thing— that is until boredom set in. Human beings of the 24th century were simply incapable of complacency. There were those, of course, who with years of training and practice could spend days or even weeks meditating with only their own thoughts for company. But Sally was not one of them. By day four she was calling up specs for all the equipment she was likely to use. From battle armor, line guns and even navy-issued toothpicks (which could be quite incapacitating when shot from an ARG). If Sally was going to be stuck in solitary confinement, she was going to make the best of it; even if the notion of doing so had come from her dad.

She was so engrossed in the assembly of a portable milspec drone sweeper that she hadn't noticed the intruder.

"You'll need to tighten the guard plate on the intake port."

Without thinking, Sally shoved her elbow backwards, followed by a well-aimed round kick. But Thomas had anticipated the move and was nowhere near the point of impact.

"Hey, hey. Relax, Cookie." he said. "It's just me."

"Don't call me that," she snarled, eyes narrowed. "You don't get to call me that, *ever.*"

Cody sighed. "Fair enough. But in return could you try not to beat me to death every time I want to talk to you?"

Sally considered the request. "Fine." Then added, "as long as you don't sneak up on me."

Thomas nodded. "Excellent. Then I'll just stand here in silence and you can go back to practicing."

Sally looked confused and was about to ask a question but was curtailed by Cody bringing his index finger up to his lips. He subsequently activated a small box on his belt. "Okay, we can talk. This," he said indicating the box on his belt, "will make it appear as if I'm observing you practice."

"How?"

"I accessed and recorded about three hours of your activities. Splicing myself in was easy. We have about three hours."

Sally turned her back. "You may as well turn it off. Your box has the right idea. I really have nothing to say to you."

Thomas sighed. "Well, can I at least get a 'Thank you?'"

Sally froze. She closed her eyes and tried to count to ten but only made it to three before spinning back around. "Thank you!? Thank you!?"

"You're welcome?" answered Thomas weakly.

"What do I have to say thank *you* for? Oh, that's right. Let's see," Sally started to count off on her fingers. "Should I thank you for abandoning us for your group marriage when I was five? Should I thank you for all the birthdays you weren't at?"

Thomas winced.

"How about for all the baseball games you missed? You know, the games where I kept stupidly looking for you in the bleachers? Guess how old I was when I finally stopped looking?"

Thomas shrugged his shoulders.

"Fourteen," she said. Her laugh was an odd tincture of sadness and disbelief. "It took me nine years to finally realize, in my heart of hearts, that you weren't ever going to be there for me."

Thomas said nothing, head lowered.

"So what do I need to thank you for?"

Thomas mumbled something.

"I'm sorry, Recruit Foster, I didn't quite get that."

"I did save your life," Thomas whispered.

Sally grabbed her father by his shirt and shoved him against the wall. "You do not get to claim credit for saving me from the live charge you threw at me in a training exercise!" Then she noticed something strange about his face and, releasing his shirt, took a step back. "What the hell's wrong with your nose?"

"You like it?" Thomas's eyes lit up.

"No, it's crooked."

"It should be," he answered with his smile growing wider. "You broke it."

"That's stupid," she said, releasing him. "Why didn't they just fix it?"

"Didn't let 'em."

"It looks ugly."

"Does not," he answered, bringing his hand up to the appendage in question. "I think it gives me a bit of distinction. Besides it's …" he seemed to think better of it, and his voice trailed away.

"It's what?" demanded Sally.

"Well …" he fumbled. "It's just that …" Then he finally blurted, "it's the first thing you've given me in fifteen years."

Sally stared at her father, dumbfounded. "Fix it. I don't want to give you anything."

"Then let me at least pay you for it."

Sally's brow scrunched. "Pay *me* for breaking *your* nose?"

Thomas nodded. The stupid smile, noticed Sally, still hadn't left his face.

"I thought I'd made myself perfectly clear. I don't want or need anything from you."

"You got it, Cook …" he stopped himself when he saw her face tense up once more, "Sally."

"If you have to call me anything," she said, "it will be 'Recruit Meadows' is that understood?"

"Yes, Recruit Meadows, it is."

"Was there anything else, Recruit Foster?"

"Yes. I may have gotten us flunked out of basic training."

"May have?"

Thomas' mouth formed into a wan smile. "We're going to have to take it again … right here."

If Sally had a weapon, she may have been tempted to use it. Instead she spent the next two hours and fifty-six minutes in abject silence—a far more effective means of hurting her father than any weapon she could have dreamed of.

O O O

Two days later Sally had another visitor, one she welcomed with open arms.

"Gemmy!" she shouted and as soon as her friend crossed the threshold, almost tackling her in a bear hug.

"That's *Private* Suttikul to you, Recruit Meadows," answered Gem with mock severity.

Sally laughed but there was little joy in it.

"Hey, it's okay," said Gem giving her friend a gentle hug. "You can call me 'Gemmy' as much as you want."

"It's not that."

"Then, what?"

"I was supposed to be with you," answered Sally. "I can kick myself for going through school and not having you as a friend."

"Me too," smiled Gem.

"But at least I was going to fight the war with you and that would've made up for school."

Gem nodded. "A thousand times more."

"But now thanks to my … to Cody, that's not going to happen!"

Gem sighed and touched a small box tucked within her belt.

Sally shot her a look. "You do realize he's the reason I'm still stuck here."

"And the reason you're still alive," Gem whispered softly.

"He threw me a live charge!"

"Did *he* activate the annealer?"

"I … don't know," Sally began, "maybe." Then honesty got the better of her. "No."

Gem took Sally's hand, "Correct. And when it happened, he ran straight towards you. No one else did."

"No one?" asked Sally, looking at Gem for salvation.

"No one," answered Gem as a single tear ran down the length of her face. "I'm so sorry, Sal. I should have. I don't know why … I just … I didn't."

Sally grabbed her friend by the forearms. "Gemmy, don't you for a moment blame yourself."

Gem's lips curved slightly downwards. "I do and I always will." Gem then extricated herself from Sally's grip and took a half step back. "But I will *never* abandon you again."

"Stop it, Gem. You did nothing wrong. Anyone would have acted like you did. It was a live demolition charge. *I* would have run the other way."

"Anyone but your father. He didn't hesitate for a second, Sal. He saw you were in danger so that's where he went."

"Then why did he throw me a live charge?"

"You dope," said Gem with enough affection to soften the blow. "He tried to tell you but you wouldn't listen."

"Listen to what?"

"He wanted you to blow up that building."

"Well, yes. That was the exercise."

"No, stupid. *Actually* blow it up. Not theoretically."

"Why the hell would he want that?"

"So you'd flunk out of basic training and have to do it all over again." Gem said this as if it were the most obvious thing in the worlds.

"What?" Sally said, her brain suddenly feeling fuzzy.

"Honey, we're not ready for war. Eight weeks is just not enough time."

"But they said we'll get additional train …"

"Not enough," Gem interrupted. "Your father did this to increase your odds of surviving. At least listen to him."

"Why should I? He wasn't there when …"

"Oh, for Damsah's sake," shouted Gem, "he's here *now*. I don't know if you realize this but your life is in danger *now*. He wasn't there when you were growing up and yeah, that sucks. But the worst you really had to fear was spinal injuries and broken bones; big deal. In case you don't remember, my father chose to stay in the outer orbits and fight for the enemy. I may very well have to kill him and never know it. Or," Gem continued in a smaller voice, "he may kill me." She then comported herself. "Yours chose to change his face, risk death on occupied Mars, come back to Earth and volunteer for a war we both know he doesn't really believe in and become an extraordinarily well-trained soldier. Why?"

Sally shrugged.

"To make you one too, dipshit. He's not perfect but from my point of view he's pretty damn good and the least you can do is talk to him." Gem's eye's grew wide for a moment as she scanned an incoming message. "Gotta go."

"Wait," said Sally, grabbing Gem's arm. "If I'm not ready for war, how can you be?"

"I'm not. Cody got me assigned to a lunar Repo/Depot unit and arranged for them to lose my paperwork. And I plan on taking advantage of that for however long it takes them to figure it out."

"Wait. How did he …?"

"Sally, for Damsah's sake, talk to him!" And with a kiss to the air Gem was gone.

Moscow, Russian Federation

Sally wasn't sure how to speak to her father but figured she'd use the 48 hours leave they'd been given to figure it out. He had other plans, however, hardly saying a word to her on the trip away from their Siberian base. As they left the station, bundled up in thick overcoats and scarves with only the sound of snow crunching beneath their feet, he finally spoke.

"Thanks for waiting," he said, "walking in the snow actually plays havoc with general listening devices, but this will take care of most anyone specifically listening in."

"This?" she asked in a frustration-tinged voice.

"Ah," he answered, realizing she couldn't see through his coat. "The box."

"You've got issues," Sally said trying to be sarcastic, but failing utterly.

"More than you can imagine," Thomas answered dryly.

"Are you some sort of corporate spy? I used to imagine that you were and that's why you had to leave us." Sally realized that she was starting to sound very much like the five-year-old girl she'd spent so many years of her life being. She hated that girl.

Thomas's eyes crinkled slightly. "I was tempted to tell you exactly that when this moment arrived. It was going to be filled with all sorts of hazy, yet convincing evidence to support the lie. But I can't lie to you anymore, Cookie." His face tensed slightly, waiting for the tongue-lashing that never arrived.

"Then if you're not a corporate spy what are you?" The question was as plaintive as it was painful.

"A con man."

"A what?"

"I trick people into giving me their money."

"So you're a common thief?"

"No, Cookie. I'm an extraordinary one. And I can assure I have never ever stolen anything from anyone who couldn't afford it."

"Uh, huh."

"Really," said Thomas. "It's also, by the way, how I met your mother."

Sally stopped walking and turned to face him, eyes piqued.

"Alright, alright," he answered, genuinely enjoying the moment then indicated a bench in the distance. "Let's talk."

O O O

Two hours later Sally sat quietly and digested the fact that, but for the someone illegally having acquired an original printing of the Declaration of Independence, she would not be alive.

"So let me get this straight," she said, "you gave up an exciting life, filled with danger and adventure to marry … mom?" Her confusion was complete.

"Yes, Cookie. Your mom's ability to find joy in the most ordinary things is what attracted me to her. In that respect she opened up a world I'd rejected long ago."

"How long?"

Thomas laughed. "You get answers to many things, Cookie. More than most, actually. Just not that."

Sally allowed herself an uncharacteristic pout.

"However," Thomas said, "that's not what caused me to stay. It was Emily at first. Then you and your siblings. When I held each of you in my arms, so small and so amazingly perfect ..." he sighed, his mind wandering off for a moment. "I gave up nothing to be with all of you."

"Then why did you leave?"

Thomas reacted to Sally's question as if it were a body blow. He then spent the next hour telling her rest of the story.

O O O

By the time Thomas was finished, the sun had gone down and the weather had turned markedly colder. Had it not been for the internal nanites adjusting Sally and Thomas's metabolism, the clothing they wore would not have sufficed.

"I can understand why you left," Sally admitted grudgingly, "but how come you never came back? How come you didn't give any of us the chance to go with you?"

"Cookie I was not bragging when I said I was extraordinary. There are maybe fifty of us left in the entire solar system."

"Us?"

"Extraordinary thieves. And the Incorporated system does not take kindly to anyone threatening their monopoly on theft."

"You don't think I could do it," she laughed. There, was, however an earnestness about it that demanded an answer.

"Actually, of all my children," answered Thomas "I'm pretty sure you're the only one who could. I can tell you I had daydreams of coming back in to your life and bringing you into mine. I would teach you all about the art of the con in the modern worlds. We would all go through the solar system and find the stupid and greedy and redistribute their wealth in our favor."

"So Why didn't you?"

"Because I was happiest when I had you and the family. My life as a con man brought me pride and adventure, but not happiness. And above all else I felt you should at least have that." Thomas shook his head. "And then you and your sister had to go and join the fucking marines?"

"You know why I joined."

"Yes. To avenge your sister. And I joined to protect you. I was too far away to help Ems. But not too far to help you—even if you didn't want it."

"I want it now, Daddy," she said softly.

Thomas smiled and gave his daughter a hug. "I can get us out of the marines and under new identities in less than a week. We can ride out this war in relative safety and impressive comfort." For the first time in a long time Sally could discern real hope in his voice.

"No, daddy," Sally insisted, putting her hand gently on his shoulder, "that's not what I meant. You're a great soldier."

Thomas snorted.

"Don't do that, Daddy, you are. And if I'm going to be a great soldier, if I'm going to survive this war and keep Holly and Lee out of it, I'm going to need your help."

"Baby girl," he said forgetting in his distress that it was her call sign and not his special nickname anymore. "Please. This war is going to last a long time. I've lived as much of my life in the outer orbits as I have in the Core worlds and I can tell you, the Outer Alliance will *never* surrender. We can blow them to pieces and take asteroid after asteroid and even some of their worlds and they'll fight to the bitter end."

"But they killed Emily."

"No, Cookie. The bastards who sent a teenage girl with eight weeks of training into combat against people who'd had a lifetime in space killed her. And those same bastards will do the same to you."

"Not if you keep on helping like you have. You can teach me enough to survive. Enough to make them pay."

Thomas Meadows sighed. He knew this was likely and he knew that until his daughter had seen and experienced more of this war, he was not going to be able to change her mind. "Okay, Cookie. I got a contingency plan for this. Remember how I told you that there are fifty people like me in the solar system and that they really don't like me very much?"

"Of course, Daddy."

"Well, the good news is they were the ones I was most fearful of hurting our family if I stayed with you. Of the fifty, guess how many are in the Outer Alliance?"

Sally shrugged. "Twenty?"

Thomas shook his head.

"Twenty-five?"

He shook his again, pointing his thumb upwards.

"For Damsah's sake, Daddy, how many?"

"Forty-nine."

"Why is that good news? Forty-nine 'you's' on the other side sounds like terrible news."

"It is for the war. I shudder to think how much of an advantage the Alliance will have if Kirk Olmstead can get even a quarter of them to sign up. But the good news is that since they're there …"

"Thomas Meadows can come back here!" Sally finished, happily having to resist the urge to clap her hands in joy.

"Technically, he already has. A man matching my old description with my ident code has signed up and is about to start basic training. It's going to cost me almost all the funds I have access to and some favors I never thought I'd have to call in, but in eight weeks he'll become Cody Foster and I'll become Thomas Meadows again. Hopefully, for the last time. And Sally and Thomas Meadows will be posted to the same Marine combat unit."

Sally leaned across the bench and gave her father a hug that, judging by his reaction, was worth every credit he'd spent and was yet to spend. But then she stopped and leaned back, looking at him quizzically.

"What is it, Cookie?"

"Daddy," she paused. "What's my name?"

"It's Sally. Sally Meadows, Cookie."

"No, Daddy, it's not."

Sally knew she was asking him the one piece of information her father had never shared with anyone. The one secret he'd kept above all others.

"Your name is Ryan. Sally Ryan."

Sally digested that all-important piece of information, understanding the enormity of what had just been shared. "Thank you, Daddy."

"You're welcome, Cookie."

Asteroid 17-43A7-9234 (aka Leary's Casino)
Year 3 of 7 of the Unincorporated War

"Get your ass's down!" shouted Private first class Thomas Meadows at what was left of his squad. The five marines, including Sally, were on the surface of an asteroid famous for having the only casino/whorehouse in an area known mainly for its religious adherents. If the local population had any say in the matter they would have happily closed the place down and put up a seminary or hospital in its stead. Thomas amused himself with the fact that the locals had finally gotten their wish in that all the whoring had finally ceased on the God-forsaken rock. The gambling had continued though, only this time they were playing for lives and the ante had been his daughter.

Thomas was very pleased to see that all the practice with Sally had paid off. After reeling in the line and dragging herself to the surface, she'd made sure that her whole body hugged the rock and not just her arms and face. The first couple of times they'd practiced the maneuver she kept forgetting to pull in her legs and hips. So Thomas programmed a shock droid to zap any part of her not hugging the ground. It worked.

But the other three members of Thomas's squad did what their terribly wrong, born-and-bred-at-the-bottom-of-a-gravity-well instincts told them to do—they *threw* themselves to the ground. The problem was that the slight forward leap, which made perfect sense in gravity, ended up with them flying across the landscape like superheroes in the 0.03 gravity of the six-kilometer long asteroid. Actually, Thomas saw that the recruit from Luna did manage to use her linegun after she'd leapt to ground but since she hadn't attached it to her belt she'd ended up with both legs dangling high above her head, making a perfect target for the Alliance bomblets dropped from on high. The munitions were primitive but smart enough with rudimentary guidance and programming. If something were moving in their target area, they'd veer towards it. For instance, two UHF assault marines flying across the landscape like supermen. Now Thomas had to admit that UHF battle armor was impressively durable. He could testify as to how much damage it could take and still keep its occupant alive and fighting. The shielding could probably survive an attack by two, maybe even three of the Alliance bomblets. But by the time dozens of them had done their job, all that remained of the two marines were floating and expanding composites, liquid, gasses and gnarled bits of frozen flesh. The marine from Luna had been smart enough to stop moving her legs, which had probably saved her, but her oddly prone status had managed to attract the attention of two bomblets and as a result the legs she'd stopped moving were now missing and all that was left of them were two bloody stumps. Her screams over the com were deafening.

Thomas checked to see that his daughter was okay and then he checked himself. Only then did he use his command overrides to take control of the injured marine's battle armor. It had already sealed the breaches were her legs had once been but he ordered her Med-Kit to inject the max tranq dose—both for her comfort and the relief of his and Sally's eardrums. Once the immediate perimeter was clear, he dragged the comatose marine to the shallow depression he'd found for Sally and himself and then secured her to the ground.

"Something tells me," Sally said, looking over at the unconscious marine and then back to the barren landscape, "that we won't be linking up with Bravo squad."

"What?" said Thomas, absent-mindedly trying to rub his long-healed broken nose. He then smiled awkwardly on Sally's you-can't-do-that-with-your-helmet-on look. Thomas moved his hand away and continued. "You're upset we won't be breaking the bank at the blackjack tables?"

"It's not that," said Sally, the corners of her mouth twisting downwards. "I was hoping to get to the whorehouse.

Thomas's eyes widened. "The what?"

"I heard the men were enhanced and genetically designed to be longer-lasting. Called 'em 'Eveready Bunnies' or something."

Thomas stared at his daughter, slack-jawed until the corners of her mouth crept back upwards. He started to laugh and then a moment later they both were.

"We're the only ones left, aren't we?" his daughter asked suddenly.

Thomas pulled out his camo blanket and motioned for Sally to hand him hers. He then combined the two and once beneath it, the three marines looked to all the worlds, and most Alliance sensors, like just another pile of rubble on giant rock filled with them.

"Yes," he finally said.

Grief, sobriety and anger flickered across Sally's face like fire pit shadows on a moonless night. "But there were 5,000 of us when we landed."

Thomas sighed heavily. "And now there are three. Well," he said looking over to the comatose marine with a lopsided grin, "maybe two and a half."

That elicited a brief smile from Sally.

Both Their HODs flashed a perimeter breach warning. They went silent as Thomas activated the blanket's passive scanner. One second later they had their answer.

Sally's eyes took in the Alliance frigate then went as cold as the asteroid's surface. "We're going to get captured and spend the rest of the war as corpsicles orbiting Eris, aren't we?"

"We should be so lucky, look again."

As Sally did, the ground began to rumble. The Alliance frigate was emptying a multitude of tiny objects from its bowels. Typhoeus, the monstrous immortal storm-giant imprisoned by Zeus, was back and his ship was a metal cloud unleashing a torrent of exploding rain.

"Oh, fuck me," she whispered, "they're sanitizing the whole Damsah-cursed rock."

"Guess we put up a better fight than we thought. I give us four minutes, five tops."

"Fucking Alliance bastards,"

"It's not as if we haven't done the same to them." Thomas's words hung for a moment. "Or worse."

"You keep on defending them!"

"All things being equal, I think they're right." Sally knew this wasn't a death's door confession, just her father's forthrightness.

"But you've killed so many of them."

"Your point?"

"I dunno. In my book that makes them wrong."

"3 minute, ten seconds. Because they're trying to kill you, Cookie. Right or wrong has nothing to do with it. So, we going to stop this frigate or what?"

Sally's face betrayed her irritation. "How? By scolding it to death?"

Thomas smiled. "Me? I'm just going to provide the distraction. *You're* going to destroy it."

"With?" she asked.

He handed her a grenade. "This."

She looked at it and her father with incredulity.

"I agree," he said before should could speak. "But luckily that is not an Alliance frigate. It's one of ours that they've captured. Two minutes, forty-seven seconds."

Sally looked at the image in the HOD and nodded. "So it is, and that matters how?"

Thomas sighed. "Too much time with Eveready Bunnymen, not enough time with manuals."

"Thomas Meadows Ryan!" She whispered, nostrils flared. That she'd used his real name revealed just how on edge she was.

"Okay, Cookie. That's a Raider-class frigate. When it stops propulsion, it opens a small exhaust port on its lower section near the rear anti-missile defense battery."

Sally's eyes narrowed. "Really."

"Yes," he said, sharing an image on her HOD. "It's open."

"And?" she asked through gritted teeth, "when we fire this thing, the battery will get it way before it reaches the port, assuming it's even open."

"I said nothing about firing it."

"But …"

"You're going to throw it. No weapons exhaust plus some clever programming means the grenade will look like just another piece of floating debris."

"I'm going to …" Sally's face twisted further into confusion. "The second I stand up, they'll hone in on me!"

"Which is why I've slaved every one of our squads' weapons left on this Damsah-forsaken rock to mine. Right before you get up, they'll all start going off. The friendly fire mechanism will keep them from tracking on you and the grenade but the melee should confuse the frigate's targeting scanners quite nicely, especially with all the debris floating up from the surface. That should give you time to make the throw. One minute fifty."

"That is a *two-kilometer* throw against a moving target not much bigger than what I'd be throwing. It can't be done."

"Cookie, of course it can. You pitched baseball."

"I didn't have to throw the ball two kilometers!"

"Sally, we don't have gravity here. Well, not much anyways. You could throw that grenade a million kilometers."

"But I can't hit that target," she said, beginning to wilt.

Thomas took her hand into his. "Cookie, I've seen you pitch no hitters against schools with GE's." He'd used the nickname given to anyone who'd obviously been genetically enhanced.

"Wait a minute. You saw me? Holo-vid?"

Thomas shook his head.

"I didn't see you," she said, lost in memory.

"You were fourteen. You'd stopped looking by then."

"Daddy, I never stopped looking."

"You wouldn't have recognized me, Baby Girl. I wasn't even the right gender."

"But why … the danger."

"60 Seconds" flashed in their HOD's. They both knew it was only an estimate but that was of little comfort.

"Sally," Thomas said, "I came to every game I could—thirteen in all—and they were the best games I ever saw." He moved his hands up to the side of her helmet and stared deeply into her eyes. "You can do this."

The ground started shaking more violently as the frigate drew closer and its deadly cargo emptied onto the barren landscape.

"You son of a bitch," she said, her face lighting up. "You were at my games."

Thomas nodded with a shit-eating grin.

Sally looked down at the grenade in her hand and nodded back.

"Okay, in three, two and GO!"

All at once every weapon still loaded and working started going off. Private Sally Meadows stood up, used her helmet's scanner to locate the target and, adjusting for the asteroid's movement against the ship's, made the second best pitch of her life.

The grenade sailed into the exhaust port and detonated with two seconds left to spare.

UHF Capital of Burroughs
Mars

Father and daughter were walking away from an awards ceremony where they'd both been onstage almost as props. The story Thomas had convinced Sally to follow would have allowed for no other outcome.

"So Amy gets the UHF order of Valor and all we get is a seven-day pass."

"Rather generous, if you ask me," answered Thomas dryly.

Sally shook her head. What seemed a convoluted mess of a story to her, the UHF High Command had bought lock, stock and barrel: When the UHF had gotten to Leary's Casino they found 5,000 dead UHF marines, a crashed Alliance frigate with the crew safely evacuated and the ship stripped of almost all equipment that could be salvaged, one legless hero and two unconscious dimwits who couldn't even hold on to their weapons,. The badly degraded battle data did tell enough of the story for the Central Command to piece together what had happened. Apparently when all seemed lost, Private Amy Fromage had managed to throw a grenade into the exhaust valve of the enemy frigate. She then dragged the surviving two incapacitated UHF marines to safety (the Central Command refused to use the word 'faint'). Unfortunately, some falling debris had pinned her down, forcing the amputation of her legs. But she'd still been found with an asteroid-pellet loaded ARG down to a 3% charge, her mutilated, unconscious body protecting her two perfectly healthy and utterly useless comrades.

The UHF had a hero, whom they extolled to the heavens. They also had two, at best incompetents or at worst cowards, who they'd effectively pushed under the rug. If it weren't for the fact that every trained marine was needed and that cashiering the two out of the service would have proved too embarrassing, both Sally and Thomas would've been court martialed and thrown out of the service.

Thomas had been hoping for that outcome, actually. But in the end, Sally agreed to go along with the story. If anyone looked too closely at his background he would not have been able to answer questions that in normal times would have been asked. But the need for heroes was too great and the need to ignore cowards was almost as strong. So when "Asteroid Amy's" story was told and told again, Thomas and Sally were either completely ignored or merely referred to as the two incapacitated marines. They'd each gotten a six-month reprieve from the war and now that the publicity show of Amy's medal ceremony was over, they'd both been given a seven day pass with one real order—"Do not draw attention to yourselves." Any reporters who did manage to track them down were to be directed to the hero. Although this suited Thomas just fine, his daughter was still smarting over it.

"Doesn't it bother you," she asked as they walked down Sambianco Boulevard.

"The 1/3 gravity?" answered Thomas. "Not that much."

Sally's eyes flared. "I'm not asking about the gravity and you know it."

"You're not?" asked Thomas coyly.

"No one knows what we did or who we are. Worse, if they do know, they think we're cowards."

"Better that than a psyche audit, don't you think?"

"Yes, but …"

"But …" he coaxed.

"Dammit, I took out an Alliance frigate with a Damsah-forsaken grenade and a two kilometer throw. And no one knows I did it!"

Thomas mouthed her exact words as she said them, causing Sally to gut him with her eyes.

"How could it not bother you?" she asked, "It's bugging the crap out of me!"

Thomas's face registered a conviction and resoluteness she hadn't yet seen. "Because," he answered calmly, "the only thing I care about is you. It makes my life much simpler and my ego much smaller. I don't need to be a hero. I need …"—Thomas's voice cracked—"I need to be a father."

Sally stopped walking, forcing Thomas to turn back towards her.

"I love you, Dad."

"I love you too, Cookie. Now can I please arrange for us to disappear? Keeping you alive is getting harder all the time."

O O O

Sally didn't answer immediately. "But we're finally making a real difference in this war—even if no one notices."

"An unjust war."

"A war that cost Emily her life," Sally answered through thin, bloodless lips.

"It's not worth yours, Cookie."

"But what if that's what it takes?"

Thomas smiled sadly and they walked on in silence, still not agreeing on the point, as always.

O O O

Coffee had become the main drink of the UHF, given that the best plantations were still on Earth. But Tea had become the drink of the Outer Alliance as Saturn had developed dozens of asteroid farms dedicated to growing the plants. Cody Foster would have been more daring and ordered tea but now that Thomas Meadows was back, new face and all, behavior had to change. He ordered a cup of patriot blend coffee just like a marine in dress uniform should. He and Sally were discussing their "out" plan. Taking a boat cruise of the 1,000 Canals, one of Mar's most spectacular sights, was one of them. Sally wanted to hit the clubs and go "flirting" as she referred to it, sparing her father's humorously prudish feelings. They were just starting to reach a point of compromise when someone tapped Sally on the shoulder.

"Gemmy!" she shouted and bounced up out of her chair to hug her friend, forgetting the 1/3rd gravity. Gem had to grab Sally and bring her back to the ground.

Gem's face was pure marine. "That's Field Sergeant Suttikul to you, Private."

Sally looked at Gem in momentary confusion until Gem broke the spell with a radiant smile.

"Asshole!"

"Shitwipe!"

After the two hugged, Sally looked over to her dad. "Oh, uh, Gem, this is my father, Thomas."

"It's an honor to meet the man who's taking such good care of his daughter." With a knowing glance, Gem activated a switch on her belt. "And, I might add, disguising himself so well." Then she slapped Thomas hard enough that the sound of her hand striking the back of his head echoed across the room

Thomas laughed through his obvious pain. "Not well enough, apparently."

"That," said Gem, "is for being stupid enough to keep the broken nose. It's a direct link to Cody!"

"Who's Cody?" asked Thomas innocently.

Gem raised her hand for another blow.

"I had to keep it."

"What on Mars for?"

"It was from my daughter," he answered softly.

"Of all the stupid, sentimental, pointless, dangerous …"

Gem's use of adjectives was inventive and seemingly inexhaustible but Sally noticed her best friend's hand was now lowered.

O O O

"I can't believe High Command bought it," Gem said, relaxing on the luxury deck of the ER Burroughs. Sally and Thomas had parked themselves in deck chairs next to her. The Cruise ship was filled with soldiers on leave, their "friends" as well as a leavening of corporate executives. "I mean we are supposed to have an Intelligence Department in the military aren't we?"

"We're a lazy species by nature," answered Thomas. "It's one of the traits I relied on in my old profession."

Sally looked over at her father and raised her brow slightly. He never hinted to anyone about his past—ever. Sally figured he'd either had too much to drink—doubtful—or perhaps Gem had managed to fuck her way into family status—probable. Gem and her dad had been spending a fair amount of time together. Sally should've been upset that it wasn't with her mom but that quickly passed. Sally no longer thought of her father as the man Augustine Cooper had married. He was in a totally different class now: Thomas Meadows—warrior/conman.

"Give 'em an easy enough script," continued Thomas, "and they'll follow it."

"And now," grumbled Sally, "no self-respecting unit will have me."

"More time away from the war," Thomas said, contentment evident in every line of his face.

"It should bug you, T.M.," said Gem, using the new nickname she'd given him. "The war needs bodies. Which means no matter what, you'll eventually end up right back in it. Only this time with some idiot no one else wants to work with who'll get you and Sally killed."

"I've got my connections," answered Thomas.

Gem was unimpressed. "That'll only take you so far. What's your plan after that?"

Thomas raised his drink. "We're supposed to be relaxing, right? I'll think of something, I'm sure."

Gem's eyes were fixed and determined. "Why don't you join my unit?"

"Uh," began Thomas, "Given our activities over the past couple of days I may have a tough time separating the private from the professional."

"Don't worry, T.M. You may but I won't." And for a brief moment the tiny, bikini-clad woman relaxing on the deck chair with the sugary sweet drink had all the menace of the trained killer who'd left countless bodies in her Valkyrian wake.

Thomas twitched a nervous a nervous smile. "I guess not."

"Besides it won't be permanent," continued Gem. "Once you both get a few missions under your belt, I'll have no problem transferring you to another unit in my fleet."

"*Your* fleet?" Sally said, eyebrow raised.

"Okay, Admiral Trang's fleet. But it's the best in the UHF. He wouldn't have let 5,000 marines to die on a rock like that idiot Tully. If he couldn't have supported the landing, he wouldn't have done it."

"I hear Tully's taking credit for the successful conquest of Leary's Casino," said Sally. "Like he planned it that way!"

Thomas raised his glass. "Damsah help the poor souls who end up in that idiot's fleet."

Gem nodded. "Which'll be you if you don't take me up on my offer." Then she used the one argument she knew was going to work on the man who was currently Thomas Meadows. Looking over to Sally she said, "And that will be her."

It took Thomas and Sally a moment to realize they'd been had. That Gem had arranged everything—the "chance" meeting, the cruise, the lovemaking, the evening's deck soiree—all in order to make her irrefutable point. The father and daughter smiled knowingly.

"What are your orders?" said Thomas.

"Why don't you carry me back to the cabin and we'll figure something out?" she said, smiling mischievously. And that is exactly what he did.

Year 4 of 7 of the Unincorporated War
Fourth Battle of Anderson's Farm

Sally and Thomas were on the rock for three hours—a record for a UHF force on Anderson's farm—when Sally's world came crashing down. She'd entered a warren and had managed to clear it using grenade-shaped charges. It was at the moment of feeling good about another job well done when she saw the body. She could tell by the blood-damaged eyes that the brain was beyond repair—a permanent death. It was a boy who could not have been more than sixteen and even more horrific, looked eerily like her younger brother, Lee. It was not an exact likeness but it was close enough, especially the way the kid had worn his hair—grown long, set it in place with a saucer-like depression at the top; like having a bowl permanently balanced on your head. It was such a stupid look that Sally was convinced that Lee had gotten it just to bug her. It had never occurred to her that the Alliance could have stupid, annoying teenagers too.

"Dad," she called out over their private com.

Thomas was over in an instant.

She pointed at the body. "I killed a kid."

Thomas nodded serenely then pointed to another one further down; a girl, not more than 12—clearly the sibling. Sally threw up in her helmet. The suit cleared the mess in seconds.

"Sergeant," barked Thomas over the com, "The tunnel's clear, front and back about fifty yards. Private Meadows got her head rattled by the blast. I'm taking her back twenty meters till she settles."

"Understood, Corporal," came Gem's crisp reply. "Good job. Take all the time you need. Just so long as it's not more than ten minutes."

"Yes, Sergeant," said Thomas, gently moving Sally back down the tunnel. He toggled them back to private communications. "Cookie, you had no choice. They would've killed you."

"Why does the Alliance recruit and send children to fight us? What's wrong with them?"

"I don't think they recruited anyone," he said gently. "I saw the names on the suits—Anderson."

Sally stopped looking down at her feet and looked up at her dad.

"Baby Girl, they weren't sent here. "They never left."

"Home," whispered Sally, trying to understand and desperately trying not to.

"The home we came to … and attacked."

"We came to their … home," said Sally finally beginning to understand. "And … and I killed them. I murdered that little girl. Oh God." Tears pricked the corners of her eyes. "She … she didn't even get to be as old as Emily."

Thomas waited patiently for the tears to stop flowing before he continued. "Sally, my dear darling girl, yes you killed them. But if you hadn't, I would've. Them and everyone else on this cursed rock. I don't care about the UHF or the Alliance. I'll kill everyone I must to get you out of this war alive. As long as you have to fight this war I will fight it with you."

A heavy sigh escaped from Sally's downturned mouth. "I don't have to … *want* to … fight this war anymore, Daddy."

Thomas Ryan closed his eyes and nodded, a barely perceptible smile could be discerned through the battle-scarred helmet. "Once this battle is over, Honey, you won't have to. We're going to go back to Mars and Thomas and Sally Ryan will disappear."

Sally nodded. "We have to talk to Holly and Lee. I have to let them know. They can't join up."

Thomas patted Sally on the shoulder. "We'll send them a coded communication. You can tell them what they need to hear. Maybe they'll even hear it if it comes from you."

O O O

Neither of them saw the boy. He was as silent and undetectable as only a lifetime spent on a rock he called home could make him and he was going to avenge his brother and sister even if he'd die trying. The boy dropped behind Thomas and Sally, charge in hand. The father and daughter's HOD's instantly made them aware of the intruder. They both spun to face their foe, ARG's raised to fire, but Sally knocked Thomas's aside as the boy's charge landed at their feet. Thomas nodded at his daughter in pride.

O O O

The emergency cryo-units were prepped and ready by the time Gem cleared the tunnel. The Medic leapt to the prone forms. "Sell me for a penny stock," he said, relief evident in his tone, "they're alive."

Gem closed her eyes and thanked an uncaring universe. She supervised the placing of her two most important humans in the universe, making sure they were safe and secure.

"You're safe now," Gem whispered over Sally's body. "I told you I wouldn't abandon you again." She kissed her fingers and touched it to the top of Sally and Thomas's helmeted foreheads and ordered the units sealed. She then made sure that the units were taken to the secure triage area.

Gem had been tempted to go with them just to make 100% sure that nothing went wrong. But at the end of the day, she was still a sergeant in the UHF Marine Corp and she had a job to do.

O O O

One hour, fourteen minutes later Sergeant Suttikul's job was over. She'd missed the signs; missed the telltale signature of nanite subterfuge and so had missed the Alliance assault miners waiting in ambush. She remained alive long enough to watch her unit slaughtered before her eyes. Even as one of the attackers plunged a mining laser through her back and out her chest.

"Die, you child-murdering piece of shit," snarled the attacker. He expertly flipped her body over in order to shove the drill into Sergeant Suttikul's brain, making the death permanent. But as the drill was poised over Gem's helmet, the attacker suddenly stopped, his face paling to a shade of gray almost as deathly as the landscape he'd suddenly sprung from.

"Oh, dear God, no," he whispered, as the drilled floated down to the ground. "MEDIC!" he screamed.

The medic was at his side in moments, surprised to see his commander cradling a fallen UHF marine in his arms. "Sir?" he asked in confusion.

"Save her."

"But, Captain, we may not have enough cryo-units for our own wounded. Why waste it on a fucking …" then the medic saw the name stenciled on the marine's armor and realized at once what was going on. "Jesus."

"Save her," pleaded the officer once again.

"You got it, Captain." And he bent down and activated the suit's protocols to oxygenate the brain and reduce its temperature. A cryo-unit was rushed up.

As the body was placed inside, the captain put his hand on the woman's helmet. "You'll be safe now, little one. You'll be healed and put in secure storage far, far away from this war. When you wake up again it will be over and you'll be safe."

He stifled his tears. His greatest nightmare had happened, and it was over. Exactly one hour and fourteen minutes later a thermite charge exploded, vaporizing Captain Mel Suttikul and most of his unit. His daughter would never know the man who'd both killed and saved her.

Ceres: Capital of the Outer Alliance
Year 7 of 7 of the Unincorporated War

She remembered the explosion, remembered killing her father, or at least allowing him to be killed. But she couldn't allow the boy to be hurt. She'd killed far too many innocent people. She'd chosen to be killed rather than kill again. It had brought her such peace, that decision.

But Sally Meadows Ryan had not expected to wake up—and certainly not in pain. *This doesn't happen*, she thought to herself.

"I'm sorry about this." The voice was strangely mellifluous—almost in direct contrast the extraordinary amount of pain. "You will not be awake long, but I needed to talk with you."

"It … it burns!"

"You and your father have been purposely infected with nanites by an entity that had planned to use you both to horrible ends, a side effect of which has been to make your nervous system even more efficient."

"Side effect!?" screamed Sally, as sweat began pouring off her body.

"I have managed to limit your suffering quite a bit, but any more intervention and you will not be cogent enough to make the decision."

"Who ... did," she let out a scream as the pain of what felt like a thousand needles exploded through every one of her joints.

"His name was Al," the voice answered. "He was killed by my"—there was a slight pause as the voice seemed to search for the proper word—"father. That may be the closest analogy you would understand."

"Questions ..." uttered Sally through her clenched teeth. It was the only word she could manage.

"You can call me, 'Pam,'" said the decidedly masculine voice. "You're here because in trying to undo the horrors committed by Al I discovered you and your father."

"But ... we were killed ... Anderson's Farm."

"Not killed. I can assure you. I have the records from your sergeant." Then Sally saw and heard Gem's efforts to find and secure them. Even though the blaze of pain she was touched by Gem's parting kiss and parting words. "You survived but I must ask you to decide for you and your father if you wish to continue to survive?"

"What?"

"Sally Ryan, you and your father were diverted and the records changed. As far as the human race is concerned you died on Anderson's Farm."

"But ... Gem ... she saw."

"Everyone was either killed or suspended. Sergeant Suttikul is frozen in a prison cryo-center in orbit around Eris."

Safe, thought Sally. A smile appeared momentarily through her clenched jaw.

"Please, this is taking too long and I can't keep up the pain abatement for long. Listen and answer. I can save you and your father but it will take time."

"How much time?"

"Long enough that history will have moved one. I can give no specific answer, but your time and place will be long gone. Do I have your permission to suspend you and begin the healing process?"

"Gem," said Sally.

"Your sergeant is fine," said Pam. "She is due to be awakened soon."

"She'll … know we didn't die. She'll … search." Sally then let out a scream as the shockwave of pain hit her once more.

"She won't find you. You're going far away. Farther than you can know."

"Won't stop. You … don't know her … can't stop."

"I can't tell Sergeant Suttikul where you are. I have another I must protect," Pam answered. It was evident in his voice that he was not sure what to do with the unanticipated complication.

"Let us die … leave … bodies where they'll be found," answered Sally. "Gem deserves … life."

The voice of Pam sighed. "I cannot take that risk. I'm sorry. I can grant you your death, but I cannot let you be found—at least not right now."

"Not … location. Hope," Sally said to the surrounding shadows.

Pam chuckled. "Humans," he said with obvious affection. "Very well, Sally Ryan. I promise that your Gem Suttikul will have 'hope' concerning you and your father."

Sally nodded her assent and collapsed, a weak smile forming at the edge of her lips.

It was the last sentence she heard before fading into blessed, if somewhat temporary oblivion.

The End

EPILOGUE

Archeologist 1st class Katherine Black had returned after far more years than she would've thought possible. It was like wandering through the halls of a legendary castle. But she remembered these halls and it wasn't legend, it was home—one she hadn't visited since childhood.

It had taken Katherine and her companion the better part of a week to find the chamber. There'd been rumors of its existence but she wasn't foolish enough to believe in them. No, what Katherine chased were leads; leads that had led them to this one spot, on this one asteroid—the most famous in human history. They could have spent a thousand years looking and not found it. But technology had gotten better in the time since the room went dark and find it they had, guarded by an avatar no less; one as much out of legend as the place itself. Unlike the legends of old, this guardian was friendly. Indeed it seemed he'd been waiting for them for quite some time.

Katherine turned to her companion. "Well?"

Her friend nodded nervously. There was a strange calm about her that Katherine had never seen in their centuries-long friendship.

"So, what are you waiting for? The Blessed One to come back to life and give you an invitation?" Katherine looked over to the suspension chamber. "Wake her up!"

O O O

Sally's eyes flittered open. Her last memory rose up like driftwood from the depths of a sea. It was of a voice talking to her, but how long ago? Her vision was blurred and now there was a new voice, one more gentle and familiar. Then her vision cleared.

"Gemmy!" she said as loud as her unused vocal chords could muster. She tried to raise herself out of the suspension unit but could not. Her body was still unwilling. Gem, tears now flowing freely, reached in and with the delicacy of a mother cradling her infant for the very first time, pulled Sally up into her arms and didn't let go for a very long time.

"I told you I wouldn't abandon you again," Gem whispered softly and then with her achingly familiar mock stern voice, "and by the way, it's Archeologist 2nd Class Suttikul to you."

"My dad …"

"In the chamber behind this one."

Sally's eyes widened. "Nanites … infected."

Gem gave her friend's shoulders a reassuring squeeze. "He's fine. Pam told us everything. The only nanites left are the good ones. We'll wake your dad next."

Sally nodded gratefully. She was able to slowly move her head. "Where … are we?"

"Ceres," answered Katherine. Sally looked over her.

"That's my friend, Katy," said Gem. "You can thank her later."

Sally thanked the stranger with her eyes and looked back to Gem. "Ceres." Then the rest of her conversation with Pam returned. "I … thought Pam said we were going far away."

"Oh, we are, you have no idea."

"Not near Mars?"

"Not even close."

"And the Outer Alliance?"

Both Katherine and Gem giggled. "Well, let's just say it hasn't been a factor in galactic affairs for a long, long time."

"Galactic affairs?" Sally repeated in confusion. "How long have I been down?"

"Discounting relativity factors," Gem said as if discussing the weather, "10,826 years,"

Sally desperately tried to wrap her mind around the number. "Impossible."

Gem's lips drew back impishly. "You think that's impossible?" she asked, turning her back to indicate the far wall, "Just wait till I tell you who's in *that* chamber."

ESCAPE HATCH

KEVIN J. ANDERSON

1

The mass of alien tentacles writhed over the side of the Earth Planetary Navy destroyer. When the *Far Horizon*'s Admiral Bruce Haldane saw the vicious things crash onto the deck and scatter in all directions, he knew the battle was lost. There was no stopping the swarm of Sluggos.

Rough seas rocked the destroyer, but the grim crew who manned the guns against the worm things were not worried about getting seasick.

The enormous cluster of alien creatures also attacked from beneath the surface, hammering the *Far Horizon*'s armored hull. The thunderous clang was even louder than the explosive artillery. *How could something so soft and squishy sound so loud?* he wondered, then stalked along the deck, a weapon in each hand as he shot the swarming slugs. Each creature exploded with a disgusting splat of oozing protoplasm. The ship's crew were running up and down the open deck, wading through smashed Sluggos, but the things kept coming from below.

Unstoppable.

Each alien was the length and thickness of Haldane's forearm, looking like a beige banana slug with teeth. The Sluggos combined and moved in concert, wrapping their wormlike bodies together to form a larger organism. Thousands of Sluggos braided into a giant tentacle that rose up from the rough seas to wrap around the destroyer, and then dissolving into countless ravenous components again. The Sluggos squirmed forward, mouths chomping. They were blind, but they were hungry, and there were so many of them that the doomed crew had no place to hide.

Admiral Haldane was grim, but he drove back his panic. As their leader, he had to focus on the fight. His crew was yelling, some clearly fearful because they had just begun to realize they were all going to die. They didn't have an escape hatch. Knowing he could give his all and still live to fight another day let Haldane concentrate on the crisis and do what was necessary, without being crippled by fear of his own mortality.

"Keep shooting! By God, there's no shortage of targets!"

The lower decks had been infested, and evacuating sailors had come out into the open. One of the nearby seamen, his dungarees splotched with yellow-green ichor and bright red blood, fired his sidearm until it was empty, then snatched another still-hot weapon from the hands of a dying seaman on the deck. The wounded seaman's abdomen had been ripped open, and his guts spilled out like another swarm of Sluggos. Without pause, the desperate seaman continued firing, each bullet exploding one—or more—of the squirming aliens.

"Aye, sir. It's not a shortage of targets we're worried about, Admiral," he shouted over his shoulder. "It's running out of ammo."

Haldane kept firing his own sidearm, not even making a dent in the invasion. He shouted back, hoping he sounded encouraging, "According to the weapons locker manifest, we should have ten thousand rounds aboard the *Far Horizon*." The number sounded impressive, objectively, but not in comparison to the million hungry Sluggos swarming over the destroyer. He had opened the armory and distributed weapons as widely and as swiftly as possible, to the Marines as well as to any other sailor with fingers and thumbs.

Everyone aboard would be alien food before long. Haldane felt sorry for them, but he'd make sure they got a nice memorial ceremony back in La Diego.

After humanity had ventured away from Earth and set up fledgling colonies on the Moon, Mars, and the asteroid belt, nobody ever guessed that an alien invasion would target Earth's oceans. The invaders had landed in the Pacific, emerged from their interstellar spaceships, and began swarming through the seas.

The slimy creatures moved like a gigantic school of fish, thousands of separate pieces that formed a sentient community organism—an incomprehensible alien creature that managed to build starships, travel across space, to plunge into Earth's oceans, where they reproduced at a furious pace—whether by fission, or breeding, or eggs, no one knew—and swiftly became a terrible hazard.

They attacked ships, sinking commercial freighters, cruise liners, fishing vessels. The Earth Planetary Navy was little more than a token force, peacekeepers and emergency responders. It had been a long time since battle fleets went on a full-scale war footing. Now, the EPN went on the hunt, combing the waters in search of the enemy.

Sonar could detect the large clusters of Sluggos, which then vanished with each pulse and then re-formed elsewhere. Admiral Haldane had already led two preliminary engagements, each one disastrous. He was about to make it three for three.

Reaching this point in the South Pacific, the suspected location of the original Sluggo starships, the *Far Horizon* had dropped dozens of depth pulsers hoping to destroy the underwater alien base. The explosions had been wonderful, creating rooster-tails of water like massive geysers. The shock waves should have ruined any Sluggo structures on the ocean floor.

The excitement was short-lived, though. The individual aliens had combined into a monstrous body, countless squirming components adding together like cells. Then the community organism rose up like the most twisted nightmare of any sailor's legend and attacked the *Far Horizon.*

The shapeless beast shifted and rearranged its bodily blueprint, first engulfing the destroyer with tentacles and then smashing onto the deck in a huge flat mass like a manta, which then dissolved into an overwhelming slimy army of individual Sluggos that could attack—and devour.

Constant gunfire continued to ring out, and even ten thousand rounds didn't last very long. When the crew ran out of ammo, they used metal pipes, tools, even small storage pods, to smash the things. Someone had rigged a flamethrower and jetted fire that fried the wormlike aliens. When their protoplasm boiled, they exploded, but the Sluggos did not feel pain or fear, and more of them came forward. One young seaman thrashed as a dozen of the worm-things chewed into the meat of his thighs and calves, then tunneled through his chest. He kept screaming until one crawled down his throat.

Other seamen had better luck with fire extinguishers, driving the Sluggos away, briefly, but there was no place to hide. Each extinguisher ran out within minutes, and the crew used the empty tanks to smash more Sluggos.

"Turn the heavy-caliber guns down," Haldane yelled. "Fire into the water!"

"But, sir, that'll do nothing!"

"It'll make some big explosions," he shouted back. That was something at least.

At central fire control, weapons officers tilted the large-bore the guns down, and the guns roared, but even the heavy shells did little more than stir up the Sluggos in the water. In response, a huge pseudopod composed of braided Sluggos lurched up, wavered in the air just long enough for Haldane to estimate the tens of thousands of hungry creatures that comprised it, then it dissociated in midair, creating a rain of hungry Sluggos that fell onto the *Far Horizon*.

Haldane had found shelter under the bridge wing, but he watched the crew get slaughtered. He had emptied both of his sidearms, and he had no other defenses but his bare hands and his boot heels. The squirming aliens came at him like an unstoppable invertebrate tide....

No one in the EPN had had more direct experience with the Sluggos than Admiral Bruce Haldane. He had studied their movements firsthand in three engagements now, seen how they attacked. He made mental notes. Even though he didn't understand what he saw, his knowledge was irreplaceable. If Earth was going to win this war against the undersea invasion, *he* had to survive.

The overburdened destroyer was groaning, listing to starboard, clearly taking on water from belowdecks. The pounding Sluggos had chewed and torn through the lower hull and were even now swarming through the breach, infesting the ship even faster than seawater could fill it. Damage control crews had been devoured as they rushed to respond. The destroyer was going down.

As he backed against the bulkhead, he watched hundreds of Sluggos burst through the hatches, huge maggots writhing up the ladders and spilling onto the deck. Even with the din of gunfire, explosions, and shouts, Haldane could hear them moving around in the compartments below, feasting.

Then they came toward him.

Most of the *Far Horizon*'s crew had been slaughtered already, but Haldane stood straight and proud, facing the alien enemy. He owed it to the brave men and women who perished here: He would stay until the very last as the hordes of fleshy bodies and chewing mouths squirmed toward him. He kicked at the Sluggos, but more and more came.

The admiral raised his voice and announced to anyone left on deck who might be able to hear him, "I want to thank you all for your service. Your lives will not be lost in vain."

As the Sluggos swarmed over him, Haldane reached behind his head and hit the transfer pendant embedded at the base of his skull. His escape hatch.

He was going to miss this body, which had served him well for the past six weeks, but he gave little thought to the volunteer seaman who would transfer with him at the last moment. If Admiral Haldane timed it right, the volunteer would feel only a few seconds of pain as the Sluggos devoured him.

It was what the volunteer had signed up for: He was just cannon fodder, and he had played the odds. Haldane couldn't even remember his name. Now it was time for the man to do his duty so that the valuable, experienced naval admiral could live to fight another day.

Haldane felt the alien jaws rip into his flesh. The pain was horrific, and he was glad to be out of that body.

2

When Paulson Kenz picked up his mail, he expected to find bills, junk mailers, delinquent notices on his student loan, even another eviction threat because his low-paying job didn't earn him enough to pay the rent and eat both in the same week.

The urgent draft notice, however, was far worse than any stack of bills or legal notices.

Paulson stared at the official envelope for a long time. Some of his friends in equally dire financial straits had talked about joining the military, but in the same distant way that they might talk about travelling to the Moon or signing up for a stint at one of the asteroid colonies.

Paulson knew he wasn't military material by any stretch of the imagination. A recruitment officer should take one look at his scrawny figure and muscles that could at best be described as "bookish," and laugh out loud before telling him to find a job as an accountant or librarian.

But libraries weren't hiring these days, and Paulson had no aptitude for accounting. With the increasing attacks by the alien Sluggos, however, the Earth Planetary Navy wasn't so picky.

His dismissive parents always told Paulson he was going nowhere, and now he had arrived—at nowhere. But now, as he held the EPN summons in his hand, he felt a chill. He would much rather be going nowhere than going into the planetary navy. Only the most desperate of military forces would take a bottom-of-the-barrel recruit like him, and if the EPN was that desperate then the human race was in dire straits indeed.

Retreating into his small apartment, he thought about calling his friends or his parents, but he didn't think his voice was stable enough for conversation. The draft notice allowed for no appeal. He needed to think about this, but the more Paulson considered his fate, the more terrified he became. He had been aware of the horrific alien invaders that attacked helpless vessels in the Pacific, but since he lived in a farming city in the Midwest, with little local industry, automated agriculture, nothing to attract tourists and very few job prospects, Paulson hadn't paid much attention to the Sluggos.

The notice commanded him to report to the training facility at the La Diego Naval Yards within three days.

The draft summons was legally binding and intimidating. The fine print said that any prior employment or contractual obligations were henceforth superseded. Payments and debts would be put on hold until the end of his EPN service.

Paulson read pages of instructions, a list of what to pack, and a helpful pamphlet on ways to prepare for this "exciting new phase" of his life. He fixated on a paragraph that advised him in the strongest possible terms to prepare a detailed Last Will and Testament before departing for the training facility. "Don't leave your family and loved ones with estate entanglements. Do the last brave thing in the event that you are unable to return home. A sailor in the Earth Planetary Navy must be prepared."

"I'll be prepared to die at sea," Paulson muttered. He didn't even know how to swim, but he supposed that wouldn't matter. If he fell overboard into a sea roiling with voracious Sluggos, treading water wasn't going to be much help.

Sitting alone in his apartment, glad that he had managed to get the power turned back on, he activated his entertainment and information screens to watch the news, which suddenly seemed relevant to him. A terrible nautical engagement and complete defeat had just occurred five hundred miles off the coast of Hawaii. Paulson felt physically ill as he saw the frantic jittery footage of creatures that seemed to be equal parts teeth and slime. The Sluggos swarmed across the deck of the destroyer that had engaged the alien infestation. Crewmen snarling, yelling in pain, sprays of blood, a tentacle the size of a redwood tree crashing down onto the *Far Horizon*, collapsing the bridge deck and communication mast and cutting off the transmission.

On the report, a tall young man with haunted-looking eyes wore a pristine white officer's uniform, his chest bedecked with so many medals and decorations that he had trouble standing up straight. He stood at a podium addressing hundreds of uniformed sailors who stood at attention. Hundreds of media reporters directed their imagers in the officer's direction.

"I am Admiral Bruce Haldane," he said, "and I recently survived the *Far Horizon* engagement. I've faced the Sluggos three times now, and I've watched them destroy brave sailors, wreck civilian ships as well as military vessels. I am convinced there can be no negotiating with these creatures."

Paulson thought he seemed arrogant.

"With my experience and insights, I promise to do my best to develop an effective strategy to defeat these alien monsters. No more sailors need to shed blood into the sea. I am humbled by the sacrifice of all those who died on the *Far Horizon*, as well as the volunteer who formerly inhabited this body." Haldane touched his own shoulders and chest, as if to reassure himself of where and who he was. "That man gave his life so I could stand before you today and vow my revenge against the alien. Thanks to him, I can lead the EPN's retaliatory strike and wipe out those squirming bastards once and for all!"

Admiral Haldane raised a fist, but his movements were jerky and uncertain, as if he hadn't quite adjusted to his new body. It seemed to fit him like a stiff pair of new boots.

The crowd cheered regardless, and the media imagers captured the drawn and determined expressions on the sailors' faces as they vowed to avenge their fallen comrades.

Looking at the crowd of EPN seamen, Paulson could not picture himself as one of them, no matter what the draft notice said. He felt as if he had swallowed a hand grenade, and it was still in his stomach, ticking down the last few seconds. He couldn't run, couldn't escape the summons. He was DNA imprinted, and he had been chosen by a flawed lottery system: no exceptions. And he certainly couldn't argue that he was too valuable in civilian life.

He liked to read and ponder, but had never found the ambition to acquire a philosophy degree (which, in itself would not have led to a lucrative career). He was healthy enough, but only due to biological good fortune; he wasn't overweight, thanks to a natural metabolism. But he was sweating now, as if he had just run a marathon. Paulson didn't have many loose ends to tie up in his life, because he didn't have much of a life.

He had to figure out some way to get to the La Diego base. Because budgets were tight and all finances had to be devoted to constructing new Navy warships and weapons against the Sluggos, Paulson Kenz had to pay his own way to the last place on Earth he wanted to go.

O   O   O

The naval training center was aswarm with new recruits, herded about by junior officers as if they were a separated mass of Sluggos in human form. The chatter of conversation in the giant intake hangar was deafening; announcements over loudspeakers were garbled and incomprehensible. The background noise seemed to increase each time important instructions were given. Paulson expected this routine would have been more organized under normal times, but the EPN was undergoing quite an upheaval as they increased their ranks tenfold in response to the invasion.

Paulson stood among other recruits, some of them shiny-eyed and eager, jabbering with nervous enthusiasm. They pounded one another on the back, laughing and trying to outdo any braggadocio from their comrades. Paulson knew about such attitudes: patriotic young men and women ready to go off and kick some enemy butt. Most often that didn't turn out as planned. Some came home in body bags, others were lost forever. And the ones that did return were haunted for the rest of their lives.

Oddly, with so many disorganized people and so much chaos, the bureaucratic machinery hummed smoothly. Everyone flashed ID access cards and passed through human inventory kiosks into gigantic hangars where lines queued up, snaking around pedestals. Personnel Specialists studied each person that flowed into the larger base.

Paulson was confused and anxious, but he followed the person ahead of him, and he listened to instructions. When yeoman ran a quick gaze over him, studied his ID chip, then sent him into corpsman scan lines, he cooperated. He tried to keep his expression meek (which wasn't difficult at all). The intake officers studied the records displayed on their screens, narrowed their eyes, and frowned at him, then directed Paulson into a different line. Each time he met with more skepticism, was directed into a smaller line. He could tell he was being winnowed out.

They took blood samples and urine samples; they breathalyzed him; they performed a digital rectal examination, then a dental examination (mercifully changing gloves in between). They fitted a mesh hood around his scalp and took a brain scan. They gave him vision test, and then they clucked at all the results.

One nurse who looked as if she had retired from a Valkyrie squad loomed over him, knitting her eyebrows together. She turned to the yeoman at her side and spoke loudly enough to be sure Paulson heard her, "I thought we hit the bottom of the barrel last week."

"Sorry," Paulson said. "If you'd like to excuse me from service, I'll understand."

The Valkyrie-nurse gave him such an intense glare that his scrotal sac shriveled to the size of a prune, even though he had already been thoroughly checked for hernias.

"No one's excused," she said. "If nothing else, you'll do as cannon fodder."

3

Day by day, Admiral Bruce Haldane was growing accustomed to the new body, and he certainly had no time to waste. Fortunately, the volunteer had kept himself in good shape. The body was adequate, with a good frame, well-toned muscles. He was even handsome, in a way. Haldane was growing accustomed to what he saw in the mirror. Instead of being startled, he took the time to study his features, the dark hair, heavy eyebrows, the boyish expression of an innocent young recruit who had seen little horror in his life. But Haldane's eyes looked out from the face, and *he* had seen enough of war in the last few months.

Previously, his career had been soft and dull, but the Sluggos changed all that.

The volunteer's name had been Aaron Shelty, a seaman-apprentice who seemed a perfectly reasonable recruit for the Earth Planetary Navy, but he must have been a coward, because he refused to sign up for actual combat duty. *Too many people have grown as soft as the Sluggos,* Haldane thought.

After the mind transfer, Haldane had glanced through Shelty's dossier, looking at his grades, his performance in basic training. Everything seemed normal. Haldane couldn't understand why the man would sign up as cannon fodder. Shelty had left behind a fiancée, but she was young and pretty; she would find someone else before long. Shelty had parents and a sister, and they would all receive a compassionate and carefully-worded letter thanking them for Mr. Shelty's sacrifice aboard the *Far Horizon*. Haldane certainly appreciated the gesture, otherwise he would have died aboard the destroyer rather than his replacement.

It must have seemed like a good bargain when young Shelty had signed up for the program. The young man had gambled—whether through laziness or cowardice Haldane didn't know—that nothing would happen to Admiral Haldane. And the gamble had backfired on Shelty.

But Haldane benefited, and therefore the EPN benefited, and therefore the human race benefited. The admiral was alive, and he still had his expertise. The Earth Navy could count on him.

Yes, he was glad for Aaron Shelty's sacrifice, but was that sacrifice any more dramatic or extraordinary than that of all those seamen who had died, devoured or crushed under the onslaught of the alien slugs? Haldane didn't think so. Every person needed to do his or her duty, and Haldane needed to do his, even if it meant he had to swap bodies at the last minute and let the old body die on the battlefield. The war depended on him, and so it was worth the hassle.

Haldane looked in the mirror again, ran his fingers through the dark hair, made different expressions as he practiced the movement of his facial muscles. Yes, this body would do. Maybe he'd even pay a visit to Shelty's pretty fiancée. Now wouldn't *that* be a surprise!

But he didn't have time for that. There was a war on. After all the alien creatures were wiped out, however ...

Unless something terrible happened again to him on the battlefield.

This time, the shock of the body transfer hadn't been as dramatic as when his original body was killed, when he'd been forced in that awful last second of indecision to push the transfer button on the implanted pendant, to give up his actual physical form, the one that had emerged from his mother's womb, the one he'd lived with all his life. But during the explosions, the firefight, and the horrific swarming Sluggos, after watching so many uniformed men and women torn to pieces around him, the decision hadn't been so difficult after all.

New body, same old job. He was back at EPN Headquarters in the La Diego main base, briefing world leaders, requesting new ships, more armaments, more depth pulsers, and an expanded fleet to attack the Sluggos.

As he drove in that morning, two Marines had tried to stop him at the outer gate. Though he had a new ID, the system had not updated his fingerprints, photographs, and DNA scans. Haldane made three increasingly angry calls until revised credentials were transmitted back to the guard shack.

After the *Far Horizon* tragedy, he had delivered his grand speech in this new body. Didn't they recognize him? Everyone on Earth should have seen the images of how the destroyer had been torn apart and sunk, all hands lost. How could these Marines not recognize Admiral Haldane's new body? He hated to be reminded that he wasn't as famous as he believed himself to be. Earth itself was under attack! Why wasn't every human being glued to their media and entertainment screens? Didn't they know that the fate of their planet was at stake?

After the fiasco at the guard shack, he finally made it to his office. As he entered, he still met the questioning stares, the double-takes from his staff as they tried to readjust to his new appearance. The Admiral's uniform had been altered, but the rank insignia and name plate were transferred over, same as before. Haldane was still himself, with his demeanor, his facial expressions. They would have to get used to it.

He sat behind his large desk and called up the day's intel reports of aerial flyovers and deep-water scans. His chief of staff, Ms. Tenn, entered the office and stood before his desk, running her eyes up and down his face and uniform. "I have your calendar, sir. If there's anything you need, please let me know."

"I need concentration time to reassess these images. Is there full documentation regarding new intel on the Sluggos? I need to plan our next strategy. There's some piece missing, and because I have the most experience, I'm the one to find it."

"It's all here, sir." Tenn leaned over the desk to activate Haldane's screen, calling up the messages he needed and spreading them out so he could sort and review them in whatever order he chose.

She brought him his usual bitter black coffee, but when he took a sip, it tasted strange. "Are you using a different blend, Lieutenant? Or does the brewer need cleaning?"

"No, Admiral. Same as always."

"Taste it."

He pushed the cup toward her, and she dutifully took a sip. "Tastes awful, sir, just like always."

Haldane shook his head. "Must be these new taste buds. Bring me a variety of coffees, lattes, cappuccinos, espressos. I need to sample them until I find one that tastes right on Aaron Shelty's tongue. Can't do my work without caffeine."

"Certainly, Admiral." She departed.

Haldane took another gulp of the bitter brew, struggled to swallow it, then pushed the cup away. That wouldn't do at all, and the inconvenience was troublesome. He'd have to compile a more detailed dossier about the next volunteer waiting in the wings. Shelty had passed all the required tests and his brain scan had been a match for Haldane's, but no one had thought to ask about his favorite foods or drinks. The admiral made a note of that.

On the screen, he called up the new messages. The Sluggos were damned difficult to locate under the water, but they were such a huge mass, millions of them writhing together, spreading out, moving a gigantic school of fish. Each time sonar bursts tried to pinpoint the location of the main mass, the swarm faded away and reappeared elsewhere. As soon as the mass of Sluggos was spotted, attack aircraft would drop explosives, which would kill a lot of fish and individual Sluggos—thus the military scientists had plenty of specimens, but very few answers. Even after the most horrendous explosions, though, the main Sluggo body would reappear and continue to attack.

All the EPN efforts thus far had only pissed off the squirming invaders, but Haldane wasn't going to use that as an excuse to relent.

Even ineffective explosions were far superior—from a PR standpoint if nothing else—than letting the Sluggos do whatever they liked. The aliens had not proven to be good neighbors.

As humans expanded into the solar system, no one found any evidence of ancient Martian races or prehistoric Venusians, no Selenites under the craters of the Moon, no civilizations under the ice sheets of Europa, no bizarre creatures drifting among the asteroids.

No one knew where the Sluggos came from. Their ships were detected at the edge of the solar system by bored teams of asteroid mappers, but no one noticed their speed or incoming trajectory until the invaders had almost reached Earth orbit. Though the human military scrambled, the metallic teardrop ships hammered into the atmosphere like shotgun pellets and plunged into the Pacific Ocean.

Ships were dispatched to the area to see if they could find wreckage of the alien vessels, while news pundits demanded rescue efforts. Subs and diving bells went down to the crashed ships to save the benevolent alien visitors before they drowned. (Even then, Admiral Haldane knew it was a brash notion to assume that any alien visitor would breathe air instead of water.)

Considering the size of the alien ships, they should have been easy to find even in the deep water, but sonar detected nothing. The vessels seemed to have vaporized on impact.

The first attack struck a far-ranging Japanese whaler, the *Dragon Pearl*. The terrified crew transmitted images and distress signals, wailing for help as squirming conglomerate tentacles rose out of the water to smash the decks. After the initial horror subsided, Haldane thought that the scenes reminded him of a clip from a bad low-budget Japanese giant monster movie, some horrific rubber behemoth rising from the sea to toss about a toy model of a boat.

But the destruction of the *Dragon Pearl* was real, the Sluggos were real, and the alien mass had attacked other cargo ships, an oil tanker (causing great consternation among environmentalists who insisted that the resultant spill was a greater threat to Earth than the alien invasion), and even a large cruise ship—all passengers and crew slaughtered on formal night. Recovered surveillance cameras showed frantic, swanky passengers trying to flee in their fancy tuxedos or slinky cocktail gowns and high heels.

Admiral Haldane had led the first unsuccessful responses against the aliens, embarrassed because he couldn't even find the Sluggos.

When he finally did locate the enemy, they had destroyed his ship, killed his crew, and forced him to evacuate into a different body.

But he was the first one to notice that the Sluggos were pulling some equipment down into the water after destroying the ships, as if they meant to use the components, metals, antennae, even some of the weapons pieces.

The *Far Horizon* had been the Earth Planetary Navy's most heavily armed destroyer, and that too had been utterly destroyed, but Haldane did not feel defeated. He was back again in a new body, and he would continue to fight—although if he continued to die during engagements against the enemy, it would look bad on his record.

Ms. Tenn returned carrying a tray with seven cups of various coffee drinks. "I brought you a variety of options, sir. One of these should do."

"Thank you, Lieutenant," he said, then had a horrible thought. "God, I hope Shelty wasn't a tea drinker." He decided to be methodical about his testing. He closed all the records displayed on his screen. He would review them later.

Haldane fingered the implanted pendant at the base of his skull. Sooner or later he would go out on another brutal engagement. He couldn't put this off. "Ms. Tenn, I want you to go through recruiting records so we can prepare for the worst-case scenario. This body is certainly adequate, but there's no telling what might happen to me. Find me a new volunteer."

4

Boot camp was hell—and Paulson meant that literally, as well as figuratively. (Yes, he did know the proper usage of the term.)

Throughout his life, Paulson was always the last person picked for any team sports activity. He played a good game of archaic chess, but no one considered that a "sport," despite his protestations. Any activity that required coordination, speed, strength or other physical prowess was not his forte. He had done a good job as a statistician, however. When he suggested that he be considered for such a role in the EPN, the training officer simply scowled at Paulson as if he were a form of nematode even lower than the Sluggos.

Because the alien invasion was now of immediate relevance to him, Paulson wanted to spend every spare minute scouring information about the alien invaders infesting Earth's oceans, but that plan quickly went out the porthole. All day long, the training officer tortured the recruits, forced them to do appalling exercises, tested their endurance. He did his best to kill every single trainee through exhaustion, screaming muscles, and cardiac failure before they had a chance to confront their first Sluggo.

Paulson struggled to memorize the rank system of the Earth Planetary Navy—no, EPN called it a *rating* system, just to make it more confusing, he supposed. He struggled to understand who outranked (or was it outrated?) whom. As a practical matter, it made no difference, since as a seaman-recruit, Paulson Kenz was lower than absolutely everyone. Even among the trainees who had been inducted on the same day, Paulson's performance set him apart— and beneath them all.

Inside the gigantic hangars, the recruits marched in ranks, drilling like robots, following nonsensical orders—moving back and forth, side to side, and around in circles, as if that sort of regimented pageantry would impress the alien hordes.

Paulson was in the lowest pay grade, but had no opportunity to spend what he earned. He was too sore, too exhausted and too miserable to read in the evenings. He felt nauseated, so he couldn't even eat the ill-seasoned chow they fed recruits. It seemed a sort of irony—perhaps intentional, perhaps a coincidence—that they had to eat seafood for every meal. Paulson plunged a fork into his fish sticks with a vengeance, as attacking a surrogate Sluggo.

His fellow recruits sat together, growling as they watched footage of the carnivorous slug creatures massacring Earth Navy ships. Some of the pale recruits whimpered in terror and recorded desperate messages for their sweethearts, but Paulson was simply too weary, wrung-out, and broken. He didn't know how he would get through another day.

If he ever did face a mass of Sluggos, he would be too bruised, battered, and weary even to lift a sidearm.

The next day was worse, and so was the day after that. The training officer was trying to toughen them up. The recruits practiced in the shooting range, trying to bull's-eye holographic Sluggos and receiving points for each kill. Paulson proved to be a poor marksman in every respect, although his score improved when they gave him scattershot guns. Paulson fired so many pellets in so many directions that he couldn't help but hit some of the aliens.

"You're lucky," the training officer said. "If the Sluggos attack, there'll be so many of them even you'll be able to cause some damage."

Paulson shuddered. Yes, that made him feel very lucky indeed.

Some of the recruits called the storm tank *fun*—the psychopathic recruits, as far as Paulson was concerned. The training tank simulated a storm-swept sea, cold churning waves complete with whitecaps. The recruits were thrown into the tank and told to struggle their way to a rescue buoy. Once they reached the buoy, they had to key in a safety code and solve some sort of puzzle before they could be retrieved from the freezing water and blowing winds.

Paulson could barely keep himself above the surface, flailing his hands, going under, inhaling water and then coughing it up. Simulated rain splashed his face so he couldn't see, but he felt stinging ice crystals. He shivered uncontrollably. He kicked his feet and tried to swim, but his sodden uniform was heavy and dragged him down. He could make out the other sailors reaching the rescue buoy, completing their tasks, and being yanked out by hover slings. Paulson couldn't do it, though. He went under, struggled back to the surface for a deep breath, and saw that he was drifting farther from the buoy. Even if he made it, he certainly couldn't remember the safety code. At the moment, he couldn't even remember his name.

He drowned during the exercise, one of three failures in the group.

But they revived him, and Paulson rolled over onto his hands and knees, retching onto the deck. He was still wet, freezing, miserable. All his muscles ached. His mouth tasted like vomit and seawater.

The training officer stood there, arms crossed over his chest, shaking his head. "Even a turd knows how to float. You're dumber than a turd. A complete and utter disgrace."

Paulson wasn't going to argue. He sucked a lungful of air and croaked, "I wouldn't want to do anything halfway, Sarge. Glad I'm not only a partial disgrace."

The training officer was not amused. On his pad he called up Paulson's records, then frowned to spot a fresh set of urgent high-priority orders.

"I'm just not cut out to be a seaman, sir," Paulson said.

The training officer roared, "Don't call me 'sir'! You don't deserve to call me 'sir,' turd!"

"Sorry," Paulson said. "It's all so confusing."

The training officer turned the pad around, showing Paulson's brain scan and a high-priority request from Admiral Bruce Haldane himself. "You see that, turd? You're a match—for better or worse, though I don't know why the Admiral would accept someone like you. I can't force this decision on you, but I can offer to transfer you."

"I … I don't know what you're talking about."

"Of course you don't, turd. You don't need to know. But here's something you actually *can* do—I suggest you take it."

O O O

When he met Admiral Haldane, Paulson recognized the man who had delivered the speech honoring the sacrifice of those who had lost their lives on the *Far Horizon*. In earlier media glimpses, Paulson had also seen images of Admiral Haldane's previous incarnation. This new version seemed younger, taller, less salty, but the hard expression was the same, as was the swagger of his movements … and of course the nameplate on his chest beneath all the medals.

Haldane did not seem to be impressed. "You're the volunteer."

"Seaman-recruit Paulson Kenz, sir." He saluted, then hesitated, considered his words, and realized that 'sir' was indeed appropriate in this circumstance.

"You realize what you're being asked to do, seaman?"

"No, sir. No one's briefed me at all."

Haldane shot a glare at his chief of staff, a female officer who stood looking as prim as a mannequin in a department store window. "Sorry, Admiral, he must have slipped through the cracks. Seaman Kenz, you are being offered a chance to be Admiral Haldane's next alternate-in-waiting. We would like to install an interchange conduit at the base of your skull, which is linked to an identical one in the Admiral's head."

Haldane turned, showed Paulson the implanted disc at the base of his skull.

"The Admiral has a great deal of direct experience and innate knowledge about our enemy, about the tactics used by and against them. Such knowledge cannot be lost, nor can it be replaced. Therefore, the Earth Planetary Navy has developed extraordinary measures to preserve that brain trust—and you will help us do it."

"You mean, I'm going to become cannon fodder?" Paulson said.

"That is an inaccurate term," Haldane said. "The Sluggos don't use cannons."

"Why would I want to do that?" Paulson asked. "If you get in trouble, then I'll die, right?"

"That's a big 'if,' seaman. Until recently, I lived my entire life without dying, and I've learned a great deal with each successive engagement against the enemy. I believe we come closer to finding the key to their ultimate defeat with each encounter."

"In the meantime," Tenn interrupted, "you will be excused from any dangerous duty, any further training, any military drills. You'll have a comfortable existence. You'll be given quarters, food, and very few responsibilities. It's a cushy job, Seaman Kenz. You wait to be called up, and hope you won't be. If you agree to be the Admiral's alternate-in-waiting, then that will be your only duty for the duration of your contracted service."

Haldane seemed annoyed at the situation. "In other words, you just sit around and read or play games, although you're expected to keep yourself in shape." He raised his arms, flexed his muscles. "The previous owner of this body did a good job, and we'll count on the same from you. Are you willing to take the gamble? You're my escape hatch so I can live to fight another day." He paused, added a greater threat to his tone. "Your other alternative is to go back to boot camp and be put on the next ship, where you'll face an engagement of the Sluggos. In person."

Paulson swallowed hard. He'd seen the images of the *Far Horizon* massacre, listened to the howling crew, saw the chomping teeth of the Sluggos. He had watched how the aliens moved in eerie concert, forming a gigantic organism that was far more ferocious than the sum of its parts.

The decision wasn't hard for him.

"I accept, sir. It's a gamble, but it's really my only option. If I get out there facing those things as *me*, I know I won't survive." Paulson fingered the back of his head, felt the smooth hardness of his skull. He supposed the surgery was going to hurt. "I'll take my chances with you."

5

It came from beneath the sea.

The next time the mass of Sluggos appeared, they did not prey upon Navy ships patrolling the open seas; rather, the new conglomerate monster rose up out of Pearl Harbor and attacked land for the first time.

Tour boats and naval patrol ships spotted the incoming surge, but no one understood what was happening at first. Hundreds of thousands of Sluggos swam in individually like the world's entire population of eels meeting in Hawaii for a convention. The arm-length creatures glided in under the surface, choking the channels, filling the harbor.

Tourist boats were buffeted by the swarms of soft shapes with sharp teeth. Naval destroyers, missile cruisers, fast frigates, and even a huge old battleship were brought to bear. General Quarters sounded and the crew raced to their stations. The dockyards were put on high alert.

The squirming worm-like things choked the harbor, but that was just a start. The Sluggo bodies coalesced, braiding together, building up like pieces in a gigantic wriggly mosaic sculpture—until a huge and hideous monster rose out of the sea.

Rushing down to the harbor from his satellite headquarters office, Admiral Haldane screamed for fishing boats and salvage cutters to string nets that would stop the numerous individual Sluggos from joining one another, but it was too late. The things became a gigantic mound of squirming flesh, as if a mad artist had made a nightmare sculpture out of living maggots. The Sluggo mass extruded pseudopods and began smashing any vessel in the harbor.

Admiral Haldane had been sent to Oahu, not for a tropical vacation but to organize the EPN Pacific Fleet's plan to dispatch numerous search-and-destroy subs that would find the Sluggos. Unfortunately, the alien monsters decided to be found right there on the Earth Navy's doorstep.

Pearl Harbor was full of Navy ships, tourist boats, and cargo barges hauling goods in lightweight crates for launch at the Honolulu Spaceport. Like a child playing with toys in a bathtub, the conglomerate Sluggo monster crawled over vessels and pushed them under the water, crushing their hulls and sinking them. Other pseudopods snatched desirable equipment and whisked it away beneath the surface.

Admiral Haldane dispatched fighter jets loaded with missiles. As the giant monster hulked its way on top of the floating museum battleships and onto shore, the roaring jets launched missiles that blasted the huge monster, dispersing it into countless squirming Sluggos that sprayed in all directions. But the monstrous mass shuffled and reorganized itself somewhere else, heading toward the rocket launch area of the spaceport.

Haldane didn't like this one bit. "Let's try napalm. We must have some left over."

Tenn called up summaries on her datapad. "None of the new formula is weaponized yet, sir, but there may be some old leftovers in storage."

"Never let anything go to waste," Haldane said. "We might as well use it up."

"There's plenty of fuel spilled on the water from all those damaged ships, sir. Igniting that could be effective as well."

"Good idea. Let's do both."

The EPN battleships launched huge sprays of missile, and the sky became a messy finger-painting of smoke, mostly from damaged structures, exploding naval ships, even one crashed jet when the Sluggo-beast had thrashed a unexpectedly whip-thin and unexpectedly long tentacle into the air to snatch and crush the plane, before hurling it onto the deck of a snorkeling cruise boat just being loaded with a senior citizens' tour group.

The Sluggos moved like an enormous blob, rising up to capsize cutters. Large-caliber artillery guns hammered away at the mass, destroying thousands of individual Sluggos, but the overall monster did not seem affected.

"Open the weapons lockers," Haldane yelled. "Distribute weapons to anyone who won't turn and run. Rifles, shrapnel pulsers, pea-shooters—I don't care."

"We may have a shortage of pea-shooters sir," Tenn said.

"That was a joke, Lieutenant."

"Very funny, sir."

Haldane thought this might be a war of attrition: humanity just needed to kill off enough of the individual Sluggos, which were easily destroyed. But the supply of squirming aliens seemed inexhaustible.

Out in the harbor, a group of sailors were making a last stand with rifles and hand grenades. No one could understand how all those little maggot things could work together to create a single massive and apparently intelligent organism. They kept tearing apart ships, stealing components. Haldane knew the aliens had built starships that had carried them to Earth from some other solar system.

But how did these silly little worms know what to do when they were linked together? A million humans certainly couldn't cooperate like that. Often it was hard to get three people to agree.

More light bombers roared overhead, dropping explosives, including canisters of old napalm. The intensely hot flames from the jellied gasoline crisped the outer layers of squirming worms. They blackened and fell away, but new Sluggos boiled up to take their places. More and more Sluggos streamed into the harbor from the open sea, adding themselves to the monster's bulky conglomerate body. Even after so many individual aliens were destroyed, the overall bulk swelled.

The pseudopods extended outward, moving the mass away from the naval ships to the reserved spaceport area. The Sluggos snatched tall gantries and pulled rocket shuttles and girder structures down off the launch pads. The squirming creatures dragged those components into the water of the harbor.

Haldane shouted orders because he was expected to, but no one could hear him in the deafening noise. The oddest part was that the giant alien monster moved in silence. It simply created havoc without adding any extraterrestrial commentary.

Haldane considered calling in a nuclear strike. Oahu was beautiful, but there were other islands in the Pacific. And if it took such an extreme measure to get rid of the Sluggos once and for all, despite the loss of the entire population, including himself.

He had grown fond of his new body from Aaron Shelty and didn't want to use the escape hatch too soon, especially now that he had seen the alternative-in-waiting, the scrawny slip of a man named Paulson Kenz. But Haldane couldn't think of himself at a time like this.

The tentacles broke the keel of an aircraft carrier that had entered the harbor, and that was enough to force Haldane's decision. He was really getting upset now. Yes, he had to call in a nuclear strike for the good of humanity.

Before he could issue the order, though, a slimy tentacle burst out of the water right at the shore's edge and swept all of them aside, including Admiral Haldane. He found himself flying through the air, flailing. Another series of explosions roared nearby.

He shouldn't have waited! He grabbed for the back of his head, trying to find the transfer pendant. Others were sailing through the air near him, screaming, bloody, broken.

There! He found the pendant. Emergency transfer with the volunteer—

But then Haldane slammed into the side of a boat house, splintering the shingles. The pain was brief, the unconsciousness swift.

This time, he doubted he would live to fight another day …

O   O   O

He awoke in the medevac hovercopter along with a dozen other broken and bleeding casualties. Haldane felt as if someone had made kindling of his ribs and spine. A corpsman hunched over him, poking and prodding until he got the proper response to his question of "Does that hurt?" Other doctors tended the wounded.

"I see by your insignia that you're a admiral," said the corpsman.

"I am, dammit!" As much blood came out as words. He could tell this was bad. He tried to lift his hands, but his arms were strapped down. "Help me. I'm Admiral Bruce Haldane. I need to activate my exchange pendant."

"Sorry, sir, I can't let you move. There could be internal damage."

Haldane was appalled. The corpsman didn't understand what was going on here. "I don't care about my injuries! Before I die, I need to transfer." He began coughing again and felt the warm blood on his lips.

"Good news for you, then, sir—you're not going to die. Just rest easy. You suffered some broken ribs, a shattered clavicle, probably a severe concussion. But our deep scans show no obvious internal bleeding. We just want to be careful."

"So I'm going to … recover?" Haldane said. That shouldn't have been disappointing.

"Looks like it. We'll patch you up." The corpsman looked shell-shocked; his expression was gray. "You're one of the lucky ones. Over fifty percent fatality rate from the monster attack. They'll be a long time counting up the casualties. I think …" He shook his head. "… I think Pearl Harbor is gone. Half of Honolulu is gone. Fires are raging. The Sluggos sank most of our fleet, destroyed the spaceport, then they withdrew."

"Is there any good news?" Haldane asked.

"I just told it to you. The Sluggos departed, slithering back into the ocean. That's the best news you'll hear."

"Oh."

"That, and the fact that you're going to live. Should be enough good news for the day, right, sir?"

The corpsman shot him full of sedative. As he sank down, Admiral Haldane knew he would be a long time healing, which was upsetting. Thankfully he could keep this body, even though it was going to hurt like hell when he woke up. At least he wouldn't be a 90-pound weakling.

6

Even with the tension that was always in the back of Paulson's mind, his daily duties here—as in, no useful duties whatsoever, only busy work so the EPN could feel confident in their investment—certainly beat basic training. Instead of being aboard a ship hunting for voracious alien monsters, his duty station was a giant rec room.

The surgery to install the transfer pendant was as unpleasant as he'd feared: having a hole drilled in the back of his head, a sensor plug and transmitter installed with a million self-seeking wires plunging into his brain, where it found the core of personality and memories. The exchange conduit would tear out, record, and transmit everything that was Paulson Kenz, then re-upload the very being of Admiral Bruce Haldane—in the event that circumstances warranted it. Paulson kept his fingers crossed and hoped.

Paulson had healed up after the quick coagulant slather, and the pain meds had been nice until they ran out (budget cuts, with all the best stuff reserved for any EPN soldiers wounded in combat).

There were fifteen other volunteers inside the guarded recreation hall. They were forced to remain in the La Diego base, but it wasn't so bad. All fifteen of them had the exchange conduit installed in their heads, tethered to other command officers or political leaders that were deemed too valuable to lose.

Two volunteers played ping-pong, but neither was very good at it. One man, who had already put on fifteen pounds, placed orders from the galley and ate all day long. Paulson knew the food was not at all tasty, but at least the quantity was comforting. Just this afternoon, though, a dietician had come in, take control over the man's eating habits, and advise (as well as enforce) nutritious meals. "You are required to take care of your body," the dietician said in a decidedly threatening voice, "in case it should be needed."

The volunteers seemed to have a free ride, but they were obligated to take care of themselves. Although *they*, as individuals, weren't important, their bodies were considered vital to planetary defense, and the Navy had made a considerable investment in them. Some volunteers took the task seriously and worked out in the fitness center, lifting weights, jogging on the treadmill. Paulson did the required calisthenics, but he had never seen the purpose in picking up heavy things and putting them back down again, or running on a piece of equipment that went nowhere.

He remembered how his parents had told him <u>he</u> was going nowhere, that he spent too much time reading, paying little attention to practical things. They had been right, according to their own definitions. Now, they were probably proud of him for being a part of the brave Earth Planetary Navy. If he were called upon to provide the mortal escape hatch for Admiral Haldane, they would be pleased as punch to tell their neighbors about how their good-for-nothing son had become a war hero.

Paulson didn't feel particularly brave. Any heroic end on his part would be completely out of his hands. Most of his fellow volunteers had resigned themselves to an imminent and unpleasant demise, grabbing as much life as they could in the meantime, playing games, horsing around, sleeping in. Several had written up a petition demanding access to a military-approved escort service, and that request was currently working its way up the chain of command.

Paulson was the only one who cared about the war against the Sluggos, and about increasing his chances for survival, as well as the rest of humanity's, in a worst-case scenario. Because he was cerebrally paired with Admiral Haldane, he requested access to the briefings on the invasion and records of prior Sluggo attacks, in hopes of teasing out any vulnerabilities. He studied news reports, although the most detailed, and most gruesome, footage was missing.

He requested additional intel, including the full classified reports, but since he was just a seaman-recruit, with the lowest possible security clearance, his request was summarily denied. So, he submitted an appeal, documenting that he was the functional physical equivalent of Admiral Haldane, that his body—and therefore the structure of his brain—would be used by the leader of the Earth Planetary Navy. Therefore any information might be beneficial, should the admiral be forced to swap bodies with him. Paulson also pointed out that if the admiral ever did activate the transfer protocol, Paulson himself would be rapidly devoured by aliens, and therefore all secrets would be safe.

The yeoman, who was harried and overworked, didn't entirely understand the nuances of the argument, but rather than risk annoying the real Admiral Haldane, he bumped the request up the chain. Somehow, it got approved. Accidentally, Paulson supposed.

In the rec hall/prison, he spent hours poring over the records, watching the movements of the Sluggos through the water during the rare times they were tracked. But whenever sonar rigs tried to track the large conglomeration, the entire mass vanished like a puff of smoke. Maybe they just dissociated into a million little worms again, invisible to sonar traces.

The EPN knew about where the alien invaders lived beneath the Pacific, a broad general area where their starships must have landed. Supposedly, that was where their base might be.

He studied biological reports of the creatures. Many Sluggo specimens had been dissected, individual nematode-like things that had very little physical structure. Each Sluggo was just a sac with a few rudimentary organs, a digestive system, and a mouth with sharp teeth, but no eyes or other obvious sensory apparatus, not even a brain, just a small nerve cluster.

It made no sense that these things could combine into some gigantic entity that obviously had a structure and a purpose, and was presumably intelligent. The Sluggos used tools, they built machinery, constructed spacecraft, and flew interstellar distances. Not bad for a bunch of hungry worms.

In the specimen tanks or dissection trays, they didn't look any more sophisticated than extraterrestrial leeches. When Sluggos moved en masse in the water, they looked like a gigantic school of fish, somehow moving with one mind. He shook his head.

Then the pendant at the base of his skull began to tingle.

The rec hall around him fuzzed. The ringing in his ears grew as loud as church bells, and he wavered. Other volunteers in the rec hall looked up, sensing something amiss.

"It's happening!"

This was too soon! He wasn't ready. No one had even told him Admiral Haldane was going out to fight with the Sluggos. It would have been nice to have a little more warning.

He felt as if his soul were rushing down a wind tunnel. He left his body, yelling—but without making any sound.

And when he woke up he was somewhere else, inside a different body. And he screamed in agony. He felt shattered bones, torn muscles, a bashed head, nerves that clamored about all the bodily damage. He tried to open his eyes, but he was surrounded by white blurs, moving faces. Doctors? If he was going to die, he wished he could at least stomp on one or two Sluggos first.

Then the pain was too much, and he faded into unconsciousness.

O   O   O

He awoke to find his own face staring down at him.

Paulson recognized himself, saw the body at the bedside—*am I really that scrawny?*—but realized that the eyes were different. Then the pain hit him again, so he wished he hadn't woken up. The agony was somewhat diminished from before, and he was a little foggier. He could feel painkillers like slimy wet velvet working through his mind and body, but he could also feel the physical damage. He knew this body was mangled.

This wasn't his body in the first place … so many things didn't feel right. Meanwhile, Paulson watched his own body pacing back and forth in the infirmary room, studying the medical equipment and monitors that provided a discordant symphony of bleeps. His own face turned toward him, and in all his life of looking at himself in a mirror, he had never seen his expression show such disapproval before.

And his reflected image had never talked back to him, either. "Good to see that you're awake. I need to explain the situation, and then be off to a briefing." His voice sounded funny.

Paulson croaked in a rough voice, "You're not dead." This had to be Admiral Haldane. The vocal cords weren't his own, and the tone sounded wrong in his head. His throat was sore—he must have been yelling or screaming before the swap.

"I was badly injured during the battle of Pearl Harbor. I thought I was a goner there for awhile, and I almost used the transfer during the worst part, but I got walloped before I had the chance."

Paulson's body shrugged. Admiral Haldane touched his new shoulders, felt the bones there, encircled his wrist with thumb and forefinger. He clucked. "You really need to take better care of yourself, Kenz. Put on a few pounds, preferably muscle."

"I'll leave that up to you now, sir," Paulson said.

"This transfer is just temporary while that body heals," Haldane retorted. "The doctors said I was going to live, but the recovery would be hard and painful. I don't have time for that bullshit—there's a war on. And then I thought, what do I have *you* for? Now, you just lie there and heal. It's the least you can do in service to your country and your planet."

Haldane leaned over the infirmary bed and prodded the bandages in Paulson's side. Paulson gasped, nearly fainted from the rush of pain that exploded through him. Haldane continued. "A few broken ribs, lots of bruises, stitches in a half dozen places. Oh, and they removed your spleen, but you can do without that. When was the last time you used your spleen?"

"Never noticed it before, sir," Paulson said, trying to be stoic.

"The medics are pumping you full of accelerated cell growth. Your body's got so many bruises all over that your skin has natural camouflage. But that'll heal. The bones will heal. The physical therapy is going to be rough, but you can handle it. I don't have time—I have meetings."

Paulson lay back and just felt the aches piled upon aches. He had dreaded being called upon to transfer with the admiral, but this, he supposed, was the best realistic scenario. He was still alive. He could lie here and recover in the admiral's place, as he asked.

And whenever the fuzzy painkillers wore off, maybe the EPN would even provide him with a reading library so he could catch up on some of the books he'd meant to read.

"Be quick about it healing," Admiral Haldane said, before turning around. "I'll want that body back again as soon as you've fixed it."

7

Something about the scrawny body of Paulson Kenz inspired disrespect despite the medals and rank insignia on the uniform. Kenz was bookish, shy, the sort of person who simply begged to have beach sand kicked in his face by a bully of even modest proportions.

The more days Admiral Haldane lived inside the other body, the more he noticed the subtle attitude shifts toward him.

When the admiral entered the La Diego base headquarters, he carried his revised ID and temporary access cards, with Paulson's fingerprints and retina map transferred over to his diagnostics records. It was just a temporary situation, though, since he expected to swap back to his preferred body as soon as the damaged one was healed in sick bay.

Previously, Admiral Haldane's very presence had inspired instant deference, but in Paulson's body he had to work at it. As he marched down the passageway, a pair of junior officers strolled by, engrossed in conversation and paying little attention to him. Annoyed, Haldane placed himself directly in their path so that they were forced to look up and notice his insignia and name badge. They scrambled to give the proper salute accompanied by hasty apologies.

Haldane walked on, not entirely satisfied. War was all about sacrifices, he supposed. He could endure this one.

It wasn't just the fact that he felt physically weak, that he grew winded after climbing only five flights of stairs, that simple acts such as opening a pickle jar or carrying a box of classified printouts to the shredder were more difficult. He didn't like the way he looked when he took a shower, couldn't imagine suavely trying to pick up a woman in a bar or, even more embarrassing, taking her home where he would have to make bedroom excuses: "This isn't really my natural body. My normal endowment is much more impressive." He could already imagine the seen-it-all-before looks of skepticism....

He was still trying to get his office in order, breaking in a new chief of staff, since his adjutant Ms. Tenn had been inconveniently killed during the Sluggo attack on Pearl Harbor. Her death had caused innumerable problems.

In his office, the interim replacement had brought him the morning coffee, a cinnamon cappuccino, which, after thorough testing, was what Haldane and Ms. Tenn had determined best suited his Aaron Shelty taste buds. He gave a grunt of thanks and sipped the coffee as he sat down—but it tasted awful. He had forgotten. Paulson Kenz's body preferred something else entirely. Haldane growled in his throat and drank the cinnamon cappuccino anyway, forcing it down because he simply didn't want to bother to get it done right.

He had work to do and a world to save.

The morning's reports made the day seem much brighter. He studied the new images and grinned, then he immediately called together his highest-level advisors.

○ ○ ○

The briefing room was full of high-ranking EPN officers, prominent politicians, and even businessmen in charge of massive amounts of funding—all the important people who could make the proper decisions without the delay of red tape. The secure conference room felt like a cave; the original design had been to evoke the comfortable camaraderie of an exclusive gentlemen's club.

"Gentlemen," Haldane said, before nodding toward the lone female in the room, "and ma'am. We have wonderful and fascinating intelligence—our reconnaissance has finally borne fruit!" In his ears, Kenz's voice sounded squeaky.

The lights in the briefing room dimmed further as he displayed images on the wall screens.

"With the attack on Pearl Harbor, the Sluggos showed their real intent. They are going to infest our oceans, then swallow up our islands, then devour our coastlines. Who knows, they may even chew canals wide enough to bring them all the way to Kansas. And as you well know—" He narrowed his eyes and swept his gaze across them. "—we have no naval bases in Kansas."

He saw the determined faces around the room nodding gravely. An unnamed man in a business suit folded his hands and leaned forward. "You've already convinced us, Admiral. No one disputes the magnitude of the alien threat. Our shipyards and weapons factories, our naval construction operations have been blossoming like weeds. Just tell us what you *can* do, and we'll give you everything you need."

Haldane smiled. Throughout his EPN career, his ideas had been met with reluctance and resistance, thanks to narrow-minded individuals and the web of red tape they spun. Now, Admiral Haldane had everything he could possibly ask for. All he had to do was ask. Even in his scrawny body, these advisors looked to him, respected him, understood the weight of experience and wisdom he brought to these discussions.

Among the inner circle gathered here, he knew that at least six of them had transfer circuits implanted, because they were deemed to be powerful and influential enough to be classed as irreplaceable. They had their own escape hatch volunteers.

"I have faced the Sluggos several times in person, at the cost of two previous bodies and damage to a third. I've looked them in the eyes …

well, at least in the slimy membranes. I have watched men and women die all around me, and I've felt myself die. I know what it's like. I was aboard the *Far Horizon* until its last moments. I was there at Pearl Harbor. And I'll be there again at our final engagement."

He changed the images on the screens to show blurry sonar readings. "After the attack on Hawaii, the Sluggos withdrew with many vital spaceport components, dragging them beneath the sea. We've been trying to find their secret base. A fleet of fast mapping survey ships cruised over the surface, covering thousands of square miles of open sea. They were ready to map every inch of the damned Pacific if they needed to. And this is what they found."

He zoomed in. The sonar trace showed the gigantic mass of Sluggos that had formed the conglomerate monster. The echo was bigger than a hundred giant squids as it moved along the ocean floor. The first image of the huge alien mass was sharp, the second was fuzzed and blurry.

"With the third sonar ping," Haldane continued, "the Sluggo mass had vanished—as usual. But this time it's different, because we found where those creatures go to bed."

The sonar trace showed the ocean floor, a low-resolution image that nevertheless revealed a city of permanent undersea structures, a hodgepodge assembled from wreckage the creatures had stolen.

"Knowing where to look, we dropped off submersible micro-cameras, self-guiding imagers that dove down to the coordinates. They were small enough to remain unnoticed—for a time."

Haldane displayed crisp video feeds as the submersible cameras dove to where the invaders had built their submerged fortress. At such a depth, the water was dark and murky; activating bright lights to penetrate the gloom, the microcameras revealed bizarre free-form sculptures, towers and domes that were welded together with mud and coral. The structures incorporated the wreckage of ship hulls, including the bridge tower of the *Far Horizon*, along with sunken wrecks dragged hundreds of miles from Oahu.

The buildings themselves, however, seemed to *squirm*. As the microcameras flitted closer, they revealed that the walls were also built out of Sluggos. The worm-like creatures piled up like soft flexible bricks, many of them dead, others dissolving and oozing into organic cement. Gantry structures stolen from the Honolulu spaceport served as frameworks, and individual Sluggos crawled up the girders, wrapping around them like putty.

"Unfortunately, the lights the cameras used to obtain these images attracted attention," Haldane said.

The images on the conference room screens switched to static one at a time. The last microcamera zoomed in on one of the eel-like creatures swimming toward it, its mouth gaping wide until it swallowed the camera, which valiantly transmitted a last few images of the alien digestive sac until the acid destroyed it.

Haldane crossed his arms over the many medals on his now-scrawny chest. "So there you have it, gentlemen." He nodded to the woman again. "And ma'am. We pinpointed their base. We know where they're lurking." It felt good to grin. "We have a large expeditionary sub being converted into a battle vessel. It was originally designed to complete a full sonar map of the ocean floor, but now we have more important work for it."

The man in the business suit nodded. "Ah, the *Prospector*. We funded that. One of our subsidiaries is developing domed underwater housing as condo time-shares, and we were going to lay claim to all that undeveloped real estate. We're having trouble selling shares, thanks to the Sluggo infestation."

Haldane nodded. "We know sonar does little good to track them, but we can arm the *Prospector* to the teeth. It's got a reinforced hull and expanded magazines to accommodate more than fifty torpedoes. I'll find a determined crew. We'll be ready to make our final assault within a week. I intend to lead the expedition myself and blow the living slime out of those Sluggos!" He smiled. "If I have your permission."

They gave him their exuberant approval, but the lone woman asked, "Why wait a week if we know where the Sluggos are now?"

"It'll take that long to get ready, ma'am. We have to give this our best shot."

Admiral Haldane had an ulterior motive. In a week, the infirmary would release his other body. Paulson Kenz had finished the basic healing process, and he was completing the final physical therapy schedules.

If he was going to defeat the alien invaders once and for all, Haldane certainly didn't want to be wearing this scrawny body for the history books.

8

After all the snide comments and complaints Admiral Haldane had made about Paulson's original weakling form, the young seaman-recruit wished the admiral had been more careful with this one. If Haldane hadn't let himself get so smashed up or killed—twice in fact—then Paulson wouldn't have to spend his days here in the infirmary being tortured by a Spanish Inquisition of physical therapists who used enhanced healing therapies and supercharged hormones that pummeled his muscles and bones until they knitted themselves together—or else.

The physical therapists had a bedside manner more appropriate for the Marquis de Sade than Florence Nightingale, and Paulson was very quickly convinced that he wanted to be released from their clutches as soon as possible. He longed to be back in the rec room hall again with nothing to do except study reports on the Sluggos.

Even here in sick bay, however, as soon as he grew strong enough, Paulson called up all available images of the Honolulu attack. Because so many vacationers spent time in Hawaii, most of the footage had been confiscated from homemade tourist videos. Paulson watched the rampaging conglomerate monster that had destroyed the ships in the harbor, the spaceport, the buildings on the shoreline.

He was more interested in poring over clips taken prior to the assembly of the Sluggo monster. He watched how the myriad organisms drew together like some kind of group mind, how the individual worm-things assembled into a much larger and adaptable body that reorganized itself according to circumstances. The Sluggo organism was clearly intelligent en masse, though the individual creatures showed only the most rudimentary brain activity. After the harbor attack and ransacking the ships and spaceport, some of the retreating Sluggos had maintained enough physical integrity to haul off the wreckage they desired, while the rest of the creatures dissolved like a mist of maggots.

Even if sonar couldn't track the massed alien organism underwater, fast ships could have followed the sunken ships and the spaceport gantries as the Sluggos hauled them away. But with Pearl Harbor, the EPN base, the waterfront, and the spaceport destroyed, no one managed to think that far ahead.

Paulson walked on a treadmill, limbering up his legs. He still felt lingering broken-glass pain in his ribs and shoulder. His numerous bruises had turned an alarming bouquet of colors, but the flesh tone was returning. The therapists often studied his body, finding patterns and designs in the discolorations. One even exclaimed that he saw the face of the Virgin Mary there. Paulson thought he was joking, but the man's voice held no sarcasm or humor whatsoever.

During the treadmill work, he sweated heavily and his pulse raced. He was ready to drop, but the therapists egged him on and threatened him. Paulson was surprised they enhance his sessions with a bullwhip just to keep him moving. After weeks of physical therapy, he began to long for the days of boot camp, which had been miserable enough, but at least he'd been able to sleep at night.

On the other hand, if he hadn't signed on to the escape hatch program, he would have been doomed to go out and fight the alien monsters. He probably would be a statistic from Pearl Harbor. In most ways, being dead was worse than physical therapy.

According to the doctors' estimates, given additional enhanced jolts of healing chemicals, in a few days he would swap back into his own body and return to the rec hall with all the other transfer volunteers. And wait.

Admiral Haldane appeared in the therapy center just as Paulson stumbled off the treadmill and the therapists yanked the monitor electrodes from his scalp and chest.

The admiral regarded him with obvious impatience.

"Hurry up and finish healing, Seaman Kenz. The clock is ticking, and I want that body back. I'm due to head into battle again, and I'd rather face the Sluggos wearing that—" He jabbed a finger toward Paulson's borrowed body. "—than this."

"Healing as fast as I can, sir."

"He'll be ready on time Admiral," said the physical therapist who had seen the Virgin Mary in his bruise patterns. "I'll give him a double maximum dose tonight."

Haldane seemed to consider Paulson as little more than a piece of equipment; he paid attention to the medical specialists instead. "And have you scheduled the cranial reset surgery yet?" He tapped the pendant on the back of his head—Paulson's own head—and glanced at Paulson, who stood panting and sweating beside the treadmill.

"Cranial surgery again, sir?" Paulson said. "I didn't agree to that."

"Yes, you did," Haldane said. "It's in the fine print. The transfer conduit is set for one-way transmission only, one-time use. It has to be that way, if you think about it. After I evacuate from a critical last-stand situation, I can't have my volunteer just hit the pendant again and reset."

Paulson ran his fingers along the small disc on the back of his head. "So now that we've transferred, we can't just switch back?"

"We'll just pop out the device and put in another one," said one of the medical techs. "Easy as replacing an eyeball. Piece of cake."

"You'll be happy to get your own body back, Seaman Kenz," said Haldane, "and I'll certainly be glad to have that one. We located the main undersea base where the Sluggos are building their fortress, and I'll be taking an expeditionary sub there rigged as a battleship with plenty of megatorpedoes and missiles. It'll be glorious!"

Paulson decided it was time to share what he had gleaned from his research on the aliens. "Sir, I've been studying the enemy behavior. The Sluggos seem to be a group organism, collectively intelligent but individually not much. The Sluggos are just like cells, bound together by some kind of telepathy. They cooperate, bond with synergy, and—"

"Yes, yes, very nice, Seaman Kenz," said Haldane. "With all the megatorps loaded aboard the *Prospector*, we'll blow the Sluggos to hell and level their undersea base. The ruins will be the next best tourist attraction since Atlantis."

9

They didn't have time for a proper commissioning cruise aboard the *Prospector*. The crew would get accustomed to their battle sub, and he would get reacquainted with this body, by the time they reached the coordinates of the sunken alien base.

Admiral Haldane touched the sore spot in the back of his skull where the transfer conduit had been replaced. His freshly healed body still ached; he could feel the lingering remnants of bruises, and his bones twinged when he moved the wrong way. Nevertheless, it felt good to be out of that weakling form. These aches and pains were a good sort of hurt, like after a heavy workout. In the body of Paulson Kenz, his tired soreness just felt like hopeless surrender.

In the week since the discovery of the alien undersea base, the Sluggos had remained quiet, though aircraft and high-resolution satellites made several tentacle sightings.

Admiral Haldane was the EPN's highest-ranking officer and he insisted on commanding this mission, but he had never served aboard a sub before, so he let the actual captain, XO, navigator, and weapons officer do their jobs without interference. Normally, a admiral with Haldane's clout and experience would never have been risked on such a dangerous mission—and at least half the *Prospector*'s crew was convinced this would be a one-way trip. Admiral Haldane, though, intended to face the squirming enemy one last time. He wanted to see them all splattered into plankton-sized pieces.

The *Prospector* needed his background and experience during what was sure to be intense fighting. He knew the sub's crew might panic at the wrong moment, so he had to lead them with his proven abilities. Besides, he always had his escape hatch.

During the long and tedious voyage, Haldane spent much of his time on the bridge, watching the screens. The navigator sent sonar bursts, but the waters remained clear. He called for numerous drills and targeting simulations, loading and unloading torpedoes. The admiral also worked out in the sub's makeshift exercise area, limbering his restored body and working through the last aches and pains.

When the *Prospector* reached the coordinates of the Sluggo base, the sub, the crew and Admiral Haldane's body were ready for action.

"We'll strike fast, and repeatedly," he said over the horn from the command deck, glancing over at the captain and XO. "Like ninjas. One megatorp after another after another. You all saw the size of that monster that attacked Pearl Harbor. I'd say twenty megatorps should be sufficient, and that leaves thirty more to obliterate the base." He waited for the resounding cheer, then glanced at the captain. "Captain, prepare your firing pattern."

The captain snapped, "Weps, Fire Control, you have your orders."

When they approached the target, the sonar technicians sent out pings to map the alien structures ahead. For an instant he saw a shadow of the monstrous conglomerate creature, but it disappeared by the time of the second burst.

In the blurred sonar images, he saw the huge alien structures, which seemed significantly larger than what the microcameras had recorded a week ago. Some of the towers appeared to be falling, the domes collapsing.

"That sonar resolution really sucks," he said.

"We're close enough that we can see with our own eyes, Admiral," said the XO. "Lighting it up now."

Haldane smiled with pride at the efficient crew. "Captain, I'll turn operations over to you. Handle all the details, please."

The sub's brilliant lights stabbed into the deep, dark water, illuminating the bizarre alien fortress. Around them, the water was aswarm with millions of the squirming eels, but the gigantic conglomerate monster was not in sight. The dismantled ship hulls and spaceport gantries stood on the sea floor—and they were slowly toppling down. The base seemed to be falling apart by itself.

Everyone stared at the startling images, momentarily frozen. Haldane roared, "What are you waiting for? Fire control, launch megatorps!"

The crew had been tense and waiting, with hair-trigger fingers. The first megatorpedoes soared out like javelins on a tail of foam. The weapons crew was already loading the second volley even before the first had hit.

Haldane muttered to himself, "This is going to be good."

The torpedoes arrowed straight on target and struck the Sluggo base with glorious detonations. Haldane caught his breath as bright shock waves blossomed like an explosive cluster of flowers. The sonar techs switched off their ears before the close-range blasts rang out, and thunder reverberated through the *Prospector*'s hull. Haldane was caught off guard, but the rest of the crew hunkered down at their stations. Fire control shouted a succession of orders.

As admiral, he wanted to be in control and direct all activity, but the others reacted so quickly without him, like a well-oiled machine. Within seconds, another volley of megatorps was away. This would be a constant punishing brawl, and the squirming aliens didn't have a chance.

Explosions wrecked the undersea structures. The broken hulls and gantry frameworks were already toppling, but then he saw a flurry, as if the megatorps had startled a flock of carrion birds. Individual Sluggos boiled up from the patchwork structures by the thousands—tens of thousands.

Haldane realized that all those huddled invertebrates had been *holding the base together*, like living building blocks. Sluggos had covered the scrap components, but the explosions had stirred up all those creatures, which now abandoned the structures and swarmed toward the sub like angry hornets from hundreds of disturbed nests.

Contradictory orders echoed throughout the *Prospector*. Haldane intended to give some kind of brilliant insight that would allow the crew to make a wise and instantaneous response, but the best he could vocalize was "Uh-oh. Keep firing megatorps."

The weapons officer yelled, and the crew aft in the torpedo room kept frantically loaded volley after volley into the launch tubes like a fire brigade. Explosions hammered the crumbling alien base, but the uncertain and scattered cloud of free-swimming Sluggos simply swirled around. Then the swarm came toward the sub like an angry school of fish.

"Keep firing!" Haldane yelled, as if the crew needed any encouragement.

Countless writhing shapes formed a cloud that congealed around the *Prospector*. The squirming bodies in the swarm wove together, fastening one body to another, and another conglomerate alien creature formed itself like a giant fist around the battle sub.

The last three megatorps launched, but became caught in the thick amorphous mass. The detonations were like sledge hammers pounding the *Prospector*'s hull, and throwing the crew to the deck. Haldane lost his balance and slammed into a control station, knocking the sonar tech aside. He climbed to his feet, shaking his head. On the main screens, they saw all the water go dark as the mass closed in.

"All megatorps gone, sir," said the captain. He looked sickened.

"Already? This is not possible!" Haldane said. "Fifty megatorps struck their targets! We destroyed the alien base!"

Nobody argued with him. The fire control and weapons officers knew the explosions had caused damage, but the huge squirming mass of Sluggos just reformed into a giant and powerful mass of angry flesh.

The *Prospector* groaned and shrieked as even the reinforced armor was bent beyond its tolerances. The intercom was filled with shouts.

"Watertight doors closing! Breach on Deck Five!" the XO yelled.

The battle sub lurched, and the deck tilted at an angle. The huge alien creature had grabbed the hull and was squeezing and shaking the *Prospector* as if it were nothing more than a toy.

"Another hull breach on Deck Three, Admiral," the XO yelled. "Water's coming in."

"And so are the Sluggos!"

The *Prospector*'s captain gave him a beseeching look. "You've faced the Sluggos before, sir. In your experience, how should we fight off this thing? We need you to tell us."

Haldane didn't know, but he was aware that he had to escape. The sub would collapse any minute, and someone had to return with a full report to the main EPN base. Humanity would count on him to debrief his fellow admirals. With each engagement, Admiral Haldane learned more and more, and now he had to tell someone that even megatorps didn't work.

"Even failed missions can be instructive," he said, making sure he sounded brave. "But we have to keep fighting until the last possible second. Full ahead. Can we use our engines? Maybe we can break free of this slimy mass."

The captain gave the order while shaking his head. The engineer yelled through the horn." The Sluggos are caught in the propellers, This vessel is frozen and shut down, and our reactor's at 110%. Any more of an overload and it's going to go critical—fifteen minutes, max."

Haldane thought fifteen minutes sounded highly optimistic. "If the reactor goes critical, maybe that'll take out these things. We all have to be brave right now." Their bravery, of course, would manifest differently from his own.

"Sluggos inside the sub!" yelled someone from the torpedo room. "They broke the hatches, pushed their way through the tubes! We're taking on water—water and Sluggos. Compartment's filling up!"

Haldane wanted more details, but the torpedo officer spent too much time screaming and so wasn't very helpful. More damage reports came from other decks. "Thousands of Sluggos are aboard!"

Haldane thought of the wriggling forms, slithering along the decks like carnivorous maggots, attacking anything that moved. The *Prospector*'s hull groaned and lurched again. The captain and XO looked at each other, expressions white.

Haldane was amazed at how swiftly the invading Sluggos reached the command deck. He had faced these awful things before, had seen the horde wipe out Pearl Harbor, and seen them take down the *Far Horizon*, had felt them squirming over his body and sinking fangs into his flesh in the seconds before he activated the escape hatch transfer.

Knowing there was nothing to do and no point in delaying, Haldane faced the bridge crew. This was their last stand. They were out of weapons; alien invaders had breached the hull. Without question, the *Prospector* was doomed.

Haldane accepted the inevitable. Although he wasn't looking forward to escaping into the scrawny body of seaman-recruit Paulson Kenz, he knew that even a weakling form was better than a dead one.

"Thank you for your service and bravery, crewmen. Your deaths will not be in vain. I shall deliver the story of your brave final battle, your last stand for humanity."

The weapons officer gaped at him. "You're just bugging out!"

The XO glowered. "He's saving his own skin."

Haldane lifted his chin. "I'm living to fight another day. It's the only way Earth will defeat these monsters."

Twenty of the squirming, sharp-fanged Sluggos lurched onto the bridge, and several crewmen yelled in terror. Haldane touched the transfer pendant in the base of his skull.

As reality faded around him, he was indeed proud of the *Prospector*'s crew. He saw their faces … but for some reason, they didn't seem particularly glad to know that he, at least, would survive.

10

When Paulson Kenz felt the wrenching inside his head and found himself whisked back into Admiral Haldane's surrogate body, he knew the poop had hit the fan—industrial-sized cargo load of poop.

Struggling with disorientation, he found himself was on the command deck of the battle sub that had gone to attack the Sluggo undersea base. It was a shocking transition from his comfortable padded chair in the rec hall, where he'd been studying reports of the mission, looking at the parameters of the *Prospector*.

He had gone over the list of added weapons, the reinforced hull, the fifty megatorpedoes loaded aboard. From what he suspected about the alien biology, Paulson was skeptical that explosive kinetic weapons would solve the problem at all. But Admiral Haldane had not demonstrated much ability to think outside the box.

He would assume he had enough firepower to level the alien base, then return to cheers and parades. The problem was, blasting the Sluggo monster to pieces wouldn't help, because it was already in pieces. The alien swarm was fundamentally composed of countless individual units bound together by some kind of common telepathy.

Admiral Haldane had not been interested in hearing any suggestions from a scrawny piece of cannon fodder, though.

Knowing the sub intended to engage the invaders' base, Paulson had watched the meager intel as it came in, preparing himself for the worst, since the admiral's previous engagements had not turned out well—especially not for the "escape hatch" volunteers. The waiting was maddening.

The other volunteers in the rec room amused themselves by playing ping-pong or engaging in interactive games. None of them bothered to become friends, sure that any one of them could be called to duty and dispatched at any time.

Paulson could feel them looking at him with pity. Admiral Haldane's track record, and his recklessness (which Haldane tried to characterize as bravery), was no secret. Right now, he was leading his battle sub to the monstrous horde. Paulson hoped for the best, but he didn't get his wish.

This time, when the conduit in his head activated, he knew exactly what was going on—and he was ready.

He braced himself during the transition, and when he gazed out through a different set of eyes, this time he wasn't in a safe sick bay, nor was he being evac'd from a battlefield.

Instead, he saw several slithering, eel-like creatures with round hungry-mouths and white diamond-like teeth. They squirmed forward along the deck, bursting onto the bridge, or command deck, or whatever it was called on a submarine. The alarms were deafening, as were the shouts of the *Prospector*'s crew. Uniformed men and women made their last stand and fought the Sluggos, stomping and hammering, using any possible weapon. The sub's captain had a handgun and shot into the soft masses, and they exploded like snot-filled water balloons. Some bullets whanged and ricocheted off the bulkheads, making the other crewmen duck.

Through the main port, Paulson saw only a solid writhing mass of interlinked Sluggo bodies, as if someone had placed the worm aliens into a trash compactor and smashed them up against the *Prospector*.

Paulson only had a second to assess the situation. More Sluggos slid through the hatch onto the bridge; twenty were already making their way to the controls. Two bloodied seamen threw themselves against the bulkhead door, ramming their shoulders and pushing the heavy metal hatch into its jamb, slicing two Sluggos in half.

The captain, the XO, the weapons officer, the fire-control officer, the sonar tech—all of them were completely disregarding Paulson. He had an idea, but he needed their help, and their attention. "Captain, give me a situation report," he barked, surprised at the sound of his own voice.

The startled captain turned to look at him. "You're not the admiral—you're just cannon fodder."

"We're all cannon fodder, but I'm wearing the uniform. I've got the rank, I have the authority … and I have an idea. What's our weapons situation? Tell me what's happened and where we are."

"We're up a creek without a paddle," the XO cried. "Megatorps gone, and our hull is completely engulfed by Sluggos. At least four hull breaches, and the aliens are swarming through all the decks."

The engineering officer wiped sweat from her forehead. "Structural failure imminent, sir. Catastrophic hull collapse in three minutes." Her voice was hoarse. "Or less."

"I predicted the megatorpedoes would be ineffective," he said.

"I wish you'd been in the Admiral's body before we got in this mess, then," the captain said.

Paulson didn't want to argue. "Do we still have sonar?"

The sonar tech climbed back to his feet, held onto the anchored chair. "Sonar didn't do any good, sir."

Paulson believed they'd been misinterpreting the results. The Sluggo monster didn't know how to become invisible to the sonar pings; rather, the massive organism had actually *broken apart* and then reacoalesced.

"I want a sonar burst, the loudest boom you can make, Mr. Lieutenant—Ensign … sorry, I don't know your rank."

"My rate," said the sonar tech.

"Does the sonar work or not?" Paulson snapped. From the design specs, he knew the *Prospector* had been built as a survey vessel, with a full complement of sonar mapping gear.

"We can send out a ping as loud as bad rap music coming from a car stereo."

"Then let's hope it sounds as annoying as that."

As the sonar tech scrambled with his controls, Paulson yelled to the communications officer, "Send a message throughout the ship … the sub, or whatever. Close all compartment doors, seal off the bulkheads. We need to separate the clusters of Sluggos." He had noticed that after the crew sealed the door to the bridge deck, the individual worm creatures were less lively, more disoriented, and without a driving goal. "We need to divide and conquer. The Sluggos are a conglomerate organism. If you separate the pieces, the pieces are no longer intelligent."

The sonar tech removed his ears. "Here we go." He activated a loud pulse that thrummed out. The response was immediate and startling.

The Sluggo mass surrounding the *Prospector* shivered and broke apart like flies taking flight from a pile of manure. At the main port, Paulson saw hundreds of the things peel off from where they'd been compacted against the view port, and they scattered away from the sub. Even the Sluggos inside the command deck were dazed from the sonar blast, which gave other crew enough time to stomp on them and pop their body sacs.

"Another ping! Keep it up!" Paulson shouted.

The tech stared wide-eyed at the controls. "Did you see that?"

Paulson ran over and grabbed him. "Keep pinging! The sonar disrupts whatever binds them together into a collective organism. It may be our only chance!"

The tech launched another loud boom, and most of the remaining Sluggos drifted away from the sub's hull like flakes of dandruff.

"I can keep pinging all day!" the tech yelled excitedly.

"You may have to do that. Call the engine room—see if that freed our propellers so we can get the heck out of here."

"They're called screws, sir," said the engineer.

The reactor room called up to the bridge. "We're free—and the reactor's running at peak. I'm going to burn off some of our excess by setting off at top speed."

While studying so many reports, Paulson had tried to determine what held the Sluggos together like a million brain cells in a single coordinated organism. Now he was grinning. "Keep hitting them with sonar blasts, and they won't give us any more trouble. Our pulses are scrambling the single intelligent creature into countless unintelligent cells. They won't be able to reassemble into anything big enough to threaten us."

Now that the main port was clear, Paulson could see the ocean around him. He saw the wreckage strewn on the sea floor, the components and debris the Sluggos had used it as a structural framework. The megatorps had indeed destroyed the base at least, but if the big structures were held together by conglomerated Sluggos, the aliens could just rebuild as soon as the individual worm-things settled down. By then, though, the *Prospector* would be far away. So long as the sonar pulses kept scrambling the Sluggo mass, the sub could move unimpeded.

Another sonar boom resounded through the water. The sea around them was a boiling swarm, but the scrambled creatures didn't attack the sub. Inside, the crew were rapidly dispatching the Sluggos one at a time.

"Blow all ballast," Paulson ordered in his loudest command voice, then turned to the captain and whispered, "That's the best way to get us to the surface, isn't it?"

The sub's captain turned to look at him with a dawning respect. "Indeed, Admiral. I'll take it from here, sir. You've already saved the day."

"You may have saved the human race," the XO added.

The captain ordered, "Put us on the ceiling!" He nodded at Paulson. "You might want to hold onto something."

Soon, the *Prospector* breached the surface like a humpback whale. It was a short but exciting ride, and for the first time Paulson felt excited about being part of the Earth Planetary Navy. On the scope, the seas were peaceful and Sluggo-free.

"Our comm systems are damaged," the XO said. "Can't send anybody the good news until we make repairs."

"Then we have to get back to port and report," Paulson said, glad to be getting out of this with his skin intact. "We're going to live to fight another day."

11

From the main press podium at the La Diego Earth Navy base, Admiral Bruce Haldane wore his formal uniform again, the one that had been re-re-tailored to fit Paulson Kenz's scrawny body. It was his body now, a permanent swap now that the *Prospector* had been lost. But he could always upgrade. He had already sent out a call to the recruitment offices and among the current sailors. Thanks to the Sluggo threat, new recruits were being drafted by the tens of thousands, processed as quickly as was bureaucratically possible. Certainly, with so many choices available, there must be someone better qualified than this wet-noodle bookworm.

Still, the escape hatch had worked, and Haldane was relieved to be safe again. He vowed to carry on the fight for Earth....

As soon as he had transferred out of his body aboard the battle sub, he found himself in the recreation hall along with the other lazy slobs who took the easy way out, all those young men who were too afraid to face down the voracious Sluggos as Haldane had done— several times.

Settling into the bookworm's body, he brushed himself off, glared at the rest of the volunteers, and marched to the guarded door, demanding to be taken to base headquarters. Medical monitors would have picked up the transfer signal, so they would come to investigate before long, but he needed to meet with the advisory board, issue his report, and add his new information to the growing backlog of data. Someday, his experiences might allow teams of human geniuses to discover some small weakness in the aliens.

And he also had to make his announcement, putting forth a brave face for the people of Earth.

At first, the guards didn't want to let him out of the rec-hall prison. They looked at Paulson's scrawny body and regarded him with skepticism.

"I am Admiral Haldane, I tell you! Let me loose, I have to make my report."

The guards raised their eyebrows. "Sure, you are. And you expect us to just release you without confirmation?"

"I'm *me*, dammit! That's all the confirmation you should need." Haldane realized that he would have to correct this flaw in the system.

One of the other volunteers looked up from a suspended game of ping-pong. "That one's been acting awfully strange. Could be an adverse reaction to the conduit surgery."

The others nodded. "I wouldn't believe him."

These cowardly slackers didn't respect him! "This is nonsense!" Haldane shouted at the guard. "I outrank you. I'm your admiral!"

"I heard him talking," said another volunteer. "He said he was going to escape and find a black-market surgeon who would pop out a plug for a fee."

The lazy bastards were setting him up! Haldane was furious.

Finally, a signal from medical command informed the guards that Haldane's transfer protocol had been activated, and that the escape hatch swap had been successful. He gave an annoyed huff toward the slovenly volunteers who thought it was all a joke, then he stormed out. This was an emergency, not a minute to lose!

Ever since the *Prospector*'s launch, all of Earth was waiting to hear the news. They expected to learn that the invaders had been annihilated, their base destroyed, and any other Sluggos from the Sluggo planet would see that the Earth Planetary Navy was nothing to mess around with.

When he delivered his speech in his weakling body, though—not the one that had departed aboard the battle sub—he could see dismay ripple through the crowd. They'd already figured out that the mission had failed, that the Sluggos were still a threat … and they assumed that the *Prospector* had been lost with all hands. That much was obvious, because otherwise the admiral would never have used his last-ditch escape plan.

The captain of the submarine would have gone down with his ship, as expected, but a war hero like Bruce Haldane had survived to rouse the troops, to inspire the populace and honor the sacrifices of those who had fallen in battle, as well as to advise the EPN's tactical experts.

Standing at the podium, he activated the loudspeaker systems. His words pounded out across the gathered crowd. "You may not recognize me, but I am Admiral Bruce Haldane. And I have just come from the embattled submarine *Prospector*. With fifty megatorpedoes, we wrought terrible damage to the alien base, but the Sluggo retaliation was swift and overwhelming. They engulfed the sub, and I … I regret the loss of all hands."

He cleared his throat. "A list of all names will be made available to you in subsequent press packets." He lifted his chin and kept his tone stoic. "However, even failures are instructive. We believed that a megatorp bombardment was our best possible hope, but now we'll just have to try something else. Maybe undersea nuclear saturation. It's worth a try."

He drew a breath. "Let us pause for a moment of silence to honor all those who sacrificed themselves aboard the *Prospector*." He closed his eyes, bowed his head—and then an actual signal from the *Prospector* spoiled the moment.

The excited announcement broke through on the loudspeakers. The media reporters were abuzz. The battle sub had survived after all, had surfaced intact and was now making its way at best speed back to land!

Admiral Haldane straightened his cap, squared his shoulders and forced a smile. "Oh … well, then. This is wonderful news."

12

An escort of EPN destroyers met the *Prospector* as it approached the La Diego harbor. People gathered on public docks to welcome the victorious vessel with remarkable fanfare. The cheers from the crowd were deafening.

When Admiral Haldane went to greet them as part of a formal reception party, he was all smiles and pride.

In the days it had taken the battle sub to return, the *Prospector*'s crew had become heroes. No further Sluggo attacks or even sightings had been reported. The sub's captain had transmitted that they had only escaped by using the "sonar defense suggestion" of "Admiral Kenz" to great success, and they believed they had found a way to eliminate the alien invaders once and for all.

"Admiral Kenz" indeed! Haldane fumed inwardly.

As the *Prospector* docked and Admiral Haldane stepped out to greet them, the captain and the XO disembarked with an altogether too smug looking seaman-recruit Paulson Kenz. The sailors looked battered and bruised, their uniforms tattered. Haldane thought their disheveled appearance was strictly for dramatic effect, because even after the Sluggos had swarmed through the decks, the officers and crew must have had a clean change of clothes aboard.

Haldane said, "I'm so pleased you all made it." He waited for the sub's captain to salute, and the man did so, but reluctantly, keeping his eyes fixated on the Admiral's insignia rather than his face. "We welcome your return home, and we look forward to your report about the end of the engagement."

The XO blurted out, "Our report will include how you abandoned us, Admiral Haldane—how you took us into danger with reckless disregard for the lives of the *Prospector*'s officers and crew."

Haldane was shocked. "I led an attack that had a reasonable probability of success, but it didn't work. Such are the fortunes of war."

"Excuse me," said the sub's captain, "but Admiral Kenz said he advised against your method from the outset, but you refused to listen to his advice."

"His *advice?*" Haldane spluttered. "*Admiral* Kenz? He's just a recruit, cannon fodder! I'm the real admiral!"

"As far as I'm concerned, you relinquished that title when you abandoned the ship and crew." The captain cleared his throat. "Sir."

"I was required to survive," Haldane said. "I waited until the last possible moment, when there was no hope for survival. I saw no other way."

"And yet …" The XO nodded at Paulson Kenz. "After you fled for your life, this untried seaman-recruit assessed the situation, solved the problem, saved all our lives, and defeated the Sluggos— in about two minutes. I believe that's called a battlefield promotion, sir."

With a sinking sensation in his gut, Haldane realized that all of this was being recorded and transmitted live.

In the familiar strong and handsome body, Paulson Kenz said, "I've even worked out a way that we can use continuous sonar for complete victory. You see, each pulse scrambles the Sluggo hive mind, breaks it apart. If we bring in numerous subs and keep hammering them with sonar so that the individual creatures cannot re-coalesce, then we can use nets or tanks as a harvesting system. If we winnow down the individual Sluggos so that no more than a hundred or so can gather in any single place, the group intelligence won't come back. Divide and conquer. It may take time, but we can simply whittle them away until there are no more Sluggos left."

"Thank you for that interesting suggestion, recruit." Haldane put all the scorn he could possibly muster into his voice. "We'll have our experts take it under advisement. For now, it's best if we initiate the transfer protocol again, swap back so you can have your original body, and I'll make my announcements and appearances in—"

Paulson raised his head. "Sorry, sir, but as you informed me, it's a one-way transfer protocol. We'll have to reinstall and surgically reset the conduits, but there's no time to go through that now. I need to present my findings to all the command advisory board. There's a war on, you know."

The captain and the XO ignored Haldane and looked at Kenz. "What are your orders, Admiral?"

Paulson looked flustered. "Well, we need the submarine fixed up and cleaned, for one thing. Then we have to discuss how to implement my sonar strategy so we get rid of the Sluggos."

"I demand my body back!" Haldane said.

Paulson plucked at his sleeve. "I don't believe this is your original body any more than that one is. Meanwhile, you can spend time in the recreation hall with the other cannon fodder volunteers. You should have plenty of time to write a personal letter of sympathy to the families of each of those *seamen* who died during the attack on the *Prospector* ... and on the *Far Horizon* ... for starters."

"But you're just a ... a nobody!" cried Haldane.

The sub's captain said, "We believe Admiral Kenz has valuable insights and irreplaceable knowledge and experience. The EPN could not afford to lose him, so he must be preserved at all costs."

"Yes," the XO added, "it would be a grave threat to the human race if Admiral Kenz were to be lost in combat. I'm sure the escape hatch conduits can be adjusted. You can wait with the other volunteers." He narrowed his eyes and gave Haldane a withering look. "Don't worry, you'll be called to do your duty, if needed."

ABOUT THE AUTHORS

Michael A. Stackpole is best known for his Star Wars and BattleTech books, garnering legions of fans in particular for his X-Wing series. He has a BA in history from the University of Vermont. From 1977 on, he worked as a designer of role-playing games for various gaming companies, and wrote dozens of magazine articles with limited distribution within the industry. "Remains of the Dead" is a continuation of his Star Tigers series, which was also featured in the novella "Out There" in *Five by Five* volume 1.

http://www.michaelastackpole.com/

Sarah A. Hoyt is the author of 23 novels from various publishers. Most recently she's concentrated on the Darkship space opera series and the *Shifter* fantasy series for Baen books and the Magical Empires (multiverse fantasy) series for Goldport Press. Her most recent books are *Darkship Renegades*, *A Few Good Men*, *Night Shifters*, *Noah's Boy*, and *Witchfinder*. She lives in Colorado with her husband, two sons, and a variable clowder of cats. She is hard at work on sequels for all her series.

Doug Dandridge is a veteran of the US Army and Florida National Guard as an Infantryman and Infantry team leader. He has multiple degrees from Florida State and the University of Alabama. He self-published his first two novels, *The Deep Dark Well* and *The Hunger*, in 2011 and has sold over 100,000 copies in two years. He has been a full-time writer since March 2013. His Exodus: Empires at War series has placed five consecutive books at #1 on various amazon bestseller lists. Doug is currently working on more Exodus novels and stories, as well as future efforts in his Refuge fantasy series.

Critically acclaimed siblings **Dani** and **Eytan Kollin** have drawn comparisons to the biting political themes of Heinlein and Rand and the grand space operas of Weber and Asimov. Their debut novel, *The Unincorporated Man*, was designated a SciFi Essential and went on to win the Prometheus Award for Best Science Fiction Novel of 2010.

Kevin J. Anderson is the author of over 120 books, 51 of which appeared on bestseller lists; he has 23 million copies in print in 30 languages.

Kevin coauthored thirteen Dune novels with Brian Herbert, as well as their original Hellhole trilogy. He followed his epic Saga of Seven Suns series with his Terra Incognita fantasy trilogy, and wrote the novel *Clockwork Angels* based on the new Rush album. He recently launched a hilarious new series featuring Dan Shamble, Zombie PI. In addition to numerous Star Wars projects, he wrote three *X-Files* novels & collaborated with Dean Koontz on *Frankenstein: Prodigal Son.*

ADDITIONAL COPYRIGHT INFO

OTHER WORDFIRE TITLES

Our list of other WordFire Press authors and titles is always growing. To find out more and to see our selection of titles, visit us at:

wordfirepress.com